About the author

Christopher Downey was born in Glasgow on 31st July 1991 and raised in a town called Penicuik in Midlothian, Scotland. Christopher has spent much of his life coming up with characters locations and stories and has wanted to publish his ideas to share with everyone. An avid gamer, video games influence his stories along with many other inspirations from the various types of fiction of which he is a fan.

FROZEN FIRE

Christopher Downey

FROZEN FIRE

Vanguard Press

VANGUARD PAPERBACK

© Copyright 2018
Christopher Downey

The right of Christopher Downey to be identified as author of
this work has been asserted by him in accordance with the
Copyright, Designs and Patents Act 1988.

All Rights Reserved

No reproduction, copy or transmission of this publication
may be made without written permission.
No paragraph of this publication may be reproduced,
copied or transmitted save with the written permission of the publisher, or in
accordance with the provisions
of the Copyright Act 1956 (as amended).

Any person who commits any unauthorised act in relation to
this publication may be liable to criminal
prosecution and civil claims for damages.

A CIP catalogue record for this title is
available from the British Library.

ISBN 9781784654078

Vanguard Press is an imprint of
Pegasus Elliot MacKenzie Publishers Ltd.
www.pegasuspublishers.com

First Published in 2018

Vanguard Press
Sheraton House Castle Park
Cambridge England

Printed & Bound in Great Britain

Dedication

To Lauren, Matthew, Michael and Steven. Thank you for letting me base characters on you.

And to my family, Mum, Dad, Grandad, Aunt Rosie and my brother Jonathan, for helping make this a reality.

Book one

The World Within the Web

If you were to use magic to power the electrical devices of the world would it not have some side effects? The magic would run through the machines and get into the Wi-Fi's perhaps even create a new form of magic. In the world the floating island Kerozonia is part of, this did happen and a new world was born known as the Data Realm. Kerozonia's world is filled with magic, already just about anyone can learn magic or acquire magical powers; it is part of everyday life. This is the start of the tale of the worlds born from the meeting of magic and the internet and the group of friends that wielded great magic and who would come to call themselves Frozen Fire.

Zack was happy that he was having four of his friends over that day. Zack was an awkward and uncomfortable boy with a loud voice who found it hard to talk to new people. He was odd and loved video games greatly. For some reason he always wore goggles on his forehead. Five years ago, he and his friends gained magic in different circumstances that allowed each of them elemental powers. For instance Zack himself had ice and snow magic. There was a knock on his door as his first friend arrived.

"Hey Eric," greeted Zack as he opened the door.

"Hello," replied Eric in a voice the others called his camp voice. Eric was Zack's second oldest friend, he was also a fan of video games and a lover of animated musicals and theatre. He cares more than you might think at first and likes to act like a diva. Eric's magic was that of fire. Soon the next friend arrived.

"Hello Patrick," greeted Zack.

"Good to see you guys," answered Patrick. Patrick was a year older than the others and was a massive fan of what he and Zack considered to be the greatest sci-fi tv show in the world. He had a little touch of smugness in his nature but valued his friends a lot. His magic was known as the time element, temporal energy that was known to look like clocks.

This meant among other things he could slow down or speed up movement. About twenty minutes passed before the third friend arrived.

"You're late, Malcolm," Zack pointed out.

"Yeah sorry," said Malcolm. Malcolm was a good friend of Zack's; like Zack he was not too good with people but was more of an outdoor person. Malcolm had a bit of a quiet voice and didn't seem to speak much. His powers were lightning magic. About an hour passed and Zack's last friend arrived while he was making lunch for the others.

"You're always so late, Gretchen," said Zack with a sigh.

"At least you still know when to expect me," responded Gretchen. Gretchen was Zack's oldest friend, she was friendly, artistic and had a bit of a violent streak in her which she was not afraid of turning on those who hurt whom she cared about. Gretchen had shadow magic. The group could use their powers for all sorts: Zack made ice cubes for the drinks, Eric used small flames to keep his food warm, and Patrick froze time in small areas to make his plate float. Malcolm would often use his lightning to power things like his phone while Gretchen would occasionally make her shadow move by itself for her own amusement. After lunch came the time to find something to do.

"All right, guys let's get to it!" exclaimed Zack.

"We haven't decided what we're going to do yet," Gretchen pointed out.

"You vetoing several ideas didn't help," added Eric.

"Like you didn't do that," said Malcolm.

"I believe we all did," said Patrick.

"Yeah, that sounds about right," said Zack glumly.

"Say, Zack is your console supposed to have that light?" asked Gretchen pointing over to the TV where one of Zack's home consoles was.

"I must have left on. Which is odd for me," mused Zack.

"It's not the power light, or a stand by light," said Eric with a hint of concern. Everyone else turned to look at the console. The slot for inserting discs was emitting a white light.

"I think there's some strange magic in that light," stated Patrick.

"What the fudge?" said Zack staring at the light as it grew. Before they knew it the light surrounded them completely. And the room seemed to disappear and the group seemed fall through nothing.

And just like that they landed on something. The light cleared and they could see where they were. It looked like they were outside but things were different from what they might expect. They were standing in a field but all the grass was indigo and looked like a pixelated picture, yet the sky, the sun, the calm breeze, the gentle scent of grass and all the clouds seemed oddly regular in comparison.

"Where are we?" asked Gretchen, not expecting an answer.

"Did we get pulled into a video game?" wondered Eric.

"None of the worlds in any of my video games look like this," replied Zack.

"Who'd of thought a games console would have a larger inside," mused Patrick.

"Err I... I don't think we're inside Zack's console," said Malcolm.

"No, you're not. You are in another realm," explained a voice that seemed to come out thin air. The group jumped and before anyone could ask who was there, there was a flash of light and a figure appeared before them. It was a woman who was very tall, taller than Malcolm the tallest of the group. She wore a long silver dress, golden bangles on her wrists and a white ribbon wrapped around her waist that trailed behind her. Her navy hair surrounded her gentle face.

"I am the one who brought you here. My name is Astral." Everyone was dumbfounded.

"Where are we?" Gretchen finally managed.

"Like I said, you are in another realm," explained Astral. "Another plain of existence that is very much part of your own world."

"Did you bring us here?" enquired Eric.

"Yes, I just told you that. I need your help," replied Astral.

"What are you talking about? We need a better explanation," said Zack after struggling a bit. "What is this place? What help could you need from the five of us?"

"This world has become known as Miyamoto," began Astral. "This land and all in it is made from the data from the video games in your world. The people of your world use magic as a power source; as such it has gotten into all your machines and through them onto the Wi-Fi creating a new plane of existence. Which is where you stand now."

"Hold on, are you telling us we're in the internet?" asked Eric in disbelief.

"In a sense. Miyamoto is part of the Data Realm," explained Astral. "A world sculpted by much of the data on just about everything in your world."

"A world made out of video game data," said Gretchen absently.

"That's the most awesome thing I've ever heard!" exclaimed Zack.

"Another world," said Malcolm quietly.

"Wait. What was that about needing help?" asked Patrick.

"Yes, I do," replied Astral. "All worlds have both good and bad peoples and creatures and one being who falls into the latter category is seeking to cause devastation in both our worlds." The group began to suspect what she was going to ask of them. "An evil that manifested in this realm fused itself with all manner of viruses and malware to increase its power and gain dangerous magic. This creature calls itself The Anti-Gamer."

"For real?" exclaimed the group in unison and surprise.

"He wishes to destroy all video games within your world and destroy Miyamoto too," explained Astral. "I have power, a lot of power, but none with which I can fight. So I used my powers to summon one with a great love of video games and their closest friends to help protect this world alongside the peoples of this world. With the age of the internet it's not hard to learn all about people. And I've spoken to you through social media and forums; believe it or not, I know you all quite well."

"I knew joining that website would be trouble," grumbled Zack.

"Sounds more like more like it's your fault," said Eric with a hint of sarcasm. "Mr 'I love videos games more than the rest of you'."

"Oh shut up, Eric. But Astral, I'm telling you, you've got the wrong group. We won't be any good at fighting monsters."

"Speak for yourself," retorted Patrick.

"I... I'm with Zack, we're not right," added Malcolm.

"Well, the boys maybe useless but I think I could take this guy on," said Gretchen jokingly.

"I have not got the wrong group," said Astral firmly. "I searched for a long time for a group of friends with goodness in their hearts and great magical potential. And I found the five of you. I told you I've spoken to you all over the internet. I can read people really well; I know you're who I'm looking for."

"Oh, you've been on that elemental's discussion forum," said Zack who was still struggling with talking to her.

"I knew these powers would get us into something like this," grumbled Gretchen.

"Now, I know your names already but please introduce yourselves," requested Astral.

"I'm Zackary Glacis," replied Zack.

"I'm Gretchen Shadows."

"Eric Flare."

"Malcolm Spark."

"Patrick Tempus."

"Zack, Gretchen, Eric, Malcolm, Patrick," Astral repeated. "It's nice to finally meet you in person. I know this is a lot to suddenly spring on you and a lot to ask of you but I know the five of you can defeat even the most dangerous of villains."

When no one replied Astral offered to show them more of her world, which they accepted. She led through the field towards a building that looked like a temple.

"What's this?" asked Gretchen.

"This is my home," answered Astral.

"You live in a temple?" enquired Eric.

"I was born from the data of video game goddesses. Goddesses of power, wisdom, courage, light and order. My home was built from the same sort of data so it ended up taking the form of a temple."

"I believe I know those goddesses," Zack mused to himself.

"There's a surprise," muttered Patrick rolling his eyes.

"Nice place," said Malcolm. Astral led them inside. Within they beheld a large room with marble walls and floor, windows with deep purple curtains, a grand chandelier and tapestries each depicting a different video game hero.

"I think I just walked into my dream home," said Zack. "Do you have a gaming room?"

"I'm afraid not," replied Astral.

"Scratch that dream home comment then."

"Out of all the people in our world with magic why us?" enquired Gretchen.

"Because the five of you have the potential to be the greatest wielders of your respective elements," explained Astral. "I've heard the stories of how you got your magic."

"Well, be that as it may, I don't think you'll convince us like that," said Eric.

"Flattery usually does the trick with you," remarked Gretchen.

"Quiet, you!"

"Sounds to me like confidence problems," observed Astral.

"And health problems for the ones who live on junk food," added Patrick.

"That's rich coming from the guy who only eats celery and jelly babies," remarked Zack.

"You've never been able to prove that."

"It's more than just confidence," said Gretchen.

"Looks like I'll just have to help you find some for a start," said Astral. "I know you can make a difference and though you don't know what to make of all this, you most certainly want to learn more about this world. And I can tell you want to give this adventure a chance. Please will you at least try?"

"My grandad always encouraged me to at least try," said Zack.

"We've done stupider things," mused Gretchen.

"Only half of them were as dangerous," Eric pointed out.

"Yeah, trouble always seems to find us."

"And we've all dreamed of adventure all our lives," added Zack. "I know I have."

"It sounds like you're going to try," observed Astral. The group said that they would do this, despite their doubts. Astral told them that she would give each of them a weapon to help in their battle. She them lead down a long hallway to a small room at the back of the temple. The room was filled with dust and two empty shelves at either side and a table all made of rotting wood.

"Not the most impressive armoury I've ever seen," observed Gretchen.

"What other armouries have you've seen?" enquired Zack.

"I'll tell you later."

"Where are these weapons?" asked Eric.

"On the table," answered Astral. The group walked over to the table and there under the dust were five old weapons: a staff, a halberd, a scythe, a long bow and a good old-fashioned sword.

"They're a little worn," mumbled Malcolm.

"And I'm sure a scythe is a gardening tool," Patrick pointed out.

"They're all I've got; I didn't really need an armoury until recently," explained Astral. "Really I should have asked around a bit more. But I've put a spell on them so as soon as you grasp one it'll become infused with your powers and be made anew. Also, you will be able to summon them and dismiss them at will. And another spell that will help you realize some of the things you should be able to do with your powers, as I have noticed you haven't done much research into them. Now choose carefully."

"All right how do we do this?" mused Zack.

"Surely we can come to some sort of agreement," said Patrick.

"Can we ever?"

"No time springs to mind," responded Gretchen.

"First of all, does anyone have a preference?" questioned Eric.

"I do know some archery," replied Malcolm. "The bow could work for me."

"Sounds fair enough to me," said Zack. "All right then, go for it." Malcolm picked the long bow and a spark issued from his hand. Electricity surged over the bow and in flash the bow changed. The bow was now yellow and blue, that looked like lightning bolts running across it.

"Awesome," said Malcolm quietly.

"Who's next?" asked Zack.

"I believe the scythe is just my style," stated Eric.

"It was bound to be you or Gretchen."

"Nah, I'm leaning towards that halberd," replied Gretchen.

"All right Eric, go ahead," said Zack. Eric picked up the scythe. Fire covered it and when it cleared the scythe had changed. The handle now looked like a long winding flame.

"My turn!" exclaimed Gretchen. She picked up the halberd and shadows covered it. When they dispersed the handle was black and the blade was purple, oddly enough. The others pondered the nightmares this would give them.

"That'll give me nightmares," said Zack. "Gretchen with a sharp object usually means trouble."

"I guess you would like the sword?" Patrick asked Zack.

"No no, if you want the sword you have it," answered Zack.

"Ace! Thanks, bud," responded Patrick. He picked up the sword and it was covered with what the group recognized as his temporal energy. The energy cleared and the blade of the sword now resembled a clock hand.

"Well, that makes this mine. Staffs are pretty awesome," said Zack as he reached for the staff. When he picked it up it froze over. The ice shattered and revealed the staff's new look. It was now an icy blue with white tips resembling snow. And what appeared to be a snowman face in the centre.

"First of all, you lot have each had your magic for five years but you haven't really explored what you can do with them," said Astral making the group rethink the number of things they shared on social media. "I think to start to boost your confidence you need see what it is you can do."

"That doesn't sound too hard," mused Gretchen.

"You'll need practice more than anything," explained Astral. "And I know just the place."

Astral used her powers to transport them somewhere else. The sensation was much the same that they experienced when they were brought to Miyamoto. They were now standing a large sheet of concrete on the field behind the temple.

"Was there really any need to teleport?" Zack managed to ask when he saw where they were.

"I suppose not," mused Astral. "Anyway I set this up as a practice area." She clapped her hands and in flash of light, several targets and large dolls on wooden poles appeared. "Practice as see you fit. I'll be back to check in a little while." And with that Astral vanished in another flash of light.

"Quite an interesting situation our group is in," observed Patrick.

"I wouldn't say we're a group," remarked Zack. "As we're in a world made from video game data I'd say we are a party. Because in video games a group of characters is usually referred to a party."

"Can't argue with that logic."

"I could, but I can't be bothered having that conversation right now," said Gretchen.

"Right then, might as well start, dearies," said Eric.

The party had a go at swinging their weapons at the various practice objects. They then tried using their greatly underused magic. They could almost feel the knowledge in the weapons giving them ideas they had never even considered before. Malcolm learned he didn't need arrows as the bow made new ones for him, plus he could charge them with electricity. Eric began to practice burning things as the fireball was the most basic of his moves. Zack had always found it easy to make snowballs so he tried his less practiced icicles and tried to make them rather sharp. Gretchen knew she could multiply her own shadow and decided to try making shadow projectiles which she had trouble with in the past. Patrick had plenty of experience summoning temporal energy but not a lot when it came to slowing down or speeding up and, as they were practising on inanimate objects and the others refused to let him try it out on them, he decided to just concentrate on his energy which was a fierce golden energy.

"Why us? Why did she choose us?" wondered Zack.

"Our information on social media," said Gretchen.

"And we just agreed so easily. Every day I get convinced we're crazier than I thought."

"We've always dreamed of adventure. No matter how reluctant you pretend to be."

"Do you think we're making any progress?" asked Patrick.

"Backwardsly perhaps," mused Zack.

"Could be worse," said Malcolm.

"Yeah, with the way Gretchen swings that halberd we could all be shorter," joked Eric.

"You'd be first," retorted Gretchen. The party laughed but they stopped when a dark feeling fell over them.

"What's this, humans in the Data Realm?" said a dark voice that came through the air. The group jumped and a figure appeared before them in what seemed to be a surge of magic. The figure was a man with short dark hair, a small moustache and small beard below his bottom lip. His attire was quite unusual: he wore a black pinstripe suit,he had metal gauntlets, armoured boots and a large pale grey cape with a fuzzy collar. There was no colour in his eyes, just white with two black spots. "I come to see what Astral is up to and instead find the first humans in the Data Realm."

"What have you got to do with Astral?" enquired Gretchen.

"I suppose you could say I am her opponent," replied the figure. "Certainly, an enemy; after all I want to destroy her, this world she watches and all those in it." Realisation came over the party like a thunder cloud over a nice day.

"You're the Anti-Gamer," stated Zack whose fear had overridden his usual struggle to talk. The figure smirked coldly as if there was no real emotion.

"I am indeed. But please call me Visrel," responded the Anti-Gamer. "And you must be the youths with great magical prowess that Astral has summoned to this world in an attempt to stop me." His voice was calm, cold and unchanging.

"You might say that," replied Eric. The party tried to hide their fear.

"You don't look like much, but then again there's that whole thing about looks and deceiving," stated Visrel "I can't help but wonder if it'll be easy to end you all here." In another surge of magic he summoned a weapon and pointed it at them. It looked like a sword but the blade wound round in a circle.

"A… A spiral blade!" stammered Malcolm.

"Technically it's a helix blade as a spiral gets wider and a helix stays the same size like that," Patrick pointed out.

"Shut up."

"If you're quite done quibbling over the shape of my blade I'd like to continue. Hmm, quite the magical potential you oddballs possess. But you don't strike me as fighters," observed Visrel.

"What's wrong being oddballs?" demanded Gretchen.

"And with enough practice we could become very good fighters," added Zack.

"Practice? It will take an awful lot; in fact allow me to help you," said Visrel. "True monsters like myself can always make lesser monsters to do our work. And it just so happens I've got a big one on standby." The Anti-Gamer's blade disappeared and he held his arms aloft. Energy sparked out of his hands and there was a dark flash and there in front of the party stood a large monster. It took on the form of an eight foot bear with putrid green fur and tusks coming out of its bottom jaw. Visrel swung his cape over himself and disappeared as the creature loomed down on the party.

"GREAT SHAKESPEAR'S BALD SPOT, THAT THING'S HUGE!" cried Zack.

"You may have made it deaf, though," remarked Gretchen.

"W... what should we do?" asked Malcolm.

"Fight it probably," suggested Patrick

"We're gonna die," said Eric glumly. The creature swiped at the party with one of its massive arms. They managed to just get out of the way; they then tried to retaliate. Malcolm pointed to the space above the creature and concentrated; he summoned lightning bolts that struck it. Eric sent as much fire as he could muster at the monster; it did do some damage. Zack managed to create some icicles which were shaped like kunai, a sort of throwing blade often associated with ninjas. The creature swiped at them again and knocked everyone, except Gretchen, down. Gretchen held her right hand up summoned as much power as she could and blasted a shadowy sphere at the monster. It struck the monster and while it was dazed Patrick got to his feet, mustered his power and sent a small amount of time distortion energy at the creature which managed to slow it down a little. The others staggered up onto their feet and Zack directed his powers at the creature's feet causing ice to form on the bottom. The monster began to slip and wobble and with help of Eric's fire and Malcolm's lightning the creature fell on its back with a loud crash. Gretchen and Patrick took this chance and rushed forward and stabbed the creature with their halberd and sword. The monster let out a loud cried and exploded in a burst of magic, this knocked everyone over again.

"Oh my stars! Are you all right?" came the voice of Astral who had just returned.

"More or less," groaned Zack.

"Using our powers isn't usually this exhausting," moaned Gretchen.

"I guess you're not used to using powers so extremely," explained Astral. "As you use your powers more and get better with them it will take less out of you and you'll be able to fight for longer and do more powerful things."

"As anyone in our world can learn to use any of its forms you'd think our bodies would be already used to magic. Especially seeing as we've had ours for five years," Eric pointed out.

"I'd say it's likely due to you neglecting your powers. I'd imagine it's the same for anyone who learns magic. Anyway where did that monster come from?"

"The Anti-Gamer showed up," answered Patrick.

"With his funny looking blade," added Malcolm. Astral gasped

"Well, let's be glad he didn't fight you himself. You've only just started using your powers properly; you're far from strong enough to face him," said Astral. "I'm sorry, I didn't mean for you to encounter him yet. You must be exhausted and it's beginning to get late; I should return you home now, I'll send for you tomorrow if you're still willing to try."

"Could you give us a warning beforehand this time?" requested Zack.

"I guess I should," answered Astral. The white light surrounded them and again after falling again they found themselves back in Zack's living room.

No one had noticed that the party had been gone for a couple of hours. This was mostly because Zack's mother and brother had gone out. Soon everyone went home knowing full well that tomorrow they could encounter even more fierce creatures. Their dreams were filled with what they had seen in Miyamoto and the possibilities that it may hold. They were all scared but they did not want to back out. Despite the suddenness of it all they wanted to see this adventure as far through as they could.

The morning came, though it was hard to tell due to the grey clouds that always hung over Kerozonia. Of course, no one on Kerozonia was bothered. When they woke up everyone got ready to meet up with the others. Nearly all of Zack's clothes were blue as he loved the colour, even his goggles were a particularly bright shade. He got ready to head out and meet his friends when the time came.

"See you later, Marcus," Zack called to his older brother when he was about to leave.

"You're going out? You don't go out," stated Marcus suspiciously.

"I'm going to meet my friends."

"Ah, so you finally caved in to them telling you to get out more."

"I figured I'd better before they resorted to the violence."

"It always is better to head that off at the curve."

"Or before it gets a chance to start."

Gretchen dressed herself in her purple and black clothes usually with a pair of cherries on it and said goodbye to her family before going out.

"I'll be back later, Oswald," Gretchen called to her big brother.

"Have fun with your friends," Oswald called back.

"I will."

"Try not to cause too much trouble."

"You're one to talk."

"I don't know what you're talking about."

"Oh yes you do."

Eric liked to dress in red. Malcolm, like Zack, just wore what he could find (but didn't have a predominate colour). Patrick liked to mimic the style of his favourite TV character, which usually led to him wearing large coats and shirts adorned with question marks. The party lived in a city called Reekie, Kerozonia's capital and second biggest city. They met up in the local park.

"All right, then; we just need to wait for Astral to call us," stated Gretchen.

"Yeah, but she'll need something to call us through," Zack said.

"A games console or a computer of some sort," mused Patrick.

"Plenty to choose from," said Malcolm.

"Could be a problem as we all told our families we were going out for the day," Eric pointed out. "Though my mother, sister and brother are also out for the day." Everyone had that grin that told Eric he had just inadvertently volunteered his house and the party headed there. They weren't there for long when the white light emerged for one of Eric's consoles and the party found themselves back in Miyamoto.

They were greeted by Astral.

"What happened to our warning?" Zack managed to ask.

"Oh! I knew I was forgetting something," replied Astral. "Anyway, I meant to tell you I am working on a series of enchanted stones that'll allow me to communicate with you wherever you are and will also let you enter and leave Miyamoto at any time."

"Now that would be a good thing to have," said Patrick.

"Can we use them to talk to each other?" enquired Zack.

"Yes, you should, but they are quite a way off from being complete," explained Astral.

"We do all have mobile phones for communicating with each other," Eric pointed out.

"Do they even work in this world?" wondered Gretchen. "We should probably check that at some point."

"We should," added Zack. It was a long time before they did. "Anyway what part of Miyamoto are we in this time?" The group had been brought to a different area. They stood under a larger cliff face on which the sun shone. The cliff was a good twenty feet tall and stretched off in both directions with a deep chasm running in front of it. Also nearby was a forest with trees that had curved trunks and green or pink leaves. Sights like this made the party think that Miyamoto got some of its data wrong.

"This is Edge Forest, named such because this cliff is the edge of Miyamoto" explained Astral.

"What's beyond the cliff?" asked Eric.

"The ocean," answered Astral. "Our world is a sphere as well, but this cliff is nicknamed as the wall next to the rest of The Data Realm."

"Why here?" asked Malcolm.

"The Anti-Gamer wants to destroy Miyamoto, so I doubt he'd look for a way to do it at the edge of this world," explained Astral. "It seemed like a good place for you all to practice without risk of coming under attack from him again."

"I guess you know what he'd do," mused Patrick.

"But do still be careful, he has sent monsters everywhere," said Astral.

"Of course he has," grumbled Zack.

"I'll take my leave now, as I still have to work on those stones and try to learn more about the Anti-Gamer's plot," Astral vanished and left the party to get on with their practice.

"First of all we should try summoning our weapons," said Zack.

"Just by willing them right?" checked Gretchen.

"Yep, that's it." confirmed Patrick.

Zack held his arm in front of him and thought how he would need his staff at this time. And in a flash of snowflakes his staff appeared. The others summoned their weapons and they appeared with a burst of their respective element. A swirl of shadows for Gretchen's halberd, a burst of fire for Eric's scythe, a surge of lightning for Malcolm's bow and a pulse of temporal energy for Patrick's sword. Once again they thought they could feel their weapons helping them come up with new ideas. The party found the training equipment amongst the trees and began. During their practice the party inadvertently knocked some of it far away so they moved further through the forest. They came across something they did not expect to see. There was a large door in the cliff side. It was rather imposing even though it was just wood, with a mental frame and onyx steppes leading up to it from across a stone bridge which was above a chasm that ran along next to the cliff. The door was covered in heavy chains with a mighty lock on it. When the party moved closer they noticed a small wooden sign which read:

'Doorway to the larger part of the Data Realm.
Better known as the Free Space.
Access is strictly prohibited to all. No exceptions.
This is due to its unstable nature. Where nearly anything could happen.
Signed: Astral, she who watches over Miyamoto.'

"Wonder what it's like?" mused Malcolm.

"Unstable nature? I wonder what it refers to," mused Patrick.

"With the internet? Take your pick," replied Zack.

"It's not that bad," stated Gretchen.

"No, it's worse," added Eric. "But still why not let anyone at all in?"

"Isn't it where the Anti-Gamer came from? Maybe Astral is scared of something else just as bad coming through?" said Zack

"Sounds about right. Look at how video games made this place turn out; who knows what sorts of villains could be through there thanks to the rest of the internet," claimed Eric.

"Well, one way or the other we've been asked to only protect this particular part of the Data Realm," Patrick reminded them.

"We won't see it anytime soon," said Malcolm.

"Too bad. Oh well we've still got all of Miyamoto to see," said Gretchen. And with those words the party decided to explore a little bit.

After wondering aimlessly through Edge Forest for about an hour the party finally came to the other side, groaning and sore from wandering around.

"Right, I think we can all agree we all took a turn getting us lost," stated Zack, very irritated. There was a general sound of agreement.

"This is the wrong side," Malcolm pointed out which was met with loud groaning.

"I'm not going back in there anytime soon. Not with all the whining you guys did," declared Gretchen.

"At least not without a map for one of you to read. That's assuming any of you can read a map," added Eric.

"We'd better see if we can find Astral's temple," said Patrick.

After resting for a bit the party headed off again. Eventually it dawned on them that they had no idea where they were going. While wandering aimlessly the party came across an odd sight. It looked like a large crater. Though it could very well have been dug, the large stone indent in the grassy plain was an odd sight. Stranger still was the fact that this 'crater' was filled with odd-looking buildings, built from steel but still big enough to house a whole family. A large family. There were so many of them it looked like a city built out of metal.

"Maybe we can find help here?" suggested Patrick.

"Even if we don't I'm not moving again for a week," said Zack who was almost serious. The party descended into the city.

"Hello? Can anyone help us?" called Gretchen. There came the sound of large thuds; it took a moment for them to realize they were footsteps. The residents of the city came into view.

"What the...?" was all Patrick could manage. The residents weren't humans. They were large creatures made of metal, large bodies with short legs. Large arms and heads that were just separate from the body.

"Well now, this is unexpected," stated Eric.

"Ah, a group of polygons; did you get lost nearby?" said one of the metal begins, examining the party. Its voice was deep and sounded like it was echoed from within.

"I'm sorry, what?" said Gretchen puzzled and surprised.

"Are you not polygons?" asked the metal being.

"No?" replied Zack unsure of what it meant. "We're humans."

"Humans! You will not have seen anything like us before?"

"No," said the party together.

"We are the ore.rar, grand beings of living metal born from ore within the ground," explained the ore.rar. "I am known as Iron, for we are all named after kinds of metals. And this is our city, The Steel Crater."

"Metal people. This place really out does itself in strangeness," observed Gretchen.

"I take it you're the humans Astral summoned to fight the Anti-Gamer?" asked Iron.

"That's us."

"Well then, I imagine you may have some questions? I shall try to answer them. But let us get a seat," said Iron gesturing for them to follow.

The party followed the ore.rar inside one of the steel houses. They found themselves in what resembled a living room, though the floors walls and ceiling were made of metal and all the furniture was made of stone. The party sat down on a large stone couch while Iron sat down on a stone chair across from them. Most likely due to the ore.rars' short legs, the seats were quite low to the ground.

"Firstly, why did you call us polygons?" enquired Eric. Zack, Malcolm and Patrick got nervous around new people so Gretchen and Eric usually ended up doing most of the talking until they warmed up a bit.

"Polygons are the equivalent to humans you find here in the Data Realm," explained Iron. "The polygons are born from the data on humans and are themselves identical to humans apart from the fact that they are made from data and come from the Data Realm. And of course, in Miyamoto you can find we ore.rar, the metal people, as you called us. There is also the acorn.ris wooden beings who live in trees. And finally there are the cloud.tiff the cloud dwellers."

"If there are so many people in Miyamoto why did Astral need people from our world?" wondered Patrick.

"I can only guess," replied Iron. "Perhaps because there are stories in the data that made her, someone from the secret other world, always summons humans to help. She may simply think we need all the help we can get. Or perhaps this is simply her way for our two worlds to finally meet. You had better ask her, I suppose."

"I suppose we should once we find our way back," said Zack.

"Better head back to the forest," said Patrick.

"I think getting lost in there once was enough," replied Eric.

"Astral's temple?" suggested Malcolm.

"Yep. Though I have no problem with the forest," said Gretchen.

"You got us lost in forests enough times for a lifetime when we were younger," remarked Zack.

"It wasn't that bad."

"Marcus had to come and find us each time."

"Sounds pretty bad to me," said Patrick.

"I got dragged along with them once or twice, so I can vouch for Zack," added Eric.

"And, surprise surprise, she was the one who got us lost in Edge Forest in the first place," said Zack.

"OK you've made your point!" yelled Gretchen. There came an almighty thud and the whole village shook. "Huh, I thought only Zack's yelling could do that."

"Oh, you're hilarious," responded Zack flatly.

"The whole village shook; it must have come from underground," stated Iron. Everyone went outside to see what was happening. There were ore.rar running to one particular spot and the party followed. "Cobalt, what's going on?" Iron asked one of the other ore.rar.

"The Anti-Gamer's minions and a terrible coal monster that's leading them," replied the ore.rar who must have been Cobalt.

"How many monsters has he got?" questioned Eric.

"As we understand it he uses his powers to animate virus programs to make him monsters to do his bidding," explained Iron.

"The coal creature has burrowed underground, that's what the noise was," added Cobalt.

"Everyone better get ready to fight," said Iron.

"Something tells me we not going to be able to go a day here without fighting monsters," observed Eric.

"Guys, the hole's over there," said Malcolm pointing. The party went over to where Malcolm had indicated and sure enough there was large hole in the ground. When they arrived at it several monsters dashed in front of them to block their path. These creatures were rather strange, their small round bodies were predominately giant moths with sharp teeth, supported by four spindly legs with talons on the end. They snapped at the party.

"Everyone else is seeing them right?" asked Gretchen slightly joking.

"I don't know whether to be scared or just weirded out," said Zack unsure. The party summoned their weapons and began to fight the monsters they later would find out were called talon-teeth. One of them lunged at Zack and bit down on his staff; he then used this opportunity to smack the creature on the ground. Malcolm shot a barrage of arrows at the talon-teeth. Though not knowing a thing about swordplay, Patrick was still able to use his sword to defeat one. Eric used his fire to keep a talon-teeth at the exact point where the blade of his scythe would hit. Gretchen simply rammed the one she faced with her halberd.

"OK, that's the little ones taken care of now we need to work out how to get the big one out of the hole," said Patrick.

"Sounds like it's coming up," stated Malcolm.

"That's convenient. Sort of," observed Eric. Sure enough the creature surfaced revealing its lizard like face made entirely of coal. It crawled out and loomed over them. "Great big coal lizard. That's pretty odd."

"I'm going to start freaking out now," said Zack.

"Could you do the screaming in your head?" asked Patrick.

"We'd still be able to hear him," said Gretchen.

"Uh guys, it's attacking," Malcolm pointed out. The coal lizard swiped at them with one of its front legs. The party ducked just in time. Eric was the first to retaliate mustering a small fire twister which he threw at the coal lizard and was disappointed when despite being made of coal it seemed immune to combusting. Zack managed to freeze part of it which he smashed with his staff. Malcolm and Patrick summoned lighting and small temporal pulses above the lizard which broke more of the coal. Patrick's temporal pulses were flaring spheres of the golden energy. Gretchen managed to make a duplicate of her halberd using its shadow and then used the pair to strike more coal off the creature.

"Nice trick," complimented Patrick.

"Thanks, I'll have to remember this one," replied Gretchen. "I could duplicate just about anything." Something orange glowed inside the creature, which shone between the coal. There was a crackle of energy across the lizard and it suddenly had new coal where the broken ones were.

"It regenerates!" cried Malcolm.

"I hate healing enemies!" exclaimed Zack. "And it's usually the final boss in RPGs. It's a really irritable and in many cases cheap trick."

"Rant later, Zack," Eric cut across.

"At least it stopped him from making a loud deafening screech," said Gretchen. The orange glow started again only this time the lizard opened its mouth wide and fired an energy blast at them. The party were knocked off their feet. They scrambled to their feet to try and avoid further blasts. The party went for cover.

"How are we going to beat something that can heal its self?" cried Patrick.

"Usually the trick is to do more damage to it than it heals," replied Zack.

"I don't think that'll work in this situation," said Gretchen.

"We're going have to attack its core," stated Eric.

"We could fire a shot into its mouth," suggested Zack.

"It'll be though with those blasts." Gretchen pointed out.

"You just need to time it right."

"Then let's give it a try," said Eric. The party got ready, they waited for a blast to pass and then made their move. Zack threw the sharpest icicle kunai he could muster but the coal lizard saw it coming and knocked out the way. Patrick tried a pulse of temporal energy but it hit one of the lizard's beams. Malcolm summoned an arrow and began charging it with lightning. He waited and when the orange glow started he fired the arrow right at the lizard. The arrow flew like a bolt of lightning with a crack of thunder. The lizard had opened its mouth right as the arrow reached it and ended up swallowing it and all the lightning. The coal lizard collapsed and exploded into a burst of magic and vanished.

"Nice shot, Malcolm," complemented Zack.

"Nicely done," added Patrick.

"Thanks," mumbled Malcolm.

"I've found you at last," came Astral's voice and she then appeared next to them. "What have you been doing?"

"They did it; the humans beat the coal monster," Iron was calling to the other ore.rar.

"Well, I suppose that answers that," stated Astral. "But how did you end up here?"

"We decided to explore Edge Forest and got lost," answered Gretchen.

"When we got out of the forest we wandered for ages before ending up here," added Eric.

"Quite the knack for trouble you all have," said Astral. "If you don't find it, it finds you. I suppose it's partly my fault for asking you to fight monsters. Oh it's getting late I better send you home."

"Wait can we ask you something first?" said Zack after struggling for a moment.

"Of course."

"If there are so many people in this world why did you need humans to battle the Anti-Gamer?" asked Gretchen.

"Based on all the information I gathered from across the internet, I came to the conclusion that teenage humans made the best heroes," explained Astral.

"I can see how she came to that conclusion," mused Eric.

"Perhaps I sensed you were destined to battle evil anyway and brought you here. I don't know why but out of all the people from your world I talked to, you five seemed right. Like somehow you were meant for this. But it's said we make our own destiny; perhaps you made this yours."

After that exhausting day the party took a good long rest back home. The following day came and they met up once again. Zack's house was free due to Marcus going to hang out with Oswald at his and Gretchen's. When Zack went on his laptop he noticed something strange.

"That's odd," observed Zack. "There would appear to be some kind of strange energy on the internet."

"What are you on about?" asked Gretchen.

"Come take a look." The others stood behind Zack and looked at his computer screen. "Now watch; it happens every time I click on a link." Zack clicked on a link and during the brief second when one page transferred to the next there was a surge of some kind of energy.

"Isn't that the same magic we saw Visrel use?" said Eric.

"W… what's going on?" stammered Malcolm.

"What is that monster doing?" wondered Patrick. Just then a different energy covered the screen. A shining white brightness and a familiar voice began to speak through it.

"Zack, Gretchen, Eric, Malcolm, Patrick, can you hear me?" came the voice of Astral.

"We can hear you Astral," replied Zack.

"There's major trouble going on that's affecting both our worlds," explained Astral. "I'm going to bring you into Miyamoto straight away." Before anyone could ask they were transported.

When the party arrived in Miyamoto they were face to face with Astral again.

"What's going on?" asked everyone.

"The Anti-Gamer has begun a plan to destroy the video games in your world," answered Astral. "He is at a location called Connection Tower. While he is there he is able to access the internet in your world. He is casting a dark spell on the internet through the tower's connections to destroy the video games. He says it's a test of his bigger plan for destroying Miyamoto."

"We'd better get to this tower then," said Eric.

"We're not strong enough to fight him yet," Zack pointed out.

"We've got to do something," stated Gretchen.

"Let's go to the tower then!" exclaimed Patrick.

"We can't go just yet," replied Astral.

"Why not?" questioned Malcolm.

"The tower is a connection between the Data Realm and your world. As such it has a powerful protection spell on it. Only those with permission may enter. The Anti-Gamer is powerful enough to get past the spell but you are not. Which is why first of all we must go see the king of Miyamoto, the only one who can give permission to enter the tower. I've brought you to the city where he lives. It is called Adlez.Follow me to his castle."

They were standing on the outskirts of a city and they could see a castle rising out above it. Astral lead the way and the party followed. The city was bustling with people, who must have been the polygons. They were indeed just like humans with just as many differences in size personality and hair skin and eye colour,though there were some unique combinations. The buildings came in all shapes and sizes. Adlez was just as modern as the party's home. There were all sorts of shops, street lights of varying designs and a generally good atmosphere.

"This place is fancier than Reekie," observed Eric.

Before they knew it they found themselves at the entrance to a magnificent castle, built from mighty white stone, that struck an imposing air. It was quite tall and wide with several towers and blue slate on the roofs. There must have been more rooms than people knew what to do with. The whole thing was a sight to behold.

"I have brought these humans to see the king," Astral told one of the guards at the door. They were allowed in. When inside the castle they were lead straight to the throne room. It was a large room, with a golden carpet, a throne that looked like it had been cut from diamonds and paintings of former monarchs that made them wonder how old the Data Realm was.

"You stand before his majesty, King Hud the Ninth," announced one of the servants. They managed to resist saying "For real?" There on the throne sat the king. He was an aged man with the years he had seen clear on his face. He still had plenty of hair but it had all turned grey and upon his head sat the crown all the past monarchs were wearing in their paintings, golden with a gem at the front shaped like a game disc. The party bowed. Zack started to fiddle with his goggles something he did when he was nervous.

"Ah, at last, the young ones Astral has requested to help in the duty of protecting our world," stated Hud. "I do hope you're up to the task otherwise I've gone and had my garden re-wallpapered for nothing. Incidentally do they have names? You never know."

"Of course, your majesty," confirmed Astral. "This is Zack Glacis, Gretchen Shadows, Eric Flare, Malcolm Spark and Patrick Tempus." She then lent down to the party and whispered. "I forgot to mention the king is a little mad and likes to ramble."

"We are well met young elementals," greeted Hud.

"Over here, your majesty." said Astral with an air of having to put up with this sort thing all the time. The king turned.

"Indeed! I knew that. And let no one ever question whether or not I did. Anyway, tell me, for what reason have you come to see me?" There was a moment of silence but after a bit of struggle Zack managed to get himself to speak.

"We need your permission to enter Connection Tower your majesty," replied Zack.

"The Anti-Gamer has invaded it and has started a dark spell that's already affecting our world," explained Eric.

"It may have a specific target but it could do all sort of damage to other things," added Gretchen.

"And, of course, after that all his attention will be focused on this world."

"So it is very important that we get there." The king mulled over these words.

"Those are indeed very good reasons," said Hud at last. "Which is good, otherwise you would be in trouble. You know there any many in our world who are learning to fight monsters, even my own grandchildren. It fills me with pride watching them beat people up. Now, none of these people are any worse at fighting monsters than you; some are probably better, yet for whatever reason Astral has entrusted this task to the five of you. But she claims that teenage humans make the best heroes but in my experience so do the peoples of this world. But when we are faced such a dangerous foe we should use everything at our disposal and not just start knocking out teeth left, right and centre. Then again it may be better if the centre was struck first. I should look into that later. Where was I? Oh yes! Well you lot should be given a chance to prove yourselves and I have nothing against you myself, so, why not, you have my permission."

"I think he said yes," whispered Zack confused.

"Thank you, your majesty," the party said in union.

"Yet I must tell you," began Hud. "I sense there may be more to the Anti-Gamer's plan than you know. And it may have something to do with his plans for your world. So be careful and if you get eaten by a monster count your lucky stars you'll be dead when you come out the other end. Good luck and I hope you find the strength of heart you will need."

"We will try, your majesty," said Gretchen.

As they left Hud thought to himself, "I like 'em. They seem like a right bunch of oddballs. Like me I'm a whole bunch. They're perfect for our world."

"Is the king going a bit senile?" asked Patrick once they were out the throne room.

"No, he's always been like that," explained Astral. "I've known him his whole very long life and he's been like that for all of it. It's about twenty percent put on and eighty percent for real."

With the king's advice ringing in their ears (among the other things he said) the party left the castle. Astral warped them to the tower for quickness. Connection Tower stood over them tall and somehow mighty. Made from black stone, the architecture made it look as though a wire wound around it and on top they could make out what resembled a portable Wi-Fi connector.

"The Anti-Gamer will be at the top," explained Astral. "There's likely to be several talon-teeth on the way up."

"Talon-teeth?" asked Malcolm.

"Probably those four legged mouths we fought in the ore.rar city," replied Patrick.

"There's no time to waste, you must go now," said Astral. The party went straight to the door, and heaved it open. Inside they were surprised to find simply a staircase straight to the top.

"That's most convenient," observed Eric.

"Apart from those bitey, scratchy guys," added Zack gesturing to the large number of talon-teeth on the stairs.

"Always the pessimist, Zack," mocked Gretchen.

"I'm with him on this one," said Patrick.

"Me too," added Malcolm.

"Oh shut up," snapped Gretchen. "Let's just go fight the bad guys."

"All right,all right," said Zack.

"Let's go then, dearies," Eric said camply. And so they began to climb the stairs and fight the monsters. talon-teeth came at them from all angles. One lunged at Zack but he managed to freeze it before it could bite him. The one that tried to drop down on them were met by Eric's blazing fire balls and the ones that tried to climb up were struck by Malcolm's lighting. A couple jumped at Patrick but he used his powers to reverse their movements and send them backwards until they were above nothing and he let them drop. Gretchen sent waves of shadows ahead to clear the way. Finally they made it to the top of the stairs which lead on to the roof of the tower. The sculpture that looked like a portable Wi-Fi connecter was suspended above and there in front of them was the Anti-Gamer. He had made a dark sphere of magic which was sending energy into the sculpture which in turn was directing it towards the sky. Visrel turned to face them.

"We meet again, young interference," sighed Visrel. "No doubt you're here to try a stop my spell from wiping all those detestable games from your world."

"That's right, whack job," remarked Gretchen.

"You had better get ready for a thrashing," said Eric.

"No, I don't think I'll fight you myself," replied the Anti-Gamer. "I have someone else to do the deed. Come out spring snake." Replying to his call a large creature appeared from over the side of the tower. The creature, true to its name, was a large snake that must have coiled itself round the top of the tower and taken on the form of a large spring with a serpentine head.

"Not another one," moaned Zack.

"Those fangs look nasty," groaned Malcolm.

"Might as well beat this one too," said Patrick. The snake lunged down at the party but they got out the way just in time. They threw their respective elements at it but they didn't seem to have much effect.

"You are not strong enough to defeat my spring snake it would seem," taunted Visrel. "Now, would Astral's chosen heroes like to meet their end either in the belly of the spring or by meeting the ground from a great height? Do make this decision carefully."

"Well if we can't beat it what do we do?" asked Zack.

"If we can't beat it perhaps we can trick it," suggested Eric.

"Do any of you guys have a trick in mind?" asked Gretchen. There was a pause while they thought. However, it was interrupted by the snake attacking again. It slammed its metal body down on them, they got out of the way but were still knocked down.

"This seems to happen a lot," observed Zack from flat on his back. As the party tried to get up the Anti-Gamer waved his hand and they were pressed back to the ground by his magic.

"Now, spring snake, finish them," called Visrel. The snake bared down on them; the party could not move they tried to use their powers in some way. Luckily their powers weren't blocked and Patrick's time powers managed to immobilize the snake temporarily. The Anti-Gamer advanced on them summoning his helical blade, but Zack managed to freeze the soles of his boots causing him to slip over and free the party. The party managed to get up and Zack used his powers to pile on the ice keeping the Anti-Gamer on the ground. While the others' attention was on the Anti-gamer Eric noticed that the spring snake was free of Patrick's powers and was pushing its body together to launch itself at him.

"Oh drat," stated Eric. He knew he didn't have time to get out of the way so he concentrated hard on using his powers to defend himself. The snaked sprang forward straight towards Eric but just as it reached him, his powers worked and he was covered by a large flame. The flame exploded and knocked the snake back the way it came, causing it to strike the sphere of magic, which cracked and shattered. The others had just noticed what was happening as the spring snake crashed to the floor.

"We foiled his plan," said Gretchen triumphantly.

"What do you mean we?" asked Eric.

"If we can't beat either of them maybe we should get out of here," said Zack.

"Don't think you get to escape me so easily," warned Visrel. Zack threw a snowball at the ground which burst into a large cloud obscuring the villain's view. The party turned to retreat.

"Was that a smoke-screen?" asked Gretchen.

"Technically it's a snow-screen," replied Zack.

"Another ninja-themed move?" Visrel appeared in front of them before they could reach the door.

"I do hope you're not leaving already," said Visrel. "But don't worry, I won't waste time destroying you; I'll simply leave you all trapped here." He faced the spring snake and held his hand up to it. His magic surged from his hand to the snake and the metal it was made of came apart. The Anti-Gamer then gestured towards the party and the bits of metal divided up into five and wrapped up each one of the five of them.

"I'm fairly certain this counts as cheating, said Zack.

"I'd like to examine the 'source' of the Data Realm so I'll be heading to your world," said Visrel. "I can use this tower to send myself there and return to the Data Realm later to destroy this world. Now then, sweet dreams, foul heroes." And with another wave of his arm everything went dark.

Zack was the first to come to; the loud cry he made when he saw where they were revived everyone else. After knocking them out Visrel had hung them off the edge of Connections Tower's roof.

"AAAAAAAARGH!" Zack continued yelling.

"Zack you hurting my ears! Quiet, down!" said Eric.

"ARE YOU KIDDING? WE'RE HANNGING OVER THE EDGE OF A TOWER I'LL YELL IF I WANT TO," was Zack's response.

"Somebody's bound to have heard that," said Gretchen.

"Even if someone pulls us up I don't think they could break this metal easily," Eric pointed out.

"Yeah, it's some sturdy stuff; we'd better use our powers," said Patrick "You know, from what I understand about my temporal energy, if I use it right I should be able to teleport us."

"You're thinking of space powers," said Eric.

"No, I've read up on this sort of thing: you can warp through which ever element you control."

"But for you doesn't that mean time travel?" said Gretchen. "Which you said was extremely advanced stuff that barely anyone has tried."

"Eric, do you think you could use your fire like a jet to get back on top and then go get help?" enquired Zack.

"I think I should be able to," replied Eric.

"Oh, come on, guys, why won't you let me try," cried Patrick.

"Because you're mistaken," said Malcolm.

"Yeah, we don't wanna risk ending up in a time without video games," said Zack. Everything around them went white and they felt like they were floating; the same sensation as when they were transported between their world and the Data Realm.

And when everything cleared they saw they were on top of the tower again free from their metal bonds.

"What part of 'don't try teleporting' didn't you understand?" demanded Gretchen. "If we end fighting dinosaurs you're never gonna hear the end of it!"

"I didn't do anything," Patrick pointed out.

"It was me who transported you," came Astral's voice. They turned around and there was Astral.

"Gretchen was right, someone did hear your screeching, Zack," joked Eric.

"Yes. I knew he was loud but I didn't think I could hear him from all the way down at the bottom."

"That's nothing; you should hear him when his games go wrong," remarked Gretchen.

"You're the first to go, Gretch!" growled Zack.

"What have I told you about calling me Gretch?"

"You'd better tell me what happened with Visrel," said Astral cutting across the next remark. The party explained what had happened.

"Can he actually go to our world?" asked Eric.

"He can. This world and everything from it was born from the magic and data in your world," explained Astral. "Anything from the Data Realm can go to your world just as anything from your world can come here."

"Where in our world would he have ended up?" wondered Gretchen.

"I can use my powers to search for him." Astral returned them to her temple to begin the search.

Astral did what she said she could and located the Anti-Gamer; he was in Reekie. She returned the party to their home city straight away. Based on the information Astral gave them the Anti-Gamer was in the power plant over on the western part of the city.

"What is the Anti-Gamer doing in a power plant?" wondered Patrick.

"Don't you remember? The Data Realm was born from our world's magic," replied Eric. "He wanted to see the source."

"And this happened because the magic got into the Wi-Fi through the world's computers due to us using magic to power everything," recalled Zack.

"What does he think he's gonna suddenly learn by looking at a giant crystal?" wondered Gretchen.

"Don't want to know," said Malcolm.

"Whatever he's doing we can't just leave him there. It's bound to end badly for someone," said Zack. Reekie had a tram system which the party utilized to get to the right part of the city. "Can you imagine the trouble if they ever had to rebuild the tram system?"

"What makes you think they'd rebuild it if they had gotten rid of it?" asked Gretchen.

"Are you kidding? That is exactly the sort of thing the barmy lot who run this city would do." When they arrived outside the power plant they began to plan how to get inside.

"Anyone got any ideas?" asked Eric.

"Nope."

"Nada."

"Not a thing."

"I'd have a go at you guys if I had any ideas myself," said Eric.

"Maybe my shadow powers can get us in," suggested Gretchen.

"Let's go with that seeing as the rest of us don't have so much as a crazy idea," responded Zack. Gretchen began to concentrate and her magic began to build. Her shadow began to grow and became a large circle that surrounded the party on the ground. The party then sank into the shadow and before they knew it they were within the shadow. Inside the shadow was like being in a dream where they had no body. Except for Gretchen who was still in complete control. She directed the shadow along the ground under the gate and beneath a door to within the power plant. Once inside everyone rose out of the shadow which returned to normal.

"Just wait till I can do that alot easier," said Gretchen proudly.

"Come on, let's find that psycho," said Eric.

"Twice in one day we're seeking out a maniac with dangerous magic," observed Zack grimly.

"He's likely to have gone straight to the power source," said Patrick.

"Here's a map of the place," Malcolm pointed out. They found the room named 'Crystal Room' and headed straight there. As you may remember in this world magic is used as a power source. This is done by creating mystic crystals that generate electricity which is used to power many things in this world. The party made it to the room and burst inside. They found the Anti-Gamer standing in front of the machine; the electrical crystal was hooked up, to preparing to attack.

"Oh no you don't, captain creepy," called Gretchen. The Anti-Gamer turned round.

"So you did manage to get out of that predicament I left you in," mused Visrel.

"This place is deserted. What have you done to all the people who work here?" demanded Zack who still struggled a little.

"I simply put them to sleep while I'm here. I have no quarrel with them."

"What do you think you're going to learn here?" asked Eric.

"I wanted to know how to make these myself," replied Visrel. "Can't seem to recreate the Miyamotan variant."

"Why do you need electrical crystals?" wondered Zack.

"Something terrible no doubt," said Malcolm.

"Whatever you're doing we're going to stop you," added Patrick. Visrel smirked a fake smile.

"I've got what I need so I'll be leaving now," mused Visrel. "Miyamoto won't destroy itself. The king's not that kind of crazy."

"Can't we convince you to give up altogether?" asked Gretchen.

"No. I will destroy Miyamoto then I will return to this world and get rid of all your beloved games and then slaughter every last gamer and game developer in the world for good measure."

"Didn't know about that massacre bit," said Zack. "Just the genocide."

"And it is somewhat amusing that the ones supposed to stop me are you five," Visrel continued. "Not that I can feel amusement. I have no idea why Astral chose you lot out of all the other teenagers with magic powers, but it doesn't matter. You couldn't handle Spring Snake, you'll never be able to take me on. What chance does Miyamoto have?"

"Well, that's just plain rude," grumbled Zack.

"We'll show you, ya jerk," snapped Gretchen.

"We won't give up just 'cause of a few harsh words," growled Eric.

"Perhaps you will if you make a disastrous mistake," said Virel.

"What are you talking about, dearie?"

"Another monster."

"We've only failed to defeat one," Patrick pointed out.

"But this time there's no way for it not to end badly." Visrel snapped his fingers and a mass of dark energy appeared in the room. "You have two choices. One, you leave and the monster ruins the plant leaving your city without power for a long time or, two, you fight it and ruin the plant anyway. No matter what you do it will end in failure for you. And as a bonus it'll be harder for Astral to send for you for a while. No matter what happens remember to feel bad about it."

The Anti-Gamer threw his cape over himself and vanished. The monster emerged from the energy mass: it looked like a giant earthworm but it was putrid yellow and had a gaping mouth filled with teeth like a shark's. Zack yelled in fright at the sight of it. The worm lunged at the party and they scrambled out the way as it bit the air where they were.

"We have to beat this thing before the plant gets too damaged," said Zack.

"Yeah, we know but it won't be easy," said Patrick.

"We know that!"

"Try not to get bit in half."

"Can't guarantee that."

The worm opened its mouth and its sharp teeth fired out at them. Zack made an ice wall blocking the attack which cracked when the teeth hit. Eric moved around the worm's side and hit it with his scythe covered in flames. The worm turned to where he was and was then hit by a blast of lightning from Malcolm. The worm spat more of its never-ending teeth at them but Patrick used his powers to stop them in mid-air and then Gretchen dropped a shadow block on it. The worm was knocked to the ground but it whipped its tail around and knocked the whole party over. The worm rose above them and lunged down towards Zack summoned his staff and struck it. Malcolm shot several arrows at it and Eric threw fire balls. The worm whipped its tail again and Gretchen made another shadow block which the worm hit instead. Regrouping the party noticed that Patrick had been standing charging his magic. He then unleashed it and a huge pulse of temporal energy hurtled towards the monster. When it struck the worm, it was thrown back towards the crystal, breaking through the protective glass and slamming into the crystal. Electricity coursed over the worm and it burst into magic. The party saw the crystal had a massive crack in it just before all the power cut out across Reekie. After realizing that the plant workers would be waking up soon Gretchen used her shadow magic to get them outside again. They felt really bad.

"What do we do now?" asked Malcolm.

"What can we do?" replied Zack. "Why were we picked? What makes us so special?"

"I guess we should figure that out," said Gretchen.

"And then we'll know if we can stop him or not," said Eric.

"Let's just go home," said Patrick.

The following morning came and the party weren't feeling any better. Even though the power was out for little more than twenty minutes the felt awful. They sat on a bench overlooking a river, their reflections staring back at them. Zack looked right into his glum face, his brown hair covered by his goggles. Gretchen's long brown hair just came over her shoulders. Eric had hair which was the same colour as Zack's but was cut shorter. Malcolm adjusted his rectangular glasses beneath his gold coloured hair. Patrick had short black hair and had thin side burns. Coincidently they all had blue eyes (of varying shades). In terms of height it went, Malcolm, Gretchen, Patrick Zack and Eric were about the same height. They pondered over whether or not they had any chance.

"All my life I've wanted to go on adventures," stated Zack. "But deep down I always knew I was never meant to."

"Are we just going to give up then?" asked Patrick.

"Yep."

"What does make us any different from other teenagers with elemental magic?" wondered Gretchen.

"We're a fabulous bunch of oddballs for a start," joked Eric. "Well, I'm fabulous."

"Or maybe it's got something to do with how we got our powers." You see in their world everyone was born with the ability to use magic however it wasn't common for people to use magic, but neither was it rare. There are two ways in which they could use their magic prowess: first they could teach themselves or they could be given knowledge and a natural knack for a certain form of magic from someone or something. This is how the party gained their elemental powers. Everybody cast their minds back to how they gained their abilities. Each one is a tale on its own but for now let's just look into Gretchen's story.

It began back when she was twelve, when she used to tower over the boys; she's still taller than most of them but it was more obvious back then. As mentioned before Gretchen had a habit of getting her and her friends lost in the woods. On this occasion it was just two of them.

"Come on, Zack, there's nothing to be afraid of," assured Gretchen.

"Being in a dark forest is plenty to be afraid of," answered Zack.

"We've been down here plenty of times and nothing's ever happened to us. Why should this time be any different?"

"This could well be the time a ghost living in forest decides he hates twelve-year-olds."

"Well you did promise you'd come with me into that cave we found last time we were here."

"No I didn't, I promised if you made me go in there I'd tell both our mums."

"Fine then, you wait outside when we get there." They arrived outside the cave and Zack waited while Gretchen ventured in.

"We must have passed by this part of the woods several times before," Zack thought to himself. "So how come we didn't notice this cave until last time? Could it be some sort of magic cave? Knowing our luck that's where the ghost lives. Sort of." It would be some time before Zack would learn that it was a magic cave, the sort that changes its location every month. Gretchen had ventured into the cave; it was not deep and at its back she found a torch that cast a large shadow.

"That's it?!" Gretchen thought to herself. "It's just a torch? Hey what's that?" Gretchen had spotted the writing on the torch just below the flame.It read:

'This flame casts what is known as the Deepest Shadow.

It is rich with magic that can only be used by some.

You must prove yourself if you wish to claim its power for your own.'

Gretchen began to wonder what that meant.

"I wish to take this challenge," declared Gretchen wanting to see what would happen. The flame flickered and the writing on the torch faded and were replaced with new words.

'You must face the trials in the shadows.

To prove your heart is strong enough to wield this magic.'

The shadows surrounded Gretchen and she could only see herself when, suddenly, three other people appeared in front of her. Gretchen stared in shock as all three of them looked exactly like Zack.

"There's three of him now?" she yelled. "Is this a trial? Come on one's loud enough!" In the darkness before her more words appeared.

Which of these would your best friend say?

"Being in this cave is tremendous fun," said the first Zack. "It's dark, I don't like it, can we go please?" said the second. "I bet all sorts of cool things are hiding in here," said the third.

"That's not even a challenge.It's clearly the second one. Zack is really scared of the dark; he'd be trying to get out of here," said Gretchen. The Zacks smiled and then vanished. Three other figures appeared.This time they each were her older brother, Oswald. New words appeared.

'Which of them is your brother?'

This time the figures said nothing. They each smiled then frowned.They cycled through various different expressions,but they each looked a little different on each face. Gretchen, realising what the trial was, stared closely at each face until she knew.

"It's the one on the right. I'd recognize the look in his eyes anywhere; the other two are far to normal," The three figures smiled one last time and then vanished. The shadows shifted and a third message appeared.

'Save your friend and brother.'

This time the shadows formed a large chamber with cages hanging from the ceiling. In one was Zack, in the other was Oswald.A strange figure stood before her; it just seemed to be a large shadow.It was looking at the two cages.

"If this was real I'd be freaked," thought Gretchen. Gretchen looked around her to see what she could do. However, she was drawing a blank so she just started to yell, "Hey you! That's my big brother and my best friend you got there. Give 'em back before I give a good hard kick right where you don't want me to." The figure turned around and moved towards her. She was shaking a bit but she mustered her courage, picked up a large rock and smacked the figure with it. While it was dazed she ran past it to the cages. She saw that they had been hoisted up by the same chain held in place by a rope tied to a weight. The creature was advancing on Gretchen again as she fiddled with the rope. She managed to untie it and then the cages dropped down right on top of the figure. The figure was trapped and the cages were open and Zack and Oswald climbed out. Before anything else happened, everything shifted and the cave returned to normal with one last message.

'You have a good heart.

You can be trusted with this great power.

The deepest Shadow shall go through your heart.'

"Go through my heart, what does that mean?" thought Gretchen. The shadow rose up off the ground and shot into her heart. Gretchen found herself lying on the ground and the torch had strangely disappeared. She realized she must have passed out. She headed over to where Zack was still waiting.

"About time," said Zack when Gretchen emerged from the cave.

"Zack, there was this strange flame and this magic shadow in there," Gretchen began.

"ZACKARY! GRETCHEN!" came the voice of Marcus from somewhere nearby.

"Tell me when we get back to the house. Mum's sent Marcus to find us," said Zack. Gretchen didn't know what to make of what happened in that cave. Over the next few days Gretchen came to realize that the Deepest Shadow had given her shadow-based magic. She was rather surprised at first but soon she realized that she loved being a shadow elemental; however, in the long run they were a little neglected.

Back in the present Gretchen knew now why they could save Miyamoto and what Astral had been telling them.

"I know why," she stated.

"Know what?" asked Eric."

"Why Astral chose us."

"We know why, because we have magic and we're teenagers," Zack reminded her.

"Something about our potential," added Malcolm.

"Exactly.She knew we had greater potential than most others," said Gretchen. "Because of what we've done."

"You mean because of how we got our powers?" asked Patrick.

"While most people taught themselves all sort of magic spells to master an element we were given our powers. I got my powers when the Deepest Shadow passed through my heart. Zack, your magic was made to match the most powerful ice elemental who ever lived. Eric you wield the fires of the sun itself. Malcolm, you were gifted your lighting when you befriended the thunder birds. Patrick, only you could have your way inside the crystal meteorite and only you could have gotten those time powers. We each faced a trial and earned our powers. We might not realise it, but we all have courage inside even those of us who don't believe it. Your courage appears when it's important: when we think our friends are in danger or when we're about to fight a monster. Like Astral said we have the potential to be greatest wielders of our respective elements and that could make us great heroes. For once we just need to believe in ourselves."

"I always knew we'd die doing something stupid. Might as well be while fighting a powerful monster," said Zack feeling some rare confidence. "Maybe we were always meant to fight insane creatures. And for whatever daft reason we're in this, we don't want out. Let's go save Miyamoto."

They realised what Astral meant when she suggested they had already made their destinies. She believed that the way in which they each got their elements they had made the decision to be a hero. So the party set off, not sure if they could do it but more willing to try than before.

When they got to a computer Astral summoned them right back into Miyamoto. They were once again in Astral's temple.

"I know you all have trouble believing in yourselves but I will always be grateful for you have done," said Astral. "And what happened at the plant was Visrel's fault alone. I've been able to access the plants records which made it say that the break in the crystal was due to a fault in the spell that made it, causing a freak energy surge." The party thanked her.

"Well we're not going to give up quite yet," assured Eric.

"Who better to save this world than a bunch of gamer oddballs," added Zack who didn't struggle as much.

"Even if we can't beat him we'll at least mess up his plans," said Patrick.

"We'll fight to the end," stated Malcolm.

"And we will show him not to mess with us," claimed Gretchen.

"I think your team should have a name," suggested Astral. "What was it you called your group on social media?"

"That's a great idea! We are now the Frozen Shadowy Temporal Lightning Fire Club!" said Gretchen who was probably joking.

"You know full well it's just Frozen Fire," said Zack. "And that the name had nothing to do with any of our powers."

"It's absolutely perfect," agreed Eric.

"All right then, Frozen Fire if you're up to it, it's time to continue your fight," said Astral. "The Anti-Gamer is putting the final stages of his plan to destroy Miyamoto in motion. All I know is that he plans to cut Miyamoto away from the rest of the Data Realm. I have no idea how he plans to do this, I'm not even sure where I should send you. It must have something to do with more powerful version of the spell he was using at Connection Tower. He did say it was a test." Nobody could think how Visrel was planning to utilize this spell; however, they weren't without ideas.

"Surely he'll have to do something at that cliff?" mused Patrick.

"Yeah, maybe we should head to Edge Forest," said Zack.

"I suppose it would be a start," said Astral. Just then something seemed to catch Astral's attention as she turned suddenly. She walked over to the far wall where a large painting hung, which Frozen Fire just noticed was a map, presumably of Miyamoto. "Something's happening at the ore.rar city. You better head there first."

Astral sent Frozen Fire straight to Steel Crater where it was clear some commotion was happening. They summoned their weapons and headed into the city. In the city they found the ore.rar fighting an army of talon-teeth.

"Twice in one week, these guys can't catch a break," observed Zack.

"They're large metal creatures, and it would seem they can pack a punch so I don't think the talon-teeth can cause them too much bother," Eric pointed out. Just then several talon-teeth were sent overhead by an ore.rar they recognised as Iron.

"My friends, your timing is perfect," exclaimed Iron when he saw them. "The Anti-Gamer's minions are setting something up in the centre of town; follow me." Iron lead the way to the middle of the city where a large group of talon-teeth where positioning a large black cube.

"W...w... What is that?" stammered Malcolm.

"Undoubtedly it has something to do with Visrel's plan," mused Patrick.

"Come on, guys, let's go see if we can break that thing," said Gretchen. Frozen Fire charged forward but out of nowhere a large monster landed in front of them. It was a suit of armour the size of a big man wielding a lance in its left arm and a hammer in the other. Gaps could be seen: it was an empty suit of armour despite its fearsome eyes gleaming through its helmets visor.

"That's the smallest but scariest yet," said Zack with a hint of peril in his voice. The armour leapt at them and they scattered. The helmet turned as it looked at each of them no doubt deciding who to go for first. Zack made an icicle kunai and threw it at the armour but it simply broke on contact. Eric mustered his strength and sent a great burst of fire at it but it didn't work either.

"This thing's as durable as that ugly snake!" exclaimed Gretchen.

"I guess we should expect that from a suit of armour," mused Patrick.

"We need a plan quick," said Malcolm.

"And it should probably be a good one for once," added Eric. Eric leapt to the side as the lance came towards him. Zack scrambled out the way as the hammer came crashing down. Malcolm threw a ball of lightning at it and it struck but the armour still wasn't fazed. Patrick sent a lot of temporal energy at the armour in what was an attempt to immobilise it.However it swung its hammer at him and he lost his concentration and the temporal energy disappeared. Gretchen sent a shadow wave at it while it was still recovering and knocked the helmet off. Suddenly Iron appeared, kicked the helmet and grabbed the rest of the armour and held it still.

"Strike now, my friends, quickly," cried Iron. But the arms and legs of the armour detached and floated towards Frozen Fire. Iron looked rather taken aback by this.

"Phantom armour always does that," groaned Zack.

"I suppose we'd better run until we think of something," said Gretchen.

"We are," called the voice of Eric. Gretchen then noticed the others had already started running; she then ran too while muttering insults. The various pieces of armour pursued them. The arm with the lance appeared in front of Gretchen who defended herself with her halberd. She made some shadow duplicates to help her. The right leg charged at Patrick but he distorted its time so it couldn't get near enough to land a hit. The other leg came at Malcolm who grabbed it and began sending electricity coursing through it. The torso came towards Eric who realized it was rather spiky; he held it back with all the fire he could muster. Finally, the arm with hammer approached Zack with the helmet just behind it. Zack pelted the thing with his sharpest icicles but to no avail. The hammer rose upwards ready to land a deadly blow but

Zack focused his magic and sent out a cold beam at the hammer. The ice built up on it until it was too heavy and the arm dropped it and it landed on the helmet which smashed. And with it broken the whole armour disappeared in a burst of magic. Frozen Fire staggered back to the centre of the city but it was too late; the mysterious cube had activated. Its middle rose upwards as the whole thing unfolded and became a twenty-foot tower that looked like an electric pylon. When anyone went near it they were stopped by a force field of some sort.

"What could he use this for?" wondered Iron. There was flash of light and Astral appeared.

"Frozen Fire, are you all right?" asked Astral.

"We're fine," assured Eric.

"We got all the monsters but they still set up whatever this is," explained Gretchen gesturing to the tower.

"It's filled with the same magic he used at the tower," said Astral. "But this spire isn't the only one. There are towers in the homes of the acorn.ris and cloud.tiff. What's more is that the Anti-Gamer is in Adlez. He must have one last tower to set up."

Frozen Fire arrived in Adlez which was under attack. Soldiers and law enforcers were fighting talon-teeth left right and centre.

"I think the polygons can handle themselves," said Patrick.

"We better head straight to the head jerk," said Zack.

"Guys, something's happening at the castle," Malcolm pointed out. They headed straight to the castle. In the throne room the guards were battling larger than normal talon-teeth while Visrel advanced on the king.

"Do not fret, your majesty, I will not harm you or your grandchildren. I simply wish to place something on your roof," said Visrel in a mock reassuring tone.

"This something will help you destroy this world. So, you will hurt my grandchildren and all the peoples of this world regardless," retorted Hud. "But your plan is doomed to fail. Miyamoto will never fall by your hand." The Anti-Gamer held his helical blade up to the king getting ready to strike.

"Then I guess it doesn't matter when I kill you." Lighting struck Visrel from above, followed by an icicle and a fireball in the back and then a shadow wave and a temporal pulse. He turned around to face his attackers. "Oh. Did your failure not destroy your spirit?"

"You're meant to learn from your mistakes and correct them not sulk over them," said Zack. "For once I'm skipping the sulking."

"And now we're gonna kick you out of the castle," added Gretchen.

"Do excuse me, your majesty, I think the humans would like to be destroyed," Visrel said to the king. Visrel waved his hand they felt some magic but it didn't seem to do anything. "What? You can resist being knocked unconscious by my powers already. How? You're no stronger than you were on the tower." The Anti-Gamer walked towards Frozen Fire whilst waving his hand and dark barriers appeared in front of the king and the guards, keeping them out.

"No escape now," observed Gretchen.

"Didn't seem likely anyway," said Eric determined.

"Let's show him just how strong we can be."

"By all means show me your strength, young fools," mocked Visrel.

"That's Frozen Fire to you, lord psycho!" exclaimed Zack.

"I won't bother to remember seeing as you're about to die," threatened Visrel. He lunged straight at them swinging his helical blade but Patrick blocked it with his sword. Malcolm grabbed Visrel's arm and unleashed a lot of electricity. He growled in pain and pulled away from them and then summoned a sphere of dark energy and threw it at Frozen Fire. Gretchen swung her halberd cutting the sphere in half. Zack sent his freezing energy at Visrel but he blocked it with his blade. While he was distracted Patrick used his power to send a blast of temporal energy at Visrel, causing him to buckle over and the last bit of Zack's energy covered half his face in ice. While pinned to the ground Visrel unleashed a burst of darkness that knocked Frozen Fire over allowing him to get back up and remove the ice. He then made ropes appear around the respective feet of Frozen Fire hoisting them into the air. Eric managed to summon a massive flare underneath Visrel which caused the ropes to disappear and sent Frozen Fire back to the ground.

"Ow," could be heard from several of them. Visrel sent a beam of energy at them but Zack managed to make an ice wall, for defence, in time. Malcolm sent a barrage of arrows at Visrel but he knocked a few away with his gauntlet while others managed to strike. Eric charged forward swinging his scythe and knocked the helical blade out of the Visrel's hand. Visrel held two of his fingers together and a dark energy appeared around them. When he swung them through the air the energy became sharp as proved when it struck off Eric's scythe. Gretchen sent a shadow wave at him but he just cut through it and made his way to his blade and picked it up. At this point Patrick struck him with a time blast (as he called it, it looked like a clock that burst apart then the shards went flying towards the target)knocking him to the floor. Eric and Malcolm piled on the fire and lightning but Visrel just used another burst of dark energy to escape and then knocked the next time burst out of the way. Gretchen sent a ball of shadows at him but it just hit him and didn't slow him down much. Zack formed a lot of ice on the end of his staff and then swung it and struck Visrel on the head. He staggered backwards and rubbed his face where he had been hit.

"Well done, Frozen Fire, you can have the victory in this battle," stated Visrel. "But what does it matter. I sent the order to place the final tower before the battle began and now that it is in place I can begin this world's final moments." And with that the Anti-Gamer swung his cape over him and vanished.

"Thank you, young ones," said Hud. "Well, next to me everyone's young. Except Astral. Anyway, if you hadn't arrived when you did he may have killed me and my grandchildren wherever they are at the moment, and then all the staff. There'd be no one to clean up the mess."

"He might pull it off indirectly though," Eric pointed out.

"Will you go after that well-dressed cad?" asked the king.

"Well, we've nearly gotten ourselves killed so far, so we might as well see it through to the end," mused Gretchen.

"Of course we need to know where he's gone," added Eric.

"He has likely gone to Game's Edge," stated Hud.

"Where's that?" questioned Zack.

"You've been there before, Astral tells me. Game's Edge is the name off the cliff between Miyamoto and the rest of the Data Realm," explained Hud.

"Where that massive blue door is," recalled Eric.

"Yes, he no doubt wishes to make sure his plan works. Front row seat and all that," said Hud. "From what I've gathered it would seem that the purpose of the towers in the homes of the ore.rar, the acorn.ris and the cloud.tiff is to charge massive amounts of magic and send it to the tower on top of this castle which will combine the magic and fire at Game's Edge in an attempt to cut this world away. If he succeeds Miyamoto will become unstable and he'll be able to destroy it easily. Which would be a bit of rotten day for everyone. Except for Visrel I suppose."

"I suppose you've got to go to a lot of trouble to destroy the world," observed Zack. "Still, that is a teensy bit over the top."

"We'd better find Astral straight away," stated Eric.

Astral was waiting outside the castle staring up at the roof. On the castle's roof was the fourth tower; it looked just like the other one they had seen only it was bigger and had a large dish on it that they guessed was for firing all the built-up magic. It took a moment before they remembered what they were meant to be doing. They got Astral's attention and told her what they knew. Frozen Fire were then told that the polygons, ore.rar, acorn.ris and cloud.tiff would each try to take out the tower in their respective homes. They then agreed to fight the Anti-Gamer again as a means of distracting him so he wouldn't notice the towers were being interfered with.

Frozen Fire arrived at Game's Edge. For some reason the looming cliff face seemed more ominous.

"Frozen Fire, I must thank you," said Astral. "I know you don't find it easy to believe in yourself, but please remember that you have made a difference in our world so far and as much as I want to point out you not strong enough yet to challenge him you have already bested him in a duel and walked away relatively unscathed. True, that was most likely due to his plan being ready to begin its final stage but still you should be proud of what you've done. I promise you I will get you out of there if he defeats you." Frozen Fire thanked Astral a turned their attention to Game's Edge. On the bridge leading to the door they could make out the figure of Visrel. They headed straight to him.

"I was beginning to think you wouldn't arrive before the world was destroyed," said Visrel when Frozen Fire arrived. He then turned to face them. "You seem to have unusual magical strength yet you're far from being strong enough to stop me and yet you still face me with what little chance you have."

"The odds are never in the heroes' favour," said Eric.

"But the good guys still win," added Gretchen.

"This isn't a children's fairy tale, this is real life," said Visrel coldly. "I am a true monster; you can't match my power."

"So what? We could be the greatest of each of our respective element," said Patrick with confidence.

"We'll mess up your plans," said Malcolm.

"We'll make sure you never succeed," added Zack.

"Well you're certainly welcome to try," said Visrel. "We're lucky this bridge is so large. Plenty of room to cut you down. And don't forget, monsters always have another form." The Anti-Gamer's magic surged over him and his figure turned dark. He began to grow and change. The changing stopped and the darkness cleared, he had turned into a massive beast that resembled both a bear and a wolf. He stood on all fours looking ferocious and wild, looming over them with malice in his eyes. The claws were made of metal, he gnashed his blade like teeth; he had a ridge of spikes down his back and his tail seemed to be his helical blade.

"This is it, guys, the final boss," stated Zack putting his goggles over his eyes. Visrel swiped at them with his deadly claws. Frozen Fire got out of the way just in time but they could feel the air being sliced. Next Visrel fired an energy beam from his mouth at them. Zack blocked it with a big ice shield but was knocked to the ground. Eric sent a wall of fire at him and Gretchen sent a massive shadow wave, both striking Visrel in his head. Visrel leaped around on the spot swinging his blade tail at them Patrick stalled it with a large amount of his magic Malcolm followed up with a massive lightning bolt.

"Hope that stings, Vissy," called Eric.

"We've definitely gotten stronger!" exclaimed Gretchen. "Just in time it would seem." The claws came hurtling towards them again Malcolm fired several arrows into the paw, just in time. Zack swung his staff at the spot where the arrows hit while Patrick attacked the other paw with his sword. Visrel readied to sink its teeth into them but Eric launched a fireball into his mouth while Gretchen rained shadow copies of her halberd on his head. The monster exhaled a beam of dark energy from his mouth and Eric blocked with a wall of fire. When they collided there was a BANG and everyone fell to the ground; luckily Visrel was temporally incapacitated too.

At the towers no one was having any luck destroying the barriers.

"If fifteen beings made of metal with giant arms can't break this thing then we're in real trouble," said Iron, who with fourteen other ore.rar was feeling rather exhausted. "What's worse is that the energy seems to have built up as much as it can." As soon as he finished saying that the tower fired the energy in the direction of Adlez and the towers in the homes of the acorn.ris and the cloud.tiff did the same. The three beams met at the top of the fourth tower which began charging energy. Below the king was witness to this.

"We must hurry time is running short," called Hud. "It's up to us, while Frozen Fire keep the Anti-Gamer distracted. There must be some way to break this thing. Or at least make it look a little nicer. "

The fight against the Anti-Gamer in his feral form continued. He began spewing energy balls at them. Everyone retaliated: several were cut in half by the sword, scythe and halberd; some were shot by arrows and others were knocked away by the staff. The monster proceeded to snap at them with his teeth again so Frozen Fire moved out of the way. They retaliated with icicle kunai, shadow duplicates of paint pots, fire balls, lightning bolts and time bursts; unfortunately, despite the rapidness of their attack, Visrel wasn't too fazed. Once again he swung his tail at them just missing as they fell to the ground. Zack covered the area of the bridge around the monster with ice causing him to lose his balance. Eric launched a fire twister into the monster's right eye while Gretchen threw a shadow copy of her halberd into the left one. Malcolm threw a lightning bolt that had a hand that punched on the end and Patrick mustered his biggest temporal pulse; both struck the monster in its back causing it to collapse. It was then that they heard a whooshing sound that got louder as quickly as it started. Frozen Fire looked up to see a beam of energy sailing overhead which struck Game's Edge. The fourth tower had begun to fire its energy spreading it all along the cliff which began to tremble.

At the castle the polygons were no closer to destroying the tower.

"There must be an opening in the barrier were the beam comes through," stated Hud. "We must utilize this to destroy the tower or give it a fresh lick of paint. I think I know just the thing. For the destroying not the paint." The king was known for his somewhat mad plans the always seemed to inexplicably work.

The bridge was shaking and began to come away from the cliff. Frozen Fire ran to get back on solid ground as the bridge began to collapse. They made it off the bridge and saw Visrel was manoeuvring to get off as well but was finding it hard due to his current form. And then he slipped on the ice Zack had made; when he slammed down the bridge tilted towards the them like it was a giant see-saw. Frozen Fire looked at each other and then each of them hurled a blast of their respective element at the part of the bridge that was attached to other side of the chasm. The force of the impact caused the bridge to tilt the in the opposite direction and Visrel slid off and into the energy surging across Game's

Edge. Visrel was covered in the same energy and writhed in pain.

The king's plan was being put into motion. The soldiers on the castle roof were carrying an item which they hoped to use to destroy the tower. It was a mirror known for being able to reflect magical energy. The plan was simple, but a bit mad: they were to throw the mirror into the energy beam close to the barrier so as to attempt to get the energy to reflect back at the tower in some way. They threw the mirror and then ran for cover. When the mirror entered the beam, it was disrupted and was seemingly absorbed by the mirror before being fired back at the tower. The surge of energy shook the tower which fell off the roof; luckily its own barrier contained the resulting explosion. Without the fourth tower the three other energy beams caused each other to reverse destroying the other towers. The mirror was shaking with energy; it split apart and shot off in different directions.

"Darn, I play fetch with that thing," said Hud. "Wait, I don't have a dog! No wonder he never brings it back!"

The energy surging across Game's Edge had stopped and there on the steps to the large door lay the Anti-Gamer having reverted back to his original form.

"I can't believe it. We're still alive," said Zack with a sigh of relief, putting his goggles back on his forehead.

"The king and the others got the towers," said Eric. Over the chasm the Anti-Gamer staggered back to his feet.

"As promised you did not succeed," called Gretchen.

"And you got trashed by your own spell," mocked Patrick.

"We beat you, you jerk." called Malcolm.

"I may have lost this day but I will not stop until Miyamoto and everything and everyone to do with video games in your world is nothing but memories," said Visrel. "It may take some time but the Data Realm is vast enough for me to hide in and regain my strength. You'd better practice,

Frozen Fire, if you ever wish to defeat me again; it will take real skill not great potential." He threw his cape over himself and vanished seemingly through the door to the Free Space.

Frozen Fire were returned to Adlez where their injures were treated; they were then brought before King Hud.

"All five of you have my deepest gratitude," stated Hud. "And that is truly deep. The depths of space aren't that deep."

"We didn't do much, your majesty, we just kept him busy," replied Gretchen.

"Indeed, which gave us the time we needed to save our world," said Hud. "And it is good to know we have allies who can help us. And for once they're not figments of my imagination."

"Not your imagination anyway," joked Zack who was still struggling a bit.

"Plus we all want to see more of this world," added Eric.

"Not to mention the rest of the Data Realm," said Patrick.

"If we're allowed," Malcolm pointed out.

"Perhaps if the need arises." mused Astral. "But you'll be pleased to know I've finally finished the communication stones. I turned them into pendants for you." She gave everyone a pendant with an amber stone. Zack's was shaped like a snowflake, Gretchen's a crescent moon, Eric's a flame, Malcolm's a lightning bolt and Patrick's a clock face. "With these I'll be able to contact you wherever you are and you'll be able to use them to open portals through computers to anywhere in Miyamoto you've been before, and warp straight to those places when you're already in Miyamoto."

"Why only to places we've been before?" asked Gretchen.

"Because that's the way it works in many video games," answered Zack.

"Just like flying," stated Eric.

"How is that like flying?" questioned Patrick.

"Don't ask," said Malcolm.

"For now, let me return you home. You've been here for quite a while," said Astral. "And you really should take so time to rest. There was that now familiar light and sensation and Frozen Fire found themselves back home where they took a well-earned rest.

When it was just the two of them in the throne room Hud turned to Astral.

"You really did find the right ones for the task," he said.

"Thank you, Hud," replied Astral. "I know it's a little unusual to send to another realm for help but in the long run the Data Realm is part of their world too. We shouldn't remain secret forever."

"Well, you made the right choice. I think this is beneficial to all involved, except the villains that get beaten up. HA! HA! HA!"

At the back of their minds Frozen Fire knew the Anti-Gamer was still out there and would have to face him again one. Yet they were still excited to have more adventures in Miyamoto.

"So we're in this together," said Gretchen.

"We'll protect Miyamoto and its people," said Patrick.

"However we can," said Malcolm.

"We'll fight Visrel and any other threat," said Eric.

And Zack finished with "Together we are Frozen Fire."

Book Two

The Hole in the Sky

A princess was walking along the corridors of the castle she lived in quietly singing to herself. It was a peaceful and beautiful morning; she stepped out onto a balcony closed her eyes and took a deep breath. When she opened them she saw something was wrong. She rushed off to find her brother and show him the troubling sight and then they went to find the king. Meanwhile in another world someone wicked smiled to themselves as the first stage of their plan was working.

Just after lunch Zackary Glacis was practising his magic. He was making snowflakes the size of plates which was improvement as normally they came out the size of coins; this was handy for his latest idea: the snowflake shuriken. Elsewhere in the city he called home his friends where practising their magic too. Gretchen Shadows was practising making shadow duplicates; before she only did to one object at a time, now she was trying it with several at once with varying degrees of success. Eric Flare was covering things with fire without letting them burn, a complex trick but he was starting to get the hang of it. Malcolm Spark was concentrating on generating electricity over himself, a tactic for defence from close range attacks. Patrick Tempus was yet again practising to slow down, speed up and outright stop the movement of people and things. It was then that the pendants that they each wore began to glow and a voice spoke through them.

"Frozen Fire, please come immediately to outside Adlez," said the urgent voice. All five of them heard it at once and they activated the magic within their pendants. They each pointed it at the nearest computer or games console which caused a white light to shoot out of it and surround them. There was a sensation of everything disappearing around them and floating in mid-air and then their feet touched the ground again. And just like that, the five friends had each gone from their own homes to right next each other.

It was not long ago that Frozen Fire had learned that another realm made out of computer data came into being due to the magic that their world used as a power source which got in to all things digital. It was known as the Data Realm and they helped protect part of it called Miyamoto born from video game data. They were facing the one who called them: she was known as Astral; a tall navy-haired woman who was their guide to the Data Realm.

"What can we do for you?" asked Zack. He had trouble talking to new people but he was used to Astral by now.

"We need help dealing with something very unusual," replied Astral gesturing skywards. Frozen Fire looked up towards the sky and were shocked by what they saw. High in the sky of Miyamoto there was a hole. It appeared to be just a black circle like in a cartoon and it seemed to be drawing energy towards it.

"Well now, that's unexpected," stated Gretchen.

"What is that it's pulling in?" questioned Eric.

"What is it?" asked Malcolm as they turned to look back at Astral.

"And what caused it?" added Patrick. Astral sighed.

"It's a rift between our two worlds," explained Astral. "It was just there in the sky when everyone woke up. What's most distressing is that it's drawing in all the magic of our world. It will slowly but surely drain all life from our home and then just leave us all to die." Frozen Fire found this news horrific. "King Hud has developed a plan to try and combat this situation. He has requested your help. We must go to him immediately." Astral lead them into Adlez. All around were the polygons, Miyamoto's version of humans being identical except for the fact that they were made from data. Zack was absentmindedly twirling his staff; each member of Frozen Fire had a magic weapon that appeared and disappeared on command.

"Do you think we should actually learn how to use our weapons?" wondered Gretchen.

"I think we're capable enough with them." answered Zack. Just after he said that his staff slipped out of his hand and clanged against a nearby streetlight.

"With the way Zack does things he never has to get near the enemy," remarked Eric. "Though I guess you have a point Gretchen."

"Being able to master our weapons as well as our magic would make us all the better at fighting monsters," observed Patrick.

"Exactly!" exclaimed Gretchen. "Patrick could learn sword play, Zack could learn some form of staff fighting, Malcolm says he's done some archery in the past, I could learn whatever it is you do with a halberd and Eric could find a gardener to give him some tips."

"Scythes are not gardening tools," stated Eric slightly annoyed.

"Yes they are," replied Zack. "They're a tool that can be used as a weapon like a rake or a lawnmower or even garden gnomes." The others gave Zack that look they gave him when he said odd things.

"Learning to use your weapons is a good idea," encouraged Astral. They arrived at the castle and were lead to the throne room were the king sat on his diamond throne. The king was an old wise and slightly mad man.

"Ah Frozen Fire, welcome to my home once again," greeted Hud. Frozen Fire bowed. "No doubt you have seen the rift in the sky, a most unusual threat. Still, it's nice to have a change in the aerial scenery; usually it's just the same cloudy nonsense."

"Your majesty, you should tell them what we do know," stated Astral.

"Yes, yes, of course," replied Hud. "From what we can tell the rift in the sky is being caused by some sort of vile machine and spell in your world, the location of which we cannot ascertain. We can only guess what sort of reason someone could have doing this. My guess is that it'll have something to do with art, turning us all into some sort of painting. There's a lot of morbid artists around." Zack looked at Gretchen.

"Oh, my art's a little creepy; get over it," said Gretchen.

"Still the king has told me that he does have a plan," assured Astral. "While I try and find where in your world the culprit is."

There was the sound of a door opening and someone coming in over to the king's left. Frozen Fire turned to see a young man with a stern face. He was just a bit older than them and was well built. His clothes looked as regal as the king's.

"Ah, you must be Frozen Fire," observed the newcomer when he stopped not far from the king. "We meet at last."

"Allow me to introduce my grandson," said Hud gesturing in the wrong direction. "This is the heir to the throne, Prince Hitbox." Frozen Fire bowed.

"I wasn't sure what to expect from what I'd heard," mused Hitbox. "Of course you've faced many monsters in battle and defeated the Anti-Gamer in battle twice; quite admirable. You already have my respect."

"Err, thanks," was the general reply.

"Now then," began Hud, "for this plan of mine we shall need the Rejecter Mirror. A brilliant artefact which can absorb magical energy and then rejects the energy, sending it back where it came."

"Grandad you lost the mirror," pointed out Hitbox. "In a surprisingly impressive way."

"I think he intends to have Frozen Fire find it," said a voice. No one had noticed that they were joined by yet another newcomer, this time a girl about the age of most of Frozen Fire. She had the same smile as the king and regal clothes as well and long orange hair. Something about her seemed perpetually bright; her cheerful nature seemed to irradiate from her.

"This is my granddaughter, Hitbox's younger sister, Princess Cyanna," introduced Hud, still not gesturing the right way. Frozen Fire bowed again.

"So this is Frozen Fire," mused Cyanna. "What was it? Zack, Gretchen, Malcolm, Eric and Patrick, right?"

"That's right, Princess," replied Astral.

"I'm very pleased to meet you all."

"Err, what was that about the mirror being lost?" asked Zack nervously. He began fiddling with his goggles.

"You remember a short time ago when the Anti-Gamer put that tower on this castle's roof," began Hud. "Didn't even match the others. Anyway, as you know, it was firing destructive energy at the cliff known as Game's Edge. While you were fighting Visrel there we were taking care of the tower. We couldn't get past the barrier so I came up with the idea to throw the Rejecter Mirror in to the energy so as to send the energy back to tower and destroy it. This worked which was very surprising."

"Now why didn't we ask how they did that?" mused Eric.

"And how did this cause the mirror to be lost?" asked Gretchen.

"Well, you see due to the tower constantly firing energy it overloaded the mirror faster than it could send the energy back causing it to split in three and scatter across Miyamoto," explained Hud. "It's something worth reflecting on. Ha! Ha! Ha!"

"Grandfather always has quite unusual plans," said Cyanna with a sigh.

"And something like that usually happens," added Hitbox rolling his eyes.

77

"Hey, without those plans the two of you wouldn't be here," said Hud defensively. No one really wanted to know more about that one.

"And no doubt we've to find these three pieces," said Gretchen.

"Any idea where they are?" asked Eric.

"I've begun a locator spell that should be able to find them for us," replied Astral. "As it happens we have heard from the acorn.ris that there's a piece near their home so we'll be able to get that one straightaway."

"I have already sent word to their leader, Lady Larch, to let her know to expect you," explained Hud. "She should be willing to help despite what impression she may give you with her manner. Mind you, she often tells me I give people strange impressions with my manner whatever she means by that." Everyone shared a look with someone else even Hitbox and Cyannna. "Still you must know that the rift has brought with it a terrible illness that attacks the homes of all in this world; you may have to face it."

"His majesty is referring to virus monsters that came through the rift," cleared up Astral.

"There's no sickness out there for you to worry about," assured Cyanna.

"Viruses cause illness," said Hud.

"Different kind of viruses, grandfather," said Hitbox. After Astral left with Frozen Fire the royal family were on their own in the throne room.

"What do you make of them?" Hud asked his grandchildren.

"Well, three of the boys looked a bit uncomfortable," said Cyanna. "But I could sense their magical strength and their good nature."

"Yes, they're definitely odd," said Hitbox. "But that's not a bad thing as you yourself are proof of grandad."

Astral warped Frozen Fire to where the acorn.ris lived. It was called the Assorted Tree Woodland. It was different from the other forest in Miyamoto that Frozen Fire had visited which had its own unique trees. The woodland was filled with trees that came from their world, however there were all kinds everywhere. It was a grand mixture of all sorts: tropical trees and swamp trees, evergreens and red woods. The climate was moderate; despite that there were species that are usually found only in cold or hot places. The forest floor was uneven due to the large amount of tree roots growing all around. Light had no trouble finding its way through the treetops; you could see very easily.

"Think of all the professors you could name after these," stated Zack.

"There's plenty for generations to come," said Eric in agreement.

"You've got to admire the way Miyamoto does things," said Gretchen.

"Where do the acorn.ris live?" asked Patrick

"Their treetop city is just over there," answered Astral.

"A treetop city?" repeated Malcolm nervously.

"Don't worry it's perfectly safe," assured Astral. She gestured for them move. They hadn't taken a step when the monsters jumped out in front of them. What were basically snapping mouths on four spindly legs with talons, Frozen Fire had encountered them before: the Anti-Gamer's most basic minions, talon-teeth. They knew they could take them; last time they had beaten plenty of them. However, before anyone could make a move a ball of magic fell down from above and when it touched the ground large wooden spikes shot upward destroying the talon-teeth.

"Good riddance, virus scum! Miyamoto is better off without you!" yelled a voice from above. Creatures that must have been an Acorn.ris dropped down from the trees. They was sort of human-shaped though, half as high, with tiny legs and arms, head just a little bigger than her body and made of wood. On top of their heads was an acorn's cap with hair somewhat resembling grass flowing out underneath it. The one who had landed in front of them stepped forward. "Ah, Frozen Fire, at last. I am Lady Larch. Always nice to see you, Astral."

"I see you're aggressive towards viruses as ever," observed Astral.

"Can't just let them try and ruin the place," replied Larch. "Those things could do some pretty serious damage to our homes. Anyway, I guess we had better discuss why you're here." The acorn.ris leader snapped her small fingers and then branches came down and picked everyone up and lifted them towards the tree tops.

"Those were Visrel's minions," pointed out Zack.

"Yes the Anti-Gamer's talon-teeth are still plaguing Miyamoto," explained Astral. "They're just coming in through the rift and I think that they're just being sent to cause trouble."

"So you think Visrel has nothing to do with the rift?" inquired Gretchen."

"No, the rift was not made by his hand," said Astral. "It may be the work of someone in your world but I'm convinced the Anti-Gamer is revelling in the idea of the life being drained from Miyamoto." The branches put them down. They found themselves amongst the highest part of the woodland on wooden planks that spread all around creating a makeshift street. They could sense the magic giving the streets the strength to hold up the city. There were all kinds of buildings that resembled both their counterparts in other cities and the many trees that made the woodland. Yet they looked just as secure and sturdy as any other.

"How big is this place?" asked Eric.

"Our city reaches across most of the Assorted Tree Woodland," answered Larch.

"Everything's so wooden," observed Malcolm in his quiet voice.

"I guess it should be expected with acorn people," mused Patrick.

"I shall take my leave now," said Astral. "When you get the mirror piece bring it back to Adlez to give to the king." She vanished in a flash of light.

"Right then, follow me!" exclaimed Larch. She led Frozen Fire through the city talking as they went. "I'll take you straight to where the mirror piece is."

"So the mirror just landed in your town?" asked Eric.

"Well, it missed the city but we found it the following day," explained Larch.

"But you have it now?" questioned Gretchen. Larch stopped. She laughed awkwardly and when she turned around she was grinning nervously.

"You see it was swallowed by a monster that came through the rift," she said.

"What kind of monster?" groaned Eric.

"A butterfly-like creature nothing you can't handle I'm sure."

"Hold on, if you hate virus monsters so much why didn't you destroy the thing on sight like you just did?" enquired Gretchen.

"Because we want to see you five fight. The ore.rar keep bragging about how they've witnessed two dramatic fights against nasty monsters."

"Well, it's good to know we're admired," said Zack flatly.

"The creature lurks bellow; beat it and you'll have the piece," said Larch. She snapped her fingers again and Frozen Fire were once more picked up by tree branches and were lowered down below.

"Let's get this over with," sighed Zack. They heard something moving towards them.

"Ah, it's here all ready," said Patrick.

"It never takes long," mumbled Malcolm. The creature came into view. It was indeed butterfly-like but closer to a cartoon one than a real one and of course it was much larger. It had hands on four of its arms and feet on the other two. The patterns on its wings looked like eyes that glared directly into your soul.

"This guy's got all the charm" remarked Eric. Energy surged between the creature's antennae which it fired at Frozen Fire. It just missed but knocked them to the ground.

"Every time," sighed Gretchen.

Everyone scrambled to get back on their feet as the butterfly sent another surge of energy at them. Zack sent a flurry of snow at the monster which covered its face. Eric then lashed out with his scythe which he covered in flames, knocking the creature to the ground. Though it was on the ground the creature still managed to send a sharp gust from its wings knocking them backwards. The "eyes" on its wings shot energy balls at them and they ducked for cover. Zack threw his snowflake shurikens at the monster, Malcolm fired a stream of lightning from two of his fingers, Gretchen threw a shadow banjo at it, Patrick lashed at it with time energy in the shape of a pocket watch and Eric erupted fire beneath it. The monster retaliated with more energy bursts. Gretchen, Eric and Patrick cut them out of the air while Malcolm fired arrows at its wings. The attacks weren't letting up so Zack made one of his snow-screens to give them cover. Gretchen began to concentrate; she wanted to try out a new trick. Patrick used his powers to speed himself up unleashing a barrage of sword strikes Malcolm then sent lightning at its wing stunning them. The creature was grounded but was still able to fire energy spheres at them which Zack blocked with a wall of ice. The boys moved into to attack: Zack swung with his staff, Eric brought his scythe down upon it, Malcolm fired several arrows at it and Patrick unleashed one of his trademark time bursts at it (which looks like a shattering clock). The creature retaliated with its wings knocking the four of them over. Gretchen had built up enough magic and began directing it at the monster's shadow. She shook and struggled to make it work. The creature's own shadow stretched out in front of it and a shadowy duplicate rose out of it and rammed the monster into a nearby tree. With a screech and a burst of magic the butterfly monster was gone and the mirror piece fell to the ground.

"How long have you been able to do that?" asked Zack.

"That was the first time I've done it successfully." replied Gretchen. "It was exhausting I won't be doing it again anytime soon."

"You're making a habit a throwing random shadow duplicates of whatever pops into your head."

"You've got a habit of throwing ninja-like projectiles. I just like how slapstick it all is."

"I think we could all do with a breather after that," said Patrick.

"We got the first mirror piece," said Malcolm picking it up.

"Right, we'd better go tell Larch and then return to Astral," said Eric. There was rustling from above and then the aforementioned acorn.ris jumped down in front of them.

"Bravo, quite the sceptical," complimented Larch. "You are good fighters. No wonder you bested The Anti-Gamer. And best of all there was no damage done to any of the trees. You're my kind of heroes."

"You guys must love your trees," observed Gretchen.

"Well, we are acorn people," Larch reminded them.

"Don't worry though; we'll always take care while we're here," assured Eric.

"Good. We can't have the place burning down."

"You must take forest fires extremely seriously," said Gretchen. "Goggles here freaks out at the thought of such things as well."

83

"You have to when you're made of wood. But we have plenty of spells and trained bears to help in the prevention of them."

"How do bears prevent fires?" asked Zack puzzled.

"Anyone caught starting fires around here gets mauled by the bears."

"That'll do it," mused Gretchen. Everyone backed away from Larch slowly after that last comment. Frozen Fire used their pendants to return to Astral and gave her the first piece of the mirror they then returned home to wait for another piece to be found.

The following day came and one by one Frozen Fire awoke, when they heard from Astral they were to head straight for Adlez's castle. Somewhere on someone's TV a news reporter was talking about some scientist.

"Doctor Lavender Putrice is a scientist known for her research on theoretical magical energies," said the reporter as the woman in question was shown walking around on the screen. "This morning she claimed to have discovered a new kind of energy and reports that her experiments on it are proving quite promising. She is quoted saying:'We need to do more study before we can announce what this new magic is as we need to learn more about what it can do.' Doctor Putrice guarantees remarkable results soon and claims her latest venture will change Kerozonia in surprising ways." Frozen Fire did not see this but they would hear about it soon enough. It was the sort of thing that spread. For now they were off to Miyamoto again.

They were met by Astral who lead them to the king; his grandchildren were also there.

"I have located the other two mirror pieces," said Astral. "One is at Candle Mountain, the other is at Thunderfalls Cavern."

"Why do I get the feeling they aren't easy access tourist destinations?" grumbled Zack.

"I'm sure we'll be fine; there's nothing to worry about," said Patrick.

"When has anyone ever said that and it wasn't immediately followed by something to worry about happening?"

"Where to first then?" asked Malcolm.

"I don't think it's overly important which we go to first," mused Eric.

"Exactly, though why don't we hear more about where we're going first for once," suggested Gretchen.

"Well, Thunderfalls Cavern is a bit of a labyrinth," replied Hud. "Quite nice overall. And Candle Mountain is on a small volcanic island several miles out to sea."

"VOLCANIC?! There's no way I'm going to a volcanic island!" cried Zack.

"On second thoughts maybe we should split into two teams," said Gretchen, flatly.

"I'll go with Zack to the cavern," said Malcolm. "Sounds like a good place for my powers."

"With a similar thought I'll go to the mountain then," said Eric.

"I'm gonna go with Malcolm and Zack," said Patrick. "Though that means Gretchen had better go with Eric." There were no complaints.

"Nothing wrong with a volcano," said Gretchen. "Unlike my icy friend here I'm not troubled by such things."

"Yeah, you'd probably want to set up a base of operations in a place like that," remarked Zack.

"I think the smaller group could use some help," said Hitbox. "I'll go with them."

"I knew you'd be wanting to get out there, my boy," said Hud.

"You know as well as I do the two of us are born fighters," responded Cyanna. "Think about it, he's a weapon master, of course he's gonna volunteer to fight."

"What?" said Frozen Fire all at once.

"I am referred to as a weapon master because I have learned how to use many weapons," explained Hitbox. "All my magic is used for memory management which basically means I remember the right thing at the right time. When I wield a weapon the memories of how to use it are brought to the front, so in a sense the memories are stored in my magic, making it harder for me to forget things. And through my life I have collected a large amount of weapons for me to summon with my magic and I know how to use all of them." Frozen Fire shared the same look that was both impressed and a little scared.

"You're a one-man armoury?" said Eric.

"You make it sound like you're an elemental," added Gretchen.

"The two of you are gonna get shown up bad!" Zack said Eric and Gretchen.

"No one shows us up!" declared Gretchen.

"And when you look like that you can show up wherever you want," said Eric. "Did I say that out loud?"

"Very well, Hitbox I'll warp you there as well," said Astral. "I knew you wouldn't keep taking no for an answer."

"Oh, I'm going to worry something awful," said Hud in a fluster. "Ever since we lost your parents you two are all the family I have left. And lord knows, I've done my best to raise you, well, me, and all the people who work for us. You know I don't want you to go out there but I'm too old to stop you now. Plus for the life of me I can't remember the spells that'll keep you here."

"Uh, grandad you're talking to a portrait of one of the old rulers," Cyanna pointed out.

"It's not my fault they're so life like!"

Astral transported Gretchen, Eric and Hitbox to a small island where the mountain was located.

"Doesn't look much like a candle," observed Eric. Candle Mountain rose high above them and covered the whole island. You could only just make out the top and there was an unexpected scent in the air. As you would expect it was very hot on the island. There was no sign of any life making it seem a little barren. The path in front of them led right to a cave a few feet above them.

"This whole place smells like some fragrance dispensing machine," stated Gretchen. "Or scented candles I suppose. Is there a reason for that?"

"It's called Candle Mountain because instead of molten rock this volcano is filled with melted candle wax," explained Hitbox. "It's very unusual but at least it can't erupt like the regular kind."

"You can't deny this place is unique," said Eric.

"So wonderfully odd," said Gretchen. They made their way to the cave and into the volcano. Inside was mostly hollow but there were stone pathways all along the walls and across the centre and tunnels leading to more paths. About ten feet below them was them was a crater filled with molten pink wax and in the middle was a very tall flame. The wax seemed to be flowing in from somewhere and flowing out somewhere else, in fact it was flowing in a big loop.

"This place is fabulous," said Eric beaming.

"An artistic beauty," added Gretchen.

"Hmm, I'd heard you guys were a little odd," observed Hitbox.

"Nothing wrong with being a little odd," replied Eric.

"You've met my grandfather I'm well used to strangeness," explained Hitbox. "It probably runs in the family. Speaking of strangeness are you sure the other three will be ok?"

"We may attract a lot of trouble but they'll be fine," said Gretchen. "Even without me there to bail them out." For a moment she expected a comeback from Zack.

"I'm sure they can fight monsters they just seemed a little... awkward," observed Hitbox.

"So long as there aren't a lot of people there they'll be fine," assured Eric. "And if the place has got some monsters in it there's not really much chance for a lot of people."

"And if some jerk gives them trouble I'll give the jerk worse trouble," said Gretchen.

"You know them best," mused Hitbox. "Now then, from what I know about the cave this is the lowest pathway. So we can only go up but the paths go all over so we better stick together. We don't want to get lost in here." He led the way with the other two following close behind. While inside a tunnel they saw that on all the pathways on the inside were many warning in many forms and the words 'watch your step' in multiple languages. Crossing through one tunnel they found themselves face to face with a group of talon-teeth.

"Oh joy, it's the ones who are all bite and scratch," grumbled Eric.

"At least they're not much trouble," mused Gretchen.

"Leave them to me," said Hitbox. And before either Gretchen or Eric could respond Hitbox rushed forward. There was a flash of light in his hands and suddenly he was holding a sword and with an upwards swing the first talon-teeth was split in half. Another flash and he held a large hammer in place of his sword which he brought down on the next one. The third talon-teeth felt the swing of a large axe while the one after that was knocked off its feet by a staff and thrown into the crater below. Another tried to sink its teeth into him but was knocked down by a lance and then another tried to catch Hitbox off guard but was shot by an arrow from a crossbow. The last one lunged at Hitbox but soon found itself being knocked out the air by a spear.

"He's more of a show off than we are," said Eric.

"We could have done that," said Gretchen. "Maybe."

"Remember when we first met the king and he told us his grandchildren were training hard to fight monsters? Seems like a bit of an understatement now."

"Let's just be glad he's on our side. If his sister is as good as him the bad guys don't stand a chance. Of course with us here that was true anyway."

"Quite the bravado you two display," said Hitbox. "It doesn't quite hide your self-doubt, however. But I sense it doesn't hold you back as much as it did when you first came to Miyamoto."

"I guess we weren't the obvious choice but Astral went for us anyway," mused Gretchen.

"Can't help but wonder how many other candidates there were," said Eric.

"Astral has always liked learning about people," explained Hitbox. "She never looks for people's secret information and she always respects people's privacy but her empathic abilities allow her to always understand what people are feeling. At first when she said she wanted help from your realm me and my sister weren't keen of the idea. But she was convinced Visrel could only be defeated by our two worlds working together. Regardless of what we thought at first you five saved our grandfather's life so I know Astral made the right choice." Gretchen and Eric mumbled some thanks and they carried on. It was a long climb up the winding pathways through the volcano and soon they found themselves at the highest point. But there was already a monster there.

"I'm willing to bet this thing has the mirror piece," declared Eric.

"Whelp it's not gonna beat itself. Let's get it," said Gretchen. The monster in question was made of metal and looked almost like an overweight person but instead of a head it had the top of what appeared to be a gas fuelled street lamp and its arms looked like piping. The monster attacked.

It sent flames at them but the trio moved out of the way and then Eric sent his flames back. Hitbox then charged forward and struck the monster with his hammer but this didn't seem to do much. Gretchen assaulted it with her halberd and the metal was scratched.

"So it can withstand force but not the sharper of weapons," observed Hitbox as he switched his hammer for a small dagger. The lamp monster and sent flames at them again and Eric sent his flames back; they were both engulfed by the fire and when they cleared neither Eric nor the monster were so much as singed.

"The thing makes fire; it's gonna be resistant to it!" yelled Gretchen. "You can't roast it any more than it can roast you!"

"I'm sure my scythe will be able to do plenty damage," said Eric brandishing his weapon. "It's the monster that can't do a thing to me." The monster then swung its arm at them knocking them over except Hitbox.

"Can't do a thing, huh?" remarked Gretchen.

"Quiet, you!" As she got up Gretchen sent a shadow wave at the monster's head causing it to stagger backwards. Hitbox unleashed a barrage of strikes with his dagger scratching the monster's metal. Eric had got back up and began to scratch the monster too. The monster shot fire from its head Eric wasn't affected and stopped it from getting to Hitbox. Gretchen made a shadow duplicate of her halberd and struck the monster rapidly and managed to make tiny indents around the many scratches. The creature swung its arm at her knocking her over and swung the other at Hitbox who dived out the way stopping just at the edge of the ground. The monster shot a flood of fire from its head and arms; while Eric didn't need to move, it was all Gretchen and Hitbox could do to avoid being horribly burned. Eric moved through the fire and started hitting the monster at close range making it stop its stream of fire and trying to hit him instead. Gretchen took this chance to place her two hands together thing we want is someone with wicked intentions getting a hold of it as they could do all sorts of damage."

"I'm twelve, I'm hardly an evil wizard."

"Sorry, I'm a bit on edge. Some kind of creature has being trying to get it. I never get a good look at it but it's always attacking. I manage to drive it off but it's persistent. I'm not sure I'll be able to keep it away."

"How much damage could a wild animal do?"

"It's most definitely a magical being. It might cause the magic the run amuck and destroy half the city."

"That's a scary thought. If you knew what it was you could figure out how to drive it off properly."

"It doesn't seem to be intelligent so I'd guess it's some kind of creature that is drawn to magical things and tries to eat them. Look you'd better go before whatever this thing is returns." Eric headed home with the intent of researching any creatures known for eating magical items that might be found in Reekie but he could not find anything that fitted. Eric decided to return and try to help the sun spirit. He grabbed something from out of the house that he thought might help.

"Hello?" Eric called when he returned to the site of the solar flower. The sun spirit appeared above the flower.

"What are you doing back here?" the spirit asked.

"I tried to find out what sort of creature it might be but there's nothing that's likely to be found in Reekie that eats magical items."

"So it must be something from outside the city!"

"I also brought this." Eric pulled out the item he brought from home; it looked like a small coin. "This coin has a spell on it that can paralyze creatures, well, small creatures. My mum bought it on holiday to repel the fireflies that can actually make fire. These days it's mostly used on midgies."

"Thank you. That could be helpful in identifying it." Suddenly there was a rustling noise nearby. "It's here!" Eric aimed the coin at where the sound had come from. They waited and when there was movement again Eric squeezed the coin and it shot a wave of magic. The creature was paralysed allowing them to get a look at it. The creature may have been humanoid but it was without question not human. It almost looked like a skeleton despite being covered in blood red skin. It was covered in rags and moved with its arms low to the ground. Its fingers and toes all had sharp claws and its mouth was full of matching teeth.

"Is that a bloody bones?" asked Eric quite scared.

"It is. They're usually found in Reginland. What is it doing here?"

"Never mind that, they don't eat magical items they eat magical creatures. It's not after the flower it's after you." The bloody bones was freed from the spell and attacked. With a swipe of its arm it knocked the coin away from Eric it then turned on the sun spirit. The spirit fired a beam of light at the creature but it moved out of the way. It lashed out with its claws and the spirit responded with more shots of light. Eric picked up a large rock and hurled it at the creature and struck it on the back of its head. It turned and lunged at Eric knocking him to the ground. Eric noticed the coin, grabbed it and used it on the creature again. It broke free a lot quicker this time and chased after Eric. He tried to paralyse the pursuing creature but it just avoided the waves of magic. The spirit appeared between them and shot a beam of light right into the creature. The creature was angry, ready to unleash an attack upon both of them. It viciously slashed with its claws leaping at both Eric and the Spirit, from one to the other, dodging both the shots from the coin and the shots of light. It threw Eric to the ground and turned to the sun spirit who was beginning to get exhausted and grabbed it. The creature was about to sink its teeth in when Eric struck it with another rock knocking it out and freeing the sun spirit. They breathed easy as it was seemingly over.

"Thank you. I believe you saved my life," said the spirit.

"You're welcome," said Eric. "How did it grab you? You're made of light?"

"It has magic that allows it to prey on anything smaller than itself."

"Did I kill it?"

"It's just unconscious; I'll make sure it's sent to people who know how to deal with it. Listen, I wasn't to reward you for your help."

"A reward you say? Thanks! What is it?"

"I'd like to give you the solar flower."

"Aren't you supposed to keep it from people?"

"The wrong sort of person. That's not you. If you eat the flower you'll be able to recreate the fire of the sun itself."

"It'd make me a fire elemental? That's awesome." Eric picked the flower, thanked the sun spirit and headed home, leaving the sun spirit to transport the bloody bones to the appropriate authorities. When he was home he placed the flower it a bowl of water which dissolved and seemed to turn the water into a kind of potion. Eric drank it all, it felt warm like the light of the sun. Soon he could feel the magic within him had the same warmth. Eric had become an elemental and had great fun with his magic. Yet he neglected his potential until he came to Miyamoto.

At the same time as the events at Candle Mountain occurred Zack, Malcolm and Patrick were at Thunderfalls Cavern. They found themselves on rocky area on a hillside that was covered with plant life and were faced straight at a large cave mouth. Everything seemed quiet and still making it hard to believe that anyone had ever come here before.

"I wonder how long it will be before the others get themselves into trouble," mused Zack.

"Hitbox might keep them out of it," suggested Malcolm.

"I don't think he's miracle worker," said Patrick.

"Odds are we're gonna get into trouble as well," Zack pointed out.

"Probably some monsters waiting for us," said Malcolm.

"Better get it over with then."

"Into the cave we go then, lads," said Patrick.

They climbed up the rocks and through the cave mouth. Inside the air was cool and damp. There were tunnels stretching off in all directions. The walls were a navy grey coloured stone and despite the damp air were as dry as a new towel. The ceiling had lighting on it. No doubt, this place was a tourist attraction but at that time it was deserted, bar the three of them. They followed a sign indicating the way to the falls deeper into the cave.

"Can you hear that?" asked Malcolm.

"Sounds like something moving around," observed Patrick.

"Look up, guys. It's our ol' pals," said Zack. Above them on the tunnel walls were some talon-teeth that lunged at them. The first ones that jumped met Malcolm's arrows and the ones that stayed on the walls slipped on Zack's ice and were caught by Patrick's sword. They were finished off by icicle kunai, a stream of lightning and a temporal pulse. With a sigh of relief the boys moved forward cautiously in case any more talon-teeth jumped out at them. They entered a gigantic chamber and saw where the cavern got its name from. At the back of the chamber a stream of brilliant white lightning was coursing down like a waterfall. No flash, no rumble of thunder, just constant electricity pouring down. Out of one hole in the ceiling and into another hole in the floor, seemingly out of nothing and into nothing, definitely both a magical phenomenon and a natural one.

"I don't know whether to be amazed or terrified," said Zack uncertain.

"This place is a tourist attraction I'm sure it's perfectly safe," assured Patrick.

"It feels so powerful," said Malcolm. "Never felt anything like this."

"I'd be surprised if it wasn't powerful," said Zack.

"How different can it be?" wondered Patrick. Malcolm began to move closer.

"No other electricity is like this," said Malcolm.

Zack and Patrick shared a look as they realized Malcolm was transfixed by the thunderfalls. They wondered if they acted the same around their own element. However, the distraction was short lived as suddenly a burst of magic appeared nearby and a monster leapt out. This one took the form of a skeleton horse with phantom eyes, mane and tail. It floated down in front of them and the boys readied their weapons. The horse fired a beam of magic from its mouth but they dodged out the way. Patrick fired a temporal pulse at it causing it to land. It flicked its tail at them which sent an energy blast at them and it just missed giving Malcolm the opportunity to fire some electrified arrows at it. Zack the sent freezing energy at it and began to cover it in ice but it unleashed another beam at them knocking them over. The monster galloped at them and raised its front legs ready to stomp down but Patrick slowed it allowing them to get back up and he then struck it with his sword. It didn't do much.

"OK, what is holding this thing together? That should have knocked its skull off!" growled Zack.

"Some kind of spectral glue perhaps?" ventured Patrick.

"More like cement."

The monster started flicking blasts at them again and they scrambled to get out the way. Zack jabbed it with his staff rapidly while Patrick unleashed a time burst in its face. The horse fired another beam knocking the two of them over. Malcolm rained lightning bolts at it but the monster flicked a blast at him and he got out the way and ended up against the rail overlooking the falls. The horse began another beam and Zack blocked with an ice wall but neither he nor Patrick could get out from behind it. Malcolm shot an arrow with a lightning ball on it. Patrick formed a grandfather clock out of his time magic and slammed it on the monster while Zack simply threw several snowflake shurikens. The monster fired a beam again making the boys scramble all over the chamber. Zack made a snow-screen for cover while Patrick tried to freeze it temporally. Malcolm had a crazy idea. He turned to face the falls, he held up his hands and started to concentrate. He began to send his magic into the falls more and more magic and then after a few minutes several bolts flew from the falls and struck the monster causing a blast that knocked everyone over. When the air was clear the horse was gone and the mirror piece was in its place.

"Whoa! That was quite the attack bud!" exclaimed Zack.

"I need to sit down," said Malcolm.

"After that? You certainly should."

"And now we have another part of the mirror," said Patrick picking it up. They turned to leave when a thought occurred to Zack.

"Did we just literally beat a dead horse?" he asked.

"Looks that way," said Malcolm.

Everyone used the pendants to warp back to Adlez castle. They were met outside by Astral and Cyanna.

"Excellent. I hope there wasn't anything too dangerous," said Astral when she saw the two mirror pieces. "Come, King Hud and the other leaders are waiting for you." Frozen Fire were about to ask what she meant.

"The leaders of the other three races," explained Cyanna. "You know the ore.rar, the acorn.ris and the cloud.tiff." They followed Astral through the throne room up a flight of stairs and into a large room with a circular table where Hud, an ore.rar, an acorn.ris and a cloud.tiff (the first they had seen) sat.

"Ah, good. You're all here," greeted Hud. "I know you've met Lord Iron." He gestured towards the large metal creature with gigantic arms and a head that was just separate from the body. Frozen Fire realized this was the same one they befriended on their last adventure.

"Frozen Fire, how good to see you again!" exclaimed Iron.

"You never told us you were the leader of the ore.rar," Eric pointed out.

"Yes, that often slips my mind," he said with a chuckle.

"And you recently met Lady Larch," said Hud.

"I hope you gave those viruses a great beating," said Larch.

"That's how we always beat monsters," replied Gretchen.

"Yeah, from on our backs," added Zack quietly.

"And this is Elder Stratus whom of course you haven't met before," said Hud. The cloud.tiff had pale blue skin looked more human than the ore.rar or the acorn.ris and had a large beard seemingly made of clouds but no hair on his scalp.

"Greetings, Frozen Fire," said Stratus. "It is interesting to meet you at last." They returned the greeting. The old cloud.tiff seemed like he was a little annoyed about something or possibly about everything.

"So what is the plan?" asked Patrick.

"How dangerous is it?" added Malcolm.

"I can assure you it's very dangerous indeed," replied Hud. "Madly dangerous. If you think I'm mad for coming up with it you're madder for doing it. You're going to take the Rejecter Mirror right to the rift and throw it in, whilst trying not to get sucked into it."

"Uh, Grandad what are you expecting that to achieve?" questioned Cyanna.

"Well, my dear, with any luck the mirror will absorb and reject whatever energy is causing the rift hopefully causing it to close."

"Assuming it doesn't get pulled into the rift," Iron pointed out.

"The data I've gathered from the rift suggests that it won't pull anything in," explained Astral. "It only takes in magical energy; it shouldn't affect any of us or the mirror itself. I suppose there is a risk it could pull the magic right out of the mirror itself but it shouldn't pull magic out of any of you."

"Good luck with that! Myself, Iron, the king and his grandchildren won't be joining you on this venture," said Larch.

"To get close to the rift first you must come to my home," said Stratus. "The Solid Cloudbank. From there we will be able to get right up to the rift."

"First of all, the mirror needs to be repaired," said Astral. She held her hands out in front of her with the palms facing up, there was a glow of magic then the three mirror pieces which had been laid on the table floated over to her. They spun around as they were covered in Astral's magic. They joined together and the gaps between disappeared like they were lines on paper being erased and the mirror was repaired. So once again they were off

Astral warped them to the home of the cloud.tiff. They found themselves in the sky standing on clouds that were solid as ground. In fact the whole city was made of solid clouds: everything from the streetlights to statues of the famous cloud.tiff. The buildings themselves were bright white clouds while the streets and roads were darker rain clouds which actually made them resemble concrete. The cloud.tiff were all around; the younger ones had cloud hair on the tops of their head proving the assumption that the elder had gone bald. Stratus gestured for them to follow. He led them through the city.

"If you get disorientated there's not actually anything to be done," assured Stratus. "It should pass eventually though."

"This sort of thing can't disorient us," said Gretchen.

"Are you sure? It can take some time to get used to being this high in the air."

"Didn't Astral tell you we come from a floating island?" questioned Eric.

"Oh. Really?"

"Yes, Kerozonia is a floating isle," replied Astral. "I did tell him but he can't have been listening."

"And fear of heights is surprisingly common there," Zack added to himself. "And all the hills and mountains don't help."

"Despite his complaining we'll be fine," said Patrick.

"Pfft, young people always so sure of themselves," said Stratus.

"Someone's grumpy?" said Malcolm.

"We're here."

"Then take us straight to the rift elder," said Astral. "If this plan can work we must waste no time." Stratus held his arms out in front of him and clapped his hands together. There was a burst of magic and then they started to rise up, when Frozen Fire looked down they realized that a new cloud had formed beneath them and was carrying them upwards. Miyamoto expanded below them. What a view it was! The familiar indigo fields stretched off not too far away in the west. They could see how high up the Solid Cloudbank was and they could see Adlez to the south west and the Assorted Tree Woodland to the south east and even the ore.rar home, the Steel Crater to the north. They never realized how close the four cities were. And there on the horizon was Edge Forest and Game's Edge, the cliff at the end of Miyamoto. But above them the rift was hovering ominously. Even up close it looked like just a large black circle like a hole in a cartoon. It was about twenty feet across and only when you got close could you see that it was an opening. There was a sound like rushing air going into it.

"All right, Astral, do what you need to," said Stratus. "I do not wish to linger around here for any time more than we need to."

"Frozen Fire, be alert, monsters could show up at any time," warned Astral. She held up the mirror and it floated over to the rift. It touched one of the edges and there was a surge of energy around the mirror. Then it moved slightly and released more energy which was pulled straight into the rift. The mirror floated there for a few minutes both pulling in and releasing energy then it just suddenly stopped and fell on to the cloud. The rift just sat there unchanged; everyone looked from the mirror to the rift and back again.

"So, his majesty's mad plan didn't work," observed Zack.

"First time for everything," said Stratus.

"What do we do now?" asked Patrick.

"I suppose we should focus on finding out where in your world the cause of the rift is," said Astral.

"It could be anywhere," Malcolm pointed out.

"Or it could be the most obvious place in the world," said Gretchen.

"Either way you'll have to confront this one on your own," said Astral

"Can't you do something?" questioned Eric.

"I have no offensive magic, remember. I can find you the place and keep an eye on you but I can't be much help directly." Frozen Fire went back to their world to rest after the day's adventures while Astral returned to the other leaders to fill them in before heading to her temple to continue her work

The next morning Frozen Fire met up at their local park. There wasn't much they could do to help Miyamoto until they heard from Astral. And they had no idea where to even begin looking for who could be behind the rift. Although in a certain kind of happenstance another part of the puzzle as it happens was bearing down on them.

"We could try searching the internet," suggested Gretchen.

"Search for what? Are you draining the life out of a secret world on the internet?" responded Zack.

"It's not the worst thing you've searched for," remarked Eric.

"I guess we're just on monster duty for the time," mused Patrick.

"Sounds about right," mumbled Malcolm. The five of them became aware of the sound of something moving behind them. They looked round and there were five white sheets lying on the ground. Before anyone could express their confusion, the sheets rose up as if someone was standing under them. There was a ghostly glow about them. Arms suddenly sprang out from their side with sharp fingers and mouths that mimicked jagged teeth opened at the top.

"What the fudge?!" exclaimed Zack. "This is creepy."

"They've got it in for us," said Malcolm as they came towards them.

"There's one each. We can take 'em," said Eric.

"Let's show them not to mess with Frozen Fire," stated Gretchen.

"Let's do it. Allons-y," said Patrick. Everyone summoned their weapons and faced a different monster. One swung its claws at Zack but he covered himself in ice blocking the attack. He unleashed a beam of cold energy; the creature froze and then Zack smashed it with his staff. Another was trying to bite Gretchen but it kept missing. She jabbed with her halberd into its mouth, right as it bit down, it refused to let go of it but Gretchen just blasted it with a shadow wave defeating it. The one that attacked Eric couldn't quite get past his flames. Eric covered his scythe blade in flames and then cut off what was pretty much its head. One was knocking all of Malcolm's arrows out of the air. He sent a surge of electricity at it and while it was distracted Malcolm finished it with a close-range arrow. The last one blocked every blow from Patrick's sword. Using his temporal powers Patrick made himself faster allowing him to get close and cut the monster in half. Frozen Fire stood over the sheets' remains which burst apart into a pixel like energy and flew off.

"Wasn't that energy from the Data Realm?" questioned Zack.

"Yeah, those sheet things were made out of it," said Eric.

"Which means who or what we're looking for is in this city."

"And they're making flimsy monsters," added Gretchen. "They were really easy to beat."

"We'd better go and tell Astral right away," said Patrick.

Astral was watching her scanning spells when Frozen Fire came through the door to her temple. Before she could ask them anything they told her what had happened.

"Reekie has to be where this person is," stated Astral. "Someone smart with access to a lot of money has to be behind it."

"Should we ask all the rich people in town?" wondered Patrick.

"Better than the whole world," said Zack.

"Surely it would be some sort of scientist wizard," mused Gretchen.

"Most likely," said Astral. "Actually that reminds me of something. I keep an eye on some of the news feeds in your world and I recall reading about a woman who studied theoretical magical energies who lives in your home city."

"What does that mean?" asked Malcolm.

"It means she researches for new kinds of magic and studies the possibilities of ones that people have only theorized about. I've certainly seen conspiracy theories proving people think magic has had some effect on the internet."

"So, by looking into these theories they could have discovered the Data Realm?" said Eric.

"The scientist in question is Dr Lavender Putrice," explained Astral. "She could very well have discovered this world and cast a spell that made the rift. But I hate to think why she or anyone for that matter would use the magical energy to make those spectral sheets you told me about. I'm going to check the news feeds now to see if there've been any reports of anyone else being attacked. And if you are the only ones then odds are that Putrice or whoever else it may be somehow knows about the five of you. We need to find her I don't why but I really think she's behind this." There was no indication that anyone else had an encounter with the phantasmal creatures made from the energy from the Data Realm. It seemed Frozen Fire had been targeted deliberately.

As it happened Dr Putrice was the sort who was constantly updating her location through websites designed for the sharing of random information. She liked to spend her lunch time having tea in a fancy hotel. Frozen Fire went straight to the hotel as it seemed that was where she was. Using Gretchen's magic they snuck across the floor as a shadow which ran through the hotel until it entered the private room where she was and the shadow climbed up onto a couch across from Putrice. She blinked and when she opened her eyes the five of them were across from her. She coughed on her tea when she saw them.

"You darlings must be Frozen Fire," stated Putrice after regaining her composure. She was smaller than all five of them and was thin and wiry. She was wrapped in a large red coat and had a black hat with a brim twice the size of the rest of it. She wore a pair of dark glasses that she did not look through but rather looked over. It was clear how her reputation as the fashionable scientist was earned. "I knew you'd come looking for me after you met my prototypes. I call my quaint little monsters the data phantoms, quite the darling name wouldn't you say?"

"What exactly are you playing at with those things?" demanded Gretchen.

"As I said they were just dear prototypes. I needed to know how much more digital magic they'd need to make them a real threat. The next ones you meet will be much stronger."

"Do you even know you're killing a whole world?" yelled Zack after some struggling.

"As it happens I do. When I learned about the Data Realm I wasted no time in learning how to siphon its magic for my own purposes. Purely scientific, of course; can't turn up this scientific opportunity."

"Oh joy, she's completely remorseless," observed Eric.

"And you probably have some horrific endgame." added Patrick.

"I've always wanted to do the thing where the villain tells the heroes her whole plan. It looks good fun," said Putrice with a wicked smirk. "I really shouldn't but what the heck. With my data phantoms I shall take over all of Kerozonia. From Reekie to Abhainn. Every beautiful loch and every grand mountain. You see it's all to do with another theoretical magical energy. All magic is born from emotion and I've always wondered what the resulting magic would be like from those who had been conquered and oppressed. Ruling Kerozonia is the second step in this scientific venture. Conquest in the name of science. It matters not who gets hurt."

"She's an actual mad scientist," mumbled Malcolm.

"Oh, no, darling I'm perfectly sane. I simply don't care about anyone getting hurt in the pursuit of knowledge."

"How do you even know about the Data Realm?!" demanded Zack. "It's being kept a secret to everybody."

"Did you really think the inhabitants of that world could keep it hidden forever? It may be part of another plane of existence but it's still part of our world it was meant to be found. This whole thing is just perfect for my extraordinary intellect. It won't take long to make my stronger phantoms. I'll have this city before you know it. Kerozonia will crumble before me and Miyamoto will die and I shall be known as a truly brilliant scientist. Anyway, must dash. Ta-ta, darlings." And in a flash of magic she was gone.

Unsure of where to look for Putrice, as she did not share her place of work on social media, Frozen Fire returned to Miyamoto to tell Astral what they learned who then went to tell king Hud and the other leaders. While the five of them were discussing things Frozen Fire and the royal siblings were waiting in another room at the castle to see what should be done next.

"How did she know we were Frozen Fire?" wondered Gretchen.

"Someone must have told her," replied Hitbox. "She must have had help. You can't just happen upon the Data Realm. You need help from this end."

"Looks like the five of us are on our own for this fight," mused Eric.

"Wherever in Reekie Putrice is," added Patrick.

"With all those phantoms," mumbled Malcolm. Zack was sitting in a corner. Cyanna came over and sat near him.

"Are you all right?" enquired Cyanna. Zack couldn't look directly at her.

"I'm fine. Just a little worried about this battle," answered Zack. "We've never fought a regular person before. But she seems just as ruthless as Visrel. We got lucky last time." Frozen Fire began to feel doubt and the princess thought to try and help.

"At the moment you need to relax. Take you mind off it."

"I would but all my games are back home." Cyanna thought for a moment.

"Well then, you'll have to talk to me about something. Why don't you tell me the story of how you became an ice elemental? What was the trial you faced that led your magic to given its current form?" Zack looked at his friends and they gestured for him to go ahead, so Zack began his story.

First you need to know about an old Kerozonian tale about a powerful hero. This hero had taught himself nearly every kind of ice spell in the world and after many years of training he became the most powerful ice elemental in the world. He battled monsters all over the world and was known as the Blizzard Master. Now most people outside of Kerozonia don't know that this legend is actually real and that his tomb is now part of a museum in Reekie. And when Zack was twelve he was visiting there. Now Zack rarely goes anywhere on his own but on this occasion, he had gotten separated from his mum and brother. He found himself standing in front of the Blizzard Master's tomb and he realized that there was a door leading into the tomb.

"What in the world?" thought Zack, his mind racing. He crept closer to the tomb and entered the door. Magic had protected the tomb; for a long time the museum didn't need much security for its exhibit so Zack was very curious about the door. Inside the tomb was a stone casket in the centre and walls covered with trophies from the Blizzard Master's adventures. Zack looked all around impressed and scared.

"Someone has found their way into my tomb at last," said a voice coming out of nowhere. Zack yelled in surprise when he heard it.

"Wh… who's th… there?" asked Zack. Above the casket snowflakes gathered and soon formed into the shape of a man. Though his face and age were not clear this spectral image wore armour and looked very strong.

"I am the Blizzard Master," said the phantom.

"No way!"

"What other ghost would dwell in this tomb?"

"Well, quite a lot of ghosts are historians who stuck around to make sure people got it right so they could be in a museum. Most of the other ghosts are pirates guarding treasure."

"I'm neither. What is your name?"

"I... I... I'm Za... Zackary Glacis. Did you let me in here?"

"We are well met, Zackary. And, yes in a sense I was the one who let you in. The tomb's protected by a spell that would only allow the right person in here."

"Am I the first person to find their way in here?"

"Yes. In my life I was the strongest ice elemental in the entire world and I saw it as my duty to battle evil. But not all my fellow elementals were quite so kind-hearted. Once or twice I clashed with some of the others. I wanted to make sure that there was at least another elemental in the future who would fight against villains as well. So, my soul stayed on in this tomb waiting for one to pass my powers onto. The spells would only let in someone who is loyal to their friends, full of creativity, has courage in their heart and a longing for adventure. And finally, after all this time, the spell has let you in. Or you're the first to get close enough to be let in."

"Wait, what? You can't think I'm right for the job. I don't have any courage I'm scared of everything, spiders, the dark, fire, drowning, you name it, I'm scared of it. And also, you can't give someone else your magic; that's not how it works."

"Zackary it was just a figure of speech. I would in fact be giving your magic, the same form as my magic, making you an ice elemental. And there is courage somewhere in your heart otherwise you wouldn't have been let inside my tomb."

"As awesome as I think ice is, as an element and as great as I think it'd be to be an elemental I'm only twelve. I'm no hero. I have no courage." The Blizzard Master thought for a moment.

"Well then, if you don't think you're worthy then why not a test to let you earn this power? A scenario which will prove to you that you that there is bravery inside your heart and when you succeed I will give you my power. And if you don't you may leave and I will trouble you no more."

"How are you going to test me in here?" Suddenly the room seemed to vanish all around him and Zack plunged downwards. And the just as suddenly he landed in a field out in the open, clearly miles from where he had been.

"Don't worry, it's not real," said the voice of the Blizzard Master out of nowhere. "No harm will come to you."

"What exactly do you want me to do?" asked Zack.

"Just do whatever comes naturally to you." The voice went silent and Zack looked around until he found something. It appeared to be a truck of some kind and on its back was a cage with two unconscious people inside that Zack recognized.

"GRETCHEN! ERIC!" From around the other side of the truck came a large lumbering figure. This man's face may have seemed plain but the something about it that just said cruelty.

"Leave here now, boy!" warned the man.

"What are doing with my friends?" demanded Zack.

"It doesn't concern you what becomes of them. Just leave here and forget what you saw and be glad I'm not sticking you in there with them." Zack was beginning to panic and suddenly found himself talking again.

"You can't just take them away! Who do you think you are, kidnapping people for no reason?!"

"Back off, boy. There's nothing you can do here." Zack was scared and angry and suddenly he felt something like acting in spite of his fear. He punched and kicked at the man and despite his size the man was winded by the flailing limbs striking his stomach. "Get off!"

"You can't do this!" The man threw Zack off him and dropped several objects from his coat including keys one of which would have been for the cage. Zack dived at the stuff from the man's pockets but the man picked him up by the scruff of the neck and brought him up face to face. Zack didn't look at the man, he looked at what he had grabbed instead of the keys.

"You are going to meet a much worse fate than your two friends here," said the man. "No one will ever find out what happened to you."

"I take it you used this sleeping powder on my friends?" said Zack holding up the bag of magic powder he had picked up by mistake. Zack threw the powder at the man's face and he lost consciousness and collapsed to the ground in an instant. Zack landed on the ground hard. He stood up grumbling in pain. The details on the bag seemed to indicate that the man would be out for a long time and Gretchen and Eric were waking up so he knew they'd have enough time to escape. Zack picked up the key and unlocked the cage and then everything fell away again and he was back in the tomb with the Blizzard Master.

"You should be proud of what you did," said the Blizzard Master. "Even if it wasn't real."

"I think I forgot that it wasn't real," said Zack, he couldn't look at the ghost.

"You were meant to forget; that way you couldn't deny it was real courage. You don't need to start fighting monsters now; in fact you don't need to fight them at all. You can just use my powers to help those you care about." Zack finally looked at him.

"I can't believe I did any of that."

"It doesn't matter if you don't believe it what matters is you did do it and you would have done whether it was real or an illusion."

"I guess I can't refuse now."

"You could but I don't think you'd mean it." The Blizzard Master held out his ghostly hand and Zack grasped it despite the fact it was just snowflakes floating in the air. A pale blue light shone out from their hands and soon filled the entire chamber. It almost felt like everything had frozen solid but it didn't seem to affect Zack. He could feel his magic surging for the first time in his life, like frozen lakes and snow-covered hills. And then just like that everything was back to normal, but the Blizzard master was gone.

"Thank you," Zack said quietly

"You're welcome," replied the voice of the Blizzard Master. "Don't worry, you'll can keep yourself and others safe now." Zack left the tomb and the door vanished behind him. No one had noticed Zack emerging and he soon caught up with his mother. When she asked him where he had been he said he had gotten caught reading about the Blizzard Master's tomb.

When Zack finished his story a thought crossed his mind that had crossed it a few times before.

"Sometimes I think I let the Blizzard Master down," mused Zack. "He made me the heir to his powers and the main thing I did with them in the last five years was get myself a lifetime ban on snowball fights with my friends."

"You kept throwing snowmen!" yelled Gretchen.

"Oh, like you didn't use your powers."

"Only to duplicate more snowballs. You were the only one throwing snowmen." Cyanna and Hitbox shared a look that said: I know it sounds like they must be joking but I'm sure they're not.

"So why do you have a few ninja-themed moves?" asked Cyanna.

"Probably too many games and cartoons. That's why I wear the goggles. What about you, princess, do you fight like your brother?"

"No, I took a very different approach. While Hitbox uses his magic to help store the memories on how to effectively wield an enormous number of weapons, I use the same kind of spells the help me remember how to play nearly every musical instrument in both our worlds and even more songs to play on them. Magical instruments and magical songs played on them have all kinds of effects, like attacks for fighting monsters."

"So, your brother's a one-man armoury and you're a one-woman orchestra," mused Gretchen.

"Glad they're on our side," said Malcolm.

"I adore music!" exclaimed Cyanna. "I sing, I conduct, I compose; everyone always says I have a soul of music. Not every genre is for me but music is one of the greatest things in any world."

"Here we go again," sighed Hitbox.

"As you can see despite what impression his stern face may give you, my brother still has the family's sense of humour."

"We may have been a little upset when Astral first called you to our world but she just wanted our worlds to meet and she saw in all of you what the Blizzard Master saw in Zack. Visrel would have struck our grandfather down had you not intervened so from now on we're grateful that you're here."

"But you can be sure we'll be fighting with you guys," said Cyanna. "We're all friends now."

"Are you sure?" said Zack

"Yes. I know you guys naturally get on with the stranger people in life and the two of us have not quite managed to not inherit some of grandad's eccentricities."

"There aren't enough genes in an eternity to overwrite them," mused Hitbox.

"The more of us fighting monsters the better," said Eric.

"Frozen Fire are friends to the royal family of Miyamoto whether you like it or not," declared Cyanna.

"Be it upon your own heads," said Gretchen.

"Especially with her," remarked Zack.

"And his deafening voice," remarked Patrick. The door opened and Astral entered the room.

"I cannot locate Putrice's hiding place," explained Astral. "She knows magic too well. I can't locate her from my temple. I need to search in a place with a far clearer connection to your world. I am heading for the Free Space, the nearly empty part of the Data Realm."

"Beyond that giant door?" checked Zack.

"Where our pal the Anti-Gamer is hiding?" said Gretchen

"Surely Connection Tower has the best connection," said Eric.

"Yes, that is true. However, I would need to use the tower's own powers," explained Astral. "Unfortunately my knowledge of the tower's magic isn't sufficient enough for this kind of spell. Visrel may have been able to manipulate some of its powers to channel his deadly spell, but how the tower works and how to use its powers properly is a secret kept by the royal family."

"Can't you have them help you?" asked Gretchen.

"Sorry, it's a secret we keep not a secret we know," said Cyanna.

"Wait, what?" said Zack.

"We've got it written down somewhere but we haven't read it."

"Riiiiight."

"Are you sure about this, Astral?" asked Hitbox.

"The Free Space may be where monsters like Visrel came from but I can handle myself fine," said Astral. "True, I may be a little vulnerable while I'm searching but that's why I'll be bringing Frozen Fire with me."

"So, presumably we've to go with you in case he turns up?" checked Eric.

"Yes, there's chance he'll attack. He's said he doesn't want to waste any time by killing me but he's not one to let an opportunity to pass either. Odds are we'll be attacked by some monster."

"Typical," sighed Zack.

"Hey, at least we're getting to see something barely anyone has seen," said Patrick.

Astral warped them all and Frozen Fire found themselves standing on the steps to the door on Game's Edge. Behind them was a giant canyon and the bridge that was destroyed in their battle with the Anti-Gamer was still being rebuilt. Astral raised her arms and the usual transporting light surrounded them and then came the usual falling sensation but this time it felt like they were being pushed through some viscous liquid which must of been them begin pushed through the door and then they touched back down on the ground. The Free Space, as it name suggested, was mostly empty, sort of. It looked like they were standing in an aurora like the northern lights in the night sky; though there was no ground they were standing as if there was. However, it wasn't completely empty: in front of them were three gigantic doors that seemed to float in the air and did not look as though they led anywhere. Each door matched the door at Game's Edge, though they were different colours, and when they looked behind them sure enough there was a fourth door, the same large blue door the other side of which is in Miyamoto.

"There are four worlds in The Data Realm?" said Zack.

"Each one born from a different type of data," explained Astral.

"Does anyone in Miyamoto know about them?" asked Patrick.

"It's not a secret but it's not common knowledge either. I can't say who knows and who doesn't, bar the royal family and the other leaders. Each world is different and each one has someone like me who watches over it. The world beyond the yellow door to our left was born from the data of animated family musical films, a colourful place with talking animals; it's called Lasseter. The world behind the black on our right was made from the data of science fiction TV shows, a spherical world like the other but it has many floating planetoids and moons as well as its own unique races; its known as Hartnell. And through the magenta door straight ahead is a world born from e-book versions of mystery stories making it seem like there are more secrets than there are; it is named Pratchett."

"And Miyamoto is behind the cyan door," added Gretchen.

"Yes, my home world born from data of adventure and RPG fantasy games."

"So, they're completely cut off from each other?" enquired Eric.

"It was the price we paid when we hid them behind the doors. We've looked for ways to reconnect the worlds without compromising the doors but we've had little luck.

"So then why hide them behind the doors?" asked Zack.

"The Free Space is unstable," replied Astral. "In many ways it is a blank slate and while we may have been able to prevent some kinds of data from taking form, we cannot stop the never-ending flow of emotions that people express over the internet. Their emotions can take on a non-magical form and when they combine with unstable magic that's when true monsters like Visrel are born. The Free Space has been full of unstable magic and while throughout the Data Realm's history there haven't been too many true monsters it's still something we worry about." Frozen Fire had that look again when they were trying to work out why the Data Realm seemed older than it should be, so Astral kept on explaining. "When the Data Realm first came into being time was unstable and centuries passed in a short amount of time. Soon our world was seemingly as old as yours but the time stabilized some time ago and now it flows at the same place as your word. We use the same dating system that you use for easiness when our worlds met." Frozen Fire took a moment to process that amount of information.

"Lucky we've watched a lot of time travel," said Patrick. "Otherwise we might not have understood all that."

"I best get started," said Astral. She held her arms up, placed her hands together, brought them down in front of her chest, closed her eyes and began to glow.

"Now for the waiting," stated Gretchen.

"Assuming we don't get attacked by monsters," added Eric.

"We always get attacked by monsters these days," groaned Zack.

"We haven't lost yet," said Patrick.

"Yes, we have," Malcolm pointed out, recalling the incident at Connection Tower. There was movement nearby that caused them to turn; something was heading towards them. They moved in closer so it couldn't get near Astral. They reached it and saw as they suspected it was a monster, this one resembling an oversized toy robot. Metal limbs, square head and body an antenna on top and blinking lights for eyes. It slammed its large arms at them but Frozen Fire got out the way in time. Malcolm retaliated with an electrified arrow while Eric struck it with his scythe which was covered in flames. The monster started blinking its eyes rapidly and bursts of energy blasted in time with the blinking. Zack threw his icicle kunai and snowflake shurikens at its face causing the blasts to stop allowing Gretchen to attack with her halberd and several of its duplicates and Patrick to attack with his sword covered in temporal energy. The monster span its arms rapidly, knocking Gretchen and Patrick away and when the other three got close it knocked them down too. Frozen Fire scrambled to get back up as the monster began with the energy bursts again. Eric made a fire twister appear around the monster's head while Malcolm sent lightning bolts down on it. Gretchen sent a shadow wave at it and Patrick sent a temporal pulse. The monster swung its arms at them again. Zack swung his staff at it but it was knocked out of his hands. Zack focused his magic above the monster building up a large block of ice and dropped it on the robot. The monster started rapidly punching making Frozen Fire rush to get out the way. Patrick formed some time magic into the shape of a pocket watch with a long chain and lashed it at the monster. Zack threw a snowball at its face making a snow-screen appear around its head blocking its vision. Malcolm fired a stream of lightning from two of his fingers, Gretchen threw shadow hammers and Eric threw his scythe like a flaming boomerang. The monster began spinning, again attempting to knock them over. Gretchen threw her halberd and several duplicates at the monster making the monster stop. Patrick attacked with a time burst, Malcolm fired a volley of arrows and Eric made fire erupt underneath it. Zack charged his magic and made a giant icicle kunai and hurled it at the monster; it pierced the monster's head it then began to fall over and burst into magic and vanished into nothing. Pacing themselves Frozen Fire returned to Astral. After a moment she stopped glowing and opened her eyes.

"I found something," she said. "We should return to Adlez castle and let everyone know."

Back at the castle Astral explained what she had found to the king and the other leaders.

"Dr Putrice has managed to shield us from directly tracing the rift's source from Miyamoto," she began. "But from the Free Space I was able to trace a series of scientific documents that she wrote, including ones based around making her data phantoms. They seemed to be stored on a hard drive kept in an office in a building with its own laboratories which seems to be her place of work."

"Excellent. The rift will be closed by sundown," exclaimed Hud. "Although which sundown remains to be seen."

"What about the energy she has already stolen?" asked Larch.

"When a data phantom is destroyed the stolen energy should return to Miyamoto," replied Astral.

"Better get all of them as well; we can't have our world in this state rift or no rift," said Stratus. Frozen Fire grumbled as the list of things they had to do got longer.

"And you'll need to make sure she doesn't just make the rift again," added Astral.

"You'd better destroy all the data she has as well," stated Iron. "That hard drive and anything else she has."

"We wish you luck, Frozen Fire," said Hud. "Have courage, determination and remember that no matter what happens I'll make sure you have nice funerals." They ignored that last part.

"Grandad, I'm going to go with them," said Cyanna. "It'll be a good idea to have some help to make sure all the data phantoms are destroyed."

"Cyanna, no. We need to stay here in case any monsters attack Adlez," Hitbox reminded her. Cyanna sighed and folded her arms in a defeated way.

"Right then, we'd better go and find Putrice," stated Gretchen. Astral handed them a small piece of paper.

"This is the address of the building I tracked Putrice's research to," she said.

"Right, let's get this over with," said Zack.

"We've got a lot of monsters to fight," stated Patrick.

"It'll take a good while," added Eric.

"Back home then," said Malcolm. Frozen Fire each touched their pendants which glowed as they began to head home. As soon as they did Cyanna grabbed Zack's arm and she was transported along with them. They appeared back where they had left from before.

"The city of Reekie on the floating island of Kerozonia," exclaimed Cyanna when they landed. "You guys have a nice home." Frozen Fire gaped at her trying to think what to say.

"What... you... why..." stammered Zack.

"Grandad, Hitbox and Astral aren't going to be happy. But I want to help and I want to make sure every bit of life stolen from my home is returned. Not that I don't think you can do it but I won't just sit and wait."

"If something happens to you we're the ones who'll get into trouble with them," said Gretchen.

"Can we say no to a princess?" wondered Eric. "She's not the princess of our country, but still..."

"This is happening one way or the other," said Cyanna. "Now where exactly is Putrice?"

"From what I can gather the address Astral gave us is in the north part of the city," replied Patrick. And without delay they were off, Frozen Fire and the Princess of Music heading into battle against and cruel and wicked scientist.

Putrice's place of work was in a five-storey building. Even though it didn't look that unusual for a building the knowledge of the one draining the life out of Miyamoto made it seem very imposing. As they approached data phantoms swarmed out of the building and headed straight for them. Frozen Fire summoned their weapons and Cyanna summoned an ocarina that looked like it was made out of light. As Frozen Fire attacked with their weapons when the monsters got close, Cyanna played a tune on her ocarina. Zack recognized the tune from a game and when she finished playing it, magic flashed and a great tornado surrounded the phantoms and it threw them in all directions.

"They're tougher than the ones we fought before," said Zack.

"Sheesh, that was quick, what a pain," said Gretchen.

"Why couldn't we fight a bumbling villain?" said Eric. The phantoms began to regroup and more appeared.

"OH COME ON!" yelled Zack.

"She really is a fast worker," grumbled Patrick.

"We're not just going to back down," said Cyanna. She swapped her ocarina for a violin and started playing and magic exploded in centre of the swarm throwing the phantoms all over. Next she produced a folk guitar and strummed a tune that caused fireballs to drop down on them.

"I'm gonna have those tunes in my head for the rest of the day," said Gretchen. "Anyway, better head inside now." She readied her magic; her shadow grew and everyone was pulled into it. It then moved across the ground and into the building where they climbed the stairs to the floor they reached when Gretchen needed to stop and came out of the shadow again. Inside were even more data phantoms prowling the halls.

"Someone has a lot of time on their hands," said Eric.

"Better head for cover," said Malcolm. Everyone tried to quickly and quietly move out of detection range. Everyone burst into one of two rooms.

Zack, Eric and Cyanna found themselves in a room filled with filing cabinets. They looked around.

"Hey, look at this," called Cyanna. "It's physical copies of her research." She was gesturing to the filing cabinet labelled 'The Data Realm'. They inspected the files inside.

"I don't understand what I'm looking at but it appears to be a machine that powers a spell," said Zack "The things I do recognize are definitely something bad."

"We can be sure she can't be trusted with any of this," said Eric. "Best to make sure none remains. Allow me." Before he could act they heard the door opening and when they looked behind them they saw data phantoms had entered the room and attacked. They were each struck by snowballs made of dense snow from Zack, followed by fire balls from Eric. Cyanna summoned a lute and when she played this time beams of energy shot at the monsters. Soon they were surrounded by slashing claws and biting teeth. Eric made fire erupt knocking them away, Zack followed up with icicle kunai. Cyanna produced a flute which fired a bolt of lightning when she played; the phantoms burst into magic.

"That's some of the stolen energy returning," said Cyanna triumphantly.

"It won't matter if we don't hurry up and close the rift," said Zack.

"At least we're getting somewhere," mused Eric. He snapped his fingers and fire erupted out of the filing drawer. After all the documents burned away he snapped his fingers again and the fire went out.

While that was happening Gretchen, Malcolm and Patrick had ended up in another room. There was nothing in it apart from a desk and a single computer.

"This isn't much of an office, only one computer," observed Gretchen. Malcolm sat down and accessed it.

"There's nothing on here," explained Malcolm.

"Well, you can hardly expect her to just leave them lying around for easy access," mused Patrick. Malcolm opened a drawer in the desk and found a portable hard drive. He plugged it into the computer and saw it contained files on what Putrice had been up to.

"She needs to work on her security," said Gretchen. Turning around they saw data phantoms had entered the room. "On second thought maybe not." The phantoms lunged at Malcolm who shot them with arrows. Patrick used time bursts on them and followed up with his sword while Gretchen threw shadow candelabras at them. The phantoms swiped with their claws. Patrick blocked with his sword and counterattacked. Gretchen struck with her halberd and Malcolm blasted lightning in what were essentially their faces. The phantoms cut through the attacks but Patrick managed to halt them with his powers. Taking this opportunity Gretchen unleashed gigantic shadow waves and Malcolm rained down as much lightning as he could muster and this finished the phantoms.

"And good riddance to ya," yelled Gretchen.

"I think there's an enchantment preventing us from just deleting files," said Patrick examining the hard drive after removing it from the computer.

"That won't be a problem," said Malcolm. He took the hard drive from Patrick and surged it with electricity. When he stopped the device was completely ruined.

Everyone snuck back out into the hall and told the others what had happened. Now that the coast was clear they headed up the nearby stairway. Cyanna sensed something powerful and proceeded to search for what it was. However none of the others noticed and they carried on to the floor above. On this floor they found a door with Putrice's name on it and barged right in. They found themselves in a large mostly empty, yet well decorated office. Against the far wall Putrice sat at a desk nearly the length of the room and there were eight phantoms in front of them.

"You children really need to learn to knock before entering a room," said Putrice without looking up.

"We got rid of digital files and the physical copies!" exclaimed Gretchen.

"It's your own fault for not being more secure," remarked Eric.

"But you haven't closed the rift yet," said Putrice looking up at them. "You're running out of time, darlings. Do you think you'll be able to get to my spell in time?"

"We're already in the building," Eric pointed out.

"Yes, but I have hundreds of my phantoms now. On your way in you must have seen how tough they are now. Can you take on a whole army?"

"Someone's been rather busy," said Gretchen

"We're not going to let you drain Miyamoto, you hag," said Zack.

"Well, the five of you are welcome to try darling," said Putrice.

"Five of us?" Turning Frozen Fire finally noticed Cyanna's absence.

Cyanna entered a room with a large machine in it; she could feel powerful magic coming from it. It seemed to contain parts for a spell and seemed to be amplifying it. On the machine was a large glass container and inside it was a black circle floating in the air, the other side of the rift. Though it was smaller than the one in the sky of Miyamoto energy was pouring out of it and being pulled into the machine. The energy was being carried through pipes into another room where a spell was set up to make the data phantoms.

"This is it!" growled Cyanna. "This is how she's killing our world! Well, no more!" She pulled out her ocarina and started playing. Phantoms entered the room and tried to attack her but soon rays of light shot down in time with her music blasting the phantoms and striking the machine. The pipes broke, the glass shattered, parts of the spell were destroyed, the entire machine was broken beyond repair. The energy flow stopped and the hole began to shrink into nothingness.

In Miyamoto the rift closed and everyone who saw this cheered in joy.

An alarm had gone off in Putrice's office. The eight phantoms had stopped moving and began to flicker like glitching images on a computer.

"What, my machine how?" yelled Putrice. "The phantoms are destabilizing, all the energy will just go back where it came! NO!"

"Cyanna must have found the rift and closed it," exclaimed Gretchen.

"Boy, that princess really is something else," mused Zack. He realized he said that out loud.

"I think I'll remember that one," said Eric with a grin.

"And we don't have to hunt down all the phantoms now," said Patrick.

"Quite a relief," said Malcolm.

"It will be short lived, darling!" snarled Putrice. "You won't be walking out of here quite so easily. You'd be amazed at what I can do with that energy." She held her arm high above her and there was a flash of magic. The door slammed shut, the phantoms reverted back into energy but rather than fly off to return to Miyamoto they flew towards Putrice. The energy merged with her and magic surged all over her. When it cleared she had changed. She was now taller and thinner; she was almost completely white like the phantoms that had disappeared and her other clothes looked different now. She had long ribbons trailing down from her arms and she floated off the floor.

"Well, now you look plain bizarre," remarked Eric.

"Man, I was hoping we wouldn't have to fight her," groaned Zack putting on his goggles.

"We knew we would," Malcolm pointed out.

"Didn't think she'd transform though," said Patrick.

"She's attacking dumb dumbs," said Gretchen.

They quickly summoned their weapons as Putrice swung the ribbons at them which swished like whips, but they were blocked by one of Zack's ice walls. Gretchen came out swinging her halberd and struck at her. Zack then threw the ice wall at her. Putrice fired beams from her eyes at them Eric retaliated with a swing of his scythe. Malcolm fired lightning out of two of his fingers and Patrick sent a temporal pulse both struck her in the face. Putrice swung the ribbons down at them knocking them all over. There was a scramble to get back up as she fired more beams. Gretchen sent a shadow wave at her as she got up and Malcolm fired several arrows when he got up. Zack struck Putrice with his staff but was kicked over after. Patrick slashed with his sword and Eric sent a stream of fire. Everyone sent balls of their element at Putrice but she knocked them away with her ribbons; this ended up smashing her desk and breaking the windows.

Cyanna arrived on the floor Frozen Fire were on. She saw the door and found it was blocked by magic. She could hear the sounds of the battle on the other side.

Putrice continued to fire beams at Frozen Fire as they scrambled around to avoid them. Zack hurled his icicle kunai and snowflake shirukens and Eric made a sharp slice with his scythe covered in flames. Malcolm fired electrified arrows that cracked with thunder into her face then she swung the ribbons round again but Patrick and Gretchen blocked with their sword and halberd. Putrice threw her head back then brought it forward firing a stronger beam. Zack made as solid an ice dome as he could manage to protect them. The beam was not stopping and Zack was struggling to maintain the dome so Gretchen used her shadow to move them out. When they were out again Malcolm threw lightning balls, Patrick attacked with his sword, its reach boosted by time magic. And Eric had towers of fire erupt underneath Putrice. She charged the ribbons with energy and started lashing out rapidly. Zack made a snow-screen for cover, Eric threw his scythe like a flaming boomerang, Gretchen threw her halberd and several duplicates, Patrick threw a block of time magic shaped a like a grandfather clock and Malcolm shot volley of arrows. Putrice fell to the ground and frozen Fire threw balls of their respective elements at her and soon she seemed to crack. There was an explosion of magic and when it cleared Putrice was back to normal lying on the floor in a daze. The door burst opened as Cyanna entered.

"You defeated that evil hag," said Cyanna. "I hope it stung."

"And you closed the rift," said Zack putting his goggles back on his forehead.

"I think an anonymous tip to the authorities is in order," said Gretchen.

"Even if they don't know about the Data Realm, making lesser monsters is illegal," said Eric. "She's gonna get in trouble."

"But all the data phantoms are gone now," said Patrick. "We didn't leave any evidence."

"But the machine that made them is still there," said Cyanna "I only broke the rift machine. They'll know she was making monsters."

"Well then, perhaps it's time for us to leave," said Gretchen. She made her shadow grow and they sank into it and it left the building.

When Putrice regained focus she was alone in the ruins of her office. She could hear sirens coming. She picked up her smart tablet and turned it on. Magic flickered across its screen and a face appeared on it. It was that of a man with short hair, some facial hair and colourless eyes, just white with two black dots.

"It would seem you have failed, doctor," said the Anti-Gamer in his cold voice.

"Yes, Frozen Fire got the better of me," replied Putrice.

"So they've done it again. I guess the rift was too slow."

"Yes, and I had finally gotten the phantom production running so quickly. It's time for me to head into hiding to avoid prison."

"It seems it will be a while before you can begin your next experiment."

"Yes, Frozen fire destroyed a lot, but I still have plenty of resources left. What's next for you, darling?"

"I need a faster way of destroying Miyamoto. I have heard whispers of a book somewhere in the Free Space which may be helpful. I have several leads on it. I hope we can collaborate again, doctor." Visrel vanished off the screen and Putrice disappeared from her office.

Frozen Fire returned to Miyamoto and were treated for the injuries they received during the rough battle. Cyanna seemed to be in no trouble for running off to help them fight.

"Please don't do that again," said Hitbox.

"You know full well I was never gonna stay out the fight," replied Cyanna.

"Well, I'm glad you're OK, my dear," said Hud.

Frozen Fire entered the room and once again found themselves in front of a grateful king, with the prince and princess at one side and the leaders of the three races at the other.

"Once again you have saved our world," said Hud.

"Princess Cyanna was the one who closed the rift," said Zack finally able to talk easily to the king.

"I may have destroyed the machine by myself but I could not have invaded that building on my own," said Cyanna.

"And we gave the villain a thorough beating," said Gretchen.

"And set the police on her," added Patrick.

"You can be sure Miyamoto will remember Frozen Fire forever," said Hud. "And much like the Blizzard Master of Kerozonia I wish to bestow upon the five of you heroic names."

"That's cool," said Malcolm quietly.

"Do they come with riches?" enquired Eric.

"Not at all. Nothing to worry about there." replied Hud.

"Aw."

"What he means is you'll be recognized as ones who have done great service to this world," explained Astral.

"Legendary figures in both our worlds are remembered better thanks to names like these," said Hud. "Now then, Frozen Fire, I knight you and bestow upon you legendary titles. Zackary Glacis, I name you the Blizzard Ninja due to your habit of ninja-themed manoeuvres. Gretchen Shadows, I name you the Shadow Mimic for your spectacular ability to use shadows to duplicate just about anything. Eric Flare, I name you the Blazing Knight due to your actions that would make old knights proud. Malcolm Spark, I name you the Lightning Archer due to your skills with a bow even without magic arrows. And Patrick Tempus, I name you the Temporal Swordsman due to your remarkable skills with your blade." Frozen Fire bowed to the king once he had finished.

"Never heard you make so much sense for so long, Grandad," complemented Hitbox.

"Don't worry, Hitbox, it won't last long," replied Hud. "Why, by tomorrow I'll sound just like a tap dancing diamond flamingo in a cartoon cat factory."

"It didn't last at all, your majesty," remarked Larch.

"Well, Frozen Fire, you should be proud of yourselves," said Iron.

"You restored our sky to normal," said Stratus. Each leader thanked them again. Frozen Fire, the royal siblings and Astral found themselves on the same balcony where Cyanna first spotted the rift.

"I checked your home's news feeds," said Astral. "Dr Putrice got away but she is now a wanted criminal so she'll have a hard time regaining the resources she'd need to make any more monsters."

"At least we can take a break," said Zack with a sigh of relief.

"Don't you need to practice to make sure you're always ready?" asked Hitbox.

"We get plenty of practice with our magic," replied Gretchen. "And it won't be long until we're among the most powerful elementals ever."

"What about your weapons?"

"What about them?" responded Patrick.

"Don't you get any practice with them?"

"There's not really much need what with our magic," explained Eric.

"I gave them their weapons to help them with their magic," said Astral. "I put spells on them to help them develop their powers."

"Surely there'd be no harm in learning how to use them?" said Cyanna. "After all it'd be another means to fight monsters."

"Good point," said Malcolm.

"Are you volunteering to teach them?" asked Astral. "I'm not sure who to feel sorry for in that scenario."

"I say the castle," said Cyanna.

"Well if you're interested I can teach you if you want," said Hitbox.

"The two of us will always be happy to help."

"And we'll be happy to help you too," said Gretchen. "Within reason."

Frozen Fire thanked them. Frozen Fire headed home to relax feeling exhausted and proud. Astral smiled to herself knowing there were seven heroes to protect Miyamoto. As it happened Zack did actually take Hitbox up on his offer to learn how to use his staff as did Gretchen, Patrick and Malcolm. Scythes didn't count as part of Hitbox's weapon magic so Eric had to learn an adapted way of using his. Both Zack and Gretchen thought they overheard their brothers talking about fighting monsters but didn't think anything of it. Cyanna was always amazing everyone with her musical talents and was often heard singing an odd verse from somewhere in the Data Realm.

"The light from four lands, Shall put our world in your hands, Only they who watch truly know, Just where this magic did go, The rulers of each land are the key, To the colours being set free, In the empty space, You can shape its face, With the power of the light, You can feel a god's might."

Book Three

The Virus's Spell Book

Each world in the Data Realm is protected by a gigantic door. They can keep many things out, but not everything or everyone. The magic of the blue door in Miyamoto struggled to keep something out but it couldn't and they made it through. Two figures landed on the ground in front of the door, one was holding a book.

"I see they've repaired the bridge since I was last here," observed one figure. "That didn't take much time."

"Where is this place you said we could hide?" asked the other figure.

"At the bottom of the chasm bellow the bridge. Nobody ever traverses down there."

"But anyone who can teleport could make it down there. I guess we're going to run interference so this Astral can't locate us?"

"Obviously. Now let's get set up and then we can began gathering what we need for the vortex."

"Do you remember everything you need from the other three worlds?"

"Yes. And unlike you I am strong enough to pass through the doors whenever I want. I can easily return on the rare chance I forget something."

"Remember, Anti-Gamer, only I was able to retrieve this book. I broke the seal of the four who watch. Nobody else."

"I know, that is why I enlisted you. Quite curious how I can get past a spell made by one who watches and yet you can get past one made by all four but not made by one. Still differences like that are what makes our cooperation a force to be feared. Astral knows whenever someone passes through the door, she'll be gathering those heroes soon. Make good use of the viruses I am giving you."

"I will be ready for any of them, in fact I look forward to meeting them." The two figures leapt down the chasm casting their interference spells as they went.

Gretchen Shadows had met up with Eric Flare.

"Ready to head to Miyamoto?" enquired Gretchen.

"Ready when you are," replied Eric.

"Right I think Patrick and Malcolm are going to meet us at the castle."

"And Zack's already there, training with Hitbox."

"Ah, yes, more of playing ninja." Activating the magic pendants they wore they opened a portal to Miyamoto through Gretchen's computer. After being surrounded by white light and experiencing a weightless sensation they landed at Adlez Castle. They were in the castle grounds near Prince Hitbox's training area. The prince himself was standing nearby. "Hey there, your highness, where's Zack?" inquired Gretchen.

"Cooling off under that large pile of snow he made," replied Hitbox gesturing to a large pile of white powder.

"You all right, Zack?" asked Eric. There was some kind of muffled response from under the snow. "I'll take that as a long loud groan." The snow disappeared and Zack sat up.

"You a real ninja yet, goggles?" asked Gretchen.

"Quit asking that all the time," snapped Zack.

"To be fair the staff techniques I have been teaching him are a form of ninjutsu," explained Hitbox. "All the fighting I've been teaching you all is based upon the titles grandfather bestowed upon you recently. I'm teaching Eric all kinds of knightly fighting for his scythe. Of course I've had to wing it a little with you, Gretchen as your title isn't a kind of warrior."

"And along with my snowflake shurikens, icicle kunai and snow-screens I'll be real ninja before you know it," said Zack.

"Apart from the stealth, the assassinations and the fact that you're not from Sollux," remarked Gretchen. "As much as you love the culture of the home of video games."

"Oh, shut up."

"I'm already a real knight," bragged Eric. "After all, all it took was being knighted which the king so kindly did." Zack finally stood up and then there was a flash of light and Malcolm and Patrick appeared next to them.

"Ah, good we're all here!" exclaimed Patrick.

"Hope we're not late," said Malcolm.

"Not at all," assured Hitbox.

"Hey everyone," called a voice from nearby the door inside. It was Hitbox's younger sister, Princess Cyanna. "Lady Astral is here and says she has something important to tell us; you'd better head straight for the throne room. I'll go find grandad." She disappeared inside and the others headed inside too.

"Well, Zack, you're improving. You're not spouting as much gibberish when you get worn out," said Hitbox.

"He never makes any sense anyway," commented Gretchen.

"That's rich coming from the girl who's always telling people they smell like cheese randomly," responded Zack.

"If they didn't constantly smell of cheese all the time, I wouldn't have to."

"Speak for yourself," said Eric.

"She's just jealous of how well I use my Frozen Fury," said Zack.

"Your what?" said Patrick.

"Frozen Fury, it's what I call my staff. Even though there's a smiling snowman face in the centre."

"Didn't you name your weapon? We all did," explained Gretchen. "I call my halberd the Umber Fang."

"I named my scythe the Sun's Reaper," said Eric.

"My bow is the Thunderbird's Wing," said Malcolm.

"Well, actually I've been referring to my sword as the Clock Blade," said Patrick. "But I was thinking of Time's Talon."

"Go with the second," said Hitbox. Everyone agreed and proceeded to the throne room. Cyanna found her grandfather, King Hud, in the midst of using all the charm his old, unusual mind could muster.

"I must say, you are a truly beautiful woman," said Hud with charm and honesty.

"Uh, grandad," interrupted Cyanna.

"Yes, my dear sweet princess?"

"That's a suit of armour." The king looked back at the armour he had been talking too with a genuine look of surprise and shock on his face

"She flirted with me first," he said defensively. Cyanna just rolled her eyes and dragged her grandfather to the throne room. When they arrived at the throne room Astral, she who watches over Miyamoto, was waiting for them. The king sat on his throne, the prince and princess stood at either side and Frozen Fire lined up in front of the throne.

"All right then, Astral, you seven-foot navy-haired watcher, what is it that we need to know?" asked Hud. Astral took a deep breath before speaking.

"The Anti-Gamer returned to Miyamoto," she said. Alarm ran through everyone, and all of Frozen Fire tried not to panic. "We all knew Visrel would return sooner or later. However, I did not expect him to leave almost immediately after he arrived."

"Wait he just showed up and then left?" questioned Zack.

"He wasn't alone."

"Well, yeah, he's got like an army of wired creatures," said Patrick.

"No, he brought someone else with him. Another true monster, one I do not recognize."

"So he brings in a new monster and leaves it here to do his work?" wondered Hitbox.

"If they want similar things then there's no reason they can't work together," suggested Cyanna. "Visrel was born from hatred, perhaps the creature was too."

"I suspect Visrel left this other monster to begin the plan while he attends to something else," said Astral.

"So they're both death and destruction mad?" asked Eric.

"Perhaps, perhaps not," said Astral. "Monsters are born when emotions that have been given form combine with unstable magic. Barely anyone knows about the Data Realm so they do not realize that often the expressions of emotion would take form here. And the Free Space is filled with unstable magic; if we who watch hadn't placed great firewalls of protection all over by now we'd be overrun by monsters. My point being that this monster could have come from any kind of emotion. It could be a greed born conqueror or a despair born misery spreader."

"Whatever its deal it'll have to deal with us first," declared Gretchen.

"So long as we don't fight it and Visrel at the same time," said Zack.

"We can all agree that the sooner this plan is thwarted the better," said Hud. "We can't have monsters destroying the world, it's not hygienic. And let's not forget how seriously we take our recycling laws. It'll be very hard to recycle the whole world. Especially if everyone is dead; we'll never get anything done. Confrontation maybe the best way to find out what its so-called deal is. We may not be able to get rid of it straight away but any info is a start."

"The monster is currently in the Iwata Snowfields," said Astral.

"Then off to the snowfields you go, Frozen Fire."

The Iwata Snowfields were spread across a group of hilltops. Always covered in a blanket of snow, snowing more often than not and always, always at a low temperature. Regarded in Miyamoto as a truly beautiful place, it was left largely untouched with a few tourist spots and a small town on the edge of the snow fields. In a bright light Frozen Fire and Astral appeared and all their feet sank into the snow.

"Wow, this place is amazing," marvelled Eric. "I wonder what its strange quirk is?"

"Now, now, not everywhere in Miyamoto has something unusual about it," said Astral.

"Edge Forest, Thunderfalls Caverns, The Assorted Tree Woodland, the Solid Cloudbank and that Candle Mountain could lead people to this conclusion," said Patrick recalling the other places in Miyamoto Frozen Fire had visited. Though not all together.

"Most places in our world are like that too," said Malcolm.

"All right, point taken," said Astral.

"This place is colder than Kerozonia. Which is saying something," said Gretchen, pointing out the usually poor weather in her home country as many Kerozonians do.

"That's the great thing about being an ice elemental, you're never affected by the cold," said Zack ever so slightly smug. "And we can easily cool ourselves off in hot weather. Haven't needed any clothes for hot or cold weather since I was twelve."

"It's the same with fire elementals though the other way around," said Eric with the same touch of smugness. "Hot weather never bothers us and we can always keep warm no matter how cold it is." Zack and Eric shared a high five while the others rolled their eyes.

"So, are we going to visit that town?" enquired Gretchen.

"No, we need to find the monster as soon as possible," replied Astral. "I'll show you the town some other time. It's called Snowman's Town." Astral lead them into the snowfields leaving trail of footprints behind them.

"You can sense all of this snow can't you, Zack?" asked Patrick.

"Yeah, every single last flake," answered Zack. "I think there's something hiding up ahead."

"Perhaps the monster we've coming looking for," suggested Gretchen. "Or a big one sent by Visrel."

"We usually get attacked at this point," said Malcolm.

"I can sense it now get ready," warned Astral. The snow burst as a creature rose from underneath it. It was large hand made from bricks of ice. It clenched into a fist and shot towards Frozen Fire. Everyone but Zack got out of the way; he was struck with the full force of the punch but completely unaffected. He didn't even move.

"Who sends an ice monster to fight an ice elemental in a snowfield?" yelled Zack. He used his magic to shoot the snow from the ground upwards knocking over the hand. Everyone summoned their weapons.

"This thing doesn't stand a chance against me," declared Eric. Covering his scythe in flames he struck the hand sending it backwards. The hand pointed and fired an energy beam from its finger at them. Everyone scrambled to avoid it. Malcolm started shooting it with electrified arrows, Gretchen made a giant shadow paintbrush that she made strike it and Patrick blasted it with temporal energy. The hand struck the ground causing everyone to fall over. Zack made the snow propel his staff at the hand striking it allowing everyone to get up. Gretchen covered her halberd in shadows making it look like a drawing pencil and stabbed the hand. The hand started firing the beam again and Eric retaliated with a fire twister while Patrick attacked with temporally speed up sword slashes. The hand manoeuvred out of the attacks and dived into the snow picking up a large amount of it and hurled it at them. Zack sent his magic into the snow and sent it back knocking the hand out of the air; the others blasted it with their elements. But the hand wasn't beat yet; it rose up and fired beams from all of its fingers. Malcolm pointed at the hand and lightning blasted it, Patrick sent a temporal pulse at it and Gretchen slammed it with a shadow block. The ice that made the hand began to crack. Zack threw many snowflake shurikens and icicle kunai at it. The cracks spread all over the hand and with one last giant fireball from Eric it shattered. Someone was clapping a most insincere applause. There was someone standing in the snow, someone wicked.

"Bravo, Frozen Fire. I imagine Visrel would say you've improved since you last fought," said the applauder. His voice was smarmy and snide. He clearly wasn't human; his skin was a dark grey colour and appeared to be very slimy like a slug. He wore a large white coat buttoned from top to bottom, thick black rubber gloves and boots and green trousers.

"You're the new monster," said Zack.

"Obviously."

"So what's your deal? You some kind of malware reject?" questioned Gretchen.

"Allow me to introduce myself," said the monster. "Many gamers express their anger over the internet; what they didn't know is that it took form. And when it collided with the unstable magic of the Free Space I was born. The anger I came from was from when their internet connections failed. I am the embodiment of all bad connections, slow downloads and sluggish game play. I am the bane of online gaming. I am Lag."

"Right," was all anyone could manage.

"Shall we just skip to the part where we fight you?" asked Eric.

"Oh no, I'm leaving. I've got what I came for," replied Lag. "But I will let you in on one secret."

"If it's you've an army of monsters we know," remarked Patrick. Lag ignored that comment and out of seemingly nowhere produced a large book. It was old. The pages looked a little wrinkled and were starting to yellow and the dark red cover was worn in places. There were runes on it that glowed faintly. Astral gasped when she saw it.

"How did you get that?" demanded Astral.

"This can't be good," said Zack.

"Never thought you'd see this again," said Lag referring to the book. "Visrel may be able to go through any of the doors but only I could break the seal you four who watch placed of this tome. The end of Miyamoto will come thanks to the words in 'The Virus's Spell Book'." Lag vanished in what appeared to be a surge of his slime. Astral began talking before anyone could ask.

"The king and the others will need to hear this as well," she said. And then promptly returned everyone to Adlez.

Back at the castle King Hud was still sitting on his throne listening to Cyanna play her flute. Hitbox entered and before he could ask if there was any news Astral and Frozen Fire appeared in the room.

"So, how'd it go?" asked Hud cheerfully.

"I've got bad news, your majesties," said Astral. She quickly explained what happened at the snowfields. "The book he has is called 'The Virus's Spell Book'. It is a relic from the old days of the Data Realm. It contains dangerous spells and curses made by viruses, there'll be plenty they can use to try and destroy Miyamoto. A long time ago we four who watch got a hold of the book and sealed it away, but Lag somehow broke our seal."

"No doubt the two of them are gathering parts of a spell," said Hitbox.

"So we should try and stop them from taking them," said Cyanna.

"It would be helpful if we knew what they were after," grumbled Zack.

"The only ancient relic that gets to cause trouble in this kingdom is me!" exclaimed Hud. "I haven't been king for a ridiculously long time just to be killed by a couple of grouchy cretins."

"You make the Data Realm sound ancient," said Patrick.

"How old is it anyway?" asked Gretchen.

"Well the Data Realm was born in the days the internet was starting to become a common thing in all households," explained Astral. "Time was unstable at first so centuries passed quickly making our culture about as old as yours as I've explained to you before. So in the one sense it's one age and in another it's another age. In short we don't really know."

"Sorry I asked," said Gretchen flatly.

"Almost as complex as some of our stories," said Patrick

"Fighting monsters isn't all that complex" said Astral.

"I think he meant how we got our powers," said Zack. "Which is why you chose us right? Thinking the trials we did was us making it our destinies to battle evil."

"That and our collective love for video games," added Eric.

"I learned a lot about you all," said Astral. "I knew you all wanted adventure and I knew you were right for this world."

Malcolm was thinking about how he got his lightning magic. It was five years ago during a holiday to the country called Vasterra. Malcolm was staring at a mural made by the ancient native Vasterrans, of the thunder birds. A woman was explaining about the creatures.

"When the thunder birds flap their wings, they make the sound of a crack of thunder," she said. "They have been featured in many Native Vasterran myths. Their control of lightning and electricity is arguably the greatest in the world. Only the thunder dragons of the east match, and of course some of the legendary lightning elementals." After spending some time at the exhibit Malcolm and his parents left. While wandering by himself Malcolm found something curious, it was a large bird cringing in pain. It looked like and eagle but it was electric yellow and sparks were surging around it. He realized it was a baby thunder bird that had injured itself. Malcolm was a little hesitant but he moved closer and noticed there was an unnaturally large thorn in its foot.

"What should I do?" wondered Malcolm. He tried to reach for the thorn but pulled his hand back as the sparks surged. After a few attempts Malcolm finally grabbed the bird's leg, held it steady and removed the thorn from its foot. The bird stopped crying and the sparks ceased, the bird started to get up. The bird began to chirp a loud call and a moment later the sound of thunder could be heard. Malcolm realised that it was in fact the sound of wings flapping getting closer. Suddenly an adult thunder bird appeared, five foot tall with seven foot wings. It landed next to the child bird and picked it up with its talon. It turned to Malcolm.

"You helped this young one?" said the thunder bird.

"Y... y... yes," stammered Malcolm somewhat afraid. "I...i... it was nothing."

"Most would be wary of helping a scared thunder bird. Lightning is something to be wary of. You showed courage and you have my gratitude. What is your name?"

"Malcolm Spark."

"Well, Malcolm, permit me to show you a bird's view of the land as an expression of said gratitude." After some convincing Malcolm climbed onto the bird's back and it took off. "I shall return you back once I've returned this child to its nest." The Vasterran landscape stretched out beneath them, it was truly a sight to behold: the large forest nearby and the city where Malcolm was staying. The air rushing all around him, he wasn't sure if he was afraid; he was too amazed by the spectacle. After the trip, even though he was amazed, Malcolm decided not to tell his parents. Before the holiday was over, however, he would meet the thunder birds again. Two days after his first encounter Malcolm had went off on his own, obviously under strict instructions to return to certain place at a certain time. While wandering through the forest near to the tourist attraction where he was supposed to meet his parents, he suddenly got this strange feeling that something was watching him. Malcolm looked around but could see no one.

"Hello? Is anyone there?" said Malcolm. Strange noises came from nearby like the sound of something moving around but trying to stay hidden. Malcolm was very scared. He was sure there was something nearby and it was getting closer. Suddenly a thunder bird came down from above.

"Child, you are being hunted by a carnivorous beast," warned the bird and without another word grabbed Malcolm and took off.

"What did you mean? What was this hunter?" asked Malcolm.

"It's what you humans call a hidebehind. A fierce predator that is master of concealment." The bird took him to a clearing in the forest where there were other thunderbirds.

"It's you," said one. "The boy who helped one of our children. Malcolm Sparks."

"He was being hunted by the hidebehind," said the bird that had brought him.

"That foul creature. Will it ever stop?"

"W… w… what is going on?" demanded Malcolm.

"We have been plagued by this hidebehind for some time now," explained the bird he had met before. "Because those creatures are master of concealment they are excellent predators. They have been responsible for many missing people in history. However, in recent years they have taken to the mountains, living off forest creatures and never venturing near humans, let alone we who can command lightning. But this one that has been plaguing us has somehow acquired a medallion infused with magic rendering the wearer immune to the lightning element. Allowing it to prey on our kind."

"That's scary."

"I'll take you back. This is no time for you to be in the forest." The thunderbird carried Malcolm over the top of the forest.

"What are you going to do about the hidebehind?" asked Malcolm.

"We'll have to fight the creature," replied the bird. "It may be immune to our lightning but we still have our talons and beaks. The problem is finding it, even the world greatest tracker would be hard pushed to find one. Obviously the trick is to let it find you but the trouble is that by then it's most likely too late for you." As they flew something leapt up from the tree tops and grabbed onto the bird it was attacking its wings forcing the bird down into the forest. Malcolm rolled off the bird when they hit the ground. Looking around he saw what had attacked them. It was tall; towering over them, it was rather thin, it was covered in dark brown fur, it looked half way between a wild dog and a bear but it stood on two legs and around its neck was a medallion emblazoned with an image of a thunder bird. It was the hidebehind. Malcolm stared at the creature in terror but it was ignoring him and focusing on the thunder bird. The bird swiped with its talons but the hidebehind dived into the undergrowth and seemingly disappeared. There were sounds of something moving out of sight like before. Suddenly the hidebehind leapt down from a tree and onto the bird, attacking it. The bird thrashed about but couldn't shake it.

"I have to do something," thought Malcolm. He rushed at the fighters and jumped onto the hidebehind. He grasped at the creature but it simply threw him off. When Malcolm landed on the ground he noticed there was something in his hand, the medallion. The hidebehind hadn't seemed to have noticed but the thunderbird had and there was a flash of lightning and a crack of thunder. When Malcolm opened his eyes again the thunderbird was in front of him.

"That was very brave," said the bird. "If a little foolish."

"Wh... wh... what happened," stammered Malcolm.

"Thanks to you the hidebehind will never bother us again. We will destroy the medallion." The thunder bird returned Malcolm to where he was to meet his parents. Malcolm was terrified by what had happened but he soon recovered from the ordeal. On the day before they returned to Kerozonia Malcolm was visited by the thunder bird to say good bye.

"You have our gratitude and eternal friendship," said the bird.

"Thank you," was all Malcolm could manage.

"I wish to offer you a reward for helping us. It will also serve as a symbol of your friendship with the thunder birds."

"What is it?"

"I wish to give you the power of lightning. To command it the way we birds do. I can shape your magic into the lightning element and you would need never fear the thunderous skies again." Malcolm, while initially unsure, accepted this offer. The thunder bird gently pressed its beak on his forehead and electricity surged all over them. Malcolm could feel it, the surging power the coursing energy. His magic was now that of the thunder element. Malcolm returned to Kerozonia an elemental ready to see what he could do with his powers. Yet he didn't really explore it as well as he meant to. While he may have neglected his powers at first he now hopes the thunder birds would be proud of how he uses them now.

Back in the present Frozen Fire were waiting on an update. Astral appeared in a flash of light.

"I can't find Lag," she said. "And there's been no sign of Visrel either. All I know is Lag is still in Miyamoto but the Anti-Gamer isn't. I'm afraid we're just going to have to wait for him to show up somewhere. He can't mask himself forever."

"What did he even take from the snowfields?" wondered Gretchen.

"There aren't a lot of spell that use snow as ingredients," said Zack.

"I can't be sure what he took," said Astral.

"I hate it when we don't know what the bad guys are planning," said Patrick.

"We don't often know," pointed out Malcolm.

"Oh well, might as well call it a day and head home," said Eric.

"I'm sure he's going to make his next move soon," said Astral. She sighed. "If we who watch had offensive powers we would have destroyed that book as soon as it came into out possession."

"There's no sense thinking about what you couldn't do," said a voice from the door. Turning to face it there was Cyanna. "We can destroy the book when we get it off them."

"With a good aim we wouldn't need to get it off them," said Gretchen.

"Anyway, Lord Iron has asked for your help," said Cyanna. "Something's happening in the Steel Crater, and he's very fond of the five of you."

"He seems very fond of everything," mused Zack. "What do we need to do?"

"He didn't say. You'll find out when you get there."

"Well, it gives us something to do," said Eric.

"Let us leap into the unknown," declared Patrick.

"If he just wants stuff moved he's getting avalanched," said Zack.

"Surely he wants us to fight something. Which is our specialty," said Gretchen.

"Let's just go," said Malcolm.

Using their pendants Frozen Fire arrived at the Steel Crater, the home of the metal people, the ore.rar. Venturing into the city they were approached by an ore.rar wearing a sash; they recognized Iron.

"Greetings, my friends. I'm glad you've come," exclaimed Iron.

"No problem, how can we help?" said Patrick.

"There's something strange happening at the hospital," explained Iron gesturing them to follow. They set off. "I think some weird spell has gotten loose. Odd stuff has been going on for days."

"What kind of stuff?" asked Gretchen. "Something that needs taking down?"

"Perhaps. It takes the form of wired apparitions and levitating objects. But every spell used to check for ghosts comes out negative."

"Great, it's creepy," moaned Zack.

"You think everything's creepy," remarked Gretchen.

"Surely someone is doing it?" said Eric. "We could still take them down."

"We did think of that. But we can't trace it to anyone." They made their way to the hospital. Like all the buildings in the crater, it was made from strong and sturdy metal, though Frozen Fire noted on previous visits that they had all the modern conveniences. Overall it looked like any other hospital apart from the ore.rar in the nurse's uniform which was an odd sight even for Miyamoto.

"And I thought Eric wore some unsettling outfits," remarked Zack.

"Quiet you," responded Eric.

"Come on. The source seems to be at the back of the building," said Iron. When they reached the other side of the hospital they did start to sense an unusual spell.

"There's something in the air all right," said Patrick.

"It's not too bad," said Malcolm.

"At the moment," said a voice and from around a corner came a familiar monster.

"Lag!" everyone cried.

"I'm going to leave you to it," said Iron turning to leave.

"You're behind this? Figures," said Gretchen.

"Oh no, I just got here," explained Lag. "It seems some dying ore.rar left a lingering spell as some kind of prank. Floating objects and strange apparitions, harmless. Unless of course someone hijacked the spell." Lag snapped his fingers and several formless ghostly figures appeared carrying several objects "Spells that aren't given a new source and are just left to burn out are just in need of a good takeover. Oh, and I brought some talon-teeth." The Anti-Gamer's spindly-legged walking mouths minions appeared as Lag retreated. Instantly Frozen Fire were buried by piling talon-teeth and hospital equipment. But a blast of their elements knocked them all off. Snowflake shurikens, shadow waves, mini fire twisters, rings of lightning and time bursts took care of various talon-teeth, but the apparitions were throwing the objects at them again.

"These things aren't gonna stop unless we get Lag," said Gretchen.

"Let's just be glad there's nothing sharp," said Zack.

"The ore.rar are made of metal; they must need something more heavy duty," said Patrick. Frozen Fire ran down the corridor Lag went down, but a pile of objects and what was left of the talon-teeth was following. Everyone kept throwing attacks backwards to slow down the advancing enemies. Screeching to a halt at the end of the corridor they found Lag about to enter a door.

"Aha! Got ya, slimy," exclaimed Eric. However, the objects and monsters piled on top of them again allowing Lag to proceed into the room. Knocking everything away again Frozen Fire summoned their weapons and began knocking away the objects that hurled towards them. They backed into the room. Lag turned as they came in.

"Too late," Lag called to them as he vanished in a surge of slime. The talon-teeth lunged at them but Zack threw a snowball at the ground making a snow-screen allowing them to finish them off with their weapons. Malcolm threw a thunder ball at one of the apparitions and when it hit the electricity shot off and struck the others. Gretchen made a large shadow block and started pushing the objects back. Iron appeared from around the corner, saw what was happening and with a mighty punch he knocked the pile of objects apart causing the last of the apparitions to appear which were then dissipated by a fire stream and a temporal pulse. At last everything was still.

"He got away," said Malcolm anticipating Iron's first question. Iron entered the room to see what Lag had been doing. It was then that Frozen Fire noticed that on the doors was the word 'morgue'. As Iron searched they explained what had happened.

"So all this started with a harmless prank?" mused Iron. "Was most likely my recently passed predecessor as leader of the ore.rar, Lead. He could be such a jerk. But the people loved him."

"What exactly was Lag grave robbing for?" asked Gretchen.

"The answer can't be good," said Zack.

"It seems he took from one of the bodies," explained Iron. "That rather grim fellow had taken the heart from one of the deceased. At least the ore.rar in question was an organ donor."

"He stole a heart?!" cried Patrick. Everyone was disgusted.

"That's so wrong," said Malcolm.

"This spell is gonna be nasty," said Eric.

"We ore.rar do have literal hearts of gold," said Iron. "But I seriously doubt that was the reason. No spell that requires a heart is anything but disastrous. But from what Astral told us leaders, this Virus's Spell Book is full of nothing but death." The thought of what could happen sent a chill down the spines of all. After informing Astral what had happened she suggested they return home and rest.

The following day Frozen Fire were discussing their task of protecting Miyamoto.

"First Visrel tries to cut Miyamoto from the rest of the Data Realm," began Zack. "Then Putrice attempts to drain the life from it. And now Lag is putting together something that's bound to put us all right next to doomsday. Where are they getting these ideas from?!"

"Well, Lag and Visrel have gained a book which is essentially a bumper guide to evil ideas," said Gretchen.

"We are stronger than last time," said Malcolm quietly.

"We'll handle anything they try," said Patrick.

"We are fighting two of them," reminded Eric. "Still we may not have to fight them together."

"Based on what Astral said Lag'll likely be heading to one of the other peoples' homes," said Zack. "Should we split up and keep an eye on both or wait for him to make a move and take him on together?"

"I doubt we're going to get close enough to fight him directly," mused Gretchen. "Might be best to split up."

"We better check with Astral first," said Patrick.

"We'll be going all over Miyamoto these next few days," said Eric. "Sounds rather entertaining." When they went to Miyamoto they transported themselves straight to Astral's temple in the middle of the Indigo Fields. They went over their discussion with her.

"I think it's unlikely that Lag will strike both places simultaneously so I don't think there's a need to split up," said Astral. "We're in a situation where we can only wait and respond. We can't even be sure he'll head for other races' homes either, though I admit it seems kind of likely."

They barely waited half an hour before Astral's monitoring maps picked up trouble in the home of the acorn.ris. So Frozen Fire transported themselves to the treetop city in the Assorted Tree Woodland. In a flash of light they were there and almost immediately the acorn.ris leader, Lady Larch, appeared to greet them.

"Good to have you back here, Frozen Fire," greeted Larch. "But let's get going. There's a virus vermin here and I want rid of it immediately." She led and Frozen Fire followed.

"You're always so aggressive towards viruses, Larch," commented Patrick.

"Those things are always trying to destroy our world so it's hard not to be. Still if there was ever a race of proper living viruses and not these animated puppets I would try to get over this attitude. So long as they weren't all pure evil."

"Where are we heading?" asked Malcolm.

"It seems this Lag is heading to our graveyard," replied Larch

"Again with the grave robbing?" wondered Eric.

"Yeah, I heard from Iron. Sounds like this spell is quite grim. Oh, you should know that our graveyards are quite different from human, polygon and ore.rar ones. We do not rest in the ground like you do, we rest in the trees. So, we have large overturned trunks in which we bury our dead."

"That's odd," observed Gretchen. "But in a good way; there's something strangely beautiful about that thought."

"This is going to inspire more creepy drawings," groaned Zack.

"You're just jealous 'cause my art is awesome."

Soon they arrived at the large overturned tree trunk. It was closer to the ground than the rest of the city and was carved into a flat surface. When they got closer you could tell it was a graveyard. Larch reached out to open the gate inside but it would not move. On closer inspection there was some kind of dark fog like magic covering the lock.

"Argh! Those blasted monsters have locked the gate magically," growled Larch. "It's going to take a while to break this spell. The five of you, go on ahead." Larch threw a ball of green energy at the ground beneath Frozen Fire and suddenly large tree roots sprang up pushing them up and over the fence, crashing down on the other side.

"I could have gotten us through underneath the gate with my shadows," yelled Gretchen.

"Oh, you're fine. Go get the bad guy now." Leaving their harsh words for Larch until later, Frozen Fire set off. They found Lag standing in the path that ran through the middle of the graveyard facing away from them.

"Oh, I forgot you had those transportation pendants," sighed Lag. He turned to face them. "Here I was thinking I could get the next part before you got here. I didn't bother to bring any lesser monsters."

"You leave the dead alone, you jerk," snapped Zack.

"Quite ironic: the ice one is the one with hot temper," mocked Lag.

"Why don't we settle this now?" said Gretchen. "And nobody gets to insult my friends but me. And their siblings. And their other friends. And random people on the internet. But not you, you spoony slug."

"But of course you all have quite mad personalities."

"At least we have personalities, slime ball," remarked Eric snapping his fingers for some reason.

"Now, now, there's no need for me to fight. I'm sure there's something simple enough in here," said Lag producing the Virus's Spell Book. Frozen Fire hurled attacks at the book but they just crashed against some kind of invisible wall.

"Of course not," grumbled Malcolm.

"That book is in need of extermination," said Patrick.

"Ah, here we go," said Lag arriving at a certain page. "The Corridors of Fear. This spell just needs an enchanted rock and I have a spare." And a glowing rock appeared in Lag's hand and he started building magic while speaking an incantation. "See into their minds and find their terror. Let them wander lost forever." They tried more attacks but they couldn't get past his force field. "Trap them in the hall with no door. Lost in fear forever more. No come and appear, Corridors of Fear." The built up magic fired at Frozen Fire and hit them. Suddenly everything was spinning and they lost sight of each other. When everything was still again, Zack was surrounded by darkness and he couldn't see a thing.

"Gretchen? Eric? Malcolm? Patrick?" Zack called but there was no answer. He started to panic, unable to see anything not even make out any shapes. But luckily a small light appeared a short distance away. Not knowing what else to do Zack headed towards the light. When he arrived at the light it turned out to be a small flame made by Eric.

"Ah, I thought I heard someone," said Eric. Zack was catching his breath from charging full speed towards the light.

"Dark... no sign... of others..." panted Zack.

"These must be the Corridors of Fear. Based on Lag's little rhyme we can assume it's gonna be filled with things we're scared of."

"That's why it so dark," he huffed.

"You just had to be scared of the dark."

"The others can surely see your flame." He breathed deeply. "I need a minute."

"And a bath." A snowball hit Eric. "I'll put the fire out." There were footsteps again and soon Malcolm appeared.

"Guys, it's so dark," said Malcolm.

"Yeah, sorry about that," said Zack

"I'm sure I'm being followed."

"Must be one of the others," said Eric.

"Wouldn't they have come into the light?" pointed out Zack.

"It's hiding," said Malcolm. "Not this again."

"Let's find Gretchen and Patrick," said Eric. The three set off in the direction Zack had gone in, towards the light. They couldn't see anything besides each other and Malcolm was right it did sound like something was hiding nearby. All of a sudden Gretchen appeared in the flame's light holding her halberd ready to swing it down on top of someone. The boys jumped.

"Oh, it's just you, guys," said Gretchen lowering her arms and having her halberd disappear. "Sorry, I thought it was something horrible trying to get me."

"This place is gonna have things we're all scared of," said Zack very wary.

"It's surprisingly empty for somewhere that supposed to have all of Zack's fears," said Eric it a slight mocking tone. Another snowball hit him.

"Patrick must be nearby," ventured Malcolm.

"Yeah, let's find him and figure out how to get out of here before we find out just how many spiders there are," said Gretchen. They wandered some more through the darkness only hearing things lurking out of sight.

"This whole thing doesn't really work if we can't see anything," said Zack.

"Guess it doesn't account for fear of the dark," said Eric. They heard the sound of someone running fast and soon Patrick appeared.

"Finally found you, guys. There is something very unpleasant following me," said Patrick.

"What?" asked Gretchen.

"No idea but as this is the Corridors of Fear it's bound to be unpleasant."

"He's not wrong," said Zack.

"Let's just get out of here," said Malcolm.

"The question is how," said Eric. "I get the feeling we won't be able to blast our way out and I doubt there are any doors."

"We'd better brainstorm before all the fictional stuff Zack's scared of gets us," said Patrick. A snowball hit him. Everybody stood still trying to think of an idea but they were all drawing a blank. None of them knew anything about this kind of spell so they had no ideas on how to beat it. As they thought something began to creep closer towards them. One by one they became aware of its presence. Just on the edge of the light was the grotesque appearance of a rather grim-looking lion. However, it soon became apparent that there was a goat's head on its back and instead of a tail was a snake's head, a chimera. Now chimeras were known in their world but this one seem somewhat near death but just as wild and fierce as any other. Frozen Fire just flat out bolted back the way they came. The chimera pursued.

"Maybe we should fight it," said Eric.

"Knowing our luck this place'll just make it again," said Zack.

"Maybe it's just an illusion," suggested Gretchen.

"Feel free to find out," said Patrick.

"Was this one from you?" asked Malcolm.

"You'll never know." Zack threw a ball of magic at the ground coating it in ice. While Frozen Fire just ran over it the chimera slipped and collapsed allowing them to get away. They stopped to catch their breath when they lost sight of it.

"Ok, I'm going to assume that thing will catch up eventually," said Zack. "We should keep moving."

"Has anyone tried contacting Astral through their pendants?" asked Gretchen.

"I tried, they don't work in here," replied Eric.

"So much for warping out." They started to move again, moving through an endless path of terrors. They crossed over a path over a suddenly high up floor trying not to look down. Zack got dizzy every time he got near the edge. They moved through what seemed to be an area covered with daddy long legs that made Gretchen want to vomit. There was an area that despite the darkness made the impression of being trapped at the bottom of a deep body water, which Malcolm had to close his eyes for. Eric was unsettled by the creatures that seemed to be bloody bones, a creature he had met before and Patrick was freaked out by the unsettling groaning sounds that resembled the cry of a cat sith. Soon they heard the sound of thunder overhead, and the smell of something burning nearby.

"WILL THIS EVER END!" yelled Zack.

"Just wandering around isn't working," said Patrick. All of a sudden, the chimera appeared again and from the other direction was what appeared to be a giant spider and the bloody bones following close behind them. They were surrounded by all sort of creepy figures closing in.

"This is ridiculous," cried Gretchen. "We fight monsters all the time now these guys aren't going to beat us just 'cause one or more of us is sacred of it." Making a massive shadow fist Gretchen punched the chimera. The others joined in. Patrick surged his temporal energy slowing all the creatures down. Malcolm held up his arms and the air surged with electricity. And there was a flurry of fire balls and snowflake shurikens. But the creatures still closed in. Eric had fire erupt knocking most the creatures over. Malcolm sent lightning down all over and Zack threw icicle kunai in all directions. Gretchen rained shadow anvils down and Patrick fired temporal pulses at all the monsters. While they rapidly attacked in all directions a bright light suddenly appeared and soon covered the entire corridor. The monsters disappeared and when the light cleared they were back in the acorn.ris graveyard. Astral and Lady Larch were nearby.

159

"Oh, thank goodness," said Astral. "It's been a long time since someone last cast the Corridors of Fear but I can still dissipate it with ease thank goodness."

"Sorry you were in there for so long," apologized Larch. "It took me awhile to get through the gate but I got Astral as soon as I saw that thing."

"It was horrible," groaned Zack. "We were surrounded when you got us out."

"I'm glad you're all all right," said Astral.

"We were putting up a fight," said Gretchen.

"That was worse than hanging off the tower," said Malcolm.

"As you've probably guessed, Lag's long gone," said Larch. "What's weird is that he dug up the recently buried Ola Man Palm and made off with his cap." She was gesturing to the acorn cap-like part on top of her head. Frozen Fire shared a puzzled look. And then a thought crossed Patrick's mind.

"Wait, you're scared of fire, the dark and thunder?" he said to Zack.

"Yeah," said Zack in a 'duh' tone. Patrick looked at the other three.

"Boy, you guys should be offended."

"Hey, I was scared of those things before they got those powers."

They were sent to Adlez castle to recover from their ordeal.

"That slug is getting burned," said Eric.

"Hopefully next time it'll just be a monster," said Patrick. The door opened and Cyanna and Hitbox entered.

"Are you all right?" enquired Cyanna. There was a general groan of "yes."

"If he ever tries it again you'll be ready," assured Hitbox.

"Yeah, it's always been said of the Corridors of Fear that no one's is ever tapped in there twice."

"And that includes the survivors." Cyanna nudged Hitbox in the side at that last remark.

"We're gonna clobber him with that book," grumbled Zack.

"And then we're gonna stick it somewhere on his person," said Gretchen. "I'll leave you to figure out where."

"Charming," said Cyanna.

"The important thing is that we got out," said Eric. "And that we're going to get him back. Very, very painfully."

"We may never have chased away the bullies at school, but we'll send this guy packing," snarled Zack who was between angry and upset. "Him and Visrel." The temperature in the room started to plummet around Zack causing Gretchen who was sitting next to him to get up and change seats. However, when she sat next to Eric things were too hot.

"At least the temperature brothers are cancelling each other out," Gretchen muttered to herself unaware that her own distress was causing the shadows to move franticly.

"I hate those monsters," said Malcolm.

"Ok, how do you guys usually calm down?" asked Hitbox.

"Watching TV mostly," replied Patrick.

"Not easily," said Zack.

"Ok, let's just find a way to take your mind off things for a little bit," said Cyanna. She had an idea. "Amusing stories could be just the thing. You know during our grandfather's coronation he insisted on trying the crown upside down just so he could see which way up he preferred."

"A lot of the nonsense he says is probably on purpose," said Hitbox. "Like the time he kept yelling at a rainbow and then offered to take it out for dinner as an apology." Frozen Fire started to laugh a little.

"And the toast he made during our parents wedding is infamous."

"And then vows from his own wedding are known as a great comedic dialogue. Grandad can inspire a whole musical comedy and I suppose I've started."

"Have you written a song about your grandfather?" Gretchen asked Cyanna.

"Yes, I have. I call it 'The king who likes to be mad.' It's no secret that I love music, and I like to write songs about the people I care about."

"So there's a song about you?" Patrick asked Hitbox.

"She called it 'Prince of Weapons,' replied Hitbox. "It's how I got that title. Before you know it she'll be writing songs for the five of you."

"That'd be very nice of you," said Zack.

"Hey, we're all friends already," said Cyanna. "And I'm sure we'll all see each other for the rest of our lives."

"Yeah, we're in this job for life aren't we?" said Zack.

"I wonder if the king'll start paying us," said Eric.

Soon Frozen Fire were sent to the Solid Cloudbank the home of the cloud.tiff as Astral was sure Lag would appear there next. Having been there before, their pendants were able to warp them and the cloud.tiff leader, Elder Stratus, was waiting for them.

"Ah about time you young 'uns got here," said Stratus. "This Lag thing is gonna be turning up anytime soon probably with some unpleasant monster and you lot better take care of it. Not that I couldn't do it myself."

"Nice to see you again too, elder," said Gretchen. The elder gestured for them to follow and they set off into the city.

"Based on what I've heard from Iron and Larch they'll be targeting our dead too," said Stratus. "Now this goon seems to primarily go for the recently deceased and we haven't buried anyone recently so he's likely to go for our hospital."

"Ugh, I dread to think what they're making," groaned Zack.

"Something gross," ventured Malcolm.

"Boy, the elder sure moves fast," observed Patrick.

"At least he doesn't shoot off miles ahead like you do," remarked Eric.

They entered a large plaza that was bustling with all sorts of cloud.tiff many of whom respectfully greeted Stratus. Zack became aware of something and stopped. The others did too when they noticed.

"What's the holdup snow brain?" yelled Stratus.

"I can hear something," explained Zack adding a returning insult under his breath. "It sounds like flapping wings." Looking around he saw a figure moving through the air towards them. "There!" everyone looked where Zack indicated and saw it too. Soon the thing came into view and it was clear that it was a monster sent by Lag. It was some sort of bizarre looking giant owl creature: its beak looked like two hooks pressed together, the feathers in its wings looked like blunt metal and its talons appeared to be made of sharpened stone.

"I don't know where they get these ideas from," said Gretchen. "But they really need to return to sender." Elder Stratus hit the ground with his walking stick. Suddenly clouds appeared underneath everyone in the plaza, bar Frozen Fire, carrying them all away from the advancing creature.

"Give that ugly bird a good thrashing," called Stratus as he was carried away. "Don't make me have to help you if you mess up."

"This thing's no match for us," Eric called back. Frozen Fire summoned their weapons as the owl floated down to just above them. The owl screeched at them which sent at shockwave towards them causing them to scatter. Malcolm was the first to retaliate firing arrows at it; they couldn't do much against the wings but he managed to hit the head as well. The owl screeched again so Zack threw a snowball that caused a snow-screen which hit the owl's head causing it to stop. Taking advantage of the distraction the others attacked: Gretchen threw a shadow easel like a boomerang at it, Eric threw his scythe hitting its torso and Patrick blasted it with a time burst.

"You really like making shadow versions of whatever pops into your head, don't you?" Zack said to Gretchen.

"I'm not called the Shadow Mimic for nothing," replied Gretchen.

"Could have had a worse title I suppose," said Eric.

"Guys! Later!" called Patrick as the owl cleared its head of snow and advanced.

"I'm glad those aren't sharp," said Malcolm he got a feather shot at him.

"Why aren't they?" wondered Eric.

"Let's not question a good thing," said Zack. The owl swung its wings together and while they didn't hit any of Frozen Fire the resulting gust of air knocked them over. It screeched more shockwaves at them as they scrambled out of the way and tried to get back up. Gretchen got back up first and jabbed the monster with her halberd with a couple of shadow duplicates. The monster was about to swing its wings again but Malcolm called down lightning bolts to paralyse the wings. Zack whacked it with his staff. The owl then tried to slash him with his claws but Eric blocked one with his fire-covered scythe and Patrick blocked the other with sword covered in time energy. The owl was stronger so it knocked both of them to the ground but it wasn't unscathed; however, its wings were moving properly again. The owl landed and started to try and strike all of them, and there was a lot of force in those heavy wings: the ground (or clouds rather) shook every time it was hit. Trying to stay upright and retaliate was proving difficult. Zack tried to freeze the wings at the joints to slow them down but was having much luck. Malcolm managed to fire an arrow with a full blast of lightning but he couldn't aim and it just missed the owl but it still got hit by some of the lightning. The owl took to the air again and started another shockwave screech. Eric blocked it with a pillar of fire. While they struggled, Gretchen formed her shadows into a piano which crashed down onto it, stopping its screech and causing it to be hit by Eric's fire and Patrick hit it with a temporal pulse. Everyone fired one last blast of their element at the monster and in the resulting blast the owl dissipated into magic. Frozen Fire caught their breath and Elder Stratus reappeared from around a corner.

"That blasted thing was just a distraction!" yelled Stratus. "Lag attacked elsewhere!"

"Did you stop him?" asked Gretchen.

"No. He robbed a wig store."

"A wig store! Whaaaat?" exclaimed Zack.

"It'll take more than a fake hair style to fix his drab appearance," remarked Eric.

"It may seem strange but it was made of genuine cloud.tiff hair," explained Stratus. "And the donor in question passed away last week, so it was still from the dead. Poor Madam Striation." Frozen Fire shared a puzzled look.

"That book's got problems," said Zack.

"What's that creepy blighter gonna go after next?" wondered Patrick.

"Who knows," said Stratus. "Go report to Astral so she can plan your next move for you."

"Gee, thanks." Was general feeling of Frozen Fire. They returned to Astral's temple and told her what had happened. With a sigh Astral told them that they should head home for the day and gave each of them a potion that she said would prevent any nightmares they may have had due to the Corridors of Fear.

Sure enough Astral's potions worked; nobody had any nightmares that night. Everyone dreamed they were doing something with the rest of Frozen Fire. Zack dreamed he was leading the party through a snowy path to find some rare creature or something. Gretchen dreamed she was having an eccentric tea party with someone being forced to paint the scene. Eric dreamed he was directing the most overly dramatic theatre production the world had ever seen. Malcolm dreamed they were arguing with a group of disgruntled robots. And Patrick dreamed they were wandering through times of old having just escaped a famous historical villain. Now in a world filled with so much magic and with people who use magic so often dreams can end up being affected. Sometimes reminders or warnings would appear and even people's dreams would connect but very rarely a window of something that was happening at that time would happen. Well, in their dreams Frozen Fire started to get a glimpse of something that was happening in Miyamoto. The slightest of connections had formed between their dreams so they saw the same thing. In Miyamoto Lag was examining the Virus's Spell Book for what he needed next. And so Frozen Fire caught a glimpse of the book and they all saw the words 'Rotten Salamander Fruit'. The following day once they realised they had all seen the same thing they returned to Miyamoto, found Astral and told her what they had seen.

"Salamander fruit can only be found in Miyamoto," explained Astral. "They're called that because they look like the skin of a salamander. And they tend to be on fire all the time like the magical variants of the creatures. Even here they are very rare; there are only two trees that grow them, one in Edge Forrest and one by the Golden Coral Bay. I suppose rotting fruit ties in with this ingredient's theme of death."

"Which is he more likely to go for?" asked Zack

"That depends on which he is closer too. And we have no idea how much he needs. He may end up going to both. It may be best for you to split up and keep an eye on both trees."

"Astral tends to be right," said Gretchen. "Who's going to go where?"

"I think we all want to see some place new," said Eric.

"Better think of a fair way to decide," said Patrick.

"This'll go badly," said Malcolm. He was right, as when they drew straws they forgot to mark any as different from the others. Nobody had any coins on them to toss and when they tried rock, paper, scissors everyone used their own element as something to beat all the others.

"This is taking a little long," said Astral rolling her eyes. "Gretchen, Eric and Patrick will go to Edge Forest. Zack and Malcolm can go to Golden Coral Bay. I'm basing this purely on who hasn't broken anything in Adlez Castle yet." Zack and Malcolm gave the other three a certain look.

"Not my fault my throwing arm's so good," said Gretchen.

"Your weapon's magic. You can control how far it goes," said Zack.

"I still think it was an overreaction on the guards' part," said Eric.

"We're not getting into that debate again," said Astral. "You're all going immediately. Zack, Malcolm seeing as there's only two of you I'll see if either the prince or princess will help."

Gretchen, Eric and Patrick arrived at Edge Forest. They were surrounded by the familiar sight of the trees that grew in a curving fashion. They followed Astral's directions and soon came to what they were looking for, a tree bearing large fruit that were covered in fire. On the ground were several of the fruit that had been extinguished and were entirely rotten.

"So we're protecting rotten fruit," mused Gretchen. "Hardly the highlight of our heroic exploits."

"That is some weird magic in the fire," said Eric. "Never sensed anything like it. They must be pretty potent spell and potion ingredients."

"Maybe we should just destroy the rotten fruit," suggested Patrick. "Make it just that little bit harder for him." However, before anyone could comment on the idea let alone implement it they became aware of sounds in the trees. Looking at the treetops they realised they were surrounded by talon-teeth. They summoned their weapons as the monsters pounced. The first ones were easily cut down by the weapons but there were a lot of them. The ones snapping at Eric got a mouth full of fire. Gretchen sent shadow waves to knock many of them over. Patrick blasted the ones leaping down from the trees with temporal energy. But the talon-teeth kept coming. The three of them were not giving in the talon-teeth could barely get a hit in as Gretchen, Eric and Patrick knocked them all over the place. There was no sign of Lag and they were too distracted to try and sense for his magic; they couldn't tell if he was nearby or not. The entire forest must have been filled with talon-teeth there were so many and the three of them were starting to tire. Gretchen was attacking many of them with her halberd and shadow duplicates. Patrick had used his magic to speed himself up to rapidly run through the monsters and strike them with his sword. Eric made a fire twister with his scythe spinning on the top which he sent tearing through the talon-teeth. But the monsters were starting to get through their attacks and the trio were getting scratched. Gretchen made a wall of shadow to push the monsters together and Patrick fired streams of temporal energy to push the rest. Soon the talon-teeth were in a giant pile. It was then Eric noticed a still blazing salamander fruit had fallen off the tree and rolled nearby him. Suddenly an idea occurred to him and he picked up the fruit. He breathed deeply and actually inhaled the fire right off the fruit. He felt a great surge of magic and he focused it of the pile of monsters and great pillar of fire erupted underneath them finishing them off. Gretchen, Eric and Patrick collapsed to the ground to catch their breath.

"I guess it's only the big ones that knock us over," said Patrick with a laugh.

"Nice attack, Eric. You should keep some of that fruit handy," said Gretchen.

"Before you know I'll be doing that without the fruit," bragged Eric. Turning to face the tree they saw all the rotten fruit on the ground had gone. "Sneaky little train wreck."

"Hopefully Zack and Malcolm will have had better luck," suggested Patrick. "Not even I could make time to bail them out if they're in trouble."

"You know I'm never gonna get used to your time powers," Gretchen said to Patrick. "All that golden energy turning into clocks."

"I'm surprised this place doesn't have clocks flying all over the place already," said Eric.

"You know a lot of people have a theory about time elementals," explained Patrick. "They think the magic's form is based on our own perception of time. When we think of time we think of clocks and so the temporal energy takes the form of clocks. If you look at depictions of old time elementals their magic looks like sundials and other ancient time pieces. It's the same with the space element, our perception of space causes the spacial energy they control to take the form of planets and asteroids. I guess with time and space they needed a form to take unlike the other twelve elements." Frozen Fire did enjoy reading about the history of their elements and elementals of the same type.

Patrick was thirteen when he got his powers. It was because of an encounter with something called the Crystal Meteor. It was a magic crystal sent into space and returned five years later having grown in size. It landed on Kerozonia just outside Reekie. Patrick went to see it. The meteor was very large, about ten feet high and thirty feet wide. It was a foggy white colour ever so slightly transparent and glowing with a magical energy. Nearby someone, a scientist, was explaining the nature of the meteor.

"As part of a programme to see how magic would work in space we made a crystal filled with temporal energy, the time element," explained the scientist. "While most of the programme takes place on the space station this experiment was a one of a kind. During the five years the crystal spent in space it absorbed more magic of the time element and the crystal grew until it became the meteor you see behind me. A spell was placed on it to bring it home after a number of years, which is why a couple of days ago the crystal landed here. Though it was supposed to return to Vasterra." Patrick gazed in wonder at the meteor. It was quite a sight. Though it was guarded Patrick found an opening as was able to get right up close to it.

"This is ace," said Patrick looking around to make sure no one caught him. When he got close he saw something odd. It looked like a hole leading into the meteor. He realized that the magic was somehow making it very hard to see. He suspected he was the only one who had seen it. His curiosity got the better of him and he entered. Climbing up the tunnel Patrick soon found himself inside a large crystalline cavern inside the meteor. He gaped in awe at the place he had found; it was brimming with magic even someone with untrained magical senses like young Patrick could feel it. But the place was not as empty as one would have thought; someone was watching. Patrick became aware he wasn't alone. "Hello?" he called. The person watching him appeared.

"Greetings, child," said the stranger. "You shouldn't be in here."

"I get the feeling neither should you."

"How could you have even gotten in here. The entrance is hidden and I had to use a spell to find it."

"I could see it."

"Really? Well what harm could one little boy do?"

"I'm thirteen."

"I don't care. Run along and tell no one you saw me."

"Are you trying to steal the meteor?"

"This giant crystal has more temporal energy than anything else in the world. Do you have any idea what could be done with it?"

"A thief like you could never master it." The thief moved closer to Patrick and glared at him.

"Presumptuous, aren't you?"

"You're a bad guy. Someone always stops the villain." The thief turned away from him.

"No one will ever know I was even here." As the thief moved away something inside Patrick sparked, and he tackled the thief to the ground.

"You can't have any of this magic!" yelled Patrick.

"Get off me, you brat," snarled the thief.

"No! You're staying here." Patrick smacked the thief, but it didn't seem to hurt him. The thief got up pushing Patrick away. Patrick kicked hard causing the thief to collapse again. The thief tried to kick back but Patrick scampered out of the way. The thief got up and pulled out a knife grabbed Patrick and brandished the blade in his face.

"I've had enough of you!" growled the thief. Patrick was scared. His mind raced so he did what he could.

"Fine I'll leave," said Patrick.

"Smart boy." The thief lowered the knife and released Patrick. Patrick moved towards the exit and the thief turned away. While the thief was no longer paying attention to him Patrick dashed towards him and wrestled the knife out of his hand. The thief was rather taken aback, allowing Patrick to get it from him. The thief was furious and tried to grab Patrick again. But Patrick ran for the exit and was back outside in seconds and the thief soon after. Outside they came face to face with the scientist who was explaining the nature of the Crystal Meteor.

"I had a feeling you'd be here," the scientist said to the thief. She snapped her fingers and the thief's hands were bound together by magic. The scientist escorted them away leaving Patrick to wait in a room while she led the thief away. Half an hour later she returned and explained that the thief was always trying to steal unusual magic to sell to people and that he been arrested.

"You managed to protect the meteor by yourself. Thank you," said the scientist.

"I... I don't know what came over me," explained Patrick. "It was pretty stupid."

"And a little brave. But I would discourage you from doing it again. Now I would like to thank you properly and would like to offer you a way of defending yourself in case you antagonise any more thieves despite my warning." She led him back inside the Crystal Meteor right to where a crystalline stalagmite stuck out shining with magic.

"How is this defence?" asked Patrick.

"This is a concentrated point," replied the scientist. "If you want it can give form to your magic. You can be a time elemental."

"Really? You'd let me?"

"Like I said I want to thank you and give you a way to protect yourself." Patrick didn't hesitate, he grabbed to crystal. The fiery golden temporal energy surged all over him and in an instant it stopped. Patrick now had his powers and was greatly excited about it. The scientist agreed to keep it a secret. In the following days the thief was sent to jail and the Crystal Meteor was taken to a research facility in Vasterra where it has been ever since. Patrick was in awe of his new magic but was disappointed when he learned no time elemental had even learned how to time travel.

At the time the others arrived at Edge Forest Astral had sent Zack and Malcolm to Golden Coral Bay. It was a beautiful beach with white sand with tropical trees and plant life. The sky was clear and there was a large building nearby a resort. Astral had told everybody to evacuate so the beach was empty. The ocean itself was a brilliant blue colour, but a large section was golden. Had they gotten a proper look they would have seen it looked just like any other coral reef apart from being entirely golden.

"That must be the golden coral," observed Zack when he saw the shining gold colour.

"You think the reef is actually made of gold?" wondered Malcolm.

"Knowing this place, it probably is." They looked around and Malcolm spotted the tree that was on fire on the edge of the sand.

"There it is," said Malcolm. They headed over towards the tree. When they arrived, there was a flash of light and Cyanna and Hitbox appeared.

"Hey! Your back-up has arrived," declared Cyanna beaming. "The orchestra and the armoury."

"We both felt like a fight so Astral sent both of us," explained Hitbox. "How did you two get to come here and not the others?"

"Astral sent us to the new place because we haven't broken anything in the castle yet," replied Zack.

"What! You two managed to wreck a whole room by accident," said Cyanna.

"Yes, but Astral doesn't know that."

"Probably 'cause the king was involved," added Malcolm. The prince and princess rolled their eyes at this.

"Anyway these are what we need to protect," said Hitbox gesturing to the rotten fruit on the ground around the tree. "Not exactly anyone's greatest exploit but what can you do?"

"At least we have some spectacular natural beauty," said Cyanna. "Of course a reef made of gold may not seem natural, but it grew just like regular coral."

"Hey, we were right," Zack said to Malcolm. Suddenly something seemed to grab Hitbox's attention as he turned his head quickly to look around. Zack could hear something coming from beneath the sand. Out of the sand burst long slimy appendages many of them resembling the tentacles of both squids and octopuses.

"That's unsettling," said Malcolm. Zack and Malcolm summoned their staff and bow, Hitbox summoned a mace and Cyanna summoned a trombone.

"You always look a little out of place in a fight sis," said Hitbox.

"Yeah, but I'm as good as any of you," replied Cyanna. The tentacles started slamming the ground trying to hit the four of them. Zack threw his snowflake shurikens and icicle kunai at them whereas Malcolm surged the air with electricity. Hitbox smacked the ones that were close with his mace while Cyanna played a tune on her trombone and it started to fire an energy beam which actually severed one of the tentacles. The tentacle dissipated into magic but the place where it had been removed from surged with magical energy and a new tentacle grew in its place.

"AW NOT A REGENERATOR!" yelled Zack.

"Let's be glad they don't multiply," said Cyanna. The attack continued and sand was getting kicked into the air all round. Malcolm kept blasting tentacles with lightning-charged arrows and Zack struck others with his staff while it had a large chunk of ice on the end. Cyanna was playing a tune on a violin which sent large music notes bouncing around that burst on contact while Hitbox was attacking with a broad sword. No matter how much or little damage the tentacles took they were able to restore themselves. Everyone knew they had to find the main body of the monster but they were surrounded on all sides. Zack and Malcolm were knocked to the ground but used their elements to protect themselves. Cyanna had switched to a xylophone and caused small explosions around the enemy when she played her tune. Hitbox was assaulting the monster with a volley of arrows from a crossbow. Zack and Malcolm finally got a chance to clamber back to their feet, spitting out sand as they did. It was then that they noticed the movement in the sand indicating where the tentacles were coming from. The other two seemed to have it distracted, Hitbox striking everything in range with a pike and Cyanna strumming a tune on a ukulele that made razor sharp energy discs. Zack and Malcolm took this chance and followed the movement in the sand. At the water's edge they found the body of the monster in the shallows. The thing was completely spherical with features one would associate with a cartoon octopus. They picked up the monster and shared a look indicating how bizarre they found it. However, two more tentacles appeared from beneath the sand behind them and wrapped around them. As the tentacles began to squeeze Zack and Malcolm unleashed a flurry of their elements at the monster's body, bombarding it with magic. It wasn't long before it and all the tentacles burst into magic clearing the beach.

"That was horrible," groaned Zack.

"Agreed," said Malcolm. Cyanna and Hitbox came running up to them.

"Bad news, the rotten fruit are gone," said Hitbox. Zack let out a loud groan that covered up Malcolm's quieter groan.

"Hey, we'll stop him yet," said Cyanna reassuringly. "Anyway, nice work with the monster."

"I guess we're finally getting the hang of it," said Zack.

"Still fall over all the time," said Malcolm. They returned to Adlez Castle where they met up with others and everyone told each other what had happened. But Astral had some news of her own.

"I've heard from each of the others who watch over the other three worlds," she began. "Visrel has been spotted in all of them. He'll be back in Miyamoto soon."

At the bottom of the chasm Lag was going over the preparation of the spell from the Virus's Spell Book.

"I see you've gathered almost everything from this world," said a voice from behind. Turning, Lag saw the Anti-Gamer who placed down a sack of items.

"And you have retrieved what we need from the other three," said Lag.

"As well as many magical rocks to help power the spell."

"Then we need only three more ingredients before we can make the vortex." Visrel moved over to the book to look at it.

"Hmm, the only three that don't need to be from the dead." Lag was going through the ingredients Visrel had brought.

"Oh yes, magnificent specimens. I'd expect nothing less of the Anti-Gamer."

"And it would seem the bane of online games has met my expectations too. I opted to use stealth when I went grave robbing in the other worlds. Hmm, two of these will be simple enough."

"Yes but the third will be very tricky."

"Well then, I guess it's time I met Frozen Fire face to face. It has been some time."

"Do you remember the town near Iwata's Snowfield?" Astral asked Frozen Fire. They nodded. "Something strange is happening there. There's dark energy coming from Snowman's Town but it's unclear. It seems like a monster but I can't think why they'd interfere with my tracking spells; something troubling is going on. It could be Lag but I'm not sure." Astral transported Frozen Fire to Snowman's Town. They found themselves in a beautiful town covered in snow which looked very picturesque under the pale grey sky. The snow wasn't very deep and was filled with footprints. Most seemed to moving away from where the monster appeared to be. They moved in the other direction.

"Once again we're moving towards a monster instead of away," grumbled Zack.

"Ah, come on, we can handle the big monsters almost easily now," reassured Gretchen.

"It'll just be another on the long list of ones we've thrashed," said Eric.

"It's something worse though," said Malcolm.

"Hey, yeah, this magic feels tougher than the others," said Patrick. They entered a park also completely covered in snow and in the middle of it was a figure in a cape. Frozen Fire recognized it and when they approached the Anti-Gamer turned around to face them.

"Glacis, Shadows, Flare, Spark and Tempus the mighty Frozen Fire," greeted Visrel in his cold emotionless voice. "I hear the king bestowed you all with titles after you stopped Dr Putrice."

"Visrel, the Data Realm's biggest jerk," said Zack with contempt.

"You're hiding your fear better than before," mocked Visrel. "Naturally you already know I am working with Lag. Acquiring that spell book was no meagre task; it made it obvious he would be a very powerful ally. Like Putrice's knowledge of magic and inventive ways of causing chaos."

"So, that scarlet sadist was working with you," mused Eric with a touch of anger.

"Now, what are you up to?" asked Malcolm.

"Same as before, the end of Miyamoto and all gamers," said Visrel.

"Yeah, well, Lag said something about a vortex so we know that," said Gretchen.

"And as before we're ready to thwart you," added Patrick.

"That is why Astral brought you," mused Visrel. "During our first encounter your confidence was barely anything and your powers practically untouched. But now this is the third time you're helping defend this world. Your courage doesn't falter as easily I've heard. I'm curious to see how your powers have improved." Visrel summoned his helical blade and attacked. He charged right at them and swung his blade but it struck against a wall of ice made by Zack.

"You're fighting us in my element you clod," snarled Zack.

"I could just melt the snow," said Visrel. The shadows made by the ice wall moved rose up formed a fist and punched Visrel knocking him back.

"You can't get rid of my element!" exclaimed Gretchen. Visrel was then hit by a blast of lightning and time burst and a flaming twister.

"You are stronger than when we fought on the bridge," observed Visrel. Frozen Fire summoned their weapons.

"And we know how to use these now," declared Patrick.

"Sort of," mumbled Malcolm. Zack and Gretchen ran forward swinging their weapons, Visrel blocked the staff with his blade and grabbed the halberd with his other hand. Eric charged next and struck Visrel with his scythe.

"Aw, I wanted to ignite his suit," said Eric.

Visrel pushed the staff and halberd away; he then clasped together two of his fingers on his free hand and started swinging them while they surged with razor sharp energy. Patrick blocked the attacks with his sword and Malcolm fired arrows at him while he was distracted. But Visrel is not human so while they caused damage he wasn't so much as scratched. The Anti-Gamer jumped backwards putting distance between them. He then made spheres of energy and threw them at Frozen Fire. Frozen Fire returned fire with icicle kunai, shadow paint cans, exploding sparks, fists made of lightning and clocks made of temporal energy. Visrel was bombarded with attacks but he threw his cape over himself and disappeared and reappeared behind them. Frozen Fire turned and Visrel swung his blade. Though they managed to dodge the attack there was a magical force from the swing that knocked them over. Zack sent his magic into the snow which rose up and turned to ice covering Visrel up to the knees, and he was floating a foot off the ground. Visrel struggled against Zack's ice harder than last time. Frozen Fire got back up and at the same time several halberd clones and electrified arrows struck Visrel who with a surge of magic finally broke free. He was then hit with a blazing strike of Eric's scythe and a strike of a Patrick's sword which burst with time magic. Visrel punched the ground causing a blast of magic to rise from the ground. It didn't hurt Frozen Fire much but it moved all the snow. Although Zack had already frozen the soles of his boots, he fell over and got a smack with the staff for good measure. As Visrel got up Gretchen kicked him with a large shadow boot. Then with streams of fire and time energy pushing back and then bolt of lightning from above he was knocked into a nearby wall. Visrel fired streams of energy from his hands chasing Frozen Fire away. He returned to the ground and fired more streams at them and Frozen Fire sent streams of their elements back at him. Visrel then jumped over the attacks, swinging his blade down towards them. There was a mighty crash as he collided with another one of Zack's ice walls. Suddenly the ice wall vanished and Gretchen gave him a full force shadow wave. And then WHAM! A temporal pulse followed by fire balls and then a blast of thunder. Visrel staggered but wasn't done yet. He struck his blade into the ground sending a shockwave in all directions. When it cleared he was face to face with Frozen Fire. Everyone was waiting for someone to make the next move. But Visrel suddenly realized he was only facing four of them. Zack leapt from his hiding place, spinning his staff and struck Visrel several times. The others followed; slash with the halberd, then the sword, then the scythe and finally several arrows. Visrel fell to his arms and knees.

"If I could feel emotions I might actually be impressed," said Visrel. "You've trained well but it won't help against the vortex." Visrel leapt backwards away from them. "Time to go see how Lag is doing at the castle." He threw his cape over himself and vanished.

"He was distracting us!" cried Gretchen.

"That cheating.... jerk!" yelled Zack who struggled for an appropriate word and the end there.

"Let's not waste any time," said Patrick.

"He was probably stopping Astral from calling us," said Eric.

"Let's go," said Malcolm.

While Frozen Fire were in Snowman's Town things were happening at Adlez Castle. The king and his grandchildren were discussing events so far when the doors to the throne room flew open and Lag entered.

"My goodness, Astral, your age has caught up to you in a horrific way," said Hud when he saw the monster. "And I realise it's pot, kettle and all that coming from me, but still. Dang!"

"No, your majesty, I am Lag the Bane of Online Gaming," said the monster.

"Oh well, in that case you can go away you deranged bag of slugs! Oh, wait, that's a picture of me I'm yelling at."

"No, Grandad that's a picture of Grandma," corrected Cyanna before turning back to Lag. "You can leave our world."

"Unless you'd rather me and my sister throw you over the wall," said Hitbox. He summoned a scimitar and Cyanna summoned a sousaphone.

"Ah, but I need to be here," explained Lag. "While Visrel reacquaints himself with Frozen Fire I am following the directions of the book. It's quite a good read, a true classic. Anyway, it tells me we need Knil blood. That's nil with a K which the Anti-Gamer tells me is the surname of the royal family of Miyamoto, the three of you."

"Well, the joke's on you 'cause we don't have any blood! Ha!" exclaimed Hud. Everyone just ignored that one. Lag made energy cubes (oddly enough) in his hands and threw them. Hitbox cut them in half and Cyanna played a tune that sent blast of magic from her instrument. Lag was hit but simply shook it off and then exhaled some kind of burning slime. Cyanna played a tune that protected her from the attack, whilst Hitbox moved round behind Lag and struck him with a war hammer. There was hammering on the doors. Evidently Lag had sealed the doors keeping the guards out. Lag staggered backwards. Hitbox continued his attack by switching to a bow and firing arrows while Cyanna summoned a set of pan pipes and played a tune that rained meteors on him. Lag managed to leap out of the attacks and landed on the ground.

"Impressive," said Lag. "You really do live up to the titles, the Princess of Music and the Prince of Weapons. Your grandfather does seem to like giving those out." Hud was trying to remember something and had taken cover behind his throne. "But the two of you alone can't stop me." He exhaled more burning slime. Cyanna and Hitbox manoeuvred out the way and counter-attacked by charging him with a battle lance and playing a tune on a folk guitar that hurled a large rock at him. Lag struck Hitbox and blasted Cyanna with an energy cube, they were hurt but weren't beaten. Lag clapped his hands sending a shockwave throughout the room pushing the siblings back. Hitbox summoned a sickle on a chain. He moved towards Lag spinning the chain and then started lashing it at him. Cyanna's next tune was on her trademark ocarina which blasted Lag with beams of light. The king was still trying to remember. Lag was exhaling the burning slime yet again; while he couldn't hit his opponents, it kept them moving.

Hitbox dived under the attack and swung a spear at him. When it struck it stopped the attack. Hitbox swung again but this time Lag caught it and tried to overpower him. Cyanna had been playing a tune on a harp which caused Lag to be pelted with needles. Lag stomped on the ground causing it to shake and making the siblings lose their balance Lag then clapped, causing another shockwave which knocked them over. He grabbed Hitbox by the neck lifting him up and then leapt over to Cyanna and grabbed her too. He held the prince and princess up in front of him; though he could not feel emotion he sneered a wicked smile. However, Cyanna and Hitbox kicked him hard causing him to drop them.

"Aha! I remember now," yelled Hud coming out from behind the throne. "You just gather a large amount of magic like so, and throw it." Suddenly a massive solid sphere of magic hurtled at Lag and with a mighty thud knocked him down. The siblings were a little taken aback by this.

"I always forget he can do that," said Cyanna.

"Me too," answered Hitbox. He moved over to Lag summoning a sword and held it to the monster's head. "Ready to call it quits? I'm sure Astral will have a place for you."

"You mean she'll seal me away somewhere," said Lag. Suddenly things happened very fast and Hitbox and Hud heard mostly sounds: something appeared, a swing of a blade and Cyanna screaming. Turning they saw Cyanna collapsed to her knees grasping her left shoulder in pain with the Anti-Gamer standing over her his blade out.

"It seems we both play the distraction well," observed Visrel to Lag. With a motion of his hand a bottle formed around the blood on his blade. In a flash of light Frozen Fire appeared.

"NO!" yelled Zack. "YOU CHEATING JERKS!"

"I don't think they're too happy," mocked Lag.

"You've got a sword at your face so shut it," warned Gretchen.

"Get your filthy gauntlets away from my granddaughter," demanded Hud. "I've lost enough. You will not take anyone else away."

"It matters not, your majesty, this is our last ingredient," said Visrel. Another flash of light and Astral appeared.

"This has got to stop," said Astral.

"It will all be over very soon," said Visrel. The Anti-Gamer's attention was focused on the others and he didn't notice that an instrument appeared in Cyanna's good arm. Before anyone really was aware what happened Cyanna smacked Visrel with her cello and slammed him into the wall, falling to her knees again. Visrel floated down, magic surging all over ready to attack.

"Forget it, Visrel! They'll all be dead soon anyway," said Lag.

"Hmm, yes the Deletion Vortex will consume Miyamoto and everyone who lives here," said Visrel.

"Well, that sounds unpleasant," mused Eric.

"So that's the lunacy you've opted for this time," said Astral. "You can't possibly expect to control that!" Visrel threw his cape over himself and disappeared and Lag disappeared too in a surge of slime.

"We're in trouble aren't we," said Patrick.

"Yet again," added Malcolm.

Cyanna's wound was treated, stitched and bandaged.

"It'll heal before you know it," Hitbox assured his sister.

"It's being unable to play a large number of my instruments that upsets me," said Cyanna.

"I didn't know you could get upset," observed Gretchen.

"You're always so happy," added Eric.

"That's because I'm every bit as strong as my brother," explained Cyanna. "Though I won't be battling soon."

"That reminds me," said Gretchen turning. "You OK Zack?"

"Yeah, it's passed," groaned Zack.

"Why didn't his squeamishness kick in straightaway?" wondered Eric.

"Adrenaline most likely. You were just in a battle," said Hitbox.

"I could have used some during that incident involving Gretchen's knee and a glass of apple juice," grumbled Zack.

"Come on, guys, we have to go see Astral," said Patrick. Frozen Fire and the royal siblings made their way to the conference room where Astral was with the four leaders, King Hud, Lord Iron, Lady Larch and Elder Stratus.

"Good, Frozen Fire need to hear this," said Astral as they entered and sat down. "Your majesty, leaders, Visrel revealed the spell they intend to use from the Virus's Spell Book."

"He said the Deletion Vortex," remembered Hud.

"Yes, it's a very powerful spell. And I'm not sure if there is one more destructive. The vortex pulls in all living data and then deletes it. I only know of it from the details left behind by those who watched before me but it is without doubt the most destructive spell in the Data Realm. It tears apart everything and everyone in its path and if those two monsters have their way Miyamoto will vanish. Or perhaps they'll let it consume the entire Data Realm."

"There must be away to counter it," said Iron.

"If there is I don't know it. The only other time the spell was used it was stopped when the one who made it ended up being consumed by it as well."

"What! That creep was beaten by his own spell?" exclaimed Larch.

"The Deletion Vortex will destroy anything made from living data, even the one whose magic made it. Which in turn would cause it to dissipate."

"So the thing won't stop until Visrel and Lag tell it to?" asked Stratus.

"Yes, unless one of them is destroyed. But they are both strong enough to resist the power of the vortex long enough and are smart enough to stay away. Though odds are at least one will be nearby."

"Frozen Fire won't be affected by the vortex will they?" enquired Hud.

"No, as they're not from the Data Realm the power of the vortex can't affect them at all. So it'll be up to the five of them to try a stop the vortex but that's why Visrel or Lag will be nearby."

"We're dead," said Zack.

"So dead," added Malcolm.

"Oh, you always say that," said Eric.

"But they're right," said Gretchen.

"So right," added Patrick. Astral told them to return home because tomorrow they would once again be in for a deadly endgame and would need all their strength.

During the night the monsters readied their spell. They had a cauldron filled with a boiling liquid made from the magic rocks and trinkets used to power it and prepared the ingredients.

"Now that's a little peculiar," mused Visrel while examine the phial of blood. "It's almost as if there's another magic in there besides the princess'."

"If there was another magic within her surely we would have sensed it before," said Lag.

"Not if it was masked somehow. Oh, it doesn't matter; they'll be gone soon. Let's begin."

"Very well. Let's see what we have: ah, the frozen remains of a creature that died in the snow. Got this right before I met Frozen Fire. Next the golden heart of an ore.rar, the wooden cap of an acorn.ris, the cloud like hair of a cloud.tiff and a ton of rotten salamander fruit." As he listed

185

each one he threw it into the cauldron. Visrel proceeded to do the same.

"From the world of Lasseter we have the shed skin of a talking reptile, the wings of a talking bird and withered flowers that grow in the caves in their mountains. From the world Hartnel I've acquired the eyes of those people that are made of solid glass and the bones of an animal that lived on a meteor. And from Pratchett we have the fangs of one of their giant bats, surprisingly docile, the claws of a riddle spouting sphinx and the hair of one of those things that looks like a platypus only taller. And finally the blood of the royal Knil family."

"Should you have put the phial in as well?"

"I doubt it matters. Anyway the last two ingredients."

"Hatred and anger, the very things we are made of."

"So, our powers will do. Let us do it." The two monsters held their arms over the cauldron and their magic surged and poured into the liquid. Magic flared and swirled all around and with one last flash and the sound of rocks breaking it stopped. Lag reached into the cauldron and pulled out the results: a cylindrical container made of a metal mesh with a symbol of three arrows pointing to each other.

"A waste paper basket?" exclaimed Lag. "The ultimate force of destruction is a bin!"

"Don't you know anything about the computers in the other realm?" enquired Visrel. "When they delete something, it goes to a recycling bin where they can delete it from their computer permanently. The Deletion Vortex will work the same way, without the option to restore it."

"I guess the makers of this spell had a rather odd sense of humour. And tomorrow this 'bin' will consume Miyamoto."

"Astral will no doubt send Frozen Fire to try and stop the vortex, seeing as only they are immune to it."

"Then I'll keep an eye on it; delay Frozen Fire long enough. They may not be destroyed by the vortex but they will fall soon enough."

The morning came and Frozen Fire were waiting for Astral to call for them.

"Well, guys, it's about time for another final battle," mused Zack.

"We should be getting pretty good at it by now," observed Gretchen.

"Still need to be careful," said Malcolm.

"We can get close to the vortex and they can't," pointed out Eric.

"Better take every advantage if we can," said Patrick. They got the signal through their pendants and headed into Miyamoto. They arrived at the Indigo Fields were Astral was waiting.

"Lag is about to activate the vortex," she said. "He won't let you get past him, you're going to have to attack the spell from afar. Now go quickly; we don't have time for my usual reassurances." Frozen Fire moved in the direction indicated and soon found Lag not far away with the Deletion Vortex at his feet.

"Wait! It's a recycling bin!" exclaimed Zack. Lag turned. "What sick mind thought of that?"

"Here you are at last," stated Lag. "I was wondering how much longer you'd be."

"Make it easier on everyone, slug boy, and give up the bin," warned Gretchen.

"I've already activated it, it's just warming up." Powerful magical energy was surging from within the bucket.

"Why don't we skip the fight and go straight to part where we blast the vortex apart," suggested Eric.

"Everything me and the Anti-Gamer want is about to come to fruition."

"That's a no," mumbled Malcolm.

"What do you get out of the destruction of Miyamoto anyway?" asked Patrick.

"I get the Data Realm."

"Huh? How?" said everyone.

"It's all very simple," began Lag. "Once the vortex has consumed Miyamoto the rest of the Data Realm will be unstable due to the gaping hole where this world was. Normally I wouldn't tell you any of this but the odds of you stopping the vortex is very low. With the Data Realm unstable Visrel will be able to absorb most of its magic growing in power and leaving the other worlds in ruin. And with the extra power he'll gain he'll conquer your world to kill all the gamers and destroy all the video games. With the plane of existence where the Data Realm was empty I'll be able to create a new realm and with it control the internet. I may be made from anger but I don't need destruction. True there may not be any more online gaming for me to terrorise but everything else will be. I will curse people to sit at their computers and spend all their time on an internet where everything is filled with lag. It will take ages for anything to load hours to watch clips that last only a second and I will feast on the anger of millions." The bin rose up behind him, the surging energy spilling out of it which then began to spin around at speed. It looked similar to water going down a drain but it looked like the way electricity does in cartoons: it was a purplish black whereas the bin itself was burning with an energy that looked a perpetual explosion. Lag turned to face it. "And now, Frozen Fire, there is nothing you can do to stop it! The Data Realm as you know it will be dead and I will use the ruins to spread anger across your world." There was a flash of light and Astral appeared in the air near the vortex and a clear white bubble appeared around it.

"Quickly, Frozen Fire, get past him and stop it!" she called. "I'll contain it as long as I can!"

"No, Astral they shall be the first to die!" said Lag turning back to them. His magic surged over him and flared upwards. They could only make out part of his figure but it was shifting; it grew and changed; when it cleared he had taken on a different form. He wasn't slimy anymore. He looked like a gigantic wasp only with a scorpion's tail and stinger instead and with claws instead of its upper arms and the middle arms had hands with sharp fingers and feet had sharp toes. He was now a putrid green and mouldy brown in colour. His voice could be heard making a false laugh.

"Why do they keep changing?" groaned Zack as he placed his goggles over his eyes.

"Hey, Lag, you're a bug but we're the newspaper!" called Gretchen.

"Time to swat ya," said Eric. Lag flew down and snapped at them with his claws as large as they were. Frozen Fire were able to manoeuvre around them. Energy surged between his antennae and fired a beam at them but Patrick blocked it with a temporal pulse. Next a lightning bolt crashed down on him followed by snowflake shurikens, a fire twister and a shadow wave.

"Air's not gonna give you enough of an advantage," mocked Patrick.

"It's not an advantage," said Malcolm. He fired arrows in the air, not at Lag, but at various points nearby; when they got close they burst into electricity and then struck. Lag swung his stinger at them but clashed with a time-charged sword. Eric then attacked the tail with a blazing scythe strike. Zack smacked the legs with his staff covered in very dense ice while Gretchen hurled her halberd and a couple duplicates at the head. Lag then began exhaling his burning slime down on them. Everyone was grossed out by this but just tried to avoid it. Then he struck the ground with his stinger causing them to buckle over. However, Frozen Fire bombarded his wings with their elements bringing him to the ground. Lag started trying to crush them with his claws again. Frozen Fire had managed to scramble to their feet in time avoiding the snapping pincers. To counter Gretchen poured a lot of her magic into Lag's shadow and a shadowy duplicate of his tail rose up and struck him. Zack hit his head with dense snowball that turned into snow-screen, Eric flared up fire underneath one of his feet and Patrick attacked the other one with clocks made of time energy. Lag tried to take flight again but Malcolm called down a hand of lightning that punched him back to the ground. Lag fired a beam from his antennae again and also threw energy cubes from his lower hands. Astral was struggling to maintain the barrier containing the vortex; Lag wasn't leaving any openings for them to get past. Then came the burning slime again. Zack blocked it with a wall of ice. Gretchen and Eric sent a shadow wave and a jet of fire at the monster, a lightning ball and temporal pulse followed. Zack threw a snowball at the ground this time covering Frozen Fire with a snow-screen; when it cleared they were gone. Lag looked around and saw a shadow running along the ground towards the vortex. He struck it with his tail bringing Frozen Fire out of it and onto the ground. Lag loomed over them but, using his magic to speed himself up, Patrick made a mighty time powered slash with his sword. Eric then managed a blazing strike with his scythe and Malcolm surrounded everyone with electricity to get away. But Lag was between them and the vortex again. More burning slime was exhaled at them. They blasted him in the face with their elements. Frozen Fire then charged their weapons with their elements: then staff bash on the leg, halberd strike on the other, scythe slash on the tail, arrow to the head and sword slash on one of the lower arms. Lag dropped energy cubes on them and then tried to crush them with his claws. One claw got near Zack but he struck it with icicle kunai. The stinger came towards Malcolm but he fired a bolt of lightning from his index and middle fingers knocking it back. Lag tried to stomp Gretchen but she sank into her shadow in time and stabbed his foot with her halberd. Lag inhaled readying his slime again, but Patrick struck the underside of his head with a temporal pulse knocking his head back causing the burning slime to fall on him. With a snap of his fingers Eric ignited the slime for extra damage. Lag fired energy beam from his antennae again, but he couldn't hit them so he tried bombarding them with energy cubes. Snowflake shurikens, fire balls, shadow waves, lightning balls and temporal pulses struck the arms throwing the cubes. Lag returned to snapping with the claws and striking with his tail, Frozen Fire countered with their weapons every time he got close. Zack sent his magic onto Lag's feet covering them with ice making him lose his balance. A large fire twister from Eric and big time burst from Patrick aimed at Lag's legs caused the giant insect to fall to his hands and knees. Then with a shadow anvil and another lightning punch he was knocked entirely to the ground. Astral had reached her limit.

"I can't contain it any longer!" called Astral.

"THEN GET OUT OF HERE!" Zack called back.

"You must hurry; the vortex has grown more vicious." In flash of light Astral and her containment barrier were gone. The Deletion Vortex began to spread: it looked more violent than before. The air, the grass everything was being pulled towards it, everything but Frozen Fire. They were distracted and didn't notice Lag's antennae surge with energy. He blasted them knocking them to the ground and rose back into the air. Frozen Fire were sore all over but weren't beaten. Lag was readying his next attack.

"Let's smack him good," growled Eric. Everyone charged their strong hand with their element.

"This is for sticking us in those Corridors of Fear!" yelled Gretchen. Everyone punched their arms towards Lag and five large hands made of their elements flew towards him and punched him knocking him backwards.

"Give up yet?" called Patrick. Lag righted himself.

"We have to move," said Malcolm. The vortex was growing but then they realized Lag was actually partially in the energy. Lag's magic surged and energy was pulled from him into the vortex. There was a flash and Lag had returned to his regular form floating in the energy.

"No! How can this be?" cried Lag. "It ends in failure and death!" Magic surged one more time and then BLAM! Lag exploded in a cloud of energy which vanished. Next the vortex began to surge erratically. It was no longer growing. The swirling energy slowly vanished until only the bin was left which burned up in the energy within it. Everything was still and calm. There was a large worn part of ground where the vortex was. Frozen Fire collapsed.

"I believe we won," said Zack moving his goggles back.

"I think we did," replied Eric.

"Lag's dead," said Gretchen. "When someone dies their magic disappears with them and any spells they made stop. Sure, there are ways to make spells last beyond a person's death but I guess they didn't want the vortex sticking around either."

Astral reappeared and took to them Adlez Castle where they had their injuries were treated. They were then brought before the king again.

"Well, Frozen Fire, you have the gratitude of all of Miyamoto," declared Hud. "To thank you, you can all marry my daughter. Oh wait, I never had a daughter. And my son's gone so you can't marry him. Hmm, I'll think of something for you to marry. In the meantime let's a have a celebratory banquet. You go tell your parents you won't be home for dinner. I'll tell the chefs to stop the doomsday feast and begin the celebratory banquet." The king left.

"Well it makes a change from all the disco buffets he insists on having," mused Astral.

"Will they actually start making different food?" wondered Gretchen.

"It would be a bit daft to, surely," said Patrick.

"I'm so proud of how far the five of you have come," said Astral. "Do you remember when you first came here and I gave you those weapons? Well, I lied, I never put a spell on them to help you come up with new ideas to use your magic. I knew the five of you were more than capable. You just needed the means to do so, even just a trick." Soon the castle was full of the smell of food and King's laughter. Frozen Fire were waiting in a room with the princess and prince.

"How's your shoulder?" Zack asked Cyanna.

"It's got a way to go to heal but there's no pain," she replied.

"Lucky you. We're sore all over," grumbled Eric.

"I hope you're all pleased of defeating another deadly monster," said Hitbox.

"We will be when we stop hurting," assured Gretchen.

"At least the vortex went down with Lag," mused Patrick.

"He's not coming back," said Malcolm.

"I won't be missing him or all that slime," said Zack.

"Do you think the book's gone too?" questioned Gretchen.

"Probably.He always seemed to have it," mused Eric.

"I guess I should let the five of you get out of weapon training for a bit," said Hitbox.

"Better start practicing your fake pain," joked Cyanna.

Visrel stood alone in the Free Space staring at the door to Miyamoto.

"Lag was destroyed. The vortex stopped. Another failed plan. At least Lag left this with me." he thought as he began to browse the Virus's Spell Book.

Book Four

Their Namesake

No one really understands the magical force that keeps the island Kerozonia afloat. The strange combination of a magical fire and magical ice in perfect harmony. Usually fire and ice magics cancel each other out unless the people in control are making them work together; yet whoever cast these elements is surely long dead. There are ways to make magic last beyond the life time of the caster like tying it to the natural magic of the world making it seemingly eternal, but this would usually disrupt the harmony. The two magical forces combined in this way makes an even greater force, so much so that it lifted Kerozonia into the air even created magical barriers to stop people from falling of the edges. It is known that without it Kerozonia would fall back into the sea; there have been many books and films about such a happening. It all happened so long ago that any evidence that it was once part of the same landmass as its neighbouring country, Reginland, has been worn away by the ocean. There are plenty of artistic depictions of the island rising into the sky. It is known as the Ice Flame. Due to its location in the centre of the island, underground it is also known as the Heart of Kerozonia; a group of five friends briefly mistakenly called it the Frozen Fire.

Zack was visiting Gretchen. She was painting in a rather unusual manner, having somehow managed to use her shadow magic as paint.

"I've finally got my shadow painting working!" Gretchen proudly told her friend.

"Congratulations. I'm glad it's no longer backfiring," said Zack.

"Those were some memorable art classes. And once I learn how to tie my shadows to magic of the world my art can last an eternity."

"Too bad you always draw and paint really creepy things."

"Oh, don't be such a baby. They're not that creepy."

"I think that's for a team of art experts to decide. Them and the inevitable team of psychiatrists that will one day be assessing you."

Gretchen gave her friend a look that said "You're one to talk," before saying, "I'm sure they'll put us in padded cells next to each other. And with your voice you can talk through any walls." Zack rolled his eyes and changed the subject.

"All right, we'd better head to this thing King Hud is holding."

"Ah, yes, the festival in Miyamoto everyone insists the five of us see."

They used their pendants to transport themselves to the world Miyamoto in the Data Realm. They arrived at the castle in the city Adlez where Malcolm already was.

"Hey buddy, you done with your archery training with Hitbox?" greeted Zack.

"Yep, just finished," replied Malcolm.

"Can you remember what this festival is about?"

"No."

"Yeah, me neither." A flash of light and Eric appeared.

"Ah, you're all here," stated Eric when he saw everyone.

"Do you know what the festival is about?" asked Gretchen.

"No, I couldn't understand a thing he said." There was another flash and Patrick appeared.

"Hey guys, ready for an ace festival?" greeted Patrick.

"You don't know what it's about either?" mused Eric.

"Not a clue." They headed to the throne room where the beginning of the festival was to be declared. The room was full of people of all four races. Frozen Fire just stood at the side. King Hud sat on his throne. Princess Cyanna and Prince Hitbox were sitting in grand chairs to his left and Astral was standing nearby. After a minute the king stood up and the room fell silent.

"Everyone," began Hud. "I am pleased to begin our annual grand celebration, the Festival of Industrial Strength Toilet Cleaner!" There was silence as everyone gave the king a look.

"OK, your majesty, I know that one was deliberate," said Astral. She indicated for the king to sit down and turned to the crowd. "Ahem, as you all know it is the Festival of Programming, when we celebrate the lengthy work that went into the video games that our world is made from. Though only a very small number of people from their world know of us and there would have been a number of reasons why people made these games and certainly they had no idea they were making our world, they will always have our gratitude. So let us celebrate the games that were the foundation of our home, from the great epics that all gamers love to those daft little things on people's phones and the life in our world." The entire room cheered and Astral bowed.

"I call royal dibs on first go on the bumper cars!" yelled Hud, displaying a remarkable prowess of speed as he headed for the door. The crowd in great conversation and euphoria headed out of the room too. The prince and princess moved over to Frozen Fire.

"So, you guys celebrate the games you come from?" said Zack when they got close.

"We do. The festival lasts a couple weeks," explained Cyanna. "There are all sorts of stalls that sell celebratory foods and have plenty of games to offer and several amusement rides."

"Throughout the fortnight there are many events in addition," said Hitbox. "TV specials, live performances and the like. And of course a grand fireworks show to round it off."

"A bit like the Reekie Festival in that respect," mused Patrick.

"You had me at the food," said Zack.

"Let's go check it out then," said Eric. The seven of them headed out as well.

"Hey, as you two are royalty can we just cut straight to the front of the lines?" enquired Gretchen.

"Yes. Yes we can." They headed out into Adlez. The city had been transformed: there were stalls everywhere, lights hanging all over, music and chatter coming from every direction and in the largest park were set many amusement rides from which the king's distinctive cheer could be heard. Frozen Fire went to explore the various attractions and the royal siblings were happy to explain things. There were plenty of things familiar to them as well as many new things.

"Hey, look, they do goldfish in plastic bags as prizes too," pointed out Zack.

"There's a swordfish as well," said Malcolm.

"That's one large plastic bag."

Meanwhile Gretchen was beginning to salivate. "That is some awesome looking chocolate," she said admiring the finely crafted chocolate sculptures.

"This stall belongs to the finest chocolatier in all Miyamoto," explained Cyanna. "Her shop in Snowman's Town sends regular deliveries all over. The craftsmanship is something else; it's almost a shame to eat it. Almost."

"It occurs to me that we don't know anything about Miyamoto's monetary system," mused Eric.

"Uh oh." Elsewhere Patrick had wandered into a hall of mirrors. "I look like an ore.rar," he mused examining his reflection in a distorting mirror. "Hey, there aren't any magic mirrors in here?"

"No, we keep them out of our fun houses like in your world," replied Hitbox. "Grandad wouldn't stop arguing with them."

"Some parts of ours still have some kinds of magic mirrors in them. The ones that show it how you'd looks if you made certain forms of confectionary." In the theme park Astral was sitting next to the king.

"I don't know why I let you talk me into this every year," sighed Astral.

"Don't pretend you don't enjoy yourself," said Hud. "Besides chair-o-swings are awesome."

"If we go on the ferris wheel this time no attempting to juggle while we're on it. It never ends well when you're firmly on the ground." Frozen Fire had regrouped.

"NOOOOOOOOOOOOOO!" exclaimed Zack.

"You never want to go on any rides," grumbled Gretchen. "You'd think after the monsters we've fought you'd be fine with a roller coaster."

"NOOOOOOOOOOOOOO!"

"Oh, you goggle head."

"Let's move onto something where Zack doesn't deafen us shall we?" remarked Eric.

"That's every ride out then," observed Patrick.

"There's no need for everyone to do the same thing," said Cyanna. "If you all still want to go on the roller coaster 'Cloud.tiff Plummet,' me and snowman can go get ice cream or something."

"Ah, a smart idea," said Hitbox.

"Thank you, maestro," said Zack.

"I'd like ice cream too," mumbled Malcolm. Everyone else said they'd rather have ice cream too. The princess rolled her eyes.

"Should have seen that one coming," muttered Cyanna. Astral and Hud were eating candyfloss between rides. However, a troubling feeling suddenly came over Astral.

"Something wrong, Astral?" asked Hud.

"I can sense something," she replied. "Someone's interfering with one of my spells. Oh no! I got distracted, I didn't notice something happen at the door to Miyamoto.

There's trouble at Connection Tower." Meanwhile Frozen Fire had arrived at the ice cream stall.

"Dear sweet tundra bounty," rambled Zack. The place was a blaze of colour, an extreme variety of ice cream flavours, and plenty of serving options. All sorts of ice cream dishes, cones, topping and sauces.

"This place has got all the whacky flavours and then some!" exclaimed Gretchen.

"I think we've found a new home away from home," said Eric. A flash of light and Astral appeared.

"Everyone, we have a problem!" stated Astral. "Someone has taken down the shield around Connection Tower."

"Can it wait half an hour?" asked Patrick.

"It's Visrel."

"Well, that's another reason to hate that guy," grumbled Zack.

"Your highnesses, you'd better go and find your grandfather," said Astral. "He might start juggling on the rides again." A look of worry came across their faces and they left in a hurry.

Astral took Frozen Fire to Connection Tower. It seemed different from the last time they were there, no doubt it was because Astral's barrier that kept everyone bar those who had permission from Hud from entering was now gone.

"What's that psycho up to now?" wondered Gretchen.

"We better get up there and find out," said Patrick. They climbed the tower's stairs momentarily wondering why Astral didn't take them straight to the top and soon came out on top. The scene was very reminiscent of last time: the Anti-Gamer was doing something with the stone sculpture that was the focus point of the tower's powers and its connection to the other world and Frozen Fire were ready to stop him.

"You must be feeling some of that déjà vu," mused Visrel without looking.

"You interrupted us when we were getting some epic ice cream so you're getting beat good!" yelled Zack.

"I'm afraid you won't be beating me at this time," said Visrel finally turning towards them.

"And you're not gonna tell us what you're up too?" said Eric.

"Indeed I will not. Anyway allow me to introduce you to Bone-Branch." The Anti-Gamer snapped his fingers and dark energy appeared blocking both him and the exit from Frozen Fire. Then a monster appeared: it took the form of a tree but it looked like it was made of bones, wooden bones. The trunk looked like bones, the roots it moved on looked like bones, two large branches looked like skeletal arms and there was even a skull like carving near the top.

"Where does he get these monster ideas from?" said Gretchen.

"From your art going by this one," remarked Zack.

Gretchen was about of retort when Malcolm interrupted. "Later! Do it later."

Frozen Fire summoned their weapons and readied themselves for battle. Bone-Branch screeched loudly which sent an energy wave at them. Gretchen rushed forward and attacked with her halberd and a duplicate. Eric fired a jet of fire at its face. The tree tried to smash them with its 'arms' but they manoeuvred out the way. Zack made a lump of ice on the end of his staff which he smashed against the monster, Patrick held its arms in place with his time energy making easy to strike and Malcolm pointed above the monster and a bolt of lightning struck it. The tree screeched again knocking them over with another energy wave. The monster came towards them, raised its arm and swung it down at Gretchen, but Gretchen suddenly turned into a shadow version of herself and the attack passed through her taking the tree by surprise. She then swung her halberd around which still did damage despite being a shadow as well; this gave the others the chance to get back up. Next Bone-Branch was subject to arrows and scythe slashes, followed by an extra-large temporal pulse and an oversized icicle kunai. Ghostly fruit appeared on the tree's top branches. It then swung hurling the fruit at Frozen Fire which exploded when they struck the ground. Zack and Eric spun their weapons around and covered them in their elements and then threw the spinning weapons at the monster hitting with enough force to knock it over. While it was toppled over Malcolm fired a stream of lightning from his fingers at it while Patrick punched it with a hand made of time energy and Gretchen dropped a shadow piano on it. The monster screeched again and continued to do so until it got back up; when it was upright again it launched more fruit at them. Zack blocked with an ice wall and then covered everyone's movements with a snow-screen. Eric made fire erupt underneath it, Gretchen hit it in the face with a shadow wave, Patrick hit it with a time burst and Malcolm fired an arrow that burst into lightning. The monster screeched again, so Patrick conjured up a lot of his time energy to slow down its movements. It was then hit with a fire twister, a lightning bolt punch and a snowman moving it back. Finally, Gretchen made shadow spring board appear underneath it which she made spring upwards toppling the tree over, but this time it was at the tower's edge and fell right off and it burst into magic when it hit the ground. Frozen Fire turned back to Visrel as the force-field blocking them vanished.

"Now it's your turn, jerkbag," said Patrick.

"My bony tree bought me the time I need to finish my spell," said Visrel holding up a ball of magical energy. "When she catches you be sure to tell Astral that Connection Tower is mine now." He threw the magical energy at the tower and when it hit another barrier erupted and hurtled outwards. Before they knew it Frozen Fire where pushed away by it and knocked off the tower. Frozen Fire plummeted but just as quickly as they were pushed off they were surrounded by a white light and then landed safely on the ground. Looking at the tower they saw it was now surrounded by Visrel's barrier.

"There is no way that can be good," observed Astral.

Astral returned everyone to Adlez castle where they filled the king in on what happened.

"He's taken over Connection Tower?!" cried Hud. "Gadzooks, that's where I keep my old letters from my late wife!"

"No, your majesty, they're in the secret room behind the library," said Gretchen.

"Oh yes, that's right."

"How do you know that?" inquired Astral. Frozen Fire were trying not to laugh as they remembered something funny they had read. "In any case the Anti-Gamer can do a lot of damage in that tower. Not only will he be able to freely move between our two worlds but he could cause any number of disasters with its powers."

"I get the feeling it's not gonna be what he last tried at the tower," mused Zack.

"Yeah, he's never struck me as one to retry thwarted plans," agreed Eric.

"If he's taken over the tower he's probably got a plan that involves your world," said Hud. "And we all know what a scoundrel that Visrel can be. Before you know it he'll be stealing sweeties from children, tape over peoples favourite movies, write rude words on all the important documents and kill us all. So go, Frozen Fire, return to your home on that giant floating space turtle and protect it from his misdeeds and chaos. Punch that twit right on his nose."

"Floating island," corrected Patrick.

"Whatever."

"The king's right. Partially," said Astral. "I'd better keep an eye on both Miyamoto and your homes as well."

"So much for the festival," grumbled Zack.

205

"Yeah, talk about a real party crasher," said Eric.

"Next year guys," said Malcolm. So Frozen Fire returned home and for the rest of the day there was no sign of trouble from Visrel.

The next day Astral contacted them and brought back to the castle where the prince and princess were.

"Visrel has gone to Kerozonia," explained Astral. "I've tracked him to Sky Depths."

"Sky Depths? What sort of thing is that?" questioned Hitbox.

"It's Kerozonia's ocean," replied Patrick.

"You mean below where the island floats?" asked Cyanna.

"No, it's a floating ocean," answered Gretchen. "The magic of the ice flame not only caused the island to float but some of the ocean water as well."

"The same magic barriers that keep people from falling off the edge contains the ocean," added Zack.

"Of course, Kerozonia isn't known for its ideal beach weather regardless," mused Eric.

"Anyway, I had the five of you come here so I can send you straight to Sky Depths," explained Astral.

"Hang on, why didn't you send us right where we needed to go in the past?" questioned Zack.

"Honestly, I didn't always think of it until later."

"We'd better come with you," offered Cyanna.

"I need you two here in case it's just a distraction."

"He has done that before," mused Hitbox.

"Let's go then," said Malcolm.

"Remember to be careful. He won't care if the Data Realm is exposed or not," said Astral.

In a flash of light Frozen Fire arrived at Sky Depths. As usual the Kerozonian skies were grey and dull and the ocean was calm yet the wind was strong. Off to their right was the long sand bank where people did the usual beach activities though there was hardly anyone there. And to their left was a more rocky kind of beach with rock pools and plenty of left behind seaweed.

"Well, none of those people have capes so we can rule them out," observed Gretchen as they descended onto the sand.

"I don't like the idea of asking people if they've seen a guy in a suit with gauntlets," said Zack worried. "Let's check over by the rocks first." The others agreed and they moved over to the rocks. However, this part was even quieter, just a couple seagulls and an unusually large seal. The seal was observing Frozen Fire with what appeared to be curiosity.

"Have you lost something among the rocks?" asked the seal. Frozen Fire were a little startled but not too shocked as they had heard of seals that could talk.

"We're looking for someone," explained Patrick. "Someone with powerful magic."

"The humans with the strongest magic who've been here today are the five of you. However, a dark force had entered the ocean. I fear it is a monster made from unstable magic and emotions given a non-magical form."

"That sounds like our guy," said Eric. "Unfortunately for us."

"He's in the ocean! Oh come on!" yelled Zack.

"That's not fair at all," mumbled Malcolm.

"It's not my business why five teenagers are seeking out a true monster, but the thought of a monster in the ocean is so terrifying I'd ask anyone to do something. So how about I help you get to him? There's and old selkie spell that'll let you move through the ocean."

"Really? Thank you so much," said Gretchen. The seal climbed off its rock and clapped its fins together and a large bubble formed around Frozen Fire.

"This'll allow you to breath under water," explained the seal. "It will dissipate as soon as you return to the shore."

Everyone expressed deep gratitude to the seal. "If it will help drive out a monster I'll gladly do it anytime." Frozen Fire rolled the bubble into the ocean.

"Lucky for us to run into that selkie," said Zack. "Saved us from having to call Astral."

"Assuming she can do something like this," mused Gretchen.

"Considering everything else she can do."

"Let's just be glad it wasn't a selkie from the old folktales that gives you a very romantic time before leaving abruptly," said Eric. "These days there are way more stories of humans doing it than selkies. Probably at least one occasion where both involved tried to leave quickly." There was a fair bit of quarrelling as they tried to coordinate moving the bubble. Their path was not straightforward yet they made progress through the ocean floor. Sky Depths did not have the most wonderful sea creatures or plants but they were charming in their own way and it was a rare treat to see them in this way. Finally, they saw a figure. Odds were it was Visrel as it appeared to be human and was standing in the middle of the water without the means to breath. It became clear and they were right.

"Anti-Gamer dead ahead guys, let's get him!" declared Patrick.

"How do we fight in this?" wondered Malcolm.

"Uh oh." Visrel turned around as they approached and they saw he was holding something familiar.

"Hey, that's the Virus's Spell Book," said Eric.

"Aw man, it wasn't destroyed with Lag," groaned Zack.

"Well, this is a rare opportunity," said Visrel, his voice moving through water as if it was just air. "Who'd have thought you'd dare follow me down here. This will make things substantially easier." He summoned his helical blade and thrust it with force at the bubble. Nothing happened and there was a moment where everybody just stood there. "So much for that," said Visrel lowering his blade.

"All right Anti-Gamer, time to go down," warned Gretchen.

"We still don't know how to fight in this," pointed out Zack.

"Will you not say these things in front of the bad guy."

"From what I've heard a bubble like this will only dissipate when it returns to land," mused Visrel. "Having you lot pushed back to the shore ought to buy me enough time." Something moved through the water at great speed and slammed into the bubble rolling Frozen Fire away from Visrel. They managed to balance themselves and saw they were faced with a twenty-foot-long monster eel.

"This is gonna be worse than any of those rides," groaned Zack.

"Just try not to be sick in here," requested Patrick.

"Let's fry this fish," said Eric.

"Can you make your fire stay lit underwater yet?" asked Gretchen.

"You know I've no idea. It's not exactly something I test."

"I've got it," said Malcolm. He focused on sending his magic outside their bubble and electricity surged all around the eel. While the monster writhed it managed to hit the bubble with its tail sending them rolling again. They came to a sudden stop when they crashed into a large rock and they fell into a heap. They tried to stop their heads from spinning as the eel approached. This time Gretchen and Patrick focused their magic and streams of shadows and time energy shot at the monster. It managed to dodge most but was still hit by several. Zack focused his magic on the monster and ice started to appear over it; however, it did not spread fast enough to immobilize it and the eel used its tail to flick the bubble upwards. Frozen Fire were spinning all over and they didn't notice the bubble breached the surface before falling back down. Eric managed to send his magic onto the bubble and while he made no fire he was able to heat it so it still burned when it hit the monster. When the bubble was on the ocean floor again Malcolm covered the monster in electricity while Gretchen and Patrick sent more magic streams at it while Zack managed to drop a block of ice on it. The monster lunged again but Eric managed to heat up the outside of the bubble, so the eel was burned; however, they were still sent rolling away. They were really getting dazed. They could barely get back up or focus on where the monster was. The eel coiled around the bubble and dragged it across the ground slamming it into rocks. Frozen Fire tried to unleash their magic and their elements began to shoot out in all directions except for Eric's fire which just heated the bubble again. The eel dropped the bubble and moved away. It waited for an opportunity and slammed the bubble. But the monster couldn't hit the bubble with about being pelted with attacks sent by its dizzy occupants. So finally the eel covered itself in magical energy and rammed the bubble with great force sending them rocketing away. But their attack had hit a large rock nearby which fell on the monster which then dissipated into magic. The bubble rolled at great speed and soon reached the shore. It disappeared when it left the water and Frozen Fire stopped moving around at last and lay face down in the sand. Their pendants glowed and Astral talked through them.

"Frozen Fire, Visrel's no longer in Sky Depths. Did you stop him?" she asked but all she got were groans. "Hello? Are you all right? Hold on, you're near than same discarded yet still working laptop I sent you through."

Back in Miyamoto in Astral's Temple she gave them each a potion to help with the dizziness. And they managed to explain what happened.

"I should have known he might have gone to the bottom of the ocean," sighed Astral. "It's so distressing to know he has that book. I really hoped it had been consumed by the Deletion Vortex. And you don't have any ideas as to what he was doing?"

"Nope, couldn't tell what he was doing," said Gretchen. "And we were too busy spinning around to really brainstorm any theories."

"Did he capture Connection Tower just to freely move between the realms? But why was he in the Kerozonian ocean? Hmm, I think I will head to Sky Depths and investigate myself."

"We got the eel so you should be fine," assured Zack.

"It'd take Visrel himself to harm me."

"Then why did we need to protect you that time?"

"They can still break my concentration." Frozen Fire warped to Adlez Castle to wait for Astral's return, getting some food from the festival now that their stomachs were feeling better.

"I'm glad you've recovered from your ordeal so quickly," said Cyanna watching the five of them stuff themselves with chocolate.

"I guess the five of you have gotten rather used to these things," mused Hitbox.

"We haven't done a whole lot of being tossed around in a bubble," Patrick pointed out.

"It's typical, I get out of the rides and then that happens," grumbled Zack.

"I'm just glad you weren't screaming; our ears would still be ringing," remarked Eric.

"Oh, shut up."

"I can't think of anything he'd want from the ocean," said Gretchen.

"With that book? Who knows?" said Cyanna.

"Visrel knows," said Malcolm. A flash of light and Astral appeared.

"He's left some kind of spell in the ocean," she explained. "Despite all my thorough examination I couldn't tell its purpose. And if he is creating a spell from the Virus's Spell Book he wouldn't need to get anything from your world."

"So we've gotta figure out what he's doing in the tower and why he's gone to our world," said Zack. "And of course stop him doing whatever either of them is."

"And get the book," added Malcolm.

"I guess we're waiting on him making his next move," said Eric putting his feet up. "Zackary be a dear and get me something to drink, there's a good boy."

"Get it yourself, flame brain."

Astral interrupted before Eric could respond. "I don't want you just sitting around," she said. "I'm sending the five of you to Signati Island."

"Why there of all places?" asked Cyanna looking a little troubled.

"There's something there that may help us find out Visrel's plot."

And so Frozen Fire and Astral appeared on a large deserted island in the middle of Miyamoto's ocean. They were standing on a cliff overlooking a bay but they didn't notice most of the island's features because their eyes were drawn to the cliffs opposite them. There was a giant stone door on the cliff face like something from a really old movie. They could sense it was sealed by powerful magic. It was covered in carvings that all seemed to be a variety of warning signs, the ocean seemed harsher around it and while the stone was clearly aged there was no sign of erosion.

"What is the deal with that door?!" asked Gretchen.

"It is often referred to as the Other Door," replied Astral. "Because it reminds people of the door to the Free Space at Game's Edge. However, this door does not lead to the Free Space. A long time ago one of my predecessors sealed away something terrible behind it. Anyway, we're here for something else."

"We're gonna find out what's behind there, aren't we," grumbled Zack

"Undoubtedly we will indeed," answered Patrick.

"Wait. What do you mean predecessors?" questioned Eric.

"I am not the first to watch over Miyamoto," explained Astral. "There's always been one who watches for each of the four worlds but they haven't always been the same one."

"Huh, I thought you were immortal," said Eric.

"Or at the very least frozen in time," said Zack.

"I've only been around for about three centuries," said Astral. "I'm the only person actually older than King Hud."

"So how do you pick a new watcher?" asked Gretchen.

"We're born into it. You see like the phoenix when we die we are then reborn. Our bodies disappear and our magic forms into a new one with a new heart and a new soul, with generations of memories to guide them. That's why I know much about Miyamoto's history even though I wasn't actually there." Frozen Fire were in surprise of this 'biology lesson'.

"But why are we on this island?" asked Malcolm.

"We are here to find the Desire Pearl. A sphere sealed within some ruins on the island that can show you what a person's after. Obviously you have to be very specific but we should be able to use it to find out what the Anti-Gamer is up to. The reason why we haven't used it in the past is because of the rather complex way it works and seeing as Visrel doesn't actually feel 'desire' I could be sure it'd work on him; but what I learned from the spell left in Sky Depths should be enough to get it to work." They continued onwards until they came to the ruins of an old building, with barely any walls and plants growing through the cracked stone floor. It was hard to tell there was ever a building here. It was completely empty; no writing, carvings or signs to explain what this place may have been for.

"Uh, Astral I think this is the wrong place," said Zack.

"The pearl is here, it's just out of synch with the rest of reality," explained Astral.

"Right, obviously that's a thing," said Gretchen flatly.

"So how do we re-synch it?" asked Patrick.

"First of all I use my magic to make five 'keyholes' appear," replied Astral. "Then the five of them need to be filled with a lot of magical energy. Any kind of energy, but it has to be a different kind in each, so the five of you just need to send your elements into them."

"Well, you can't say it's not secure," said Eric. "If you did this to all of Miyamoto you'd never have to worry about Visrel again."

"It's not possible to use that kind of spell on that scale. Besides we want our two worlds to meet one day. Shall we begin?" Astral held her arms aloft and her hands glowed; with a surge of light five stone object appeared. They looked like wells, but despite being on the solid ground they did not seem to have a bottom. Frozen Fire each stood next to one, held their arms over it and unleashed their magic. The elements surged from them and down into the holes. After what seemed like ages of pouring magic into the wells there was a flash of light which caused them to stop. The wells were gone and now there was a pillar in their place. On top of the pillar was a pearl swirling with magical energy.

"Uh, we're surrounded," said Malcolm. Everyone else looked and saw they were encircled by a swarm of Visrel's talon-teeth.

"I'll start using the pearl's powers," said Astral. Frozen Fire grumbled as they summoned their weapons and headed towards the talon-teeth. They knocked several over with their weapons as other leapt at them. The ones that leapt at Zack were met with his icicle kunai, the ones that grabbed Malcolm were electrocuted, the ones that went for Patrick were stopped mid-air by his magic before being cut down with his sword, the ones that attacked Gretchen were swatted away by a shadow road sign and the ones that jumped at Eric landed in a wall of fire he protected himself with. Frozen Fire had fought many talon-teeth but now the monsters could barely hit them any more despite their numbers. Zack slammed several with his staff, Gretchen slashed many with her halberd, Eric cut a lot with his scythe, Malcolm shot plenty with his arrows and Patrick struck down a bunch with his sword. Astral was floating up by the Desire Pearl, her eyes closed, her hands held up to it aglow with magic as she did what needed to. The talon-teeth formed a pile as to try and drop onto Frozen Fire but they were knocked down by their elements. No matter how much they tried the monsters could not get any closer and in the end they were all gone; it was certainly one of their shortest battles.

"You'd think Visrel'd retire those guys at this point," mused Zack.

"I don't think he relies on them too much anyway," said Gretchen.

"All right, everyone, the pearl is ready," said Astral and with a wave of her hand Frozen Fire floated up towards the pearl. After a bit of near tumbling from the initial surprise they all gathered around the pearl and looked into it. Through the swirling magic they could see something, fire and ice.

"It's just fire and ice," said Patrick. "A little underwhelming."

"Hmm, does it just mean Frozen Fire," wondered Astral. "Has this been a waste of time?"

"Either that or he's singled out Zack and Eric," remarked Gretchen.

"There's something else," said Malcolm. Looking again they could see that over the ice and fire there was a transparent image which they soon recognized as Kerozonia.

"We already know he's doing something on Kerozonia," sighed Astral.

"Unless it means fire and ice within Kerozonia," observed Zack.

"In that case it doesn't mean us, it means the thing we're named after," said Gretchen.

"The Ice Flame, the Heart of Kerozonia," said Eric.

"He wants to knock our home out the sky!" said Patrick.

"But why would he do that?" wondered Malcolm. Everybody tried to think of why, but they could not think why Visrel would send Kerozonia falling out of the sky, nor how it's linked to his taking over of Connection Tower and his long-term goal of destroying Miyamoto. So everyone just went home for the evening.

The following day everyone was taking it easy at their own home. However before they knew it their pendants glowed and Astral connected the five of them allowing everyone to talk to each other despite not being in the same place.

"Frozen Fire, I have detected Visrel on Kerozonia," said Astral. "You're not gonna like where he is. He's on Great Bard."

"He's on the biggest mountain on Kerozonia?" yelled Zack. "Forget that!"

"He may not be at the summit," reassured Astral.

"He's still on a ruddy mountain," said Gretchen. "We don't exactly climb those often."

"Most of these guys can't climb stairs," remarked Eric.

"This coming from the guy who ideally would be carried everywhere on a pillow," replied Zack.

"It simply proves who's the best, deary."

"It simply proves who thinks they're a cat."

"I've seen your mum scratch you behind the ears."

"Guys can you save it for after the mountain?" interrupted Gretchen. "As I doubt we're getting out of it."

After first transporting to Miyamoto, Astral transported them as close as she could to where Visrel was. They were now on the mountain called Great Bard, covered in plenty of trees and grass, but it was still a mountain with steep slopes and craggy rocks at a height Frozen Fire did not want to be at.

"I guess we should be glad we're not on an even bigger mountain," mused Eric.

"They probably don't think of this as much of a mountain," said Patrick.

"What Wi-Fi device did the Astral even use to transport us here?" wondered Zack trying to ignore his nerves.

"Perhaps a hiker with a mobile phone," suggested Eric. "Or perhaps she's got great range and transported us from the visitor centre."

"Guys, I found the path," said Malcolm. Following Malcolm's lead, they headed down the safest pass they could find, not a good time to have no experience in mountains. They moved very carefully across the mountainside and finally they found Visrel. Not liking the idea of fighting on the steep hill they instead hid and watched to see what he was doing. The Anti-Gamer was finishing off a spell, perhaps the same kind of spell as the one from before. When he stopped an expression came over his face and he began to look around.

"You do realize I can sense the magic from the five of you?" announced Visrel. "Just because you've managed to sneak up on me in the past doesn't mean I can't sense you coming."

"We didn't think of that one," grumbled Zack.

"Might as well see if he's willing to share," suggested Eric. Frozen Fire moved slightly out from their cover.

"We know you're targeting the Ice Flame," said Patrick.

"Care to tell us why you don't want Kerozonia floating?" enquired Gretchen.

"Of course I'm not going to say," said Visrel. "All you need to know is thanks to the Virus's Spell Book, Miyamoto will be no more."

"That's what you thought last time!" said Zack loudly.

"Last time Lag and I tried the direct approach, this time I shall be indirect."

"We'll figure it out," said Malcolm.

"Perhaps you will but first you must get off this hill." He held up his hand and a sphere of energy appeared in it. It was different from Visrel's magic but they recognized it. "It's fascinating the things you can do with the power of Connection Tower and a book with a few ideas." Visrel threw the sphere at Frozen Fire. It struck the ground near them and soon they were covered by it. The tower's energy did not affect them but the space all around them warped and twisted. When it stopped everything had changed. It was as though the entire mountain had been unravelled into a single straight path winding off in front of them; it seemed to be suspended in the air without anything above or below.

"Ok, what? This is crazy!" exclaimed Gretchen. "King Hud level crazy."

"Usually even an incredibly powerful space elemental would have trouble conjuring this," came the voice of Visrel from somewhere.

"NO! YOU CAN'T DO THIS, YOU CHEATER!" yelled Zack.

"If you can escape the Corridors of Fear you may find your way out of here. But I'm done on the mountain you won't find me."

"AARGH!" Zack stomped the ground furiously with his feet. "Oh that, viral jerk I... argh!"

"Zack, try to calm down, breathe deeply," suggested Gretchen. Zack did so. "We can get out of here."

"Has he actually warped the mountain, or just created this?" wondered Eric

"Well, if he warped the mountain someone's bound to notice," mused Gretchen.

"Not the whole mountain," said Malcolm.

"I doubt we can contact Astral," said Patrick. "But she'll probably find us again."

"I don't think we should just wait though," said Eric. "Vissy won't have been decent enough to give us an exit, but there's bound to be away to force our way out. Let's go find it." Frozen Fire sent off down the winding path. Everything seemed so flat, there wasn't steepness anymore it was like walking down the street. The path was not straight; it twisted in every way, sideways, upside-down. They were glad the gravity changed too.

"This is very disorienting," said Patrick. "Are we even the right way up any more?"

"I don't think there is a right way up anymore," groaned Zack.

"He couldn't just send a monster after us," said Gretchen. "This time we make sure that book goes."

"Maybe smack him with it before we destroy it," said Eric.

"What happens when we get to the end?" questioned Malcolm.

"Probably nothing," said Zack "If there is an end."

"Good thing there's something there." Malcolm was gesturing beneath the path. When the others looked they saw a sphere that resembled the one Visrel threw at them only it looked more solid, but it was clearly made from the same magic.

"That must be the generator for this place!" exclaimed Gretchen.

"Let's hope he forgot to put in defences," said Eric.

"Only one way to find out," said Patrick.

Everyone took aim and fired a burst of their element at the sphere; unfortunately, when the attacks got close they veered off and bypassed it. Everyone grumbled. The ground began to move: the part they were standing on rose up and soon they saw the whole path had split apart and had begun to move about in all directions. They fell over when the part they were standing on suddenly moved. When everything settled down they saw the sphere was now far above them and the path had completely reshaped.

"OH COME ON!" yelled Zack. In his anger he threw another attack at the sphere. When it missed the path moved all over again; when the thing stopped the sphere was now surrounded by the path.

"Let's not do that again," instructed Gretchen glaring at Zack.

"If we can't attack it from here perhaps we can get to it," suggested Patrick.

"Space may be warped but that's still a long way down," said Eric.

"Maybe Gretchen can duplicate that path," said Zack.

"Surely it would be redirected as well," said Gretchen.

"We have to try something," said Patrick who had misjudged his footing and fell off the path. "YAAAAAAAAAAH!"

"Patrick!" cried the others. Patrick missed the sphere and the rest of the path and fell into nothing and vanished. Before anyone could react, there was a surge of energy and Patrick reappeared face down next to them.

"Ow," was all he managed. Everyone else let out a sigh of relief.

"At least it looks like we can't fall to our death," said Zack.

"Maybe we can get to that thing after all," mused Eric.

"So, what? We just keep leaping at it until we land on it?" said Gretchen. It was decided that this is what they'd try. They'd each take turns trying to get to the sphere and they figured once one of them was on it they'd be able to help the others get to it. First up was Zack, after some coercion. He moved towards the edge and got ready to jump but slipped and fell off and completely missed the sphere. Next was Gretchen; she dived right off the path but misjudged her aim and missed. Eric tried to use his fire to propel himself towards it, but the warped space made him fly away from it. Malcolm had better aim due to his archery lessons but he couldn't get past the warped space either. Patrick jumped off the path trying to protect himself with his time magic; however, he veered off in one direction and the magic covering him went in another. Zack managed to jump this time with an extended icicle to try and get a hold in the sphere, but the warped space made him drop it. Gretchen made some shadow rope and tried to lasso onto the sphere, however, she ended up tangled up in the rope. Eric jumped swinging down his scythe to try a get a hold, and the scythe did almost touch it but it fell away at the last second. It was Malcolm's turn again and this time he was going to try something he had never done before. He closed his eyes and concentrated building up his magic. He surged with electricity making the others wonder what he was up to and then he opened his eyes and BLAM! He vanished, a bolt of lightning shot through the air and crashed into the sphere. And there where the lightning had hit was now Malcolm.

"WHOA! That's quite a trick bud," Zack called down to him.

"Thanks, it's not an easy one to do," replied Malcolm.

"Now, how does he help us get there?" wondered Eric.

"Should have given him some rope so he could tie to an arrow and shoot it up to us," mused Gretchen.

"Back to jumping it is then," said Zack. "Your turn again Patrick."

"Malcolm try to grab me when I get close," called Patrick. He leapt off the path and Malcolm threw out a line of lightning from his hand which latched onto Patrick.

"I can make thunder rope," he explained. He was able to pull Patrick through the warped space onto the sphere and thanks to his thunder rope everyone was soon on the sphere.

"Let's bust this thing open," declared Gretchen.

"I hope there's not a monster on here after all that," said Zack.

"Surely the lightning would have alerted it," said Patrick.

"Good point." Frozen Fire started to pound at the sphere with their elements. The entire thing was shaking so they had to be careful in case they fell off and had to start again. The sphere was tough but with all five of them assaulting it, it soon began to crack. They focused their attacks on the cracks making them bigger and bigger and soon it burst open. And with one final large blast into the sphere itself the energy exploded and the sphere shattered. Frozen Fire were thrown backwards and were soon falling again but all around them space was warping like when they were first trapped. Finally, it stopped and they found themselves rolling downhill. Fortunately, they had ended up at the base of the mountain so they didn't go far before they stopped. The five of them lay there groaning.

"How did none of us realize the thing would explode with us still on it?" cried Zack.

"Let's omit that part of the story when we retell it," said Eric.

Back in Miyamoto Frozen Fire recovered from their latest ordeal while Astral paced around thinking about what they knew; she was near to a breakthrough.

"Obviously he's keeping us out of the tower so we can't stop his plan like last time," Astral thought aloud.

"Something about his scheme involves a lot of the tower's magic, and it involves knocking Kerozonia from the sky? Unless... those spells, they seem to be some kind of energy discharger. Oh no. I can't be that? But it makes sense."

"We're not gonna like this are we?" said Zack.

"Not as such, no."

"Best get it over with," said Malcolm.

"It's just a theory, there's no way to be sure. He could use Connection Tower to open a rift between our worlds, and unlike the one Putrice used one that could actually cross between our worlds. He could tear open the sky of Miyamoto to the space below Kerozonia. He's going to send Kerozonia plummeting into Miyamoto destroying both our homes at the same time."

"That'll ruin our save files," said Gretchen. "And you know, kill everyone we love."

"Clearly he's learning to warp space, from what you've just been through. If he creates a rift and then warps space Kerozonia could fall quite a distance. Which along with those spells that seem to be for energy discharge, could cause it to fall at quite a velocity. The devastation would be so great there wouldn't really be anything left of Miyamoto or Kerozonia and any survivors, which is beyond unlikely, he could easily pick off."

"That's a thought that'll keep you up at night," said Eric.

"Do you remember when I was the maddest person we knew?" asked Zack.

"How would Visrel even get to the Ice Flame?" wondered Patrick. "It's not exactly a tourist attraction."

"Perhaps he'll make more than one rift," suggested Gretchen.

"That's very likely," said Astral. "Still if this is his plan then perhaps we can get a rough idea of where else on Kerozonia he would place these spells and maybe get there before him and stop him before he sets another up." So Astral set to work trying to figure out what to do next.

Before she did she sent word to Adlez castle about her theory. Cyanna and Hitbox received the message.

"It's only a theory. Should we tell Grandad?" pondered Cyanna.

"I think so. Astral is usually right when it comes to the Anti-Gamer," said Hitbox.

"Let's go see what part of the festival he's at then."

"He's still there? He's got a meeting with the other three leaders soon."

"We're gonna have to keep them busy again. Try not to do this sort of thing when you're king."

"I don't think I should make that promise." They heard footsteps and the leaders of the other races, Iron, Larch and Stratus, appeared.

"Your highnesses, where is the king?" inquired Iron.

"He's... running late," explained Cyanna trying to think of an appropriate wording.

"Told you that was his voice coming from the helter skelter," said Larch.

"Hmph, trust Hud to run around like a child, while the Anti-Gamer is up to who knows what," grumbled Stratus.

"Yes, you weren't doing something similar half an hour ago," remarked Larch.

"There's nothing to do but wait," said Iron. "We could find him and carrying him back, but all that kicking is kind of annoying." Somewhere in the distance a crashing sound could be heard followed by a loud yell.

"That's Grandad now," said Hitbox. The royal siblings went off to meet the king leaving the other leaders to wait in the meeting room. They found Hud dusting himself off nearby some people clearing up a mess. He was muttering something about needing a less complex way of tying his shoes. Cyanna and Hitbox told Hud about the leaders already waiting for him and explained Astral's theory.

"Well, that's another reason to hate Astral, always being right," grumbled Hud. "Right, that's it, I'm putting a plan into action. While I tell the leaders the doom and gloom I need the two of you to head to the subterranean library and find an old tome. By which I mean a book not my first girlfriend."

"But the subterranean library is for the king's eyes only," protested Hitbox.

"Yes, but anyone with royal blood can get in. I assumed the two of you have snuck in, in the past."

"He's not wrong," said Cyanna. "It must be a pretty big plan if we need a book from there."

"The book is called the Connection Tower Instruction Manual." Cyanna and Hitbox shared a look that said "We have one of those?" "We're going to turn the tower off and stop Visrel's plan in its tracks. And leave him on those tracks until another train comes along." So the princess and prince headed down to the lowest part of the castle which was underground. Down a dimly lit set of stairs was a large door sealed shut by magic. There was no indication as to what this door was for, as the library was predominately a secret known only to those whom the royal family trusted and those who have a habit of learning secrets they're not supposed to know. No handles on the door, no keyhole, it only opened by the touch of a royal. So Hitbox pressed his hand on the door and the stone slabs swung inwards. The room was filled with a dusty smell and lit by a magic light. Overall, despite its underground location it looked rather plain apart from the wear of age. Across all the walls and in the centre of the room were stone shelves that had stood the test of time, filled with old books with worn covers and aged pages, all still readable, all full of things meant to be secret.

"Can you remember seeing the book before?" asked Cyanna.

"No, I only remember where great grandmother's diaries are," replied Hitbox.

"That queen loved mud wrestling and pickled sardines."

"Learning about our ancestors always reveals too much." They browsed the shelves going over each and every title until at last, success.

"Ah, here it is," said Cyanna taking the book from the shelf where she had found it. The book had a rough drawing of the tower and the lettering had come off in places. "This is different from most other instruction manuals." She flicked through some of the pages. "Well, it's worded like one. No extra languages though. Hitbox?" she noticed her brother had not come over when she called. Turning round a corner she found Hitbox looking into a book.

"What?" he said to himself. "That's behind the Other Door? Why is that thing in our world?"

"Hitbox?" He finally noticed his sister and she saw the book was about Signati Island.

"Sorry, I got distracted. Have you ever seen this book before?"

"A long time ago. It gave me nightmares for a while."

"I can't believe that's been in our world all this time."

Meanwhile Astral had sent Frozen Fire to Abhainn, Kerozonia's largest city. She suspected Visrel would place another spell in city on the banks of the River Uisge. They were waiting under a bridge; though the air was filled with the sound of the city the bank of the river was empty apart from the five of them. It seemed like the kind of place Visrel would place a spell so as not to draw attention.

"Wow, that's some crazy graffiti," said Gretchen looking at the wall. "There's much nicer artwork in the alleys back home."

"Neither you or I can judge anyone on the craziness of their artistic expression," said Zack. "Assuming it's that and not just plain vandalism. And your stuff is still creepier."

"I don't think it was an artistic flare they were expressing," said Eric. Everyone turned their heads slightly.

"Whoa!" said everyone.

"Getting back to the matter at hand," said Patrick "Has Visrel thought about it being more likely that someone could find the spell in the city?"

"He'll probably mask it," said Gretchen.

"Yeah, but beforehand someone could find him. We're still in the middle of the city, it won't be subtle to fight him here."

"Unless he masks the fight," suggested Malcolm. Suddenly the Anti-Gamer appeared and was taken aback when he saw Frozen Fire.

"You're here first?" said Visrel. "That is very troublesome."

"We're on to your plan tough guy," said Zack.

"You're going to use our home to wreck Miyamoto," said Gretchen.

"Typical. Astral gets couple of the pieces and make the whole picture," sighed Visrel. "Yes, I'm planning to plummet this whole floating rock into Miyamoto ending it at last. And as a bonus I get rid of the five of you at the same time."

"Charming," said Eric in a flat tone. "A real sweet talker this one."

"Now that we know your plan it won't be hard to stop it," said Patrick.

"Oh, I disagree," responded Visrel. "You see all I need is monsters to keep you busy long enough at each turn and you won't be able to do a thing. Speaking of which..." He snapped his fingers and a cardboard box appeared of the ground. "Oh, and a little spell to make sure no one stumbles upon us." He raised his arms and what appeared to be a dome of magic covered the whole area, and though you could not see it after a moment you knew it was still there. Suddenly the box flew open and something came out. It was like a body from the waist up coming out of the box made out of plastic waste. The torn up packaging and broken wires gave the creature a rather bulky look.

"A trash monster? Seriously!" exclaimed Zack. The monster lunged and pushed Frozen Fire away from Visrel.

"Oh no, he was right," said Malcolm.

"We'll make him wrong," said Gretchen. They summoned their weapons and got ready to fight. The monster swung its arms at them but they dodged. Eric sent a wave of fire at it trying to melt it but it swung at him making him stop. Gretchen and Patrick charged and stabbed it with their weapons. The monster swung at them to get them to move and pulled the weapons out of its body, but a bolt of lightning fired from Malcolm's fingers and a block of ice thrown by Zack hit the monster in its head making it drop them. It lifted itself up and slammed its box on the ground causing it to shake and making Frozen Fire fall over. Malcolm fired arrows at the monster allowing the others time to get back up and then a couple whacks from Zack's staff allowed Malcolm to get up. It swung its arm down but it was immobilized in mid-air by Patrick's time energy. Eric slashed it with his scythe and Gretchen slammed it with a shadow road sign. The monster summoned energy balls in his hands and threw them at Frozen Fire. Zack covered them with a snow-screen hiding them from the monster's aim. While it scanned the area for them Malcolm hit it with electrified arrows and Patrick hit it with a temporal pulse. The monster swung its arms again, but they dodged and Eric retaliated with a huge fire ball and Gretchen, who had been charging her magic, hit the monster with a copy of its own arm. The monster started throwing energy balls again making them scatter. Patrick sped himself up and rushed the monster with sword slashes and Gretchen struck it with her halberd then a shadow frying pan. Next came a lightning bolt punch from Malcolm and then Eric struck the ground with his scythe causing fire to erupt underneath it and finally Zack hit it with several icicle kunai and a large snowflake shuriken. The monster tried slamming the ground with its box again, trying to knock Frozen Fire over. But before it could slam the ground again Eric threw a fire ball underneath it which exploded when the monster struck unbalancing it. Malcolm sent a bolt of lightning down on it before it could steady its self and then Zack and Gretchen hit it with a block of ice and a shadow wave knocking it to the ground. Patrick stabbed the monster with a time magic boosted sword and it burst into magic. Frozen Fire were left alone, There was no sign of Visrel.

"Great, he got away," complained Patrick. "I hate how it's become the norm to chase him all over Miyamoto and Kerozonia."

"Personally I don't believe in the norm," said Zack. "How can there be a normal if what's normal changes from person to person. It's just something people made to distance themselves from the more obviously different. There's no such thing as normal."

"We'd better go and report to Astral," said Eric. "With any luck she'll have a backup plan so we don't have to run all over the place.

Frozen Fire returned to Adlez Castle. While looking to find Astral they overheard raised voices.

"But why seal it in our world?" came the voice of Hitbox. "Why not in the Free Space?"

"My predecessors did not have the time to lure it away," said the voice of Astral. "It had to be sealed where it was. I know it's a frightening thought but all four worlds and Frozen Fire's world have dangerous creatures sealed away somewhere. I've heard stories of a sight monster that stole people's vision and a seaweed creature that wants to turn the sea to chaos." Frozen Fire wondered whether they should knock when Cyanna appeared around the corner and motioned for them to come over.

"Hitbox has read something a little unsettling," explained Cyanna. "Best just to leave Astral to it. Let's go check on the leaders." She lead them to the meeting room where they found King Hud, Lord Iron, Lady Larch and Elder Stratus had gathered around an old book.

"Ok, so we don't actually need to be at the tower to do this," mused Iron.

"The real question is can it be done with that barrier there?" grumbled Status.

"The answer won't be in this book, we'll just have to try," said Larch.

"I'm afraid to ask what this is about," said Gretchen.

"Grandfather is planning to try and deactivate Connection Tower," explained Cyanna.

"Can they do that?" asked Zack.

"It would seem so."

"Ok, so we're agreed we'll give this plan a whirl," stated Hud which was met with agreement. "If it doesn't work while the barrier is in place Astral can come up with a plan to get rid of it and then we deactivate it. And then I can finally get peace to have a tea party on the teacup ride."

"Not after what happened last year you won't, grandad."

"It strikes me as very likely the Anti-Gamer will try and reactivate the tower," observed Stratus.

"We just need to tighten security," said Larch. "Plenty of dangerous trap spells and some wild dogs ought to do it."

"You suggest we use wild dogs an awful lot," said Iron. "And we only get domesticated ones in Miyamoto."

"Visrel has always been able to get past Astral's shields," said Hud. "So we need to think what he can't get past. Perhaps we should just fill the tower with wasp nests. Or we could look out that really dreadful wall paper from my son's student days; nobody ever wanted to go near that." Astral entered the room and Cyanna left to check on Hitbox. Frozen Fire updated Astral on what happened.

"Well, your majesty, seems like we'd better give your plan a try," said Astral. She noticed that they were all gathered around the book. "Those books are meant to be for royal eyes only. You've got to stop showing them to everyone."

"Hogwash. It's only the other leaders," said Hud defensively. "Hardly anyone. I'm sure Cyanna and Hitbox will let Frozen Fire see it eventually. And once or twice I gave one those forbidden spells to the cleaning staff. Sure, we don't have the north-west tower anymore but you can't deny it's spotless. And I used a book of poetry from there to woo my beloved wife."

"Sounded like a book of war tactics to me," said Stratus.

"Oh, be quiet, elder."

"You showed me that book too, definitely about war," said Iron.

"That movie I lent you ages ago was in the north-west tower," said Larch. Frozen Fire were trying not to laugh.

"In any case I'm sure Visrel's barrier will interfere with the deactivation spell," said Astral getting the topic back on track. "I might be able to deal with it by myself but the Anti-Gamer will have thought of that and has probably set up an alarm in case I try. So we'll have to do it another way. I guess we better reassemble the Dagger of Claws."

"Dagger of Claws? For real?" said Zack.

"It's a dagger made from the claws of many magical beasts, dragons, phoenixes, rain birds, barghests, tengus, chimera and such gifted to our ancestors mostly. As such it's imbued with a lot of magic and can cut open just about any magical seal."

"Uh, and it's at the back of some nasty dungeon we have to deal with?" grumbled Gretchen.

"Naturally we hid it away as it could potentially be used to open the door at Game's Edge. In fact it was magically split into three smaller daggers and given to previous leaders of the ore.rar, the acorn.ris and the cloud.tiff so their whereabouts should be known to the current leaders."

"Why are these magic things never whole?" questioned Eric.

"Our part of the dagger is within an empty underground labyrinth like cave," said Iron.

"We keep our one inside a giant tree in a deep dark part of the forest," said Larch.

"And the third is in that upside down supposedly haunted mansion on the bottom of our cloud bank," said Stratus.

"Your predecessors sound really spiteful," said Zack.

"Nothing to do but blitz through them as fast as we can," said Patrick.

"Excellent, then it's all settled," said Hud. "Frozen Fire will run all over the place getting the things while I stuff my face with festival doughnuts."

"He wants us to hate him," mumbled Malcolm to Zack. Zack nodded.

"I mean they're really good doughnuts. So, so good with the sprinkles and the jam and all the other trimmings. And I'm like a hundred so there aint much left that can be done do my body. HA HA HA! Although as its traditional to get a birthday card from the king when you reach a hundred, it is a bit weird to start sending them to yourself. Sending yourself valentine's cards isn't tragic so long as you remember the chocolates. Where was I? Oh yes! Sending Frozen Fire on another dangerous task." They glared at the king. "Fear not, Frozen Fire, I shall write songs of your bravery or rather

Cyanna will write them as it was voted that I am not allowed to write songs anymore."

"We must remember to ask about that one," said Gretchen.

"Head home, Frozen Fire," said Astral. "Leave the gathering of the dagger till tomorrow." So they returned to their world and relaxed.

Before they knew it, was the next day and they used their pendants to warp straight to the Steel Crater where they were met by Iron.

"Greetings my friends, I hope this day fares well for you," said the ore.rar.

"That'll depend on the dagger's hiding places," said Eric.

"We'd better waste no time. Follow me." They followed Iron through the city.

"We're heading for a labyrinth, right?" checked Patrick.

"That's correct," responded Iron. "It's a good hiding spot, and thanks to those pendants Astral made for you you'll be able to get out with no bother."

"Isn't it protected against teleportation?"

"Yes, but not Astral's magic."

"Why not just warp us straight to it?" wondered Eric

"She doesn't know its exact location."

"At least that's one less thing to worry about," said Zack. "Though there's usually a monster in these places."

"Nope, no minotaurs in this labyrinth," reassured Iron.

"They could still have gotten in."

"Hey, there aren't any traps in there are there?" asked Gretchen.

"I've no idea," said Iron realizing he'd never considered it. "It's a distinct possibility so watch your step and maybe stay away from the walls."

"I'm gonna kick that king in his head one of these days."

"I'm guessing that's it," said Malcolm gesturing ahead. There was a large entrance into the side of the crater in front of them. On both sides carved into the stone were depictions of ore.rar holding up one of their hands as if to say "Go no further." There was a sign post next to it that read:

WARNING!

At the bottom of these stairs is a complex labyrinth.
Entrance is completely forbidden, if you enter
without permission (and get out)
You will receive full punishment. No exceptions!
(except looking for lost children.)
There is no treasure hidden here. Absolutely none
whatsoever. Not a spot of gold.
Not a thing. It's empty. Nothing to be found. So
don't bother looking.

"How many people have gone in there?" asked Zack.

"About three," replied Iron. "They came running back out, they were scared of spiders. Which is ridiculous for an ore.rar. They can't bite us and they're not even poisonous. And more to point we're immune to poison."

"Bet you're still weak to fire and lightning," said Eric.

"Time's a-wasting, boys, let's get it over with," said Gretchen. With a wish of good luck from Iron, Frozen Fire descended the steps into the cavern. The cave was dark and dry but there was a luminescent moss covering the walls allowing them to see where they were going. Apart from that there was not much to the grey stone that surrounded them, no carvings, no insect nests, no other plant life, not a sound and not a smell. They set off into the winding tunnels pausing only the decide where to go when they arrived at an intersection.

"You think Iron would've given us some directions," said Patrick.

"I doubt even he knows the way to the dagger," said Zack. "Everything looks the same down here; how could anyone tell."

"In this sort of story people usually leave a trail to find the way back," said Gretchen. "I wish we'd thought of that before we came down here. We don't have any paper or bread crumbs. And I don't think anybody brought a pen or something to help us track where we been. Oh no!"

"This moss is sturdy I don't think we could leave a trail in it," observed Patrick poking the moss.

"It must be magic, how else would it last?" said Eric. "It's probably fireproof otherwise I'd burn us a trail. And you'd all have to buy me lunch as a thank you."

"What about a trail of ice?" Malcolm said to Zack. Zack held his hand up to the wall; his hand glowed with his magic and ice began to form on the wall.

"Once again ice triumphs where fire falters," remarked Zack.

"Quiet you," responded Eric.

"Make sure it's the non-melting stuff," said Patrick.

"I know!" So they set off again, this time with Zack leaving ice across the walls they passed allowing them to avoid retreading the same path. And after a while they found themselves in a large open cave, with only one way to and from it and a stone table with a small dagger on it.

"I'm so glad there were no traps," said Gretchen. "Though I suppose the table could be booby trapped.

"Well if a boulder starts chasing us we can warp out of here," said Eric.

"Can you guys hear that?" asked Patrick perking his ears.

"Uh oh. Big trouble," said Malcolm pointing upwards. Looking up a large figure dropped down from the ceiling. It landed with a thud in front of them it was a monster, it looked like a rhino but with claws on its feet that let it scale the walls, dark red skin with thorns, glowing black eyes and what looked like a harpoon instead of a horn.

"Can't say this surprises me," grumbled Zack as they summoned their weapons. The monster rushed at them trying to attack with its horn but everyone moved out of the way. Gretchen sent a shadow bench slamming into its side and then Zack slammed the other side with his staff covered in ice. The monster swung its horn at them but Patrick blocked with his sword, and when it tried to overpower him he used his magic to slow it down. Malcolm hit it with a lightning punch and Eric erupted flames underneath it. The monster started to fire energy beams from its eyes chasing Frozen Fire around with them. Zack threw a snowball which made a snow-screen around the monster distracting it. Eric covered his scythe in fire and threw it like a boomerang at the monster. Next a large time burst from Patrick followed by electrified arrows from Malcolm, and a shower of shadow copies of Gretchen's halberd. The monster lunged swiping with its claws and swinging its horn around trying to cut whoever it could reach. Zack counter-attacked with icicle kunai and Eric surrounded it in a flame twister. The monster cleared the twister with its energy beams but Malcolm made a stream of lightning appear in his hand and threw it like a rope around the monster's horn electrocuting it. Gretchen then struck with a shadow wave and Patrick, inspired by Malcolm, used his temporal energy to form a pocket watch and spun it around, but rather than use it like a rope he used it like a flail to strike the monster with. The monster jumped and slammed the ground with enough force to knock everyone over. When it started to advance Gretchen sank into her shadow which moved underneath the monster and a large shadow boot kicked it away. It tried firing beams again but Malcolm stopped them with more arrows and another couple to hit the monster. Patrick attacked with rapid time slashes, Eric with a giant fire ball and Zack dropped a snowman on it. The monster charged horn first at them; it slammed into a wall of ice which stopped it but knocked Zack backwards. Eric slashed it with his scythe, Malcolm threw lightning balls at it, Gretchen lobbed shadow books and Patrick hit it with a temporal pulse. In a last ditch effort, the monster charged and fired beams at them but Zack covered its feet in ice making in slide over the ground. It spun towards Gretchen who knocked it away with her halberd with a shadow anvil on the end. Next it flew towards Patrick who sent it away with a blast of time magic and when it got near Eric he made fire explode beneath it. The monster finally came to a stop in front of Malcolm who readied three arrows and when he shot them they blasted like bolts of lightning. The monster burst into magic and dissipated. Frozen Fire breathed easy for a moment before at last moving over and retrieving the dagger. The dagger piece was small like a kitchen knife; it looked rather blunt and was strangely yellow.

"Sheesh, I hope the whole one is a lot more impressive," said Gretchen. "Right now, it looks like it'd have trouble with butter let alone Visrel's barrier." They warped outside to report to Iron.

"Well, there wasn't a minotaur like you said," Zack told Iron when they got outside. "But there was a spiky rhino that could scale walls."

"Really? That's what happened to it," said Iron. "That monster attacked here ages ago when Visrel was making those towers to cut Miyamoto away from the Free Space. I can't believe it's been in there the whole time."

"I guess monsters don't have expiration dates," mused Eric. "On to the next part?"

"We better get them quick," said Patrick. "Unless you want something else, Iron?"

"Well, I do have a couch that needs moving," mused Iron.

"Let's move," said Malcolm. And with that they warped with their pendants again and disappeared in a flash of light.

"If they let me finish I would have said I wouldn't bother asking seeing as ore.rar are stronger than polygons or humans," Iron said to himself.

Frozen Fire rested briefly after giving the dagger piece to Astral. So before they knew it they were traipsing through the Assorted Tree Woodland following Larch.

"Now obviously it's well guarded," explained Larch who was jumping from the lower branches. "But the five of you have beaten plenty of monsters so this should be no trouble."

"It's nice to know you have confidence in us," said Zack.

"Yep and any monster in there will get thoroughly kicked out," said Gretchen.

"Oh, there won't be any of those virus freaks in there," said Larch. "There's no way they'd get past those puzzle and riddle spouting doors in there."

"That's not what you want to hear," said Zack.

"So this tree is filled with magic doors that give you riddles?" said Eric.

"Predominately," said Larch. "They're made to, you know, give a very hard task, to make sure not just anyone can get the riddles and puzzles, just those that happen to be the most common. Some of the later doors probably do something a little more devious. I think when making them they should have just made a series of questions that no-one could answer, unless they already knew and have them passed down in secret from leader to leader. Oh hey, we're here." Ahead of them was a gigantic tree made of a reddish wood, with dull green leaves and covered in plenty of fungi.

"So how do we get in?" asked Eric.

"Obviously the entrance is hidden," said Larch snapping her fingers. Suddenly a rectangular hole appeared in the tree leading inside. Frozen Fire headed inside; it was hollow yet it looked natural as opposed to having been hollowed out.

Sticks and braches coming out of the walls, leaves sprouting all over. There were steps leading up to a door which was the only thing inside that didn't look like it had always been there. They climbed up towards the door and before they could ask how it worked words appeared on it.

Everyday I'm given a gift

But I always pass it on to you

Though I don't always look the same

You always know it's me

"Why don't riddles ever make sense," groaned Zack.

"Well, it is protecting something," reminded Gretchen. "Better start puzzling, guys."

"Quite often the answer's a trick," mused Patrick. "Though not always."

"How do we in put the answer?" wondered Eric. "Do we just say it?"

"We really should have asked Larch more," said Zack in hindsight. Everyone tried to think of people and things that are always receiving and giving gifts and no matter how they appear are always recognisable. They came up with a few ideas.

"Trees?" suggested Gretchen. "They're always getting the gift of air and giving us the same gift. And there's a lot of varieties, but you always know a tree when you see one." But the door stayed shut.

"I doubt it'll give us one with an answer that's just outside," said Eric. "Perhaps it's a shape shifter of some sort."

"Isn't the point of shape shifting is that you don't always recognize it?"

"Oh, right, yeah."

"Maybe it's snow," suggested Zack. "The gift could be cold and it gets turned into all sort of snow structures." Still nothing.

"You've got snow for brains," mocked Patrick. He then yelped as an ice cube formed down the back of his jacket.

"The moon?" said Malcolm. The words on the door vanished and the door disappeared too. "The gift is the sunlight it reflects and it changes appearance all the time."

"That's one to Malcolm," said Zack.

"Speaking of which," said Patrick. "Has anyone ever asked how the sun and moon of Miymoto work?"

"I think Astral said they're projections of the ones in our world," said Gretchen. "I think they mimic the time in the time zone we're in." They moved up to the next door and when they approached words appeared on it.

A memory for all to see

Movement made to remain still

Or perhaps you were waiting for me to be made

We may gather together in a book

"Well what does that mean?" wondered Gretchen. They started to rack their brains again. "Perhaps a diary? No they're private and it is a book not something that gathers in them."

"What about words in the diary?" mused Zack. Nothing happened. "Doesn't explain the middle parts though."

"I've got it, a painting!" exclaimed Eric. Still nothing. "OK I guess painting is to broad, though I maintain the thought of a gallery catalogue was clever."

"Oh, photos," said Patrick. The words vanished then the door. "Gathering in a book is a photo album and you can pose for them or people take them of moving things."

"Good thinking, Patrick," complimented Zack. "Though I get the feeling riddle experts would mock us for not getting so soon." They proceeded again and soon faced another door. Yet when the words formed it was not a riddle.

Make the picture.

And beneath them appeared a picture of a group of acorn.ris moving through the trees of the woodland. Next a shelf came out of the door and on the end a container filled will pieces of the picture.

"A jigsaw! Didn't see that one coming," said Eric. Zack leant in close and started to examine the pieces.

"Great, we're gonna be here for ages," grumbled Gretchen. "If this thing's got five thousand pieces I'm going into the spirit world to give the guy who made it a good thump."

"Start with the edges?" suggested Malcolm.

"Everyone knows to do that."

"Maybe we should count the pieces to see how long we'll be," said Patrick. "If it's gonna take a while we'd be as well to get the other dagger part first."

"Looks like there's only about a hundred," observed Eric.

"I'd say only about fifty."

"Guys, I'm trying to concentrate," said Zack. Looking back at the shelf they saw Zack had already made up most of the edges and had started on the middle.

"Oh yeah, he's good with jigsaws," said Eric recalling sometimes from when they were younger. Zack was quickly making the picture and before they knew it he was done. The shelf retreated into the door which then vanished.

"Wonder how many doors there are?" mused Zack. "I think the space in here's warped and all." Proceeding onwards there was yet another door. After a general grumble the instructions appeared on the door.

Sometimes you need to be shown the answer

Words are fine but don't always work

So let me see the sky

And then I shall open the way.

"How are we supposed to show it the sky?" wondered Zack.

"I doubt we can carry it outside," mused Eric. "And I am not burning a hole in the tree. Larch does not strike me as one we should cross."

"Move over, ya art deco wannabes," said Gretchen. "There's a simple enough way to show people anything." She pulled out a pot containing her shadow paint with a brush still in it. She grabbed the brush and started painting.

"Art deco wannabes? That's one of your odder insults," said Zack. "And one of the few that doesn't involve a comparison to cheese."

"Wait, why did you have a paint pot with you?" question Patrick.

"Keep getting called here while I'm in the middle of painting, I sometimes I grab it in the rush to go," explained Gretchen without turning from what she was doing.

"Gretchen, yesterday we agreed on a time to meet up," Zack reminded her. "You forgot and Astral had to remind you. That's why you were in a panic."

"We can't all have your absurdity for being on time, Zackles."

"You were the only one who was late today," Eric pointed out. Gretchen flicked some paint back at them.

"The tasks set by these doors are getting odd," mused Patrick.

"Might be randomly generated," suggested Malcolm.

"We've really got stop skimping over asking for details before we're sent off on these things," said Zack putting his hand on his face.

"Done and done!" exclaimed Gretchen standing up. "I figured it'd be best to keep it simple." On the door she had used her paint to make clear depiction of the night sky. She used a technique where she only painted the dark parts and left the light parts clear: a sky full of stars, a couple of clouds, a crescent moon shaped just like her pendant and a couple large dragons. The words on the door changed.

You were meant to find and open a window

But I guess I'll accept that

"Much more easy-going than the other doors," said Gretchen. The door vanished and they moved on. And soon enough they were waiting on another puzzle. This time the door read:

Find the false reflection

Among these mirrors that lie

To find the false remember what's true

You'll find the key hole there

Four mirrors appeared around them. The reflections in which were all different, and the reflections of the reflections were different too. Unlike the house of mirrors at the festival, some were upside down, some were back to front and others showed them in different outfits.

"Oh man, this is giving me a headache," groaned Zack looking at all the mirrors.

"Is it dangerous to be in amongst multiple reflections of magical mirrors?" asked Patrick cautiously.

"I doubt these are strong enough to be troublesome," reassured Gretchen. "Either that or we're gonna be trapped in them if we get it wrong."

"How do we know the fake?" wondered Malcolm.

"One must be different from all the others," mused Zack. "They must all have something in common."

"Nothing to do but look," said Eric. "This'll strain the eyes, what a nuisance." Frozen Fire looked at every single reflection of themselves trying to find the one with the keyhole, but it was hard to tell which was different from all the others when they were all so different to begin with.

"AAARGH THIS IS GETTING ON MY NERVES!" yelled Zack.

"So much for that keen eyesight you're always bragging about," remarked Gretchen.

"DON'T START!"

"At least take a deep breath and calm down, you're making it freezing in here."

"Hey, I think I found it," said Eric making everyone turn. "Look in that one, everybody is reflecting the wrong motions." They followed to the spot he was pointing at, the fifth reflection in the mirror second on the right of the door. "All the other reflections copy our movements exactly but in this one Zack mimics Gretchen's movements, Gretchen mimics me, I mimic Malcolm, Malcolm mimics Patrick and Patrick mimics Zack."

"Can you see the key hole?" asked Patrick.

"Can hardly see it past the first four reflections. It's a real testament to my abilities that I was able to see all the discrepancies." Everyone gathered in closer to get a better look and as they did their reflections melded together and formed a keyhole shape. The mirrors vanished and the door vanished to.

"Wait, we only need to gather round the right mirror?" said Zack

"No, we all probably had to see the right reflection," mused Patrick. They proceeded through the door and at last came to the resting place of the second dagger piece. Breathing a sigh of relief about finally getting to rest their brains they picked up the dagger and returned outside to report to Larch before heading to Astral's temple to fill her in.

Back on Kerozonia Visrel had finished another spell. He couldn't help but wonder why Frozen Fire hadn't shown up at all during the last two. He thought they must be doing something else and had better find out what.

After having a rest Frozen Fire headed to the Solid Cloudbank and were soon being transported to its underside by Stratus on a floating cloud.

"This mansion is completely upside down," explained Stratus. "And there's no warped space in there so despite the fact that everything stays in its place gravity will work normal for you young lot. The rooms are quite large so you may have trouble reaching the doors."

"I've gotten really good at moving us through shadows," said Gretchen. "Getting from room to room won't be a problem."

"Well la-di-da, missy. Heaven forbid you tax your young brains."

"Listen, you grumpy thunder cloud, we've just spent ages taxing our brains," growled Zack. "An upside down mansion aint gonna be disorienting after the few days we've had. Being knocked around the ocean floor, being trapped in warped space, lost in an underground labyrinth and the aforementioned tree our brains have been plenty taxed." The elder didn't take kindly to Zack's attitude.

"You're a rude little blighter," snapped Stratus. "Don't you take that tone with me you irritable, high strung, teenage snowball!" Gretchen intervened when Zack opened his mouth to retaliate.

"Let's not shout the skies down," said Gretchen. "Elder, we're all just a little wound up from the last couple places."

"Why is there an upside down mansion anyway?" asked Patrick trying to change the subject. "Was it built specifically for the dagger?"

"No, it was there before," explained Stratus. "It just seemed like an ideal place to hide it. It was constructed years ago by a deranged cloud.tiff mostly known as Gravity Nimbus. He liked the idea of messing with gravity and studied various form of spacial magic. After doing a great favour for one of the previous leaders he asked for his reward to be the mansion and he used his space magic know-how to keep all the furniture on the floors, which are above instead of below. And of course he managed to make it so his magic would last, so it's all still there. It'll all be a little worn, it being such a hassle to get around, it was a decent place to hide something." Looking ahead they saw the mansion. Like all the buildings on the topside of the city it was made of clouds. It looked like a grand house that Gravity Nimbus must have

245

lived comfortably in despite the fact that it was completely the wrong way around.

"It's gonna be in the top of the house isn't it?" grumbled Eric. "Or the bottom rather, you know the top floor, I mean the bottom, forget it." Stratus snapped his fingers and the large front doors swung open.

"I'm going to close the door when you're inside," said Stratus. "I'm not hanging around waiting for your lot to come back out and I'm not going to heave myself back down here to close it. Just use your pendants to warp back on top. Oh and I can't guarantee there are no monsters in there; last time I checked on this place there was a window open so one could have crawled in." The cloud they were on carried them into the mansion's foyer. It was a very odd sight, seeing the stairs going down to the upper floor and somewhat unsettling to see the furniture up above.

"Why doesn't Astral just get the dagger pieces herself if she can warp straight to them?" wondered Zack as the cloud landed.

"Ah, she's probably making sure you get plenty of training," said Stratus as Frozen Fire got off the cloud. "Sure, you train with the prince a princess every week but you need some time dealing with places like this to keep you sharp. Good luck, young oddballs." The cloud carried Stratus back up and out the door and with another snap of his fingers the doors closed. Frozen Fire turned their heads up towards the stairs.

"Shall we check upstairs first?" asked Patrick. "I mean downstairs."

"I'm gonna dig up Gravity Nimbus and kick what's left of his head in," growled Gretchen.

"I know these carpets are just dreadful, ugh," said Eric in his not serious camp voice.

"I can thunder rope us up," said Malcolm.

"Nah, this'll be quicker," said Gretchen. Her shadow spread out beneath them and they sank into it, then it moved across the walls and the stairs and they came out of the shadows when they arrived on the first floor. Looking around they saw they were in a long hallway with many doors. All five of them groaned.

"Good grief, we'll be at this for ages," said Zack. "We'd better make sure to keep track of the rooms we've checked."

"It's gonna be pretty upsetting if we check all these rooms only to find out it was on the ground floor," said Eric.

"What did he even need this many rooms for?" wondered Patrick. "I guess he might have had a large family."

"Too bad the doors are just out reach of even the tallest of us," mused Gretchen. "We're not gonna be able to check a room each. Unless you all have a way to get yourselves up?" They shook their heads. In theory they might have been able to but they had not mastered those particular tricks: leaving, moving via shadows and grappling with thunder rope, the only way to get into a room. So they did what they could to check the rooms, Gretchen taking herself Eric and Patrick up into some rooms and Malcolm taking himself and Zack into others. They searched several rooms (while cursing the high ceilings) trying to guess which most likely had the dagger piece. They saw bathrooms and were glad the various water points were unaffected by the unusual gravity. They saw a few bedrooms and were glad nothing was falling out of the cupboards. There were spare rooms made to look nice and a library with stacks of books that just fell short of the ceiling. Finally, opening a large door at the end of the hallway they found the master bedroom. Zack called for the others to join him and Malcolm.

"This seems like the place it might be," he said as they lowered into the room.

"So long as we don't have to drop into the attic or climb up to the basement," said Eric.

"Ok, let's see, wardrobe, chest of drawers, perhaps under the bed?" mused Gretchen looking around. "Oh, that chest looks like the right sort of thing." There was a small fancy chest next to the large bed.

"How are we going to open it?" asked Patrick.

"I'm sure the thunder and shadow ropes could latch onto it," said Zack sitting down on a couch. A moment later Zack noticed something. "Wait, why isn't this sofa with the rest of the furniture?" The cushion he was sitting on sprang forward, throwing Zack to the floor. A pair of red eyes opened on the back of the couch and it began to advance.

"A couch monster?!" exclaimed Eric. "Does Visrel just pick bits of paper out of a hat with random things written on them for monster ideas?" Zack scrambled back to his feet and everyone summoned their weapons. The monster began to spray coin-shaped energy from behind the cushions that burst upon contact. Frozen Fire danced around the stream of coins and retaliated. Zack threw his icicle kunai and snowflake shurikens and Gretchen lobbed a shadow anvil at it. Malcolm pointed at the monster and it was blasted with lightning bolts from above, Eric erupted a tower of flames beneath it and Patrick blasted it with time energy. The monster fired a beam of energy from beneath the cushions at them. They attacked with their weapons: smack with the staff, stab with the halberd, slash with the scythe, shot with arrows and struck with the sword. The monster spat spikes at them which stuck in the ground before vanishing. They ran around trying to avoid the attacks; Zack made a snow-screen to give them some cover. The monster searched for them through the cloud of snowflakes but couldn't find them until Gretchen leapt out of its shadow and slammed it with her halberd which had a shadow hammerhead. The monster chased after her (with surprising ease for something that was basically a sofa) but ran into one of Patrick's time bursts. It was then hit with a stream of lightning and a jet of fire. The monster responded with another energy beam. As they ran around the attack to get in close the monster realized it was surrounded and flung cushions at them knocking them over. It spat spikes again, this time into the air so they'd rain down on Frozen Fire. Everyone had to scramble to avoid the attack and they were starting to get pretty ticked off. Eric went in with a flaming scythe swipe; next Patrick immobilized it while he got in a good few slashes with the sword; Malcolm fired an arrow that turned into a lightning punch and Gretchen threw shadow duplicates of her halberd at it. The monster fired another energy beam along with another spray of coins at them, when suddenly Zack appeared out of nowhere, swung his staff, covered in a thick block of ice, down on the monster. The monster's attack stopped dead and it burst into magic and vanished. It occurred to the others that they hadn't noticed Zack since they were all on the ground.

"Hang on when'd you get stealthy?" asked Eric.

"Was I?" said Zack. "How? There's nothing to hide behind and I didn't make a snow-screen."

"OK, either you're doing that thing again where you pretend you don't know what someone's taking about, or the rest of us were being idiotic. Now I doubt I was acting idiotic but at the same time I doubt you were really being a ninja, so I don't which it is. Hm." Zack gave his friend a look.

"I'm the stealthy one anyway," said Gretchen. "I'm a shadow elemental and I've gotten real good at taking us into shadows. So, no one's out-doing me." There was a cracking sound as Malcolm latched onto the chest lid with a thunder rope; he pulled it downwards and it opened. There was something inside but it wasn't falling out, so he latched another thunder rope onto it and pulled it down to them. The final dagger piece landed in front of them and they retrieved it.

"Better report in to the elder," said Patrick. "I can't wait to relax after the day we've had." And they used their pendants to leave the mansion.

Unfortunately while they were battling the monster Visrel had arrived at Adlez Castle. The throne room was swarming with talon-teeth which Cyanna and Hitbox were fighting, while Visrel stood in front of the king.

"How about that?" mused the Anti-Gamer. "I had no idea there was an instruction manual for Connection Tower."

"You'll not be getting your hands on it, you oversized sewer pipe," said Hud.

"You grandchildren are busy? How will a frail old man stop me?"

"I may be a ridiculous number in age, but I am not frail." The king held up his arms and sent a wave of magic at Visrel which he blocked with his own. The talon-teeth were thinning out, as Hitbox cut half of them down with a broad sword and Cyanna blasted the others with shots created by a tune on her clarinet. However, they couldn't get to their grandfather.

"Well, your majesty, your magic is strong," said Visrel.

"Where do you think those two got it from?" said Hud. "You've underestimated me like you underestimated Frozen Fire."

"You can be sure I'll never make that mistake again." The two stopped their magic, and Visrel held up the Virus's Spell Book. "The manual matters not, this is the only book I require. It has everything I need to end this world, at long last." Suddenly an arrow pierced the book and it flew out of Visrel's hand. Everyone turned. Frozen Fire had arrived and the arrow was from Malcolm.

"What happened to being able to sense our magic?" mocked Zack. Visrel motioned towards the book and it flew towards him. But Malcolm snapped his fingers causing the arrow to burst into lightning, blowing the book apart. Next,

Eric threw fireballs at the pages burning them up and the Virus's Spell Book was no more.

"If you had any emotions I bet you'd be pretty tired of us thwarting you all the time," remarked Gretchen.

"I've memorized the spells I need," said Visrel his face sour and fierce. "Besides, I'm not the only one who relied on a book." In a sudden movement he threw a burst of energy at the Connection Tower instruction manual, destroying it. Everyone yelled at this.

"I was using that to hold my drinks," snapped Hud. A flash of light and Astral appeared.

"You won't ever win, Anti-Gamer," she said.

"Strong words coming from you," said Visrel barely glancing behind her. "What sort of guardian has no offensive magic." He turned to face her. "Even with all your power you just leave the people of Miyamoto to do things themselves. Like that bridge that fell apart when I first fought Frozen Fire; you could have fixed it in an instant, instead you left the polygons to do the work."

"I'm not a guardian, I'm a watcher. I act as a guide and adviser to the people of Miyamoto not as some magical fix-it-all. Frozen Fire and the royal family are the guardians."

"And we've got many great builders in this land," added Hud. "She wouldn't dream of doing those fine men and woman out of a job. They make the finest underwear I've ever worn."

"That opens up a host of questions," mused Eric.

"I should have just sealed you away in the reflection of a mirror," Astral said to Visrel.

"But you didn't, you chose to send for a bunch of oddball gamers," said the Anti-Gamer. "And look at them, ready to fight me, but we won't battle just now. Tomorrow your floating home will plummet into this world. No doubt I'll see the five of you at the top of the tower." He threw his cape over himself and vanished.

"I take it without the manual we can't shut off the tower?" inquired Patrick.

"No, it contained the only known way to do it," explained Hud. "The many ways the tower could be used were in the single copy of that book. Not even those who watch passed on the knowledge. That plan is out the window and way way down and gone splat on the ground."

"I should be able to recreate the book with the remnants," said Astral. "But he vaporized it so just gathering enough to do it couldn't be done before tomorrow."

"Now what?" asked Malcolm.

"I'd say you all need a rest before tomorrow," said Cyanna. "You're just gonna have to stop him more directly."

"What about the Ice-Flame?" wondered Hitbox. "Surely he's going to head there to shut it off, but how?"

"There's no way to get to it," replied Eric. "If you could it'd be a huge tourist attraction and everyone in Kerozonia would have seen by the time they were five."

"All that rock and earth that makes up the base of Kerozonia is in the way," said Gretchen. "And every attempt to get to it fails."

"Has he considered the fact that the Ice-Flame is protected?" wondered Zack. "It prevents anyone from falling off the edge of the island so surely it's protected too?"

"He'll most likely be able to open a rift straight to it," explained Astral. "If he's learned how to open a giant one beneath Kerozonia he should be able open one directly to Kerozonia' heart."

"Looks like the five of you'll be following him through that rift," mused Hud. "Oh, hang on, that gives me an idea! And don't worry, this one doesn't involve any wild goose chases." After listening to the king's latest idea Frozen Fire returned to their world for the night.

The following day they met up before returning to Miyamoto.

"It'll be quite a sight if we do see the Heart of Kerozonia," mused Zack. "No one in living memory has seen it."

"At least we get to see all the great sights while fighting this lunatic," said Gretchen. "Too bad there's always a monster."

"We won't really get a chance to admire the Ice-Flame," Eric pointed out. "We'll need to get right out of there if the king's plan works. And he's the only person whose plans always work."

"Everyone ready for this?" asked Malcolm.

"I don't think we're getting a choice," said Patrick. "Oh well, we've been pretty successful so far."

Soon enough Astral called them to Miyamoto and they transported themselves to Connection Tower. There was a lot of magic building up at the top.

"The tower is going to activate any moment," said Astral. "You'd better go." She produced the three dagger pieces and they floated in front of her. She held her arms either side of them and light shone from one to the other; the pieces rushed together. They swirled in a ball of light and a second later a full-sized dagger appeared from it. The handle had a bestial design and the blade looked like the claws and talons it was made from. "Here it is, a Dagger of Bones made from the claws gifted to us by magical beasts. Not a unique item, others have been made in the past, but this is the only one in Miyamoto."

"Any last advice?" asked Zack.

"You've fought him three times in the past but he's bound to have new tricks," said Astral taking the dagger. She stabbed the blade into the barrier and ran it down to the ground; it split open where it had touched and an entry way appeared.

"Here we go again," said Gretchen. "If he wasn't always trying to kill us it might actually be rather methodical to kick his rear all the time." Frozen Fire entered through the hole, burst through the door and ran up the stairs. Soon enough they emerged on the top of the tower, their weapons at the ready. Visrel had been looking at the door, no doubt waiting from them to arrive. The roof was covered in things that surely made the spell Visrel was using to help him control the tower; the whole place was surging with magic.

"Did they not warn the people that the world was about to end?" mused Visrel. "It seems unusual that the festival is still going on when the sky is going to come crashing down."

"You've had a terrible success record," remarked Eric. "Third time was not the charm for you."

"There you go again with all that bravado but you don't fool me. I know how scared the five of you really are."

"Maybe all our bragging is just to mask our self-doubt," said Zack. "You even managed to use it against us once. But it didn't work. We realized that we had all faced trials that gave us our magic so we knew we could face you as well. And using the bridge to throw you into your own magic was a real confidence booster."

"You're a monster, you wouldn't understand," said Gretchen. "You're just an empty husk of evil. We've all heard the stories; other monsters mimic emotions and make personalities, but you don't even try, you just act cold and hollow."

"I may not understand your doubt or courage," said Visrel. "But I know hatred and how to act on it most cruelly."

"We've noticed," said Patrick. "But all that cruelty never does you any good."

"We stop you every time," said Eric. "Usually at the last minute, but still."

"This time'll be no different," said Malcolm. The magic surging over the tower, fired upwards and spread over the sky.

"The rifts are opening; will you dare follow me to the depths of Kerozonia?" wondered Visrel.

"How are you even going to stop the Ice Flame?" asked Eric. "It's an unnaturally powerful magical force. Even you can't destroy it easily."

"The Virus's Spell Book had an incredibly powerful magic neutralizing spell." A hole in the air opened right behind the Anti-Gamer. He turned and went through and Frozen Fire gave chase. They found themselves in a surprisingly spacious cave and they could sense more magic than they had ever felt before. The cave was not dark, it was illuminated by something that sat in the middle of cave. It was the Ice Flame; about half the size of an average person, it was a sight to behold. Half of it was fire as hot as the height of summer the other was ice that stuck out and was as cold as the darkest winter's night. The ice and fire weren't side by side, they were mixed together in a manner similar to a chequer pattern. It floated off the ground and you could feel its never ending magic floating all over. Frozen Fire were captivated by it but only for a moment as Visrel moved in front of them.

"All right, tough guy, you're not gonna do this," said Patrick. "You've not got a chance with the five of us here."

"So this is what you get your 'team name' from is it?" said Visrel ignoring the last comment. "Truly it is the most remarkable magical force in both worlds. It's wasted here, it could do so many wonderful things."

"Not sure many would agree with what you'd call wonderful," said Zack. The Anti-Gamer turned around to face them.

"No, I don't think many would," he mused. "But it matters not." He snapped his fingers and archaic items for making a dangerous spell appeared close to the ice flame and began to build their magic. "It won't be here for too much longer."

"Oh yeah? You think so?" said Gretchen. She threw a shadow wave at the spell but it crashed into some sort of invisible barrier when Visrel waved his arm. "Would it kill you to make it easy for us?" Visrel summoned his helical blade.

"We can still get to it," said Malcolm.

"Just need to wallop one bad guy," said Eric.

Visrel charged, blade forward, but they manoeuvred out of the way. He was about to turn and attack but he was hit by sped up sword slash from Patrick. As he staggered backwards Zack hit one leg with his staff and Gretchen hit the other with her halberd, toppling the Anti-Gamer over. However, as soon as he landed on the ground he sprang back up without moving his body, but ended up getting hit by Eric's scythe. Visrel swung his arm and a wave of energy balls scattered around the cave, Malcolm managed to avoid them and sent a volley of arrows at him. Visrel swung his blade downwards which sent cutting energy towards Frozen Fire. Zack appeared out of nowhere and threw icicle kunai at him. As Visrel sent another cutting energy wave at Zack and then Gretchen threw a shadow anvil at him. The others followed, a lightning punch, an eruption of flames and being struck with a time magic pendulum. Visrel fired an energy beam at them. It wasn't easy to avoid attacks in the cave; luckily the Ice Flame prevented cave-ins. The neutralisation spell was building as Visrel sent another volley of energy balls at them. Zack made a snow-screen for cover, but Visrel waved his arm and it vanished. Eric hit him with a blazing scythe strike, and Gretchen hit him with a shadow spade. Visrel swung his blade but was blocked by Patrick's sword and Malcolm grabbed him and gave him a shock. Visrel released a burst of energy to make them move away from him, but Zack had covered his armour boots in ice, making the Anti-Gamer slip over. This time he crashed to the ground. On the ground Visrel swung his cape which sent a blast of air knocking everyone over. He got up and floated over them. Malcolm fired a stream of lightning giving them the time to get back up. Next Zack threw snowflake shurikens that struck Visrel all over. Visrel then charged at him swinging his blade which ended up clashing with Gretchen's halberd while a duplicate struck the monster himself. Next a large fire ball and time blast knocked Visrel back to the ground. The Anti-Gamer clapped his hands together and a shockwave shot through the cavern. Gretchen ran at Visrel who saw her coming and thrust his blade right at her head but was taken aback when she turned into a shadow and his blade passed right threw her. Even more so, when she still as a shadow she managed to punch him in the face. Next Visrel was hit by a temporal sword slash and was struck by a thunder rope. As he fired a beam of energy at Patrick and Malcolm, Zack leapt out of nowhere and struck him with his staff and then Eric attacked with his scythe. The Anti-Gamer punched the ground making it shake and making Frozen Fire fall over.

"Both my spells are nearly ready, you haven't the time to stop me," gloated Visrel.

"Unless something distracts you greatly," said Gretchen.

Back at the top of Connection Tower Visrel's rift spell was being destroyed. Hitbox split most of the items in half with a great axe and Cyanna played a tune on her pan pipes that made beams of light blast everything else. The spell began to fail and the tower's power began to return and the rift began to close. The siblings high fived.

Visrel turned towards the rift leading back to the tower and saw what had happened.

"No! Those blasted Knils!" he yelled. While he was distracted Frozen Fire each charged an attack and blasted his neutralisation spell, destroying it.

"I love how you always fall for our tricks," mocked Zack as they got up. Before the Anti-Gamer could respond they blasted him with more attacks and scrambled through the rift back to the Connection Tower.

"You got the other spell?" asked Hitbox when the made it to the tower.

"Yes!" replied Zack rather indignantly.

"Didn't doubt you," assured Cyanna. "But we're not done yet." Turning around they saw Visrel forcing his way through the closing rift. He stood glaring at everyone as the last of his spells vanished.

"You gonna turn into a big beast again?" asked Gretchen in a mocking tone.

"No, I'm going to let someone else kill you," snarled the Anti-Gamer. "I saved a little of the tower's powers just in case I was too close to the blast radius. Instead I'll use it to bring you with me to go see someone." With a motion of his hand energy surged everywhere and magic light blinded everyone. When it cleared the prince and princess were alone on the tower again.

"That's not good," said Cyanna.

"Better go tell Astral," said Hitbox.

Frozen Fire suddenly found themselves on the other side of Miyamoto.

"Isn't this Signati Island?" said Eric. They were back on the island near the cliffs.

"Where's Visrel?" wondered Patrick looking around. Suddenly there was a loud bang and the sound of something shaking.

"That can't be good," said Malcolm. Frozen Fire moved to where the sound came from. There was another loud bang as they emerged on the cliff top. Once again they were overlooking the Other Door and Visrel was floating in the air in front of it.

"I imagine you've heard of this door by now?" he called to them without turning around. "But I doubt you know what's kept behind it. Few do, but I'll be glad to let you in on this secret." He covered himself in magic and shot at the door, crashing into it making another bang. The door shook and began to crack.

"I don't think we want to see this one through," mused Zack. They threw attacks at the Anti-Gamer but he just moved out of the way and then turned towards them.

"As you know this realm is shaped by computer data," began Visrel. "But glitches can warp that data."

"Glitches? What are you on about?" questioned Eric.

"Glitches alter the shaping. That's why there are trees that are shaped strangely or why there are fields of indigo grass. But one glitch grew out of control and rampaged all across this world, so the one who watched back then sealed it behind this door."

"That's an unsettling thing to hear," said Patrick.

"Had she not been so unpredictable I'd have let her out the first time I tried to destroy Miyamoto."

"We're not doubting your malice," said Gretchen.

"But perhaps one rampage will do to take care of the five of you." Visrel turned back to the door. "One more and she's out." Frozen Fire threw more attacks but he just dodged them. Suddenly a magical barrier appeared around the door, looking over they saw Astral floating in the air too.

"I will not let you set that out of control thing free," said Astral.

"Oh Astral, when have your barriers ever stopped me?" mocked Visrel. He covered himself in more magic and shot towards the door again. He smashed right through Astral's barrier which shattered like glass and crashed into the door. The cracks spread and some kind of magic flared out and then seemed to flicker out. The Anti-Gamer turned back to Frozen Fire. "Glacis, Shadows, Flare, Spark, Tempus, I'd like you to meet the Absent Number." He threw his cape over himself and vanished. Some sort of growling noise started behind the door.

"Frozen Fire, I need you to subdue her so I can reseal her," said Astral. The doors began to open, the ground rumbled as they moved and stopped with a thud. Sound came from within; it sounded like both a screech and a cackle as if it was trying to do both. A hand reached out from the darkness; it was large with a bracelet that looked like a shackle. Another hand came out and the two arms pulled themselves forward and the top of the body appeared. Frozen Fire got a start. It dragged the rest of its body out of the door. For some reason it seemed to have another two hands instead of feet but they were the other way around. It had wild white hair that stuck up in spikes, some kind of cloth seemed to be pulled over the top of her face, but with holes for her four red eyes. The top two eyes were looking in odd directions while the bottom two were looking around as if to see where it was. It had tusks sticking out of its bottom jaw and teeth like blades from the top jaw; all her teeth were red. It moved around on its top arms and its knees; the bottom hands were gripping the ground too. It was covered in strange clothes, it had to have been around twenty feet tall, its skin was a dark green and round its neck was a pendant with the number zero on it. The Absent Number let out another screech-cackle.

"Great Hud's stone underwear!" exclaimed Zack moving his goggles over his eyes. The Absent Number finally spotted Frozen Fire and began to move towards them.

"This is in no way a good thing," said Gretchen. They still had their weapons from their fight with Visrel so they readied themselves for battle. The monster pulled herself up to the cliff and charged up energy in her mouth and fired a beam at them. They dived out of the way, the ground exploding where the beam hit.

"There are a lot more explosions in our lives these days," grumbled Patrick. Eric sent a jet of fire at the monster's face. Gretchen followed up by throwing a shadow mallet in the face as well. The monster slammed the cliff side with her arms shaking the whole island, Zack threw a snowman at her. She went to slam again but Patrick threw a series of clocks made of time magic at one arm and Malcolm fired a stream of lightning from two of his fingers at the other. Letting out another screech-cackle the Absent Number pulled herself up onto the cliff top and loomed over Frozen Fire. Energy flickered in her bottom eyes and they fired a stream of burning white energy at them.

"That stuff's not fire!" warned Eric after they dodged. "It'll burn even me."

"There'll be no island left," observed Malcolm looking at the scorched trees. The Absent Number fired another beam from her mouth another part of the ground exploded. Zack hurled icicle kunai and snowflake shurikens at her and Gretchen struck with her halberd covered in shadows. Eric threw fireballs at her, Malcolm fired arrows at her and Patrick blasted her with a time burst. But the monster was not about to let up. Her top two eyes glowed with magic and the same kind of energy exploded underneath the ground. Eric threw his scythe like a blazing boomerang, Patrick attacked with a temporal slash, Malcolm with a lightning punch, Zack slammed her with his staff covered in a thick sheet of ice and Gretchen sent a shadow wave at the monster. The Absent Number retaliated with more burning white energy; the forest was reduced further as she slammed the ground shaking the island again. Frozen Fire collapsed. Gretchen sank them into a shadow and moved them in closer, Eric erupted some fire out of the shadow when they got close. Malcolm had lightning struck her from above; as they came back out Patrick shot her with a temporal pulse and Zack punched with a fist covered in dense ice. The monster's top eyes glowed again and more magic exploded under foot. Frozen Fire scrambled in all directions as she tried to blast them. Malcolm pointed at her head and a bolt of lightning struck her between her eyes. Zack threw a swarm of icicle kunai at the monster's arms and Eric sent a stream of fire at her. Gretchen charged her with a shadow car and Patrick threw a ball of time magic that exploded on contact. The Absent Number fired the burning energy from her bottom eyes again. Gretchen ran around the energy and attacked with her halberd and a couple of duplicates. Eric slashed with his scythe propelled by fire, Zack struck with his staff covered in sharp icicles, Malcolm shot arrows that exploded into lightning and Patrick struck with time magic covered sword. The monster fired more beams from her mouth; she did not hit them but they were pelted by rocks from the explosions. Every one of them knew they needed to hit her with stronger attacks so they gathered a lot of their magic. Zack threw a massive snowflake shuirken that slashed the monster, Gretchen made a duplicate of the Absent Number's arm and punched her, Eric threw a large fire ball that resembled a sun covering her in flames, Malcolm swung a thunder rope that exploded into lightning when it hit and Patrick covered his head and hands in time magic and fired it as a powerful beam. The monster was knocked backwards off the cliff and landed in the water but she got back up and slammed the cliff side again. Frozen Fire fell over, and the monster's arms came up over the cliff and her head reappeared as she pulled herself up. She fired more burning white energy at them. They ducked just in time.

"Let's combine our magic and slam her in the face," said Gretchen.

"Then we need to focus on a similar thing for it to work," said Zack.

"Let's go for an energy ball, better be quick," said Eric. Everyone poured their elements together, they swirled together and formed a large energy ball, split into equal fifths of fire, lightning, shadows, time magic and the blue energy which froze stuff. The Absent Number was almost completely back on top and Frozen Fire swung their arms as if they were throwing it and the energy ball shot at the monster and slammed into her head knocking her back over with a mighty blast and she crashed into the water again. The monster was dazed and Astral appeared above her: she held up her arms and she began to shine with magic the same light that shone from the cave from where the monster had escaped. Giant chains made of solid white light appeared one wrapped around each of the monster's limbs and they pulled her up and the chains wrapped around her until only her head and lower hands could be seen. More chains flew from the cave and latched onto the other ones and dragged the Absent Number back into the cave. When she was out of sight the stone doors slammed shut, the cracks made by Visrel's assault vanished and light shone from all the gaps indicating the door was sealed shut again. Frozen Fire lay on the ground catching their breath as things seemed calm again despite the fact that the island looked a fair bit different.

Visrel stood alone in the Free Space looking at the door to Miyamoto.

"Frozen Fire have become so strong," he thought to himself. "They'll most likely survive that battle with that glitch. How am I supposed to destroy Miyamoto with those five; that blasted royal family and that interfering watcher! And once again the royal family has brought my thoughts back to that strange power that seemed to be in the princess's blood. It was not her own power. I thought nothing of it but now I wonder. And every time I think of that strange magic I remember that song they sing. The one that mentions a god's might. Why does it seem like there's a connection? Perhaps it's time I learned the Data Realm's most hidden secrets."

Back at Adlez Castle Frozen Fire had their injuries treated.

"How do we keep coming though these things with nothing broken?" wondered Zack. "Especially when you consider what happened to Signati Island."

"I guess we're incredibly lucky," mused Gretchen. "Either that or for some reason all bad guys have terrible aim." Cyanna and Hitbox entered the room.

"Thank goodness you're all all right," said Cyanna. "I shudder at the thought of that creature being freed from behind the other door. Let's hope the Anti-Gamer will never try that again."

"If he does the two of you can fight it," said Eric. "It was firing magic out of most of her face. Not the most pleasant experience."

"Astral reinforced the seal; with any luck that's the last anyone will see of the Absent Number," said Hitbox. "Oh and I must ask you not to tell anyone about her. She's meant to be a secret to everybody except the royal family and Astral."

"Not even the other three leaders know," said Cyanna. "But try not to get used to getting in on royal secrets."

"The festival is still on right?" checked Patrick. "I think it just the pick me up we need. Once we've stopped hurting."

"Not before tomorrow then," mused Malcolm.

Hud burst into the room.

"You've done it again Frozen Fire!" exclaimed the king. "You even beat that thing that's uglier than my ex-girlfriend from seventy years ago. The five of you must be real masters of your elements by now. I'd tell the people to take to the streets and celebrate but you they're already doing that what with that festival and all. This world will never forget how often you've saved it. I'll make sure you get plenty of great things from the festival like that two-foot chocolate castle." Astral arrived.

"Ok, your majesties, I really think Frozen Fire should return home," she said.

So they warped back to their world where they sat round reflecting on yet another adventure.

"Funny to think we're going to be famous throughout Miyamoto," said Gretchen. "But nobody in our world will know."

"I wouldn't be surprised if my mum somehow knew," said Zack. "Which would be just as well because how do you explain this to anyone?"

"Even in a word full of magic there's plenty of disbelief," said Patrick. "Though to be fair the whole thing is very mad."

"Better start coming up with reasons for why we're covered in bandages and plasters," said Eric. "Usually I just say Gretchen and trolley and no one questions it."

"I go with skiing trouble," said Malcolm.

"I go with Gretchen as well," said Zack. "I've been beaten up by her more than bullies."

"Pfft wimp," said Gretchen. So everyone let out a sigh of relief that it'd be some time before their next battle and that the king had promised excessive amounts of chocolate.

Book Five

The Other Worlds

In Frozen Fire's world, magic is everywhere; it has its rules that cannot be broken. Emotion is the fuel of all magic, emotions are to be felt or used to make magic. When they are turned into a form apart from these it can lead to disaster when monsters are born. There was once a gamer who was so fed up of online bullying he actually started to hate the games themselves. Be he was still a gamer so he could not stand that he was being turned against the things he loved so he searched for a way to rid himself of these feelings. He found a spell and combined it with his computer and downloaded his hatred. He deleted the enchanted computer files that were made as a result and took to the battle against online bullying. But he didn't know about the Data Realm where computer data can come to life. So even though the files were gone his hatred wound up in the data and took on the form of a computer virus with physical form. But the Free Space is full of unstable magic and when it combines with emotions in a non-magical form true monsters are born. So the hatred and magic absorbed more computer viruses and the Anti-Gamer came to be. Don't blame the gamer for Visrel's cruelty; he could not have known what would be born and perhaps trying to stop the online bullies can be seen as balancing the scales.

These days Frozen Fire spent a fair amount of time in Miyamoto not just learning how to use their weapons and improving their elements. They had befriended the royal family of Miyamoto and the leaders of the ore.rar, the acorn.ris and the cloud.tiff and spent time with them. They had also discovered Miyamoto's own entertainment industry.

"I have so many theories now," declared Eric having just watched the newest episode of a Miyamotan TV series he had discovered.

"Do you often come up with these theories?" asked Gretchen.

"You would not believe the things I've predicted. And Zack can vouch for me."

"Maybe we aren't suited to being TV buddies." Meanwhile Patrick had asked Malcolm for some assistance on a driving game they had at the castle.

"How often do you play driving games?" asked Patrick having just seen how easily Malcolm cleared the race he was stuck on.

"I play all genres," replied Malcolm.

"At least you don't go on about how great you are all the time."

"Like you've never done that." Gretchen and Eric were now heading towards the throne room. They were passing by Cyanna's room and they could hear music.

"Is she playing two instruments?" wondered Eric.

"Surely she's teaching someone," said Gretchen. She knocked at the door and a second later the princess answered ocarina in hand. "You heading to the throne room soon? Huh?" Looking behind the princess they saw someone else in the room with an ocarina that looked like it was made from ice.

"Zack?" they said together. Suddenly there was a snow-screen but Eric made it melt as quickly as it formed.

"Zack, that's not gonna work on us," he said. Zack was gone. "What the…? Since when can he actually ninja vanish?"

"Sorry, who are you talking about?" asked Cyanna feining ignorance. "No one in here but me. Better head to the throne room." Cyanna just ignored the questions and lead the way through the castle. In the throne room King Hud, Prince Hitbox, Malcolm, Patrick and even Zack were waiting.

"You're not wanting us to know you're learning the ocarina?" Gretchen asked Zack.

"What are you talking about?" enquired Zack.

"Oh no you don't. None of that pretending you don't know what we're talking about that you're so good at. Me and Eric saw you in Cyanna's room."

"What on Zaffre would I be doing in a princess's bedroom?"

"In your case not much," remarked Eric.

"They didn't even say hello," said Hud. A flash of light and Astral appeared.

"Ah, the five of you are here," said Astral when she saw Frozen Fire.

"She didn't say hello either. Does no one greet their king anymore?"

"Grandad, clearly something is wrong," said Hitbox.

"I'm sorry, your majesty, but Visrel has been sighted," explained Astral and Frozen Fire knew trouble was about to begin. "He was seen in Lasseter."

"The world of made from animated movie data!" said Hud. "Why would he go there?"

"In the past he has gathered things from there and left. But this time is different. She who watches Lasseter has requested the presence from someone who has experience with the Anti-Gamer. Frozen Fire, it is time for you to see another of the Data Realm's worlds."

"For real we're going to another one?" said Zack. Astral nodded.

"All right. Wait, anything we should know?" asked Gretchen.

"Not necessarily," replied Astral. "The other who watches will tell you anything that you may need to know."

"Everywhere we go it's to fight a bad guy," grumbled Eric. "At least we don't have to walk."

"It'd be a long bus journey," mused Malcolm.

"Never thought we'd see another one of the other worlds," said Patrick. "This'll be ace!"

"No one from any of the worlds has been to another one of the worlds," said Hud. "It's believed in the early days of the Data Realm we were four tribes of polygons. But once they realized the danger that horrific monsters could appear in the Free Space, they had those who watch seal off the lands of each tribe behind the doors and from there they grew into the worlds they are. Since then only they who watch have had contact with any of the peoples of the other worlds, but only the others who watch. Of course you guys are humans from the non-data world so this doesn't count. Anyway good luck, don't die and all that." Cyanna and Hitbox wished them luck as well and then they were off.

In the Free Space in front of the cyan door to Miyamoto there was a bright flash and Astral and Frozen Fire appeared. They had been here once before and it looked just as it had then: As if they were standing in a starry sky which was covered by an aurora. And once again there were four doors: the blue one they had just come through to Miyamoto, the purple door ahead of them, the yellow door to their left and the black door to their right.

"Lasseter's behind the yellow door, right?" enquired Gretchen recalling Astral's explanation from the last time they were here.

"That's right," replied Astral setting off towards the yellow door. "Now I have to remain in Miyamoto so my counterpart will be your guide. You may recall I was born from the data of benevolent video game goddesses, whereas Lasseter's watchers are born from data of fairy godmothers and characters that fit into that particular archetype in films. You know the helpful old lady." They had arrived at the door and standing in front of it was a little old lady. While Astral was taller than all five of them, this woman was smaller than them all. She looked like her age rivalled that of King Hud and she was hunched over, balancing on a walking stick. Her outfit made her look like a priestess or a librarian. She had a big mischievous smirk on her face. "Frozen Fire, may I present Amaranth, she who watches over Lasseter."

"Heh heh heh, it's a pleasure to meet Astral's chosen guardians," said Amaranth. "Heh heh, well let's not waste any time, let's get going."

"Remember, Frozen Fire, be careful," said Astral. "I sense Visrel has got something very dangerous in mind."

A flash of light and Frozen Fire and Amaranth appeared on the other side of the yellow door. Unlike in Miyamoto the door was not overlooking a canyon across from a forest; the yellow door was on an island in the middle of a lake and the door itself was on a large rock. Apart from that the small island was empty but there seemed to be all kinds of life in the lake and plenty on the other shore. The flowers on the lakeshore grew in the shape of musical notes.

"Welcome to Lasseter," said Amaranth. "This is Boundary Lake. First of all, we're heading to the capital city. You can meet the royal family while I check the latest info on the Anti-Gamer."

"Whoa, yet another world," said Zack amazed. "Then again we've got loads of lakes and hills back home."

"The weather's a lot nicer, though," mused Eric. "Hardly any clouds here, can't remember the last time we saw the sky back home."

"This world's got talking animals right?" checked Gretchen. Amaranth nodded. "I bet animals get great treatment here."

"You'll still deck them if they upset you," remarked Zack. "We all know that's the only reason why you never kick animals back home."

"I'd never hit an animal."

"Yet you're OK with giving your best friends a good whack." Another flash of light and they had moved again. This time they were on the edge of a city.

"Do all four of you have similar powers?" Patrick asked Amaranth. "The way you warp is just like Astral's."

"All four of us who watch have the same magic despite each coming from different types of data," explained Amaranth. "None of us have any offensive capabilities but we can restore a whole city that's been reduced rubble in a heartbeat." They noticed that a girl who had been sitting on rock nearby came over to them.

"Amaranth! Is this the help you said you've sent for?" asked the girl.

"That's right, my girl," she replied. "The blue boy in goggles is Zackary Glacis, the girl with the cherries on her top is Gretchen Shadows, the boy all in red is Eric Flare, the blond boy with glasses is Malcolm Spark and the boy in the large black coat with the question mark on his top is Patrick Tempus. You lot, this is a member of Lasseter's royal family, Princess Armillo." She was a young girl with a bright shining face. She was bit younger than the five of them and she was dressed all in yellow. Her hair matched her clothes and came down in a long ponytail while a straw hat sat on top.

"It's pleasure to meet the five of you," said Armillo. "I welcome you to my home city, Elleb."

"Th... th... thanks," stammered Malcolm. "Nice to be here."

"You'll have to excuse most of the boys, your highness," said Gretchen. "They're not so good around new people."

"Come on, come on, time's a wasting!" exclaimed Amaranth. "Let's head to the castle right away." Amaranth set off into the city.

"Do ya need to say stuff like that?" Zack asked Gretchen as the others started to follow Amaranth.

"Sorry, don't think there's any harm explaining to people why you're standing there with that awkward look on your face," replied Gretchen

"Just remember I'm not comfortable with people knowing certain things." He set off after the others. Gretchen sighed and followed muttering to herself something about Asperger's. Elleb was full of all the bustle you'd expect in a city: polygons all over the streets. Nearly everyone had an animal. It occurred to Frozen Fire that all the buildings were shaped unusually: they resembled clocks, wardrobes, candelabras, even footstools.

"All the buildings look like furniture and things," observed Eric.

"The architects of this city had a lot of laughs," said Armillo. "In fact, check out the castle." Ahead of them was the castle, as big as Adlez Castle but it looked like a gigantic teapot. It was a little impressive how the building curved in just the right way and how the roof looked like the lid. They had even managed to build to one tower the castle had in a slant to resemble the spout and the other side of the castle had a large curve to its architecture making it looked like the handle. And all the nearest buildings were shaped like teacups. Frozen Fire gawked at the spectacle.

"Well, somebody liked a cuppa," remarked Gretchen.

"You think the spout has a large whistle as an alarm?" joked Zack. They soon found themselves entering the giant teapot and proceeding straight to the throne room. It was very similar to the one in Adlez Castle: a large room full of portraits of former rulers and a large throne near the back. The throne was made of gold with cushions for comfort. On it sat an elderly woman with grey hair; she was small and round. On her head was a crown decorated to look like a film reel wrapped around. Following behind Amaranth, Frozen Fire moved forward and stood before her. Armillo walked straight forward and stood beside the throne, like Cyanna and Hitbox always did.

"May I present Armillo's grandmother," said Amaranth. "The ruler of all Lasseter, Queen Prelap." Despite hearing them a lot Frozen Fire never quite got used to the strange names found in the Data Realm. Still, they resisted the urge to snigger and bowed before the queen, low enough to hide their smirks.

"So, this is the help you sent for, Amaranth," said Prelap. She had a more sensible voice than Hud, the kind that suggested she did have a sense of humour but it was best saved for later in the day.

"Yes, your majesty," replied Amaranth. "These five are from the human world. They have spent many a day in the world of video game data fighting the very villain that lurks in our world now. These young elementals call themselves Frozen Fire. We have Zack the Blizzard Ninja, Gretchen the Shadow Mimic, Eric the Blazing Knight, Malcolm the Lightning Archer and Patrick the Temporal Swordsman."

"Ice, shadow, fire, lightning and time? Quite the little ensemble of elements. Very well then, I welcome you all to our kingdom. Now obviously you know why you're here but can you find out what this Anti-Gamer is up to."

"To be honest, your majesty," began Gretchen. "We more sort of work out what he's up to. He really doesn't like to share." The queen's eyes moved from each of them. She wondered why Zack was nervously fiddling with his goggles and not looking at anyone and why neither Malcolm or Patrick where making eye contact either. It was probably just nerves but there was something she couldn't put her finger on. The other two seemed calm but she could feel their nerves. She had wanted to see the people she knew deal with this monster but Amaranth warned her something was not right and that they'd need help. She had only heard about them recently, second hand from Amaranth, who had heard it all from another who watched. She didn't know what to expect but yet she was still surprised and she didn't know what had surprised her. Frozen Fire tended to project an air of oddness. The reason why no-one they knew in Miyamoto had really noticed is because they were all used to King Hud who didn't so much project an air of oddness, as shout it from the roof tops, take it out for dinner and the throw a party in its honour. The queen suddenly noticed the room had gone quiet and everyone was now staring at her.

"Ahem, what's the latest on the monster?" Prelap asked Amaranth.

"Haven't checked yet," replied Amaranth.

"I heard he's on Celestial Mountain," said Armillo. Everyone turned to look at her. "The birds claim to have seen a man in a suit and cape on the mountain. The birds told each other, including Ollie my pet ostrich, who told me."

"Pet ostrich? You don't hear that often," said Eric.

"The bird's news chain is usually very reliable," mused Prelap. "Very well. Frozen Fire you must go and investigate Celestial Mountain."

"Celestial Mountain is a levitating peak," explained Amaranth. "The mountain itself is gigantic but it floats barely seven feet off the ground."

"That's less than Kerozonia," mused Gretchen. She noticed she was about to be asked. "It's the floating island we come from."

"It's what, ten to fifteen feet in the air?" added Eric.

"As I was saying," said Amaranth. "The mountain is surrounded by a field of harmless energy that makes it look like it's hanging in deep space. Now let's not waste much more time, let's go." In a flash of light Frozen Fire and Amaranth vanished.

"Only the tall girl and the fire boy seemed to speak," mused Prelap.

"The other three are probably just shy," said Armillo. "I got the impression that they're full of surprises."

Celestial Mountain indeed looked like it was hanging in space. It was surrounded by a makeshift sky; it wasn't actually black but a very dark purple. It was filled with light that looked like stars that sometimes gathered to look like galaxies. Looking down you could see the base wasn't touching the ground; the resulting height would intimidate even the most experienced mountain climbers. Frozen Fire found themselves about half way up on a surprisingly flat area.

"We're definitely higher than back home now," said Zack. They could all sense malevolent magic ahead.

"That's Visrel all right," said Patrick. "Doesn't seem like he's casting any spells."

"Think he knows we're here?" wondered Malcolm.

"It really varies with him," said Eric.

"Well, let's get to the fighting," said Gretchen. They moved forward and they saw the figure of the Anti-Gamer facing away from them.

"Can't even escape you in another world!" said Visrel. "I suppose not gathering things and then leaving straightaway was suspicious. I never showed any real interest in Lasseter." He turned to face them. "But now I have something far more fascinating to acquire here."

"Uh, what insane magic item's on the mountain," grumbled Gretchen.

"By here I refer to all of Lasseter not just this mountain. And I never said it was an item."

"Come on, just tell us your evil plan for once," said Zack.

"No. Now if you'll excuse me I was about to execute my plan." Visrel snapped his fingers and a monster leaped out from behind him. It landed in front of them. It took the form of a grotesque turtle but with the head and tail of a snake, a mouth full of fangs and instead of flippers in had clawed arms and legs.

"Where was that hiding?" wondered Eric. They summoned their weapons and got ready to battle. The monster stretched its head towards them and snapped with its sharp teeth. As the monster tried to bite them Zack struck its head with his staff knocking it away. Gretchen had darted around behind it and slammed its tail with a shadow plank. Next, Eric blasted it with a flaming star while Malcolm fired lightning at its head. As the monster reeled back Patrick slashed both its legs with his sword. The monster was not done yet; it whipped its tail forcing Frozen Fire to move back and then it swiped with its claws. They cut through the air and you could feel their sharpness just by looking at them. Eric countered the claws with his scythe, sparks flying everywhere when they clashed. Patrick blasted it with a time burst and though he hit the tough shell the monster was still hurt. Malcolm shot arrows at the monster's arms and Zack threw icicle kunai and snowflake shurikens at its head. Gretchen attacked all the soft bits she could reach with her halberd. The monster retreated into its shell but it slammed the ground with it causing everyone to lose balance and for rocks to fall down nearby. It slammed again and they realised it was trying to cause a rockslide. Malcolm fired three arrows that exploded into lightning when they hit, flipping the shell over. Gretchen covered her halberd in shadow spikes and thrust it into the hole where the head came out. She hit it but a moment later the head came out snapping at her; the rest of it reappeared and put itself back on its feet. Zack covered both ends of his staff in thick ice and smacked both its legs. Using temporal energy to extend its reach Patrick slashed its head with his sword and Eric threw his scythe like a blazing boomerang at it too. The monster started with its claws again this time swiping them much faster as well as lashing out with its tail. Malcolm latched onto one of its arms with a thunder rope and electrified it. Patrick surrounded it with several 'clocks' which each turned into a time burst. Gretchen put her hands together palms facing forward and fired a shadow cannon ball at it. The monster swung its arms trying to crush them with its fists so Eric made fire erupt beneath it. Though it was burned it didn't lose balance and its arms descend on them, but Zack blocked with an ice wall at the last second. The monster swung backwards as it was in agony. Zack seemed to realize something and made the wall fly at the monster and slam its head. It burst into magic and vanished. Zack looked surprised.

"I can't believe I did it," he said looking at his hands. He noticed his friends were about to ask. "That was diamond hard ice. The best for defence and offence."

"Diamond hard ice?" wondered Gretchen. "That's a thing?"

"Well, only magically as you'd expect. But very few people have ever mastered it, the Blizzard Master being one. It's a very advanced ability."

"Whoa! Ace one, Zack!" congratulated Patrick. "Being able to use advanced elemental skills is a sign you've mastered the element." Zack felt incredibly happy. He'd never expected this.

"I know I got my magic from a legendary ice elemental but I never thought I'd ever master it," said Zack. "Fantasise yes, actually happen, no."

"I'm sure we must be close to mastering our elements," said Eric. "So don't brag too much."

"We've come so far," said Malcolm. Everyone felt more confident than they had ever done before but soon they all remembered something.

"Uh oh, Visrel's putting his plan into motion," said Gretchen.

"How do we get hold of Amaranth?" wondered Eric. In a flash of light she appeared.

"We have to get moving," said Amaranth. "That Anti-Gamer has struck Elleb. He's gone and started a full-on raid."

Elleb castle was swarming with Visrel's talon-teeth.

"Don't worry, your majesty, I'll return what I take once I'm done," Visrel said to the queen. "But you have something of great value here."

"You don't actually think we keep powerful artefacts anywhere near the homes of the peoples?" demanded Prelap. Visrel smirked a smile that almost looked genuine.

"That's where you're wrong. You have no idea the power hidden here." The doors swung open and Frozen Fire barged in. "They've gotten quite quick at fighting monsters. But there're plenty talon-teeth to keep them busy. Good bye." Visrel left the throne room and Frozen Fire gave chase.

"Get back here, you lesser monster dispensing lunatic!" called Gretchen. They charged passed the queen who called a wish of good luck to them. When they left the throne room they were ambushed by several talon-teeth. But a second later they were blasted off them but there was no sign of the Anti-Gamer.

"What is that psycho up to now?!" growled Zack.

"Who knows? Apart from him," said Eric. They turned a corner and found an odd sight, an ostrich kicking away several of the monsters.

"Ugh, can't tell where the teeth end and the legs begin," stated the Ostrich.

"Oh, the princess said she had a pet ostrich," recalled Gretchen. The ostrich turned and spotted them. "You must be Ollie."

"That's me. You must be that Frozen Fire, Armillo mentioned. Never met a talking animal before?"

"I've met talking birds before," said Malcolm.

"Usually its only magical animals that can talk," said Gretchen. "So not ostriches."

"Can you help me? I need to find Armillo immediately!" cried Ollie who set off. Frozen Fire followed. "When that guy in the suit came past he said he was after her."

"Wait, Visrel's taking up princess kidnapping?!" said Zack confused.

"This is gonna get wired even by our standards," mused Patrick. They ran through the castle fighting hordes of talon-teeth along the way. Lightning and fire shot through the air knocking them aside. The ones that got close were frozen solid, the ones that gave chase were hit by shadows and time magic. Bursting into a large hall Frozen Fire and Ollie found Visrel and Armillo who was knocking away talon-teeth with a fishing rod.

"Bit of a peculiar weapon," mused the Anti-Gamer. "I guess I should be used to it with Flare fighting with a gardening tool."

"You've been hit by enough times," called Eric. Visrel and Armillo turned. Ollie ran forward and kicked Visrel in the chest knocking him over.

"Back off, Mr tiny moustache," warned Ollie. "When I'm with Armillo we're a deadly combination."

"You've got a sharp kick I'll give you that," said Visrel.

"Don't forget us," said Gretchen. "Get out of here princess!" Armillo climbed up on Ollie.

"Come on, Ollie, they've fought him plenty times before," said Armillo and Ollie fled the room.

"Ok, nut bag, let's do this," said Patrick. Visrel stood up.

"Not right now if you don't mind," he said. "But I'll tell you this: today Lasseter, tomorrow Prachett, the day after that Hartnell, the next again day back to Miyamoto and the day following that Miyamoto is destroyed once and for all." He turned and gave chase to the princess. Using her magic Gretchen stretched her shadow beneath all of them and they sank in. The shadow raced across the floor, and quickly overtook Visrel. They stopped and came out and Zack froze Visrel's boots making him slip. Patrick gave him a blast of time magic to slow him down and they were off again. Soon enough they caught up with Armillo and Ollie.

"We need to get you out of the castle," said Eric. Gretchen was concentrating hard and building her magic. She made a shadow cover part of the wall next to them. It looked almost like a tunnel.

"Everybody in!" instructed Gretchen. Zack shrugged and went through the shadow. "Don't worry princess you won't be harmed by any shadows while I'm here." Ollie carried the princess through, the rest of the boys followed and Gretchen went through last. The shadow disappeared behind her.

Far off from the castle a large shadow appeared and Frozen Fire, Armillo and Ollie emerged from it and clattered to the ground. They were surrounded by trees and everyone was generating light. All the leaves, flowers and fruit growing on the trees were glowing, even in the daylight. They were surrounded by light and even the grass on the ground seemed to shine.

"Whoa, where are we now?" said Zack.

"We're in the Glowing Forest," said Armillo. "We're a long way from Elleb."

"You can warp between shadows now!" Eric said to Gretchen.

"I'm so glad it worked," said Gretchen with a sigh of relief. "By the by, that's an advanced shadow move. So that means I'm a master elemental too." Gretchen was bragging when they heard something move nearby.

"It was just the wind in the tree," said Ollie while Frozen Fire looked around.

"Ollie, I can feel a magic that's not supposed to be here," said Armillo worried. Something flew at them with great speed but it was knocked away by Armillo's fishing rod. It looked like a levitating sheet with arms that someone had cut a mouth shape in to. Yet the claws and teeth looked very sharp. It charged again but it was blasted into nothing by Frozen Fire's five elements.

"Hang on wasn't that...?" Said Patrick confused. They suddenly realized someone else was nearby: a woman wrapped in a red coat wearing a hat with a gigantic brim and dark glasses that rather than look through she looked over the top.

"Hello darlings," she greeted. "It's been too long."

"PUTRICE?!" Frozen Fire cried together.

"You know this person?" inquired Armillo.

"She's a scientist who studies magic," explained Gretchen. "But she doesn't have any morals. She once tried to drain the magic and life out of Miyamoto."

"But last we heard she had gone on the run from the law," said Eric. "After her unethical experiments were leaked by Astral."

"It was such a shame it failed," sighed Putrice. "And even more infuriating living in hiding. But a couple days ago dear Visrel contacted me again. He felt his latest plan require some extra help, and I could not pass on a scientific opportunity like this."

"What was that sheet thing?" asked Ollie.

"She calls them data phantoms," replied Gretchen. "They were made from the magic she stole from Miyamoto."

"Luckily, when they were destroyed the magic returned to where it belonged," said Eric.

"There's so much loose magic in the Free Space," said Putrice. "Just like how Visrel can make so many monsters, I've been able to create an even larger number of phantoms than last time. Now then, darlings, you know we're after the princess and this forest is full of light; you can't hide here."

"You might not be able to," remarked Zack. He made a snowball and threw it at the ground and they were covered by a snow-screen. When it cleared they were gone. Putrice snapped her fingers and a large number of data phantoms appeared and began to swarm.

"Spread through the whole forest, my darlings," instructed Putrice. "Search every inch, I've heard Glacis has learned some genuine stealth and Shadows can hide them anywhere with her, well shadows." In an instant the forest was full of phantoms overturning everything to find Frozen Fire. As it happens they weren't hiding yet they were moving in the hope that Amaranth would find them soon a take them somewhere safe. Unfortunately they were now in another fight.

"So much for our hasty retreat," grumbled Patrick as he cut down some monsters.

"I can't get any peace to make another warping shadow," said Gretchen unleashing a shadow wave.

"There can only be a certain amount of them," said Zack freezing several and then smashing them with his staff.

"Let's try and get out of the forest at least," said Eric as he trapped a few in a fire twister.

"Which way?" questioned Malcolm firing arrows into the monsters.

"Follow us," said Armillo knocking away several monsters with her fishing rod and climbing onto Ollie's back. The ostrich kicked phantoms out of the way and charged through the trees and Frozen Fire followed. All around them was the snapping of teeth and the slashing of claws, everything around them seemed to be sharp. Though they were nicked and scratched they didn't stop moving and they didn't stop fighting. Unfortunately, Putrice was close behind standing atop a group of phantoms pressing themselves to make a platform floating after them. Snowflake shurikens and icicle kunai went flying in all directions.

"Tut tut, it's rude to leave so early," mocked Putrice. Fireballs knocked phantoms out of the trees. Temporal pulses scattered the monsters all over. "Come now you've not got enough time for help to arrive." Shadows whipped around the ground sending monsters into the air. Malcolm pointed at Putrice and her phantom platform was blasted by a bolt of lightning from above. Putrice screeched as she fell to the forest floor. But soon the phantoms were all around them and they lost sight of each other. All they could see was the flashes of each other's elements when they made an attack.

"Princess, get out of here!" called Gretchen.

"I've been knocked off Ollie, can anyone see him?" asked Armillo.

"Just run. We'll help him," said Eric.

"Actually I'm afraid you won't," came Putrice's voice. The data phantoms stopped and moved back allowing a clear view. Ollie was floating upside down next to Putrice his legs bound together. "This oversized turkey has quite a kick."

"You put me down you great red witch!" yelled Ollie.

"You know I've always wondered what ostrich tastes like. I wonder if the magic that lets you speak adds flavour?"

"Leave him alone!" demanded Armillo.

"Why, you've majesty, I'd be happy to let him go. If you surrender to me. And Frozen Fire'd better not try anything or I'll be having quite a large roast dinner."

"YOU COWARD!" yelled Zack in fury.

"Dear me, I forgot how loud you were." Armillo looked like she was about to burst into tears. But she didn't need to make up her mind. She placed down her fishing rod.

"All right, Doctor. Just let him go," said Armillo walking over to her.

"No, we can beat her easy!" said Patrick.

"Good choice, your highness," said Putrice. "Though I think you need a better best friend. Most magic animals would never be caught this easily." In a flash of magic Putrice, the data phantoms and Armillo vanished. Ollie, freed from his bonds, fell to the ground.

Queen Prelap was upset about her granddaughter's kidnapping. She did not dare cry, not while she was in company, yet her sadness emanated throughout the throne room.

"What could that monster possibly want with her?" wondered the queen. "She's just a sweet girl with some healing magic and some that lets her read people's emotions like those who watch."

"I'm sorry. I did not know the Anti-Gamer had brought someone with him," apologized Amaranth. "I don't how they got past my sensor spells on the door, but we know he knows how to hide himself and others when he's in a world."

"We need to get her back right away," said Ollie. "We need to round up all the best heroes in our world and get going."

"I'm afraid she's no longer in Lasseter. I do not know what we should do next. However, Astral, she who watches over Miyamoto, said she heard everything through those magic pendants they wear and she has something important to discuss with me and the others who watch. If you'll excuse me, your majesty." With a bow Amaranth vanished in a flash of light.

Back in Miyamoto in Adlez Castle, Frozen Fire had just finished telling the royal family what had happened.

"Putrice is back?!" cried Cyanna. "I'd hoped we'd never see that cruel hag ever again."

"I'd like to give that woman a taste of my arsenal," said Hitbox sharply.

"Why in all five realms would he take Lasseter's princess?" wondered Hud. "I've never met the girl so I can't see how she'd destroy Miyamoto. The polygons in Lasseter aren't a hundred feet tall are they? I reckon I could still take her."

"No, your majesty," replied Zack. "There's no indication what that psycho is up to now."

"Astral seemed to know something," mused Gretchen. "She looked absolutely horrified about what had happened."

"I've got a horrible feeling for some reason," said Cyanna. "It's like I can feel his evil bearing down on us."

"It's always bearing down on us, little sister," said Hitbox.

"Yeah, but I never gotten a feeling like this before." Cyanna's attitude worried everyone; she was usually so bright and cheerful hiding her worry about what was happening. But now she was sensing something really bad. A flash of light and Astral appeared having returned from her meeting.

"I have something big to tell all of you," she said. She couldn't look at anyone. "Visrel's clues he gave Frozen Fire were meant to be worked out so easily. He was mocking those of us who watch."

"Oh boy, no one's gonna like this one," said Hud. "Never in however long I've been alive, have I ever seen her like this."

"The Anti-Gamer has learned the Data Realm's biggest secret. Only the four of us who watch know it and we've kept it hidden for so long only vague clues to it remain. Let's start from the beginning: back in the early days of the Data Realm there were four lands made from different kinds of data and once they all became aware of the real danger of the potential of monsters like Visrel and Lag, each of the lands were hidden behind the four doors where they grew into the worlds they are now. You see before then there was this great magical force that helped shape the Free Space. It took the form of a vast light covering the sky; this power could shape the very fabric of the Data Realm. It had been used to make the lands the peoples would call home. It was a magical embodiment of the living data that this realm is made from. It can't change reality but it will allow anyone to change the Free Space into almost anything. After the four lands were sealed behind the four doors the magic was split into four and used to expand the lands before being entrusted to the royal families of the four worlds to be hidden away. They chose to hide away the magic within the blood of their own families. But they did not pass the knowledge on and so the royal families soon had no idea that a great magical force was being passed down the generations. And now today the magic exists within the four princesses of the kingdoms, like

Armillo and..." Everyone turned to Cyanna. She started to breath heavily and fast her legs wobbled and she had to sit down.

"This insane power has been in her all this time!" yelled Hitbox.

"Visrel is after that magic," said Astral. "When he stole her blood, he must have sensed a magic apart from her own. He would have had to scour all four worlds for information and had to watch everyone from a distance. That song Cyanna always sings, about four lights hidden amongst four lands, is the last remaining clue about it. He used her blood to make the Deletion Vortex but he must have had a small amount left or a record of the magic he could sense in it, that he studied, that helped him decipher these vague clues. He's after the four princesses and he's going to use that power to destroy Miyamoto." Everyone was silent, unsure what to say. Cyanna stood up and left.

"So, that deranged monster is coming after my granddaughter?" mused Hud. "Well, I'll make sure this whole castle is ready for them with more security and protection spells than anywhere else. It's already set up so no one can be stolen away in the night but I'll make sure no one dares even try." He stood up. "Hitbox, make sure all those weapons of yours are as sharp as they can be and Frozen Fire, you come up with the best monster fighting attacks you can." Hud raced out of the room and they could hear him calling out to everyone else in the castle.

"I can't believe this," said Hitbox. "What were our ancestors thinking?" He left the room as well. Frozen Fire looked at Astral not sure what to make of any of this.

"You don't have to do this if you don't want to," said Astral.

"No, we've helped save this world four times before; we'll do it again," said Zack.

"Who cares what he's after. We always stop him," said Eric. "Usually at the last minute."

"All right, but I promise I won't let any of you come to any serious harm," assured Astral. "Now, those who watch the other two worlds have insisted you help in the efforts to protect their princesses. So, in a few days you'll have seen all four of the Data Realm's worlds. And obviously you're not getting out of protecting Cyanna, not on Hud's watch."

"The madness always seems to disappear when his grandchildren are threatened," mused Patrick.

"And the five of you will be setting out to rescue Armillo from Visrel and Putrice."

"All right, boys, we've got our work cut out for us," said Gretchen. "Zack and I have finally reached the point where we've mastered our elements and you three can't be far behind. Let's make sure Visrel finally realizes the days when he could beat us are gone."

So after returning home for the night Frozen Fire were getting ready to go to yet another world. Well rested they returned to Adlez Castle to meet Astral. Zack found Cyanna sitting in a courtyard by herself looking at nothing.

"Are you OK?" Zack managed after a moment.

"I'm fine overall," replied Cyanna. "I was just shocked yesterday; nobody in the whole family had any idea. I guess that's why I had such a bad feeling; the light is still connected so I could sense that Armillo was captured. I wonder how mum and dad would have reacted to this." Zack said nothing; he never knew what to say at a time like this. "But anyway, you've got another princess to worry about so try not to worry about me until the day after tomorrow. If Grandad is going to reinforce the castle in an insane way I might as well give him a hand." Cyanna left and a moment later Gretchen appeared.

"Back in those days when we used to get lost in the forest did you ever imagine we'd end up doing something like this?" asked Zack.

"Sometimes," replied Gretchen. "You and I have always had vivid imaginations. And I know full well you always dreamed of adventure but I never thought it'd actually happen; well nothing on this scale. I assumed we'd get attack by some angry ghosts but didn't think we'd fight a guy who's basically a sentient computer virus."

"There really is no such thing as normal. I'm freaking out a little."

"You're always freaking out. But between you and me so am I. And so are the others but they'll never admit it, only you admit it when you're scared. Anyone who doesn't freak out even just a little when they do what we do is a complete idiot."

"Better get on with it then."

They caught up with the others and Astral warped them to the door and then through it to the Free Space. This time they set off straight forward, towards the magenta door that led to Pratchett.

"So, what's this world like?" asked Eric. "You only ever said it was a world of mystery."

"I've never actually been to any of the other worlds," explained Astral "I've only got word of mouth to go on."

"Aren't you allowed in the other worlds?" questioned Patrick.

"It's not that. My place is with Miyamoto and, yes, I can come to the Free Space and your world and still keep an eye on my home, but in the other worlds there's the power of the others who watch not leaving any room for mine. I wouldn't be able to watch."

"What kind of data did this one come from?" asked Malcolm.

"The one who watches Pratchett was born from stories about detectives. He has keen eye and a sharp mind but he does overact a bit. Though I suppose you five are no stranger to that." In front of the magenta door stood a figure. Soon they could see it was tall man who looked like he was middle-aged. He wore a dark brown suit and a long navy trench coat with a matching trilby hat.

"Ah, Astral," said the man. His voice sounded normal but you got the feeling he was about to yell Aha! "The Anti-Gamer and his cohort are already through the door."

"Frozen Fire, this is he who watches Pratchett, Baritone," said Astral.

"Sounds more like a countertenor to me," remarked Eric quietly.

"Nice to meet the five of you at last. Astral's always singing your praises so I know you're good. Shall we?"

In a flash of light Frozen Fire arrived with Baritone in Prachett. On the other side of the magenta door was on a long steel wall just standing on its own. They seemed to be on the outskirts of a city and they could see the main volume of its buildings ahead of them.

"Our capital city is much closer to our door than in the other three worlds," explained Baritone. "The door to the Free Space is right on the edge of the city. The city's called Semiv. Come on let's head to the palace." Another flash of light and they were deeper into the city. Semiv looked old fashioned, reminiscent of our nineteenth century.

"I wasn't expecting this place to be so old," mused Zack. "The other cities were just as modern as our world."

"I can feel electricity everywhere," said Malcolm.

"The city just looks like it runs on gas," explained Baritone. "Everything's powered by electric crystals like in your world."

"So it's meant to look old?" mused Gretchen. "What would you call it? Pseudo gothic?"

"It's a pretty interesting hybrid of eras," said Eric.

"Almost like something's gone wrong with history," said Patrick. Semiv Palace came into to view. It was a grand house fit for royalty. The doors were quite tall and the windows were just as big. The stone was carved into all sorts of flowing shapes making it resemble long flower petals and further up it looked like strange creatures and bizarre faces.

"I think I've seen this in the opening of a murder mystery," said Zack.

"Nah," said Gretchen. "It looks like it belongs on the moors where it's plagued by evil ghosts." They entered through the front door and after moving though a long corridor found themselves in the throne room. Just like the other two its walls were covered by portraits of previous rulers with the throne at the back which was made from what appeared to be the finest and most expensive wood. On the throne sat an old man and to his left were a young boy and girl.

"May I present his majesty, King Alliteration," said Baritone. Alliteration was quite aged but he still seemed to retain some of his strength. His face was wide and on his head the crown looked like open books. Strangely he seemed like he'd rather be watching TV in his underwear and vest. "And these two are his grandniece and nephew, the twin heirs to the throne, Princess Magentia and Prince Orion." Magentia seemed like a bright upbeat girl, more so than Cyanna. She had big smile on her face that was probably very hard to get rid of. Orion looked like he was quite curious and inquisitive, the sort of person who loved to solve mysteries. They were both a few years younger than the rest of Frozen Fire.

"Ah, so this is the backup you promised," said Alliteration. "Excellent, we can get to protecting Magentia immediately. Nobody messes with my family so this Anti-Gamer is gonna face everyone in Prachett who can fight."

"I hope your plan works, uncle," said Orion. "Quite a few of your ideas have been a bit crazy."

"Ah, I'm sure we'll be fine," said Magentia. "There are more dangerous places to be hiding,"

"What is the plan, your majesty?" asked Gretchen.

"We're going to make it look like we're defending Magentia in the palace," explained Alliteration. "While in reality the five of you and her brother will have taken her to a hiding place. You'll be heading to a place called Bone Cliff Cove."

"Ugh, typical," groaned Zack.

"Don't worry it's just called that 'cause it looks like the cliff's a pile of skeletons," explained Baritone.

"Now obviously these bad guys'll work out that she's not here, eventually," continued the king. "So once you're in the hiding place you'll need to find and activate its security spells; it should be able to protect her until this mess is over. If there's nothing else head out straight away."

Frozen Fire, Magentia and Orion arrived at Bone Cliff Cove. The place seemed to have a grim atmosphere seeming quite cold like it was winter. The place was quiet with only the sound of the waves filling the air, not a sound of wildlife anywhere. The air smelled of salt and the sea was grey though you could see more brilliant blue waters on the edge of the horizon. Large cliffs rose out from the rocks and just like Baritone said all the rocks on the cliffs looked like bones. Arms, legs, torsos, skulls it really did look like a horrific hill of skeletons.

"Hey, you guys never got a chance to introduce yourselves," said Magentia gleefully.

"I'm Gretchen. This is Zack, Eric, Patrick and Malcolm."

"It's good to meet you all," said Orion. "Come on, let's get to the safe house."

"Not the best place for a royal beach house," observed Eric.

"Well, it's just a wooden shack." Looking ahead they could see a small house at the base of cliff made entirely from wood.

"That doesn't inspire confidence," said Zack.

"Don't worry, it's a great little place," assured Magentia. "We've spent endless hours of fun here." Soon they were entering the front door and stepping inside. The inside was only really different from the outside because it was furnished. Though it did seem to have some electrical lighting.

"The security spells must be to protect it from the sea," remarked Zack.

"We need to head to the attic to start up the spells," explained Orion moving over to the stairs. A shadow moved past the windows but everyone was facing the other way.

"You hear something?" asked Patrick. "I hope we haven't been followed here."

"We usually end up in fight where ever we go," mused Gretchen.

"I think something's outside," said Malcolm. Bang! The front door swung open and something large appeared. It looked like a beast made from ship wreckage and seaweed. It was adorned with shells and moved on all fours like a dog. However, the monster was quite large and got stuck in the door.

"I don't think Visrel's even bothering anymore," said Eric. Orion was checking something in a book.

"We can't activate the spells with that thing in the house," he said.

"It's no match for my grappling hook!" exclaimed Magentia.

"Leave this to us," said Gretchen. "We can handle flotsam here. You go, get started on those spells." The twins ran upstairs, and Frozen Fire summoned their weapons. Charging their magic they blasted the monster with their elements propelling it back out the door. The monster got back up and as Frozen Fire came outside it opened its mouth and exhaled an energy ball at them. Frozen Fire ran out of the way as the monster shot more energy balls at them. Gretchen rushed forward and attacked with her halberd and a shadow copy of it. Malcolm fired arrows from a distance while Patrick shot a time burst at it. Zack covered his staff in thick ice and slammed the monster after which Eric flung it in the air by erupting fire beneath it. After crashing to the ground the monster sprang back onto its feet and leapt into the air and when it landed with force a shockwave of energy shot towards them. Frozen Fire were knocked over but Patrick managed to immobilize the monster in time. As Zack got up he threw a several icicle kunai at it. The monster got free of Patrick's magic and lunged at them but got knocked back by a shadow frying pan from Gretchen. Eric attacked with his scythe while Malcolm fired lightning from two of his fingers. The monster raised its front legs and slammed them down causing an explosion underfoot. Frozen Fire scattered as the monster made more explosions, Zack froze the ground around it making the monster lose balance. Gretchen hit the monster with a shadow boulder on the end of her halberd and Eric followed by throwing his scythe like a flaming boomerang. Malcolm fired arrows that exploded into lightning and Patrick assaulted it with his sword. The monster fired more energy balls at them, it shot them in quick succession; it didn't have time to aim and they flew everywhere even hitting the shack, braking windows and blowing holes in the walls. Frozen Fire shared a look that said: oops! Zack and Malcolm attacked with ranged attacks, arrows and snowflake shurikens. Patrick attacked with double temporal pulses and Gretchen dropped three copies of her halberd down on it. Eric rushed forward and with one last flaming scythe slash cut the monster in half, it then exploded into magic.

"You think Visrel will know it's been destroyed?" wondered Patrick,

"Better get these security spells working," said Gretchen. Frozen Fire entered the shack, climbed the stairs and up a ladder into the attic. The attic was quite well lit, most likely due to the large hole now in the ceiling. Magentia and Orion were waiting.

"Err, sorry about that," said Zack pointing to the hole.

"Ah, don't worry about it, the spells will still work," reassured Magentia.

"We've got everything set up so let's do it," said Orion.

"What kind of security spells are they exactly?" enquired Eric. "Barriers have never really stopped Visrel."

"It's not a barrier," replied Magentia. "It's more of a spacial displacement."

"Wait! What?" said Gretchen.

The twins held their arms out with their hands facing each other and a flash of magic appeared between them. The whole house began to shake and was soon covered in a magical energy. Everything was distorted and a moment later it cleared leaving everyone blinking and dazed. Outside the house was just white nothingness. Looking outside it could be seen that the shack was suspended in this whiteness hanging by nothing with nothing else in sight.

"Whoa, that's odd," said Zack. "Course some of the things we've been trapped in were waaaaay weirder."

"We're not trapped here," explained Orion. "This small pocket dimension may be virtually inaccessible but Baritone has no trouble accessing it."

"A good hiding spot if they can't figure out how to get in," mused Gretchen. "Though I imagine boredom is a probability."

"Nah, there's a few things to do," assured Magentia. "There's a TV downstairs. Take a look around." Everyone fanned out wondering what to do and how long they'd have to stay here.

"Should probably fix that," observed Patrick looking at the hole in the ceiling. "Time magic's great for fixing things. Temporal reversing it's called. Of course it has its limits it can only go back so far and doesn't affect people or creatures but I haven't had to worry about broken things in a long time."

"Don't you need all the pieces for it to work?" questioned Eric. "I don't think they all came with us to the pocket dimension." Patrick considered this for a moment.

"Oh well. It's the thought that counts." Frozen Fire looked around at the various objects in the house while the twins turned on the TV. On the screen appeared Baritone and King Alliteration.

"That's cooler than our pendants," mused Malcolm.

"Ah, I see you got to the safe house," said Baritone.

"How are things at the palace?" asked Magentia.

"Things are fine here," assured Alliteration. "Those walking mouths and floating sheets are thinning out; barely any damage at all. Though I haven't seen either of the bad guys."

"Frozen Fire, I'll get you out once Visrel and Putrice have left Pratchett," said Baritone. "But Magentia and Orion you two need to stay there until we're sure this is over and they've given up on this plan. We'll call back once we've found out what they're up to."

"Don't worry, thwarting his plans is what we do," assured Gretchen. "With only a slight margin of error as you may note next time you see this place."

Visrel and Putrice arrived at Bone Cliff Cove.

"My word what a place," said Putrice. "I'm sure I've an illustration in a novel that resembled this place. You have to admire the rather grim atmosphere."

"I don't sense Frozen Fire anywhere," said Visrel. "But the monster I sent here was destroyed by their magic. That shadow warping is going to make things take so much longer. Wait, I can sense something."

"Now that you mention it, darling, something does seem a little off. A little disruption in the fabric of space."

"Yes, that's what it seems. Of course they're in a pocket dimension. They must have displaced a whole house, we won't be getting to them easily. If only brute force would work."

"Hm, Visrel darling, you brought all my scientific notes and devices to the Data Realm, correct?"

"Yes, though I haven't really looked at any of them."

"Well, before I fled from the law I manage to secure plenty of my work about that rift I made in the sky of Miyamoto. Sure, Frozen Fire destroyed all my records on the rift machine but there were other things. You see I had actually began work on a device to protect the rift that could be fired from my lab to the other side of the rift. It was a harpoon gun of sorts. Of course I stopped working on it after it seemed there was nothing they could do about it from that side. But the prototype I constructed should be amongst the things you brought here for me. With a little work and adjustment it could perhaps fire into this pocket dimension."

"You truly are a genius, Doctor I knew you would be a great ally. You've got better tricks than the Virus's Spell Book had."

Frozen Fire had found what they had thought was an entertaining way to pass the time.

"Wow, I thought Hud's diaries were giving a lot of detail," observed Eric as they flicked through a book they had found.

"Yeah, King Alliteration's predecessor should not have left this lying around," agreed Gretchen. "Anyone could start reading it. Keep going." They turned another page and kept reading.

"Oh, I didn't need to know that!" exclaimed Zack. "That is not a sentence you should read with a vivid imagination."

"The royal families must be glad we don't do blackmail," mused Patrick. "What would be the point? I think we've done enough to just ask for anything we want."

"Who are they?" came the voice of Magentia from another room. The royal twins had been watching the TV they had said something about it getting all the channels as well as having a video feed to the cove. "That hat has got one large brim. And why is he wearing gauntlets with a suit? The cape's bizarre enough." Frozen Fire put down the book and raced through.

"It's Visrel and Putrice!" said Gretchen. Sure enough on the TV was a view of Bone Cliff Cove where Visrel and Putice were moving something into position.

"That Anti-Gamer and the evil doctor?" said Orion.

"What are they doing with that?" wondered Eric.

They had something that looked like a canon but it was loaded with several harpoons and on the back seemed to be some sort of computer screen which Putrice was typing away at while Visrel covered the harpoon heads in magic. The canon fired and the harpoons shot through the air. They were attached to long metal cables, the sort used to suspend very heavy things. The harpoons vanished midflight the cables flowing into the spots where they vanished through what looked like ripples in the air.

"Where did they go?" wondered Malcolm. As soon as he stopped talking there was a crashing sound and the TV which was up against the wall fell over. Sticking out in the wall was one of the harpoons. There were other crashing sounds as the other harpoons latched onto the house.

"Oh criminy," said Zack as the shack started to move. "Oh bother, oh drat." Soon the whole building started to shake as it was begun to be pulled back to the cove.

"I wish they hadn't kept the place held together so well," grumbled Orion. Everyone fell to the ground and everything else followed. Malcolm grabbed the harpoon and charged it with electricity which ran down the cable back out of the pocket dimension and all the way to the canon. The canon was soon surging and part of it exploded making it stop. However, the house had already been mostly pulled through and with a mighty crash it landed and more of it fell apart. Visrel and Putrice moved over to the wreck where seven voices were groaning.

"The only way that could have been more successful is if they hadn't blown up my canon," stated Putrice. With a wave of his hand Visrel made most of the wood move revealing everyone.

"I was hoping for something more serious," mused the Anti-Gamer. He leaned over them and gave them his fake smirk. "Any last tricks?" Eric sat up. He had been building his magic and fire began to appeared all over his body. On closer inspection you could see he was actually turning into fire and soon he was completely transformed into fire, clothes and all.

"It seems to be a yes, darling."

Eric leapt forward and when he landed erupted into a wall of fire. The fire stretched out and lashed at Visrel and Putrice. The fire kept them moving to not give them a chance to retaliate. Gretchen managed to stand up and made a warping shadow and had the other five stagger through it.

"Eric, let's get out of here," called Gretchen.

Eric appeared out of the wall of fire and quickly moved forward and together they jumped into the shadow which then disappeared. The wall of fire then vanished leaving Visrel and Putrice alone.

The battered and bruised Frozen Fire and the twins collapsed out of the shadow. They realized they were lying in snow and looking around they saw everything was covered in snow. The air was cold and the sky was a pale grey and snow was gently falling down. They were in a valley made of multiple hills and right at the bottom was a frozen lake which shone a brilliant blue. The whole place looked like a card celebrating a winter time festival; everything bar the lake was so white even the few trees on the hillsides.

"Where are we now?" asked Gretchen.

"This is Ever-Ice Valley," replied Magentia. "The lake is always frozen solid yet for some reason it's never hidden by all the snow."

"You actually turned into fire," Zack said to Eric. "That's gotta be an advanced move."

"You bet your blue goggles it is," responded Eric. "And you know that means I'm the best."

"Oh, that's just what that diva needs," remarked Patrick.

"You're one to talk," commented Malcolm.

"Do you think there's a monster here like at the cove?" wondered Orion.

"I don't sense anything in the snow," said Zack. "Though I don't think my range covers the whole valley."

"Let's keep moving until Baritone finds us. He's bound to know what happened in the shack. Let's hope he finds us first." They began to move down the valley and towards the lake. Everything seemed so still, no movement except for the seven of them trudging through the snow. They reached the lake which sure enough seemed to be solid ice all the way to the lakebed. There was snow scattered across it making it look like it had been dusted with icing sugar rather than completely covering it like everything else.

"Eric, go heat things up," requested Gretchen.

"I'm not a furnace," he replied.

"Doesn't mean you can't be used as one. Come on, I've been our emergence exit recently."

"Running from bad guys and keeping your toes warm are not the same thing."

"Someone's here!" Zack cut across. "They just appeared. I can sense them in the snow. There!" Following where he was pointing two figures seemed to be moving towards them.

"That looks like them," said Patrick. "How'd they find us?"

"They may have just been warping from place to place until they found us," suggested Orion. Suddenly more shapes appeared around Visrel and Putrice as talon-teeth and data phantoms raced towards them. Frozen Fire and the twins had moved and ended up moving out onto the frozen lake.

"Hope we don't slip," said Magentia.

"Not while I'm around," said Zack. "They should know better than to follow us into my element."

"Hey, we're always surrounded by my element," pointed out Gretchen. "So really they should flee in terror from me."

"Then why don't you manipulate natural shadows more often so they would?" Before Gretchen could respond they were surrounded by the monsters taking their attention.

"Why are they both so bitey and scratchy?" wondered Eric. "Well, I guess they match."

They started attacking the monsters as all of them tried to bite and scratch. They were quite numerous but they barely got a hit as they kept getting knocked away by the weapons and elements. Magentia knocked them back with a grappling hook and Orion read out spells from his book to attack. Zack motioned with his arms and all the nearby snow moved scattering monsters everywhere. Zack kept using the local snow to knock down large groups of enemies. Visrel and Putrice reached the edge of the lake.

"Looks like our darlings are keeping them from another shadowy escape," observed Putrice.

"Excellent, I'm just about ready," said Visrel. Visrel held up a sphere of magic before calling out to those on the lake. "You know the trouble with your element Glacis? It's so changeable." He threw the sphere at the lake and in an instant the magic spread all across it and it turned into water. Frozen Fire and the twins sank into the extremely frigid waters; they flailed about as they held their breath trying to return to the surface. Then just as quickly as ice turned to water it turned back again. Everything was still; all the monsters were gone. Then a hand reached out of the ice as Zack pulled himself on top of the ice like he was pulling himself to shore. A flash of light and Baritone appeared. Zack pointed downwards and Baritone thrust out his arm and in a flash the others were on the surface too. Everyone gasped finally able to breathe again.

"Where's the princess?" said Baritone. Looking around they saw Magentia was gone.

"They grabbed her right after they thawed the lake," explained Orion. "Then they just let it freeze again."

"I couldn't see anyone else otherwise I would have brought you all to the surface," said Zack. "Didn't even know I could move through ice."

As Baritone tried to reassure King Alliteration that they would get Magentia back Frozen Fire returned to Miyamoto. Eric had generated heat to help everyone recover except for Zack who, as mentioned several times, isn't affected by cold. They sat in Astral's temple recuperating for their time in Pratchett.

"That could have gone better," grumbled Zack. "We're not going to be living this one down any time soon."

"Vissy's half way to getting that light," said Gretchen. "Half way to doomsday, there's a thought."

"Please don't lose heart," said Astral. "You've done so much for our world already. I can't promise that you will stop him but I know you'll try. And I'll make sure he never kills any of you."

"We're not quitting yet," assured Eric. "No matter how many bad guys are plotting together."

"Exactly, how much additional security has Hud ordered?" asked Patrick. "I didn't know you even had canons."

"You can't blame him for being extremely careful," said Astral. "You're all going to be in big fights the next two days."

"Better go home and rest," said Malcolm.

So back to their world they went and rested. That night they all had troubling dreams of Visrel getting his hands on the light. Of course the strangeness of the dream world took over so Zack dreamed Visrel built a magic chocolate factory, Gretchen dreamed he banished them to an art studio, Eric dreamed he died in a very operatic way, Malcolm dreamed he cloned himself and they spent eternity arguing and Patrick dreamed he accidently tied himself to train tracks while trying to tie them up. Needless to say they were all questioning their subconscious in the morning.

Things were still being set up at Adlez Castle.

"When they try to take her they'll find a world of hurt and pancakes," said Hud watching everything set up. "OK, tomorrow's when they arrive so I want Adlez evacuated now. Everybody's to hide out somewhere else unless they're told to help protect."

"Your majesty, the other leaders have arrived," informed a guard.

"Ah excellent! Time to rope some old friends into helping me out. Those bad guys will face all four of Miyamoto's races." Hud raced off.

"Well, Grandad is certainly busy," mused Hitbox.

"If only I could access the part of the light I have," said Cyanna. "I could use it to vaporise Visrel and end this once and for all."

"Visrel has a habit of fleeing right before the end. It was pure luck he wasn't destroyed by his own energy beam at Game's Edge."

"I hope our friends have better luck today. Grandad keeps getting more and more stuff. We need something to calm him down."

Frozen Fire were once again in the Free Space this time heading right from Miyamoto's door towards the great black door of Hartnell.

"So, we've had the guiding goddess," said Zack. "The helpful old lady and the overacting detective. What character archetype does the fourth one who watches come from?"

"The eccentric scientist," replied Astral.

"You told us Hartnell was made of planetoids, right?" said Patrick. "So it's the biggest world."

"No, all four worlds are the same size. There are a lot of pseudo celestial bodies there and large chunks of the ground float in the air. You'll see soon enough."

"I hope they've got a good plan to protect the princess," said Zack.

"Or we're out of a job," said Eric.

They arrived at the door. Standing in front of it was a man who look like he was in his mid-fifties. Wearing a large white coat over a very formal attire, he had white hair that stuck up in all directions and a pair of glasses that could only be described as eccentric.

"Everyone, this is he who watches over Hartnell: Bixbite," introduced Astral.

"I am very pleased to meet you all," greeted Bixbite. "It is a great pleasure to meet people Astral speaks so highly of."

"Frozen Fire, I leave you in the capable hands of Bixbite. Good luck." As Astral turned back towards the blue door of Miyamoto Bixbite gestured towards his door.

"Shall we?"

A flash of light and they appeared on the other side of the door. The other side of Hartnell's black door was on a large rock that appeared to be a meteor. The ground looked pretty bare and plain and the sky was just as blue as any other. But much like Kerozonia and the Celestial Mountain just about every landmark seemed to float in the air at varying heights giving the whole the look of a very small galaxy.

"Gravity seems to be optional," observed Gretchen.

"Let's head straight to the planetoid with the capital city and the castle," said Bixbite. Another flash of light and they moved again. The capital city had a look that could only be described as futuristic. Everything seemed to shine; plenty of tall buildings that all looked like they were made of plastic and metal somehow combined. But underneath it all it looked just like any other city, known for tall buildings.

"This place is definitely floating," said Patrick. "When you live on a floating island you learn to notice when the ground is floating."

"People don't often make that observation here," said Bixbite. "You'd think they would. Anyway this city is called Namerof. The castle is this way." They set off through the city.

"Where do they get the names for the capital cities?" wondered Gretchen.

"I know," responded Zack.

"Of course you do. I assume it's similar to the reason you gave me behind Adlez?"

"Yep." Soon Namerof Castle came into view, it was made of the same plastic-metal as the other buildings. It was covered in spires but barely any towers, making the whole place look like a pinecone made of blades. Overall the building seemed to have a light pale orange colour to it apart from the roof which was a much deeper shade.

"In the same way Pratchett masquerades as old fashioned our world pretends it's more advanced than the others," explained Bixbite. "In truth you'll find nothing here more complex than in your world."

"These guys aren't that tech savvy anyway," remarked Eric.

"Speak for yourself," said Malcom.

They entered through the castle doors that opened with a mechanical whirr. However, rather than give the impression of a spaceship which was most likely the intended impression they seemed to move more like the doors to a supermarket. They went down the corridor and into the throne room which, just like the others, was covered in portraits of former rulers. Similarly, the throne was at the back of the room but this one was made of what appeared to be solid light. A woman sat on the throne; she wasn't as old as the other rulers but was still quite aged, but her hair was only greying (there was still some of its old colour in it). She was small and rounded with a face that looked like she was holding her breath. She gave the impression of someone who just wanted to take things at a steady pace and have as much fun as possible. The crown on her head had an image of a wide screen TV screen on it.

"This is her majesty, Queen Episode the Fourth," said Bixbite. "Your majesty, may I present Zackary Glacis, Gretchen Shadows, Eric Flare, Malcolm Spark and Patrick Tempus."

"Welcome to my home, young ones," greeted Episode. "I'm glad that we have extra help in our time of need."

"We will do our best, your majesty," assured Gretchen.

"Are Visrel and Putice already here?" asked Eric.

"Yes, but I soon lost track of them," replied Bixbite. "But they're hiding somewhere in our world."

"Then we must waste no time," said Episode. "I want the five of you to stay by my daughter's side; you and she will be heading to a place where the rest of the plan will be implemented. Once there you will find a secure place where she will activate the device that'll hopefully keep her safe from these monsters."

"Ok, then, where is the princess?" asked Gretchen.

"She's in the hanger/armoury. She loves her technology and she'll be sure to use it to help in the fight. Please go meet her and go right away." Silence filled the room as everyone waiting for something to happen.

"Er, we've never been here before," Eric pointed out.

"Oh right, of course," said Bixbite. He started moving and Frozen Fire followed him through the castle to another room. It was a large room filled with all sorts of gadgets, all kinds of vehicles and weapons that looked futuristic. There was a young girl working away at a workstation. She turned when she heard everyone approach.

"Oh, you must be Frozen Fire," she said. "I am Princess Noir." She was older than the five of them and dressed all in black, even her long hair was black. She seemed friendly enough and had a somewhat gentle demeanour. Frozen Fire bowed.

"Your mother wanted you to get moving straight away," said Bixbite. "Grab your stuff and I'll transport you all."

"Where are we going?" Zack managed.

"A place called Monochrome Moon." Noir was pressing on some small tablet and mechanical arms hanging from tracks on the ceiling started moving bringing something to them.

"I understand the five of you are elementals," said Noir. "Which elements?"

"Er, Ice."

"Shadows."

"Fire."

"L...l...lightning."

"Time!"

"Quite a mixed lot," observed Noir. "I myself use what you might call a power suit." The arms brought into view what at first glance may have been a robot but was probably a suit of futuristic armour. It was larger than all of them and looked like it would be quite muscular if it was made of flesh. It was a shining silver-grey metal that glinted with all sorts of lights that all looked like they had some sort of trick to them. On its torso was a large black N. "This is my mech suit. Because of this they call me the Mech Princess."

"Surely that's an anime," said Zack. The mech suit opened up reveal an inside that was the ideal size for Noir. Just looking at it there was no way Frozen Fire could tell how to work it, but they were glad they didn't have too. Noir climbed into it and the suit closed around her. The suit made the sound of a machine activating and it began to move like a person.

"To the Monochrome Moon then," said Noir whose voice came through a speaker. With another flash of light and they were gone.

It probably didn't count as a moon but the ground looked like the moon in Frozen Fire's world. Apart from all the plant life and water. Craters that doubled as lakes, trees that grew out of the rocks and the sound of local wildlife somewhere nearby. However, the first thing they noticed about this unusual landscape was the lack of colour. Not that it was a dull looking place that might as well have been a uniform shade of grey; it was in fact entirely black and white, like an old movie. Everything in this place looked as if it was filmed in a time before they made colour TV; even Frozen Fire had turned black and white when they arrived.

"What the fudge?" exclaimed Zack.

"I guess this explains monochrome," said Patrick.

"Probably should have warned you about that," said Noir. "This whole moon is covered in some sort of atmosphere that makes everything monochrome. It's made from the data of all the really early sci-fi TV shows."

"This is really cool!" exclaimed Patrick. "One of the best things I've seen in the whole Data Realm."

"It is quite a sight," agreed Gretchen. "It'd be nice to take a look round here when this is over."

"Better find a safe spot then," said Noir. The bottom of the feet of her armour began to glow and the whole suit began to levitate. "I know a good spot. Come on." She flew ahead and Frozen Fire followed. They were quite distracted by checking how all the stuff in their pockets looked in black and white.

"Your suit got some good moves?" asked Eric.

"It all lasers with various effects," replied Noir. "Except of course the flying as you may have noticed."

"That would be a bit of a design flaw if you had to shoot yourself to take flight."

Suddenly talon-teeth and data phantoms leapt out of the treetops. They piled on top of Frozen Fire but a second later they were blasted off by their elements. Visrel and Putrice appeared in front of them.

"How fortuitous of you to come straight to us," said Visrel. "You must be Princess Noir. I am Visrel the Anti-Gamer. And this is Doctor Lavender Putrice."

"I don't suppose you'd be a darling princess and just come with us?" inquired Putrice.

"You'll have to pry me out of my mech suit!" responded Noir shaking monsters off her. A light appeared on the back of the suit's hand and a beam fired at them. Visrel knocked the beam away but Zack threw a snowball that surrounded their enemies in a snow-screen.

"Let's just find a hiding place!" yelled Zack. Frozen Fire and the princess moved away from Visrel and Putrice. When the snow cleared they began to pursue but they slipped as Zack had frozen the bottom of their feet. "How does that still work?"

Unfortunately, the smaller monsters were still pursuing. After a while they stopped at the entrance to a small cave and turned to fight. Zack slammed a block of diamond hard ice at some. Eric erupted fire underneath them while Malcolm shot lightning from two of his fingers at them. Gretchen knocking away many with a shadow wall while Patrick temporally immobilized them before blasting them away. Noir blasted many of them with her lasers which knocked them away a long way. Once the monsters were cleared they moved into the cave out of sight.

"Not a great start," mumbled Malcolm.

"Even if they find us now they won't get in," said Noir. Before anyone could ask "get in what?" Noir produced a small cube which she threw at the ground. The cube expanded in an instant to an enormous size nearly taking up the whole cave. But rather than crash into Frozen Fire when it shot towards them it passed through them and soon everyone was inside the cube. Inside was basically a large futuristic-looking empty room. Everything was still monochrome.

"A little warning would have been nice!" snapped Zack.

"This is a security cube," explained Noir. As she spoke her armour opened and she climbed out. "It's covered in a barrier that reflects magic. One of the most secure things in the world."

"I hope there's stuff to do in here," said Gretchen. "If not, we may end up with an elemental brawl. They do not end well"

"They're still repainting that room in Adlez Castle after last time," mused Eric.

"Don't worry, this place may look empty but there's plenty to do," assured Noir. "But first we need to contact my mother and Bixbite to let them know we're in here."

Sometime later Visrel and Putrice found the cave.

"Around here is where our minions were destroyed," said Putrice. "Can't sense any of their magic, however."

"No, but there is something strange in the cave," said Visrel. They moved into the cave and found the cube. "Well, this is quite interesting. Some kind of very powerful protection magic. I'm willing to bet this is where they're hiding." Visrel summoned his helical blade and struck the cube. Nothing. Not the sound of the blade striking and not a scratch or mark on it.

"What a fascinating construct!" exclaimed Putrice with admiration. "Magic-repelling barriers, one of the most notoriously difficult things to do." She began to examine the cube.

"So most of our methods won't help us get inside. Hm."

"With some of my tools we might be able to make an entrance. However, this is a very sturdy metal so it will take some time. We need to transport to the Free Space if we don't want he who watches to get them out of there first. We might not be able to transport inside but you can bet he'll be able to. Alternatively, I have a device that can drain the power out of things that might be unmagical enough to still work; the barriers could shut down with the power drained."

"Then I say we move it. We might need to put something underneath it so the talon-teeth and data phantoms can touch it. Being made of our magic there's no way they could touch it otherwise."

Time passed and Frozen Fire were keeping themselves occupied.

"This way is better than any daft video of a cat sith 'playing' the piano," said Zack.

"Yeah, who'd have thought that videos of pixies re-enacting political events could be so addictive," agreed Gretchen.

"That tiny one really captures the Reignland prime minister," said Eric with a chuckle. "Best parody of political leaders. Much better than the ones of bogles pretending to be Kerozonian politicians."

"We gotta remember this channel," said Patrick. "What's it called?"

"Pixie Politics," replied Malcolm.

"Man, the five of you are real crazy," said Noir quietly. There was a strange rumbling sound and it almost felt like the floor shifted underneath them.

"Anyone else hear that?" questioned Zack. The cube started to shake.

"We are definitely moving," stated Patrick.

Noir moved to the screen, turned off the video they were watching and switched to the cube security feed.

"Apparently pinstripe and wide brim weren't discouraged by not being able to get in," said Gretchen glumly. A stone platform has been slipped underneath the security cube and a lot of talon-teeth and data phantoms were underneath that moving it out the cave. Noir pressed a button on the screen and sound came on.

"There is no way we can get this to the Free Space without encountering someone," said Visrel. "In fact if we can't transport it magically we can't get it out the door."

"If we manage to drain it of its power and deactivate the barrier we might be able to," said Putrice. She placed a machine on the side of the cube. "I suppose transporting it is unnecessary overall. Unless of course we open it by dropping it off a cliff. Frozen Fire do have a habit of surviving; they'll probably manage to endure the fall." Her machine activated, the lighting in the cube flickered. Malcolm placed his hand on the wall and his magic surged and the lights returned to normal.

"How long will this take?" asked Visrel.

"Oh dear. We've both overlooked something," said Putrice agitated at her oversight. "There's a lightning elemental in there; he can just recharge the thing. It's pointless, darling." She deactivated her machine.

"It'll take far too long to cut a hole in it. Off a cliff it is then."

"Would it kill you to just give up!" Zack yelled at the screen. The bad guys reacted like they had heard him.

"I guess this thing has speakers," said Visrel. "Obviously you can hear us so do us a favour and plan a way to survive the drop."

"Oh and don't bother contacting your watcher," said Putrice. "I've placed another device that'll block your signals."

"We can't transport out. We can't send our magic out to attack," said Gretchen. "We're really in trouble."

"If I deactivate the cube we might be able to escape them," said Noir.

"Better increase the interference then," said Putrice. The entire screen started to flicker but they could still make out what was happening outside. They saw the edge of the Monochrome Moon came into view.

"Ah, that'll do the trick," said Visrel. "Try not to fall out as you fall over. Oh and you might as well admire the view." Noir frantically pressed the screen trying to get a reaction.

"I miss doors," said Eric. Noir climbed back into her mech suit.

"Should have just let them drain the energy," she said as her suit closed. "The cube would have just shrank and then we could have at least tried to fight our way out." Malcolm rolled his eyes and put his hands on the wall again. Electricity surged and a second later the cube shrank and they found themselves on the platform.

"Pity, I liked the idea of dropping you all off a cliff," said Putrice. She and Visrel snapped their fingers and their minions stopped, put down the platform and began to climb on top.

"Keep Frozen Fire busy and pry the princess out of her armour," ordered Visrel. Putrice threw her energy draining device onto Noir's armour which stopped a second later. Malcolm held his arms up towards Noir's armour and it sparked to life. The arms shot up and fired beams at Visrel and Putrice which wrapped around them like ropes.

"Wait, what? I didn't do that!" exclaimed Noir.

"Malcolm, are you controlling it?" asked Zack. Malcolm nodded. "That's pretty advanced."

"He's always been able to affect machines," said Patrick.

"Maybe charge them himself or remove the power all together, but to control a machine that complex as if he was piloting himself? That's pretty advanced." Visrel tried to move his arms and he tore his bindings apart and with a swing of his blade cut Putrice out of hers. Malcolm had the armour fire more shots blasting all the nearby monsters and another beam that made an energy wall blocking the bad guys.

"I think it's time we were going," said Gretchen. She made a warping shadow underneath them and the six of them fell through. The shadow closed as Visrel broke down the wall.

Everyone landed in an alleyway and once again there were other colours. Looking around they saw they were in a city but it wasn't Namerof.

"Now where are we?" wonder Eric.

"This is the Onyx Meteor," responded Noir. "This is the home of the breakless, the glass people. Their bodies are made from glass three times as strong as any bulletproof glass. Hence the name, they're not exactly fragile." You could not tell from where they were but the city was built on a meteor that was filled almost entirely with the gemstone onyx. Thanks to expert gem cutters the brakeless were able to build their whole city on top of it. Walking out of the ally they saw the breakless. At first glance you thought they might have been people in rubber costumes like in classic sci-fi (probably as a result of data from such things) but when you saw them up close they were indeed made of a thick and sturdy white glass. The glass stuck out at their shoulders and the top of their heads giving them a rather spiky look but they weren't sharp.

"Ok, now what?" asked Gretchen. No one was really sure.

"Ah, princess Noir," said a voice. A breakless was coming to them. "Nobody would ever mistake you in that armour."

"Oh, Fibre," said Noir. "Everyone this is Lord Fibre the leader of the breakless."

"I take it these are the ones who were to help protect you that your mother told me about."

"Yes. They call themselves Frozen Fire. Zack, Gretchen, Eric, Malcolm and Patrick. How did you know I was here?"

"I've been keeping an eye out for your suit's signals in case you showed up here if something went wrong with your mother's plan. We'd better get you someplace safe and contact your mother and Bixbite." The breakless began to move and Noir followed with Frozen Fire behind her.

"It didn't take them long to find us last time," said Zack in a pessimistic tone.

"There were probably already monsters in the snow back in Pratchett," suggested Gretchen. "I guess there's a good chance there are monsters nearby keeping an eye out for us."

"We'll end up in another fight no doubt," said Patrick. "Let's hope they don't get the princess when we're busy."

They found themselves in front of a building that was probably where Fibre did all his official work. The breakless pulled out a phone and talked into it.

"What's going on?" Fibre demanded down the phone. "What, a monster is on the roof? What do you mean no one can hurt it? I'm coming right up." He hung up. "This building has a roof garden on top some creature is tearing apart."

Everyone followed him into the building and straight to the elevators which took them up to the roof. The garden had indeed been torn apart. Soil and flowers lay everywhere with tress hanging over the edge. In middle of it all several breakless were confronting the culprit. It looked like a pile of bricks forming a humanoid shape that was muscular and would have fittingly be described as built like a brick wall. It was hunched over, its arms close to the ground and it large head did not seem to have a neck.

"My suit's scanners say that thing has been made immune to standard breakless magic," warned Noir.

"I doubt it's immune to the five of us," said Gretchen. Frozen Fire summoned their weapons. The monster turned towards them.

"Just leave this to us. This pile of bricks is no match," said Eric.

"Very well," said Fibre. "Your highness, I must insist you come with me to contact your mother and get you somewhere secure."

"Good luck Frozen Fire," Noir called as she and all the brakeless began to leave.

"I hope this roof is stable," said Zack. "Otherwise I think we might be back inside without taking the elevator or stairs." The monster held up its arms and swung it down at them. It missed Frozen Fire and instead hit Zack's diamond hard ice. But the bricks it was made of did not crack; it seemed to be shielded by magic to allowed to endure such hits.

"How did they know Zack could do that?" Gretchen yelled to no one in particular.

"Well, they are made of data," mused Patrick. "Perhaps they send out error reports when we destroy them."

The monster started swinging its arms again and Eric blasted it with a jet of fire to its head. Malcolm sent out a lightning punch while Patrick slammed time energy in the shape of a grandfather clock into its side. Gretchen used her shadows to make the front end of a car which she had run into the monster. The monster gathered energy to the centre of its torso and fired it out as energy bricks. Frozen Fire danced around avoiding the assault. Malcolm shot his exploding arrows while Gretchen attacked with a shadow wave. Zack threw multiple icicle kunai, Eric slashed with a blazing scythe strike and Patrick blasted it with a temporal pulse. The monster tried to punch them and hit the ground; it turned out the roof was quite sturdy and they didn't need to worry about falling through. Eric threw a small fire twister and Patrick attacked with a time magic boosted sword slash. Malcolm dropped lightning bolts on it while Gretchen dropped a shadow anvil and Zack struck its legs with his staff. The monster unleashed another stream of energy bricks at them chasing Frozen Fire back. Zack made a snow-screen as a distraction and the monster lost track of them. The monster was hit by Eric's flaming scythe boomerang and Patrick assaulted with sped up attacks. Gretchen struck with her halberd and several duplicates and Malcolm fired a jet of lightning from two of his fingers. The monster's shield disappeared and it started flailing its arms in a mock rage. The whole building shook and Frozen Fire began to lose their balance. Gretchen fired a shadow cannon ball to make it stop. Zack threw a snowman, Malcolm shot a super charged arrow and Eric hurled a massive fire ball. The monster slammed both arms down and as the building shook things could be heard crashing inside and windows could be heard breaking.

Patrick had been charging his magic and unleashed it. It formed a ring of temporal energy around the monster and when Patrick stepped inside, there was a flash of magic. Everyone else got a start there were now two Patricks, one at either side of the monster. They charged their swords with time magic and stabbed the monster which exploded into magic. The energy disappeared and there was one Patrick again.

"What was that?" asked Zack.

"That was an advanced move called a time split," replied Patrick. "Though you don't actually split. When you're in the temporal energy you move so fast between two points you're practically in two places at once."

"Colour me impressed," said Malcolm.

"So all five of you have mastered your elements now? Bravo!" said a voice that was almost mocking. Turning around they saw Visrel floating just off the ground.

"You're never gonna beat us now!" warned Gretchen. "None of your tricks work on us anymore."

"It matters not how strong you've become. Soon I'll be able to reshape the Free Space and you'll fall like Miyamoto." Visrel pulled out something. It was the head of Noir's power suit and he dropped it to the ground. "Pried her right of it." He threw his cape over himself and disappeared.

"Oh dearie me, darlings, you're not doing too well," came the voice of Putrice as she walked out onto the roof. "You'll have to excuse Visrel. This whole thing is rather time consuming."

"Quiet, you old hag," snapped Eric. "We're much stronger than last time we fought."

"I'm stronger too, darlings. But I'm just going to give you a reminder. Tomorrow we're going to grab that orange haired little musician and after a long night's work Visrel will practically be the spiteful god of computer viruses and I will have near infinite scientific resources. Ask yourselves is it really worth throwing down your lives in a battle you can't win? Then again as gamers Visrel will kill you all anyway. Perhaps it's time you went into hiding." There were footsteps running towards them and Fibre returned.

"Give back the princess now, you scarlet beldam!" demanded the breakless.

"Ta-ta darlings," said Putrice. And she vanished in a flash of magic. Nobody knew what to say. Fibre was furious and upset and their failure to protect another of the princesses hung over Frozen Fire.

Queen Episode was upset about her daughter being kidnapped and Bixbite could do little to comfort her. The leader of the breakless could not look her in the eye.

"I'm sorry, your majesty. I've failed you," apologised Fibre. "They overpowered us so easily."

"You're not at fault, Fibre," reassured Bixbite. "Only the Anti-Gamer and that wretched scientist are to blame."

"What can be done now?" asked Episode.

"They have taken her to the Free Space hidden beneath a barrier that prevents the magic of we who watch from being used. But we are to mount a rescue operation as soon as possible. We will do everything we can to save your daughter."

Frozen Fire went straight home after returning to Miyamoto and spent a restless night in fear of what was to come. It was raining over Kerozonia as it so often did. It, along with its neighbouring countries, Islegren and Reginland, often seemed to sit under grey skies and were faced with fierce winds and the peoples of those lands often liked to complain about the weather. All five of them headed to Adlez Castle as soon as they could. The place was quieter than usual. Zack found Cyanna standing on a balcony by herself.

"Today's the day," she said without turning around. "Astral says they have a large army to attack the castle."

"I hope your grandfather's preparations will keep them out," said Zack.

"Grandfather may be a little prone to saying nonsense but he rarely makes mistakes when it counts."

"We didn't have any luck protecting the others." She turned around at last.

"No matter what happens I want you, Gretchen, Eric, Malcolm and Patrick to know how grateful I am for what you have managed to do for us. Come on, things must be nearly ready." She left but Zack didn't follow and moment later the rest of Frozen Fire appeared.

"We're not doing too well," sighed Zack.

"What was it your grandfather said about at least trying?" said Gretchen.

"I know but they've gone all out with their tricks. More so than usual."

"This has gotten to all of us," said Eric. "A little worse than that incident at the power plant. But we need to face our self-doubt head on."

"We've all reached the advanced stage in our magic," said Patrick. "That counts for something. And we all had pretty good starts."

"We fight to the end as always," said Malcolm.

"Come on boys, let's do this," said Gretchen. They headed to the throne room where Hud, Cyanna, Hitbox, Iron, Larch and Stratus were waiting.

"This is it," said Hud. "Visrel has been able to waltz straight in here in the past but not today. Every door and window in this castle now have extremely advanced security spells on them. But even their minions might make it through so we all are going to end up fighting."

"Everyone is going to have to split up and help defend different areas," said Hitbox. "Work with everyone you can. Cyanna, you know where you need to be." The princess nodded.

"Only the people in this room will be able to move about the castle freely," explained Hud. "The bad guys might find a way through but it won't be easy for them. And Astral can transport in and out as well."

"What about the royal guard and the local law enforcement?" inquired Iron.

"I had them evacuate as well. Like I said only we can pass through the spells freely as there's no need for anyone else to."

"So when faced by a siege spearheaded by two powerful villains," began Larch. "You decided only eleven people would be needed to defend the whole castle from an army." A look of realisation came over Hud's face as ten other faces gave him a rather annoyed look.

"Oops."

"Your majesty I know you like strange plans BUT THIS IS JUST PLAIN STUPID!" snapped Zack.

"Yes, that's quite a bit of oversight on my part."

"So much for when it counts," sighed Cyanna.

"There's nothing to be done now," grumbled Stratus. "Our enemies will be here soon. We don't have time to fix it and we don't have time to get annoyed with each other. We can chastise the king later."

"Then let's get into position," said Hitbox. "Soon all their smaller minions will be swarming up the castle walls and we have to send them back down. It's unlikely we can stop them from entering completely but at least we can wear down their numbers from here. OK, here's where everybody should go."

After everyone was in position they waited. Looking down at Adlez was strange; no one had seen it so empty. But it wasn't long before the streets were full again. There was a giant flash of magic and an army of talon-teeth and data phantoms appeared. Standing on a transparent platform they had magiced up, were Visrel and Putrice.

"Astral should know by now her spells are futile," said Visrel looking the castle.

"Preparations are complete, darling," said Putrice who was working with a machine. The device had a large satellite esc dish on it aimed at the castle. "Just send your disruption spell into the amplifier and all those security spells will be less effective."

Visrel held his arm up to the device and sent some magic into it. The large node on the end of the satellite lit up and it surged with energy. Unable to be seen by the eye the magic was projected at the castle.

"Well done, Doctor," said Visrel. "Obviously we should leave it here out of range of their defences." The two villains pointed at the castle.

"GO!" they shouted and their army advanced.

Everyone had divided up and were each looking out of the places in the castle at the advancing enemies. The groups were Zack, Eric and Malcolm; Gretchen and Patrick; Iron and Larch; Hud and Stratus; Cyanna and Hitbox. The monsters started to climb up and floated over the walls. Zack froze the walls making the climbing talon-teeth slide off and Malcolm fired a stream of lightning and Eric an onslaught of fireballs at the floating data phantoms.

"They're looking bigger than usual," observed Zack.

"Oh my!" said Eric.

"I hope the three of us are enough for here."

"We are the largest group," said Malcolm.

"So let the blighters try," said Eric.

At the opposite side of the castle Patrick was temporally immobilizing all the monsters he could which made them fall back down while Gretchen dropped shadow anvils on them and the occasional shadow piano.

"You're the one behind all the large objects suddenly falling on top of cartoon characters out of nowhere aren't you?" asked Patrick jokingly.

"You bet I am!" replied Gretchen. "Though I doubt the minions are quite as fond of my slapstick." Elsewhere Hud and Stratus were shifting a defensive device into position.

"How long have you had cannons?" wondered Stratus as they aimed it.

"They were a present from my late wife on our tenth anniversary," explained Hud.

"Good grief man, my wife got me a collection of vintage records for our anniversary. What did you get her?"

"That trebuchet we have set up in the courtyard."

"I guess that explains why both your initials in a love heart are carved into the side."

"It was a very thoughtful gift."

"We all thought your wife was the sensible one." They fired. Larch and Iron stood on a balcony. Larch was throwing spells that made large sharp thorns shoot up underneath the enemies while Iron launched spells that shook the ground and sent enemies all over.

"AH HA HA HA!" laughed Larch. "You useless fools are no match for any of us."

"Let's hope it takes them a while to work out there's only eleven of us," mused Iron. In the highest part of the castle Hitbox fired loads of arrows from his crossbow and Cyanna played a tune on her trombone that fired bolts of energy at them.

"Nobody's getting in the tower this way!" exclaimed Hitbox. "And anyone who does make it inside our home will have to go through all our friends."

"I think we all will be enough to stop this army," said Cyanna. "But even if we do beat them all Visrel and Putrice will have plenty of dirty tricks. We should have gone to a hiding place. I know the ones in the other worlds didn't work but it would have been harder than this to find us."

"You know as well as I do that we don't have a safe house. Besides it's too late now."

Several monsters had managed to get into the throne room where they found the trap that had been set. The spell activated when it detected the monsters which activated the energy cannons Hud had received for his fifteenth wedding anniversary. The monsters in the courtyard were met by the aforementioned trebuchet. But the monsters still managed to find ways in and slip past some of defences. Everyone bar the royal siblings headed inside the castle to battle the intruders. Visrel and Putrice noticed there were no longer attacks from certain points.

"Hud, you mad fool! You actually only let eleven of you in there?" observed Visrel.

"Unfortunately, they seem to be doing well enough," mused Putrice. "But the direct approach may yet work."

"Then soon we'll send in our big monster." They looked at the creature behind them.

"I've been meaning to ask, darling, where do you get the designs for these things?"

"I don't design them myself. They're mostly out of computer viruses and my magic but I also need to use some spare data. The monster's appearance depends on the random data I use."

"Well, I guess we should be glad the Free Space doesn't get everything that's on the internet."

"Indeed. Though this time I wanted something specific. Back when Frozen Fire first came to Miyamoto I had two monsters made from the same metal as this monster is made from. Their magic was not able to make a scratch on them. Of course it'd be foolish not to realise that they're much stronger now and they did get lucky against that suit of armour. But it should give us a large window of opportunity."

All through the corridors of the castle battles were taking place. Iron punched monsters knocking them far away while Larch attacked with magic that dropped heavy tree stumps. Zack was striking monsters with his staff covered in icicles,

Eric slashed with blazing scythe attacks and Malcolm was shooting arrows that blasted like a bolt of lightning. Stratus used a spell that covered the monsters in clouds so they couldn't see and then Hud attacked with a wave of magical energy. Gretchen was cutting down monsters with her halberd and several copies and Patrick attacked with his sword, its range increased by his time magic. The four leaders wound up meeting in the training courtyard. Hud and Stratus from one door and a moment later Iron and Larch from another.

"These blasted things are everywhere!" yelled Stratus stating the obvious. The training courtyard was on a roof three floors up on the castle. Hud looked over the edge of the wall down at the monsters.

"I can't see the Anti-Gamer and Putrice anywhere," said Hud. "Then again my eyes aren't be what they used to be. Sure I don't need glasses but I'm like a million years old so they can't be perfect."

"OK, I'm sure he's talking to the trebuchet on purpose," said Larch.

"Without doubt," agreed Iron. "Your majesty we've spotted the device that the magical interference is coming from. We need to destroy it."

"Yeah, let's grab one of those cannons your wife kept getting you and blast it," said Larch.

"With the spells at full power those two will have trouble getting in here," agreed Stratus. "And none of those monsters can get in."

"I can see the device," said Hud. "Unfortunately, it's out of range of any of our defences. We'll have to think of something else. In the meantime, there are still monsters in the castle."

Further up the castle Frozen Fire reunited outside the door to the tower where the prince and princess were. They defeated all the monsters surrounding them and they got a moment's peace.

"Criminy, who'd have thought they could make so many monsters," grumbled Zack.

"And we have been thrashing them left right and centre," said Patrick.

"Not bad for just eleven people," agreed Gretchen.

"Let's check on the others and get back to it," said Eric.

"Something's coming," warned Malcolm. A section of the wall crumbled to the ground and the large monster came through the hole. It was indeed made of metal and took the form of a giant centipede. Visrel and Putrice came through behind it.

"Steelipede here is made from the same metal I used to strand you on Connection Tower all that time ago," explained the Anti-Gamer.

"We can break that metal now!" said Eric. "We're advanced elementals now!"

"That is true, darling," said Putrice. "However, it'll still give us plenty of time to get into the tower and get Cyanna."

"That's where you're wrong!" shouted Gretchen. A large warping shadow appeared beneath Visrel and Putrice and they fell into it and it closed behind them.

"Where did you send them?" asked Zack.

"I was aiming for Candle Mountain. But I'm not one hundred percent sure that's where they'll have ended up. Still by the time they get back we'll have broken this thing."

Steelipede attacked snapping its metallic jaws at Frozen Fire. Malcolm retaliated with a lightning punch and Eric attacked with fire in the shape of claws that scratched. The monster was clearly affected and they knew they were without doubt strong enough to break the metal. Zack threw snowflake shurikens, Patrick attacked with sped up sword strikes and Gretchen unleashed a shadow wave. Energy sparked around the monster's mouth and it fired a beam of energy at them. Eric hit it in the head by throwing his scythe like a flaming boomerang. Zack jumped out of seemingly nowhere and struck the monster with his staff. Gretchen slammed it with a shadow anvil on the end of her halberd. Malcolm fired a stream of electrified arrows and Patrick attacked with a close up time blast. Magic glowed between the monster's antennae and it shot sharp bolts of metal that disappeared after momentarily sticking to what they stabbed. Zack made a snow-screen for cover as the monster searched for them and Gretchen threw a few shadow vases at it. Eric erupted fire underneath it, Malcolm fired a stream of lightning from two of his fingers and Patrick punched with a fist of time magic. The monster fired another beam of energy and the carpet burned away as it chased Frozen Fire. Malcolm dropped lightning bolts on it, Zack threw icicle kunai, Gretchen threw several shadow halberds, Eric shot multiple fire balls and Patrick sent a powerful temporal pulse at it. It went back to firing the sharp metal at them this time the shots were closers and everyone was cut by them. Eric threw a huge fireball, Malcolm dropped a massive lightning bolt on it, Zack punched with a hand covered in diamond hard ice, Patrick attacked with a sword slash extended by time magic and Gretchen slammed a shadow sofa into it. The monster fired another energy beam this time accompanied by the shards of metal. Everyone unleashed a blast of their element and steelipede was knocked off its feet and smashed through the window and it fell right down to the ground where it broke and disappeared into nothing.

"Where do you disappear to when you jump out at the monsters?" Patrick asked Zack.

"You know I'm not sure," replied Zack.

"Sheesh, Hud's not gonna be happy about this," mused Gretchen looking at the hole in the wall the broken window and the other remnants of their fight. "Or he's going to see it as an excuse to do some weird redecorating."

Frozen Fire moved up the tower and entered the room where Cyanna and Hitbox were. The siblings turned when they heard the door open and lowered their weapons: a long bow and a ukulele.

"The monsters' numbers are finally thinning out," said Cyanna.

"Yeah, but Visrel and Putrice are probably in the castle," said Zack.

"Surely if we do something about that interference machine Astral's spells will work and throw them out," said Eric.

"One problem: the machine's gone," said Hitbox. "There's no sign of it but it's still weakening Astral's magic. It must be well hidden." There came a sound from all the way at the bottom of the tower followed by another and another. Everyone knew Visrel and Putrice were trying to break in.

"Great. Now we don't have time to find it," said Gretchen. "We need to go now."

"But where in Miyamoto can we hide?" questioned Patrick.

"Maybe not in Miyamoto," suggested Malcolm.

"Your world!" exclaimed Cyanna. "They won't be able to find us as easily there."

"Not sure Reekie has any better hiding places," said Zack.

"It'll give us more time," said Hitbox.

"Let's go then," said Gretchen.

Cyanna grabbed Zack's arm and Hitbox grabbed hers. Frozen Fire grasped their pendants and in a flash of magic the tower was empty. A moment later the villains broke through the spells and found that they were gone.

Hud and the leaders had temporarily left the castle to deal with the interference device. They had Astral warp them onto a rooftop overlooking where the machine was last seen as well as one of the king's numerous cannons.

"Right, this ought to make things easier," said Hud preparing the cannon.

"Hm, an invisibility spell," mused Stratus. "I thought they'd have something better."

"Let's just be glad the cannon can still take aim at it," said Iron.

"It's gonna be pretty amusing watching all those virus get flung out the castle," said Larch.

"Right everything's ready," said Hud. "En garde you inanimate object, you!" The cannon fired a beam of energy that hit Putrice's hidden machine causing it to explode. A moment later Astral's spells were back at full power and last of the talon-teeth and data phantoms were thrown out.

This was the first time Hitbox had been to Frozen Fire's world but it was Cyanna's second.

"Still grey and wet, huh?" said Cyanna.

"Your city's architecture has quite a quaint charm," said Hitbox.

"OK, we need to find a place to hide you," said Zack.

"We're not gonna be able to hide them in any of our houses," said Eric. Everyone thought for a moment.

"We need a secure place with public access," mused Gretchen. "I am in no mood to go somewhere where we'll have to explain the Data Realm."

"I think Reekie Castle is pretty secure," said Patrick. "I seem to recall some of its protective spells are left over from the old days."

"Yeah, but it's free admission," Gretchen pointed out. "Anyone could walk in."

"Yeah, but nobody can warp in," said Zack. "And those two can hardly walk through the front door. Putrice is a wanted criminal and Visrel has all the subtlety of Iron and his wife on the dance floor."

"There's a dinner party I wish I could forget," grumbled Eric. "I still can't believe there's female ore.rar."

"I know, right?" said Cyanna.

"They might still sneak in," observed Gretchen. "But it should give us time to contact Astral. It might take her that long to work out where we went."

"To the trams then!" exclaimed Zack.

"Trams?" said the royal siblings together.

"Yeah, none of us have any bus change," said Patrick.

Back in Miyamoto the four leaders and Astral were going over things.

"So there's no sign of my grandchildren, Frozen Fire or the bad guys?" said Hud.

"I think they all went to Frozen Fire's world," said Astral "I can find them via their pendants but I can't talk to them unless they're somewhere private."

"Surely talking through pendants isn't too unusual in a world full of magic?"

"I don't want to risk it. I'll keep you informed."

Frozen Fire, Cyanna and Hitbox arrived at Reekie Castle. It sat on a large hill overlooking Reekie. It was large with many battlements and would not be easy to get into.

"Hm, it's not as large as home," observed Hitbox.

"Well, it's on top of a hill; they probably thought towers and excessive floors were unnecessary," said Gretchen.

"So long as we can hide here," said Cyanna.

"Let's just be glad we're not drawing attention," said Zack.

"Even with your goggles," remarked Gretchen.

Everyone entered, the castle was full of tourists and the like so they searched for a quiet place. They found an empty corridor on the first floor. On the wall there was a white outline like a doorway. Next to it was a plaque explaining what was known about this.

"The Last Concealment," read Cyanna. "This outline is in fact a magically concealed door hiding a chamber that was referred to as the Last Concealment. The door could only be opened by certain people so if the castle fell they would hide inside in the knowledge that their attackers could not get in."

"That sounds like a great place to hide," mused Hitbox. "I mean there is a risk that your enemies would wait outside to trap you in there until you ran out of supplies but it'd do the trick for now."

"But it hasn't been opened in centuries," said Zack. "And I seriously doubt it will actually open right when we need it." He leaned against the wall where the outline was and when he did that part of the wall glowed and vanished making him fall down. "How do I keep doing that?" On the other side of the threshold was a large room empty bar from what looked like supplies that had aged to almost nothing. Hitbox examined the doorway as Zack got up.

"I've seen a spell like this before," observed the prince. "It's aged so I doubt it does what it did originally but it looks like it only opens for those of noble blood."

"I seriously doubt I have any noble blood in me," said Zack.

"Actually you do," said Cyanna. "Remember? Grandfather knighted the five of you. That makes you nobility."

"Oh. Right. OK then." Everyone entered and the door closed. They grabbed their pendants to contact Astral.

"At last!" she said. "I see you're in Reekie Castle but where about?" They explained what had happened and what they had found. "OK, stay there until I can set up another place to keep Cyanna safe. But watch out, Visrel and Putrice have already arrived in Reekie. They could still find you."

"Well, now what?" wondered Eric. "We'll probably be in here for a while, what'll we do to pass the time?"

"No phone signal," said Malcolm.

"Yeah, you can never get any through these old security spells," grumbled Patrick. Time passed and they waited.

After a couple hours a voice magically projected itself through the door and startled everyone.

"We know the seven of you are in there," said the voice of Visrel.

"How did you jerks find us?" demanded Gretchen.

"That chamber might be able to protect you from our attacks but it doesn't stop us from sensing your magic," explained Putrice.

"You're out of luck. The door only opens for those of noble blood," explained Hitbox.

"And you two drab dregs are no way nobility," said Eric in his camp voice.

"We should have hidden in the Subterranean Library," Cyanna said to Hitbox. "Could have saved a whole lot of bother."

"Don't be so sure darlings, we've prepared an ultimatum," said Putrice.

"We knew you'd never surrender without a fight so we made sure to make you less willing to battle," said Visrel. "The doctor has prepared a machine that sends out powerful vibrations that can make whole buildings collapse. Unless you surrender to us princess and come with us I will slaughter every single person in this castle. Everyone will be buried in the rubble of this ancient house, but I guess the seven of you will still be alive." Cyanna looked at everyone.

"I can't let them do this," said Cyanna.

"If you go with them they'll kill our whole world," objected Hitbox. "You're the last part they need; you can't."

"There'll still be time to stop them from using the light from destroying Miyamoto. But we don't have any time to stop them from killing everyone here." She reached out and touched the entrance and the door opened. Visrel and Putrice were standing on the other side. Putrice was holding a device with a pair of large buttons on it.

"Excellent choice, princess," said Visrel.

"I have a condition for going with you," said Cyanna. "If you do succeed in destroying Miyamoto you leave this world alone." Visrel grabbed her arm.

"But you won't be alive to make sure I hold up my end of that agreement."

"However, I will have the device self-destruct as a thank you," said Putrice in a mocking tone, pressing one of her buttons. "Don't worry, darlings, it was far from anyone." Visrel and Putice vanished with Cyanna.

Only Hitbox returned to Miyamoto. Frozen Fire stayed in Reekie and returned to their homes. In Adlez Castle three of the leaders were discussing events. For once Hud was silent; he was not with the others he was just staring out the window with an expression that was impossible to read.

"First his son, then his wife and now his granddaughter is kidnapped," said Iron. "The king must be beside himself."

"Hitbox must be sick with worry as well," said Larch. "But there's nothing we can do; they've fled to the Free Space."

"So once again we just sit around and see if the end comes or not," grumbled Stratus. "Hmph! At least we can keep the king company."

Frozen Fire all had the same dream. For the second time in their lives they saw a projection of reality in their sleep. Out in the Free Space away from the four doors Visrel and Putrice were placing an unconscious Cyanna down. She was placed with the other three princesses in a circle, their layout resembling that of the four doors. Cyanna at the bottom, Magentia at the top, Armillo to the left and Noir at the right. They were surrounded by magical objects and devices which were activated. Magic surged everywhere and soon each princess started to emit a magical light: Cyanna a cyan light, Armillo a yellow light, Magentia a magenta light and Noir a black light.

In the morning Frozen Fire all met at Zack's house.

"Life's always been a little peculiar," mused Zack. "What with the living on a floating island and that frog in biology class which kept donning a top hat and singing show tunes. But we're about to go battle a sentient computer virus and an evil scientist who are stealing a magical light that'll allow them to manipulate the building blocks of a reality. Peculiar doesn't even cut it."

"Yep, and we swore we'd help protect Miyamoto," said Gretchen. "And no matter what doubts any of us might be feeling I know none of us are going to back out. Fighting them both at the same time is gonna be nasty."

"I hope we can do this."

"We've mastered our elements; even if they manage to beat us they won't beat us easily either."

"At least there's no way they'll have all the light by the time we get to them," said Eric. "I'd hate to think what they'd do to us if they had."

"They could get the last of it while we fight them," said Patrick.

"That's a scary thought," said Malcolm.

"And one we may have to deal with."

"We better be ready for anything," said Eric. "And it's bound to be anything." They warped to Adlez Castle and met Hitbox.

"Grandad isn't here to wish us luck," he said. "Let's not waste any time and go get my sister."

"I think we all knew you'd be insisting to come with us," mused Gretchen. "I doubt even Astral could stop you from going."

"To be fair she does send us through the door to the Free Space," said Zack.

"I hope you all know I'm still grateful to the five of you even if we fail," said Hitbox. "And I know that myself, my sister and our grandfather are glad we met you all. You're all so wonderfully unusual. Just like Grandad."

"Yeah, but the king's a special kind of crazy," said Eric.

They all warped to the door at Game's Edge where Astral was waiting for them. Without a word she transported everyone through the door to the Free Space.

"Yet again I find myself wishing you all luck as you set off to face a dangerous battle," said Astral. "I knew this was how it would be when you agreed to be Miyamoto's guardians but I still can't help but be uneasy."

"That's just the way you are, Astral," said Hitbox. "It's made you great at what you do."

"We'll make sure to break any spells and devices we see so you can help us," said Eric.

"We all will help you," said a voice from behind. They turned. It was Amaranth who spoke; she was with Baritone and Bixbite. "This could destabilize the entire Data Realm."

"Once you subdue them we will arrive," said Baritone. "We'll make sure Putrice goes to jail this time."

"We all promised to return the princesses to their loved ones," said Bixbite. "And it's a promise no one intends to break." Astral pointed in the direction the villains were and Frozen Fire and Hitbox set off, a feeling of true dread hanging over them like a cloud waiting to drop rain that would bring a flood.

Cyanna was in a strange dreamlike place. She felt alone and scared. All she could do was sing to try to keep her spirits up.

"They guard the world but not their own. They're friends with those on the throne. The ice says he's an angry oddball. But his loyalty will never fall. The shadow loves her own strange art. Her friendly spirit warms the heart. The fire sings at a diva's ball. He'd like to give hope to all. The lightning may seem silent. But no one wonders where his voice went. The time thinks he's an adventure lord. He'll even go against his own accord." But she was still with the other princesses in the Free Space trapped by Visrel and Putrice.

"We're only half way done," said Visrel looking at the magic they had got so far. "But we have plenty to destroy Frozen Fire when they arrive." The four lights emitted by the princesses were gathering together into a giant ball of light hovering in the air.

"That will be convenient," said Putrice brightly. "I tell you, darling, this is the scientific marvel of a lifetime."

"Yes, the things you'll be able to do are near infinite. The entire Data Realm and your world will tremble before the power we will unleash."

"Darling, can you hear something?"

"Apart from what we're supposed to be hearing? I think you're right."

"Is that singing?"

"Frozen Fire answered the hero's call," sang Cyanna. BLAM! Magic was blasted by the princesses. Ice spikes shot up, shadows lashed around, fire erupted, lightning bolts rained down and time magic exploded. When it cleared their magic and machines were ruined and Cyanna was standing with the other princesses getting up.

"WHAT?!" shouted the villains together.

"Didn't you know I write songs about the people I care about?" asked Cyanna in a mocking tone. "I've been working on a theme song for Frozen Fire. I don't know what to call it yet but I can use it to summon their elements to aid me. Oh and just before your assault on Adlez Castle I drank several potions to keep any sleep spells you'd use on me from working properly."

"You insufferable little minstrel," snarled Visrel.

"Those Knils really are infuriating aren't they, darling?" said Putrice. They started to advance but Noir threw a device that shot an energy which temporarily immobilized the villains. Armillo and Magentia knocked them both over with their fishing rod and grappling hook respectively and Cyanna lead them off towards the four doors. When Visrel and Putrice were freed the Princesses had already put some distance between them.

"I knew we should have broken all their limbs," mused Visrel.

"I'll get them back, darling," said Putrice. "You get to work on understanding that light and your preparations for Miyamoto's doomsday." She snapped her fingers and a giant data phantom appeared beneath her and it carried her after the princesses.

Frozen Fire and Hitbox had crossed into the area where those who watch powers were weakened. They saw four figures coming towards them.

"Hang on. Is that...?" said Gretchen.

"Cyanna!" cried Hitbox when he realized it was his sister.

"Hitbox! Zack! Gretchen! Eric! Malcolm! Patrick!" They heard her call back.

"So much for our daring rescue," said Zack.

"At least it's something to cross off the to do list," said Gretchen. The prince and princess ran up to each other and hugged. Frozen Fire and the other three princesses caught up.

"Your highnesses, we're sorry," said Zack.

"Ah, don't worry about it these things happen," reassured Magentia.

"You wouldn't think they'd happen but they do," said Armillo.

"We still want to apologize though," said Gretchen.

"Well, then we accept it and we thank you for what you did," said Noir.

"Visrel and Putrice still have half of the light," said Cyanna.

"And I'm here to collect the rest of it," said a voice. Looking they saw Putrice on the giant data phantom she was riding.

"Oh yeah, she was chasing us," said Magentia.

"And this time, darling, there are not enough tricks in the Data Realm to help you escape."

"Did you not see us?" called Patrick.

"You haven't beaten us yet," said Eric.

"Oh, it matters not, darling. Visrel has more than enough power to get rid of you," said Putrice.

"If you want my sister you'll have to go through me this time!" exclaimed Hitbox summoning a broadsword.

"Yeah, like I'm not taking part in this fight," said Cyanna summoning a bassoon. "Frozen Fire, we'll keep her busy; you go after Visrel."

"Armillo, Magentia, Noir you head back to the doors," said Hitbox.

"No, we'll help you fight," said Noir.

"We need to make it hard for them to find you again."

"Cyanna, thank you for getting us out of there," said Armillo.

"Anytime, my friend."

The three princesses turned and ran for the doors. Frozen Fire set off past Putrice and she had her giant data phantom turn to attack. Cyanna played a tune on her bassoon that paralysed and weakened the phantom and then Hitbox jumped, swung his sword and cut the monster in half. Putrice landed on her feet as if she hadn't been high in the air.

"Very well, darlings, let's get this over with," she said. With a flick of her wrist a rope of energy whipped at the siblings. Hitbox cut it away and Cyanna played a tune that shot small rocks at Putrice. The villain retaliated with two more energy ropes which made bursts of energy when they struck. Cyanna played a tune on her steel drum that put a magical barrier around them. Putrice lashed at the shield determined to break it but Hitbox swung a great axe and cut both ropes in the air. Putrice made a ball of magic and threw it and it exploded when it landed. Cyanna's barrier had vanished so they had to manoeuvre as more magical blasts were thrown at them. Hitbox charged with a lance and Putrice swung another rope and the two struck against each other. As Hitbox blocked every swing of the rope Cyanna played a tune on her trademark ocarina that rained beams of light down. Putrice was knocked over but as she fell she threw another magical sphere that when it exploded knocked the siblings over as well. Everyone got back up and the brother and sister ran at their enemy. Putrice sent her magic into her dark glasses and it fired energy beams from their lenses at them. Cyanna and Hitbox had to dodge an onslaught of attacks from Putrice. Cyanna played a song on a folk guitar that stopped the magic in Putrice's glasses, halting the beams. Hitbox moved in with a spear but hit her with the handle and used the head to cut away an energy ball she threw. Putrice made more energy balls and threw them upwards raining them down all over. Cyanna quickly made another barrier for cover while Hitbox took out some of the energy balls with a crossbow. When their barrier vanished Putrice made more ropes and began lashing at the siblings again. Hitbox summoned a war hammer and started to counter all the attacks sent their way, while Cyanna played a tune on a xylophone that made a cloud of dust appear right in front of Putrice. The next thing she knew they were right in front of her.

"What a nuisance," said Putrice.

"The feeling's mutual," said Cyanna. And they both punched her and knocked her out. "We're not going to be able to catch up with Frozen Fire."

"They're on their own again," said Hitbox. "Good luck, my friends. For all our sakes."

"Let's take her to Astral."

Visrel was standing out in the open, no sign of any magic or machine nearby when Frozen Fire arrived.

"The princesses have escaped and Cyanna and Hitbox are taking care of Putrice," said Zack

"So just give us the magic you stole and we'll go easy one you," said Gretchen.

"You think because you've 'mastered' your pretty little elements you're a match for me," said Visrel. "Have you forgotten I stopped our battles?"

"Have you forgotten we threw you into your own energy attack?" said Eric.

"We've always been a match," said Malcolm.

"All your fears and insecurities are still there," observed Visrel. "Yet you no longer hesitate."

"We backed down once at the start. But no more," said Patrick. They already had their weapons drawn.

"Good, I'd hate to have to hunt you all down. Even though it's only half the light it's plenty to get rid of you and allow me to destroy Miyamoto myself. I will act as Charon, ferrying you over to oblivion!" Magic surged over him. "You know I almost wish I had a heart." The magic shot up into a tower completely covering Visrel; only his shape could be made out. "So I could enjoy tearing you apart once and for all!" His form shifted and grew and soon burst through the tower of energy. He was now about thirty feet tall. His body was long, his head was like a cobra's complete with hood, his feet were somewhat cylindrical like an elephant's or a rhino's; instead of arms he had gigantic wings stretched out at his sides and he had a large tail which had a giant version of his helical blade on the end.

"Well, that's something else for the nightmares," groaned Zack as he moved his goggles over his eyes.

"Yeah, this is the weirdest other form yet," said Eric.

Visrel opened his fang-filled mouth and fired a gigantic beam of energy and Frozen Fire scrambled out of the way. Zack threw a block of diamond hard ice right at Visrel's head. Gretchen made a shadow copy of Visrel's tail and blade which she slashed at him. Eric turned his arm into fire which grew and punched the monster before returning to normal.

Malcolm spotted what remained of Putrice's harpoon cannon and despite its severe damage he was able to take control of it and had it fire its harpoons at Visrel. Patrick made a ring of time magic around the monster and used a time split to simultaneously attack both legs. Visrel took to the air and with a mighty swing of his wings sent a gust of air that threw Frozen Fire over. Visrel loomed over them as they started to get back up, the face-like pattern on his cobra hood glowed and a sphere fired from it and it exploded when it hit the ground; they only just got out the way. Malcolm fire electrified arrows up at Visrel and Eric followed with throwing his scythe like a flaming boomerang. Gretchen hurled duplicates of her halberd at him as Patrick used his time magic to fire his sword like a rocket which he was then able to call back. Zack covered his staff in thick ice and sharp icicles which he threw at the monster. Visrel was not letting up.

Back by the doors those who watch could sense what was happening.

"Great Scot! What has that monster done?" exclaimed Bixbite. "This is absolute insanity."

"We knew he wanted to use the light for destruction, but still," said Amaranth.

"The devastation could tear apart everything and everyone," said Baritone.

"The spell that neutralised our powers has been deactivated," observed Astral. "I will not let Visrel kill Frozen Fire. We might not be able to fight Visrel but we will do what we have to."

Visrel fired another energy beam from the air. Malcolm latched onto one wing with a thunder rope and shocked it and Patrick fired a lot of time at the other wing to suspend it. Visrel landed on the ground and started to stomp at them. Zack struck the ground with his staff and sharp icicles appeared on the ground where Visrel was stomping. Eric threw a giant fireball and Gretchen unleashed a massive shadow wave. Visrel screeched and a shockwave of sonic energy was fired from his mouth. Visrel continued screeching so Zack made a snow-screen to give them cover. Visrel looked for them, Gretchen had dived into her shadow and now she leapt out and stabbed Visrel's leg with her halberd. Malcolm fired a stream of lightning from two of his fingers, Patrick shot several time bursts and Eric made several flaming scythe blades out of fire to go with his regular one in the shape of a mouth which he had 'bite' Visrel. The Anti-Gamer swiped with his tail bringing his helical blade crashing down. Gretchen threw a shadow piano at his head, Zack threw a storm of snowflake shurikens and icicle kunai and Malcolm fired multiple arrows that turned into lightning punches. Eric made a fire twister appear around Visrel's head and Patrick fired a giant temporal pulse. Visrel screeched more shockwaves at Frozen Fire. Zack sent a beam of energy to cover Visrel's mouth in ice but he easily broke it off. Eric attacked with a flaming scythe strike, Patrick with his sword extended by time magic, Malcolm dropped a giant lightning bolt on Visrel and Gretchen fired many shadow cannon balls. Visrel began shooting more exploding energy balls at them making them scatter again. Malcolm threw multiple lightning balls, Zack extended the reach of his staff with his diamond hard ice and struck, Gretchen threw several shadow frying pans, Patrick attacked with sped up sword slashes and Eric fired a jet of white hot fire. Visrel took to the air again, flew low and swung his tail blade at Frozen Fire. Patrick threw a sphere of time magic that exploded on contact, Malcolm fired streams of lightning from both hands, Eric threw his scythe like a flaming boomerang, Gretchen used her shadows to fire her halberd like a rocket and Zack threw a snowman made of dense snow. Visrel flapped his wings making another gust of air knocking Frozen Fire over again and an instant later he was firing an energy beam right at them before they could get up. Suddenly, a flash of light and Astral appeared in the air surrounded by a protective barrier in the attack's path. The barrier shattered when it was hit and Astral was engulfed by the beam but it didn't make it to Frozen Fire.

"Astral!" they all cried together.

The attack cleared and Astral could be seen again seemingly unharmed.

"It's time to finish this," she called. "Get in a few more hits then I'm going to do something you're not gonna like."

Visrel screeched a shockwave which everyone avoided. Zack threw diamond hard icicle kunais at the monster, Eric fired exploding blasts of fire, Patrick slashed with an extended sword, Gretchen attacked with a duplicate of Visrel's helical blade and Malcolm shot a pulse of lightning. Visrel retaliated by firing more exploding energy spheres. Astral snapped her fingers and Frozen Fire vanished in a flash of light before the attacks could land. In another flash of light they reappeared on Visrel's back. They all yelled when they realized where they were.

"She's right, no one likes this," stated Gretchen.

Visrel shook himself trying to throw them off but Frozen Fire held on. They each held up their weapons and charged them with as much of their elements as they could and drove them down into the spot below the neck. Visrel screeched and lost height. He crashed into the ground and started to exploded. Astral had magic barriers appear around Frozen Fire and moved them away before the main explosion. When it cleared Visrel was back to his regular form hunched over on the ground growling like he was angry. The other three who watch appeared around Visrel and Astral joined them.

"It's time to give back what you stole," said Astral.

The four who watch held up one of each of their hands at Visrel and light erupted underneath him. The blue, magenta, yellow and black lights shot out of the Anti-Gamer and flew off towards the doors, back where they came from, the four princesses.

"But this time there will be no escape for you Visrel," said Amaranth.

"We will not let you go after the princesses again," said Baritone.

"And we certainly don't trust you with the secret of the light," said Bixbite.

Visrel managed to stand up.

"I should have sealed you away a long time ago," said Astral. "But seals like that never seem to last and I will not just leave you to become someone else's problem."

"Like one of your predecessors did with the Absent Number?" said Visrel. "How many times will that door open? And all the worlds have doors like that."

"We will find a way to keep you imprisoned Anti-Gamer."

Visrel summoned his blade. "You're all fools to think you can make a prison that can trap a monster!"

"Give it up, Visrel, it's over, you've lost once and for all," said Zack.

"You've been weakened more than ever you can't stand up to anyone," said Gretchen.

"This is as almost a big a loss as a villain can have," said Eric.

"You can't beat us anymore," said Malcolm.

"No more evil schemes for you, Anti-Gamer," said Patrick.

"Actually I have a backup device that can block their powers again," said Visrel gesturing to those who watch. "But before I go I'm getting rid of the five of you while I can." He unleashed a wave of energy at Frozen Fire. They blocked with their elements just in time; their magic clashed violently. Visrel was too weak to keep it up so he stopped. The clashing magics made Frozen Fire lose control and the Anti-Gamer was hit by a blast of all five elements.

"That was too close," said Astral.

"Ha ha ha ha ha!" Visrel laughed his fake laugh. "If anyone was to bring me to an end it would be the five of you. Well done Frozen Fire, Miyamoto lives. The king was right, it will not fall by my hand. Not many can slay a true monster. Bravo wretched heroes. Ha ha ha ha ha!" Visrel surged with energy and exploded into magic and then nothing. The Anti-Gamer was no more. No one said anything and they returned to the doors.

Those who watch each returned the princesses to their worlds and Astral brought Frozen Fire, Cyanna and Hitbox back to Miyamoto. They warped straight to Adlez Castle.

"Home sweet home!" exclaimed Cyanna. "It's been a day but it feels like so long. Probably 'cause so much happened."

"We just killed a guy," said Zack a little grimly.

"A heartless soulless monster, mind you," said Gretchen.

"I'm sure helping saving our world repeatedly will outweigh it," reassured Cyanna.

"It's kind of a relief to know he's not around anymore," said Eric.

"A strange relief," agreed Malcolm.

"One way or the other we need a long break," said Patrick.

"And grandad will be ecstatic to know you're home," said Hitbox placing a hand on his sister's shoulder.

"But there may be something else that ruins the reunion," said Astral. Everyone turned towards her and Astral collapsed. Everyone ran over to her. "I'm sorry that beam did faze me. But please don't blame yourselves for this. Yes, I took that attack to save you but it's not something that could not be helped. I'll miss all of you."

"Astral, are you dying?" asked Zack trembling.

"I'm afraid my time is at an end as well."

"No, don't you dare leave!" demanded Eric.

"I'm glad I got to meet all of you and I'm glad I was not mistaken to make you the guardians of our world."

"Isn't there anything we can do?" asked Cyanna.

"No. But Hud knows what needs to been done next. Cyanna, Hitbox, Zack, Gretchen, Eric, Malcolm, Patrick, good bye and thank you for everything." Astral's eyes closed as she was engulfed in her magical light which soon faded along with her.

Putrice had been transported to the Kerozonian authorities. She was arrested and sentenced to prison being found guilty of creating lesser monsters, unethical scientific practices, conspiracy to hold Reekie to ransom and the endangerment of human life.

There was a sense of relief over Elleb Castle now that Armillo had been returned.

"My dear Granddaughter I'm so pleased to have you home," said Prelap.

"Grandma, you've been saying that for a couple days now," said Armillo.

"You can't blame the old gal for being so happy," said Amaranth.

"Pot and kettle," muttered Ollie.

"What about the light part that's still inside me?" wondered Armillo.

"It's stuck there I'm afraid; not even I can remove it," explained Amaranth. "But we'll be keeping the secret even closer to the chest. So try not to worry about it."

"Yeah, let's just do what we always do," said Ollie.

"To the next adventure then," said Armillo.

The royal twins of Semiv were ecstatic to be together again.

"I'm sorry I wasn't part of the team that came to save you," said Orion.

"Yeah, but we got ourselves out anyway," said Magentia.

"It was the Miyamotan princess who did most of it," Baritone reminded her.

"Hey, there's not gonna be any other creeps looking for that light she has?" inquired Alliteration.

"It will always be a possibility but an unlikely one. In all of Pratchett only the four of us know this secret."

"No one will be able to take us on when we work together," said Magentia. "Me and Orion are the ultimate team.

"Though that Frozen Fire did give us a run for our money," said Orion.

Things had not been quiet at Namerof Castle since Noir had returned.

"I've finally got my mech suit back together!" exclaimed Noir triumphantly.

"You've been working nonstop since you got home dear," said Episode.

"I need to start upgrading it. Making it, so not even something with powerful magic like a monster can pry it apart quite so easily."

"You know full well how your mother gets when you work so hard," said Bixbite. "Really you should slow down a bit, your majesty."

"I've got this light inside me, I really should upgrade the security."

"Noir, it's unlikely that anyone else will find out about that light in even my lifetime. I didn't even tell Fibre why you were kidnapped."

"He took a punch in the face for her," said Episode.

"Don't worry, I gave him enough of an explanation to satisfy him."

"I guess you're right, I should relax," said Noir. "And I should go thank Fibre in person. But I'm still upgrading my mech suit."

Things were much gloomier in Miyamoto. Astral's memorial was held outside her temple; hundreds of seats for all four races had been set up and a podium in front of them just outside the temple entrance. Nearly all of Miyamoto had come. The leaders were sitting at the front with Cyanna and Hitbox. Frozen Fire were also sitting at the front but as per a request they were slightly hidden behind a tree. King Hud was at the podium ready to deliver the eulogy.

"Not even those who watch are immortal," he began. "She may have been born from the data of fictional goddesses but her life was not eternal. She would tell us not to let our grief derail our day to day lives but I will not tell you how to deal with your grief; only ask that you do not let it consume you. I am no stranger to this feeling having lost much of my family, including some who were supposed to outlive me. Astral was a friend to all so this pain will be with us all but I can assure you all we can live with this pain. She would not want anyone to be afraid to ask for help so I would ask that you try not to be. She will live on in our memories and the good deeds she did to protect Miyamoto will make sure she will be remembered forever. Like the phoenix the magic of those who watch is reborn so there is always someone looking out for us." Hud bent down behind the podium and pulled up what appeared to be a basket covered in small blankets. He moved the blankets and from within pulled out a small baby wrapped in more blankets. "So, may I introduce Astro, Astral's successor. When she is grown she will be the one who watches Miyamoto. We are supposed to place the baby inside the temple where time will be distorted until she is ready to take on the role, allowing her to grow almost instantly. It may not be right to leave her alone in there but she will be pulled inside even if we don't place her inside ourselves. She will have contact with the memoires of her predecessor so she will not grow up alone. And soon she will have a whole world and more to befriend."

After the service Frozen Fire returned to Adlez Castle with the royal family.

"The whole thing with those who watch is still messing with my head," said Zack.

"Yes, it does do the head in a bit," agreed Hud. "Oh blimey, now I really am the oldest person in Miyamoto. That's not gonna help the glumness."

"You'll perk up again before you know it," said Cyanna. "You're usually bright like me and strong like Hitbox."

"Yeah, your majesty, you're too mad to be sad for any length of time," said Gretchen.

"I'd have you arrested for treason if it wasn't true," said Hud.

"So, we're still guardians, right?" wondered Eric. "Even with all the major bad guys gone."

"You can help whenever you want," said Cyanna.

"And besides some new bad guy could show up one day," said Patrick.

"They'd better not be as persistent," said Malcolm.

"I guess our fighting's never really over with," said Gretchen.

"Not with your hint of violence," remarked Zack.

"You're asking for it there," said Eric. "Best not to antagonize her."

"Oh, shut up you lunatics," snapped Gretchen. "And you both smell funny."

"It's called soap, dear. Don't know what that is coming off Zack."

"You're the first to go," said Zack.

"Didn't take them long to get back to it," mused Patrick.

"Don't think they stopped," said Malcolm.

Frozen Fire's adventures in the Data Realm weren't over. They were always welcomed by the friends they had made. Two worlds full of magic connected to each other always full of adventures so there were always plenty for them.